Praise for Jemima J

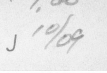

"[*Jemima J*] conveys with sass and humor both the invisibility of the overweight and the shallow perks that accrue to the thin and beautiful. Green has entertainingly updated the Cinderella story . . . Bottom Line: Sweet and Tasty." —*People* magazine

"Cleverly probes the world of a very smart, very funny, very fat reporter . . . Americans will enjoy this confection and appreciate how Green renders a certain humor-impaired California earnestness about health, happiness and love." —*USA Today*

"The perfect summer confection . . . absolutely delicious."
—*New Orleans Times-Picayune*

"The kind of novel you'll gobble up at a single sitting."
—*Cosmopolitan*

"A brilliantly funny novel about something close to every woman's heart—her stomach." —*Woman's Own*

"*Jemima J* is a fun, fast-paced novel about a woman who hates her body and decides to do something about it . . . Skinny or fat, Jemima is always endearing. Her lessons about life and love are sweet and at times ironic . . . Green's ability to evoke laughter from a serious subject makes *Jemima J* a charming, worthwhile read."
—*Lauren K. Nathan, the Associated Press*

"Compulsively readable. The ultimate makeover novel made with irony . . . one for the beach." —*Sunday Times* (London)

"Green writes with acerbic wit about the law of the dating jungle, and its obsession with image. Jolly Jemima deserves to be both slim and happy, and the novel's as comforting as a bacon sandwich.."
—*Sunday Express* (London)

"The outcome [of *Jemima J*] is one to cheer. Light, frothy entertainment." —*Sunday Mirror* (London)

a novel about ugly

ducklings and swans

BROADWAY BOOKS

New York

jemima j

Jane Green

For David

My real-life romantic hero

acknowledgments

This book would not be the book it is if it weren't for so many people who helped and encouraged me throughout those long months, only a handful of whom I can mention here.

My agent, Anthony Goff, whose wisdom, integrity, and humor made the road to hell and back almost fun, and my American agent, Deborah Schneider, without whom none of this would have happened.

Everyone at Broadway Books, especially Lauren Marino, for having faith in Jemima and me.

Graeme Weston, who showed me the real side of Santa Monica; my brother Charlie for being such a titles whiz, and of course my parents for their continuing love and support.

chapter 1

God, I wish I were thin.

I wish I were thin, gorgeous, and could get any man I want. You probably think I'm crazy, I mean here I am, sitting at work on my own with a massive double-decker club sandwich in front of me, but I'm allowed to dream aren't I?

Half an hour to go of my lunchbreak. Half an hour in which to drool over the latest edition of my favorite magazine. Don't get me wrong, I don't read the features, why would I? Thousands of words about how to keep your man, how to spice up your sex life, how to spot if he's being unfaithful are, quite frankly, irrelevant to me. I'll be completely honest with you here, I've never had a proper boyfriend, and the cover lines on the magazines are not the reason I buy them.

If you must know, I buy them, all of them, for the pictures. I sit and I study each glossy photograph for minutes at a time, drinking in the models' long, lithe limbs, their tiny waists, their glowing golden skin. I have a routine: I start with their faces, eyeing each sculpted cheekbone, heart-shaped chin, and I move slowly down their bodies, careful not to miss a muscle.

I have a few favorites. In the top drawer of my chest of drawers in my bedroom at home is a stack of cut-out pictures of my top supermodels, preferred poses. Laetitia's there for her sex appeal, Christy's there for her lips and nose, and Cindy's there for the body.

And before you think I'm some kind of closet lesbian, I've already told you the one thing I would wish for if I rubbed a lamp and a gorgeous, bare-chested genie suddenly appeared. If I had one wish in all the world I wouldn't wish to win the lottery. Nor would I wish for true love. No, if I had one wish I would wish to have a model's figure, probably Cindy Crawford's, and I would extend the wish into having *and keeping* a model's figure, *no matter what I eat*.

Because, tough as it is to admit to a total stranger, I, Jemima Jones, eat a lot. I catch the glances, the glares of disapproval on the occasions I eat out in public, and I try my damnedest to ignore them. Should someone, some "friend" trying to be caring and sharing, question me gently, I'll tell them I have a thyroid problem, or a gland problem, and occasionally I'll tack on the fact that I have a super-slow metabolism as well. Just so there's no doubt, just so people don't think that the only reason I am the size I am is because of the amount I eat.

But you're not stupid, I know that, and, given that approximately half the women in the country are a size 14, I would ask you to try and understand about my secret binges, my constant cravings, and see that it's not just about food.

You don't need to know much about my background, suffice to say that my childhood wasn't happy, that I never felt loved, that I never got over my parents' divorce as a young child, and that now, as an adult, the only time I feel really comforted is when I seek solace in food.

So here I am now, at twenty-seven years old, bright, funny, warm, caring and kind. But of course people don't see that when they look at Jemima Jones. They simply see fat.

Unfortunately they don't see what I see when I look in the mirror. Selective visualization, I think I'll call it. They don't see

2

my glossy light brown hair. They don't see my green eyes, they don't see my full lips. Not that they're anything amazing, but I like them, I'd say they were my best features.

They don't notice the clothes either, because, despite weighing far, far more than I should, I don't let myself go, I always make an effort. I mean, look at me now. If I were slim, you would say I look fantastic in my bold striped trousers and long tunic top in a perfectly matching shade of orange. But no, because of the size I am people look at me and think, "God, she shouldn't wear such bright colors, she shouldn't draw attention to herself."

But why shouldn't I enjoy clothes? At least I'm not telling myself that I won't bother shopping until I'm a size 10, because naturally my life is a constant diet.

We all know what happens with diets. The minute you cut out certain foods, the cravings overtake you until you can't see straight, you can't think properly, and the only way to get rid of the craving is to have a bite of chocolate, which soon turns into a whole bar.

And diets don't work, how can they? It's a multi-million-dollar industry, and if any of the diets actually worked the whole caboodle would go down the toilet.

If anyone knows how easy it is to fail it's me. The Scarsdale, the High Fiber, the Atkins Diet, the six eggs a day diet, Slimfast, Weight Watchers, Herbalife, slimming pills, slimming drinks, slimming patches. You name them, I've been the idiot that tried them. Although some have, admittedly, been more successful than others.

But I have never, even with the help of all these diets, been slim. I have been slimmer, but not slim.

I know you're watching me now with pity in your eyes as I finish my sandwich and look furtively around the office to see whether anyone is looking. It's okay, the coast is clear, so I can pull open my top drawer and sneak out the slab of chocolate hiding at the back. I tear the bright orange wrapper and silver foil off and stuff it into the dustbin beneath my desk, as it's far

3

easier to hide a slab of dull brown chocolate than the glaring covering that encases it.

I take a bite. I savor the sweet chocolate in my mouth as it melts on my tongue, and then I take another bite, this time furiously chewing and swallowing, hardly tasting a thing. Within seconds the entire bar has disappeared, and I sit there feeling sick and guilty.

I also feel relieved. My bad food for today has just been eaten, which means that there's none left. Which means that tonight, when I get home and have a salad, which is what I'm now planning to eat for dinner, I can feel good, and I can start my diet all over again.

I glance at the clock and sigh. Another day in my humdrum life, but it shouldn't be humdrum. I'm a journalist, for God's sake. Surely that's a glamorous, exciting existence?

Unfortunately not for me. I long for a bit of glamour, and, on the rare occasions I do glance at the features in the magazines I flick through, I think that I could do better.

I probably could, as well, except I don't have the experience to write about men being unfaithful, but if I had, Jesus, I'd win awards, because I am, if I say so myself, an expert with words.

I love the English language, playing with words, watching sentences fit together like pieces of a jigsaw puzzle, but sadly my talents are wasted here at the *Kilburn Herald*.

I hate this job. When I meet new people and they ask what I do for a living, I hold my head up high and say I'm a journalist. I then try to change the subject, for the inevitable question after that is "Who do you work for?" I hang my head low, mumble the *Kilburn Herald*, and, if I'm really pushed, I'll hang it even lower and confess that I do the Top Tips column.

Every week I'm flooded with mail from sad and lonely people in Kilburn with nothing better to do than write in with questions like, "What's the best way to bleach a white marbled lino floor that's turned yellow?" and "I have a pair of silver candlesticks inherited from my grandmother. The silver is now tarnished, any suggestions?" And every week I sit for hours on the bloody phone ringing lino manufacturers, silver-makers, and, apologizing for taking up their time, ask them for the answers.

This is my form of journalism. Every now and then I have to write a feature, usually a glorified press release, a bit of PR puff that has to be used to fill some space, and oh how I revel in this seemingly unexciting job. I pull the press release to pieces and start again. If my colleagues, the news reporters and feature writers that mill around me, bothered to read what I'd written they would see my masterful turn of phrase.

It's not as if I haven't tried to move up in the world of journalism. Every now and then when boredom threatens to render me completely incompetent, I drag myself into the editor's office and squeeze into a chair, producing these few cuts and asking for a chance. In fact today yet another meeting is due.

"Jemima," says the editor, leaning back in his chair, putting his feet on the table and puffing on a cigar, "why would you want to be a news reporter?"

"I don't," I say, restraining myself from rolling my eyes, because every time I come in here we seem to have the same conversation. "I want to write features."

"But Jemima, you do such a wonderful job on Top Tips. Honestly, love, I don't know where we'd be without you."

"It's just that it's not exactly journalism, I want to write more."

"We all have to start at the bottom," he says, the beginning of his regular monologue, as I think, yes, and you're still there, this isn't the *Guardian*, it's the *Kilburn* bloody *Herald*.

"Do you know how I started?"

I mutely shake my head, thinking, yes, you were a bloody tea boy for the *Solent Advertiser*.

"I was a bloody tea boy for the *Solent Advertiser*." And on, and on, and on he goes.

The conversation ends the same way too. "There may well be a vacancy on features coming up," he says with a conspiratorial wink. "Just keep on working hard and I'll see what I can do."

And so I sigh, thank him for his time and maneuver myself out of the narrow chair. Just before I get to the door, the editor says, "By the way, you are taking that class aren't you?"

I turn to look at him in confusion. Class? What class? "You know," he adds, seeing I don't know what he's talking about. "Computers, Internet, World Wide Web. We're going on the line and I want everyone in the office to attend."

On the line? Doesn't he mean online, I think as I walk out with a smile on my face. The editor, desperate to show off his street credibility, has once again proved he's still living in the 1980s. It's about time we got Web access at the office.

I march back to my desk passing the news reporters, all busy on the phone, my eyes cast downwards as I pass my secret heartthrob. Ben Williams is the deputy news editor. Tall, handsome, he is also the office Lothario. He may not be able to afford Armani, this being, as it is, the *Kilburn Herald*, but his suits fit his highly toned body, his muscular thighs so perfectly, they may as well be.

Ben Williams is secretly fancied by every woman at the *Kilburn Herald*, not to mention the woman in the shop where he buys his paper every morning, the woman in the sandwich bar who follows his stride longingly as he walks past every lunchtime. Yeah. Don't think I hadn't noticed.

Ben Williams is gorgeous, no two ways about it. His light brown hair is floppy in that perfectly arranged way, casually hanging over his left eye, his eyebrows perfectly arched, his dimples when he smiles in exactly the right place. Of course he is well aware of the effect he has on women, but underneath all the schmooze beats a heart of gold, but don't tell him I told you. He wouldn't want anyone to know that.

He is the perfect combination of handsome hunk and vulnerable little boy, and the only woman who isn't interested in him is Geraldine. Geraldine, you see, is destined for greater things. Geraldine is my only friend at the paper, although Geraldine might not agree with that, because after all we don't socialize together after work, but we do have little chats,

Geraldine perched prettily on the edge of my desk as I silently wish I looked like her.

And we do often have lunch together, frequently with Ben Williams, which is both painful and pleasurable, in equal measure, for me. Pleasurable because I live for those days when he joins us, but painful because I turn into an awkward fourteen-year-old every time he comes near. I can't even look at him, let alone talk to him, and the only consolation is that when he sits down my appetite disappears.

I suspect he thinks I'm rather sweet, and I'm sure he knows I've got this ridiculous crush on him, but I doubt he spends much time thinking about me, not when Geraldine's around.

Geraldine started here at about the same time as me, and the thing that really kills me is that I started as a graduate trainee, and Geraldine started as a secretary, but who's the one who gets to write features first? Exactly.

It's not that I'm completely cynical, but with her gleaming blond hair in a chic bob, her tiny size 8 figure squeezed into the latest fashions, Geraldine may not have an ounce of talent, but the men love her, and the editor thinks she's the biggest asset to the paper since, well, since himself.

And the thing that kills me even more is that Geraldine is the one woman here that Ben deems worthy of his attentions. Geraldine isn't interested, which makes it just about bearable. Sure, in a vaguely detached way she can appreciate Ben's good looks, his charm, his charisma, but please, he works at the *Kilburn Herald*, and by that fact alone would never be good enough for Geraldine.

Geraldine only goes out with rich men. Older, richer, wiser. Her current boyfriend has, amazingly, lasted eight months, which is a bit of a record for her, and Geraldine seems serious, which Ben can't stand. I, on the other hand, love hearing what I think of as "Geraldine stories." Geraldine is the woman I wish I was.

For now I settle down in my chair and pick up the phone to call the local veterinary practice.

"Hello," I say in my brightest telephone voice. "This is Jemima Jones from the *Kilburn Herald*. Would you have any idea how to remove the smell of cat spray from a pair of curtains?"

Jemima Jones pulls open the front door and immediately her heart sinks. Every day as she goes home on the bus she crosses her chubby fingers and prays her roommates will be out, prays for some peace and quiet, a chance to be on her own.

But as soon as the door opens she hears the music blasting from the living room, the giggles that punctuate their conversation, and with sinking heart she pushes her head round the door.

"Hi," I say to the two girls, one lying on each sofa, swapping gossip. "Anyone fancy a cup of tea?"

"Ooh, Mimey, love one," they both chorus, and I wince at the nickname they have taken it on themselves to bestow upon me. It's a nickname I had at school, one I tried to forget because the very mention of it, even now, brings back memories of being the fat girl in the class, the one who was bullied, the one who was always left out.

But Sophie and Lisa, in their vaguely patronizing way, continue to call me Mimey. They may not have known me at school, but they do know I hate the name because I once summoned up enough courage to tell them, but the fact that it irritates only seems to amuse them more.

Do you want to know about Sophie and Lisa? Sophie and Lisa lived in this flat long before I came on the scene, and most of the time I think they were probably far happier, except that they didn't have a permanent tea-maker in the evenings. Sophie is blond, a chic, snappy blonde with an inviting smile and come-to-bed eyes. Lisa is brunette, long, tousled locks and a full, pouting mouth.

Meeting them for the first time you'd probably think they were perhaps fashion buyers, or something similarly glamorous, because both have perfect figures, ready smiles, and wardrobes of designer clothes, but, and this is the only thing that makes me smile, the truth is far less interesting.

Sophie and Lisa are receptionists. They work together at an advertising agency, and spend their days trying to outscore one another with dates. They have both, in turn, worked through all the men in the agency, most of them eligible, some not so eligible, and now they sit behind their polished steel and beech desk, and hope for a dishy new client to walk through the door, someone to set their hearts alight, their eyelashes afluttering.

It's not unusual for them to be at home now, but it is unusual for them to be at home all evening. They arrive home at 5:30 P.M. on the dot then lounge around reading magazines, watching television, gossiping, before jumping into hot baths at 7 P.M., hair at 7:45 P.M., and makeup at 8:15 P.M.

Every night they're out the front door, dressed to the nines, by 9 P.M. Teetering on the highest heels, they totter out, giggling together, instructing me, and I'm usually either in my room or watching television, to behave myself. Every night they seem to think this is hugely funny, and every night I want to smack them. It's not that I dislike them, they're just completely inconsequential, a couple of chattering parakeets who constantly amaze me with their stupidity.

Off they go to Mortons, Tramp, Embargo. Anonymous places where they pick up anonymous men, who might, if they're lucky, wine, dine, and drive them around in Ferraris before disappearing off into the night.

Don't be ridiculous, of course I don't go with them, but, as contemptuous as I am of their lifestyles, a part of me, just a tiny part, would love to have a taste of it too.

But it's not worth even thinking about. They are thin and beautiful, and I am not. I would never dare suggest going along, and they would never dare ask me. Not that they are nasty, you understand, underneath the glitz and glamour they're nice girls, but a girl has to keep up appearances, and fat friends, I'm afraid, do not come into the equation.

Their diet, such as it is, seems to consist of bottles of champagne fueled by lines of cocaine provided by the men they meet. The fridge at home is always empty, unless I've been shopping, and in the eight months I've lived here I have never seen them eat a proper meal.

Occasionally I've seen one of them come in announcing "I'm starving!," and then Sophie, or Lisa, will pull open the door of the fridge and walk into the living room munching on a tomato, or half a slice of pita bread with the thinnest spreading of hummus I've ever seen.

You doubtless think we make an odd trio. You're probably right. The Italian man in the deli at the end of the road was flabbergasted to discover we lived together. The two beauties he flirts with at every opportunity, and the sad, overweight girl who probably reminds him of his fat mother always dressed in black.

But Mr. Galizzi has got it wrong, because for all my faults I'm not sad. Miserable a lot of the time, yes, but those who bother to get under the layers of fat know that not only does there beat a heart of gold, I'm also bloody good fun to be around, providing I'm in the right mood. But nobody really bothers to look for that, nobody really bothers to look beneath the surface appearance.

I stand in the kitchen, dropping three teabags into three oversized mugs. I pour in the water, add skim milk from the fridge, and out of habit drop in two heaped teaspoons of powdered sweetener for myself. Good girl, I tell myself, good girl for resisting the sugar, nestling quietly yet ominously in the cupboard above the kettle.

I bring the tea into the living room, and Sophie and Lisa cry their thanks, but the lazy cows don't move from the sofas, don't clear a space for me to sit down, so what else can I do but hover in the doorway, clasping my burning hot mug and wondering how soon I can go up to my room.

"How was today?" I eventually venture, as the girls stare at the television set, watching some sitcom featuring perfect-looking people with perfect white teeth and perfect figures.

"Hmm?" says Sophie, eyes never leaving the screen, even while I sip my tea.

"We're in love," offers Lisa, looking at me for the first time this evening. "We've got the most amazing new client."

Now Sophie looks interested, and I lower myself to the floor, sitting cross-legged and awkwardly in my role as agony aunt.

"Honestly, Mimey, this guy *was* gorgeous, but we don't know which one of us he fancies."

Sophie shoots a fake filthy look at Lisa, who smiles broadly.

"He definitely fancied one of you then?" I don't really need to ask the question, because who, after all, would not fancy one of these beautiful girls at first sight?

"Oh yes," said Lisa. "After his meeting he stood at the reception desk for ages chatting."

"I think he was chatting up Lisa," says Sophie.

"No," says Lisa. "Don't be ridiculous, sweetie. He was interested in you." But it's completely bloody obvious she doesn't mean it, and even I can see that he was mesmerized by Lisa's pouting lips and tumbling, just-out-of-bed locks.

"So did he ask you out?" I ask, wishing for a fleeting second that some handsome stranger would stop at my desk and chat me up. Just once. Just to see what it feels like.

"No," Lisa says ruefully. "But he did ask if we'd both be there next week when he comes in for a meeting."

"We were sitting here before, planning what to wear," says Sophie, turning to Lisa. "So, what about the red suit?"

"I'm just going upstairs," I say, feeling well and truly left out as I heave myself to my feet and edge out the door. I'm no longer needed, the courtesies of greeting have been dealt with, and I would never be asked an opinion on clothes, because as far as Sophie and Lisa are aware I haven't got a clue.

I climb slowly upstairs, stopping at the top to catch my

breath, walk into my bedroom and lie on the bed, staring at the ceiling, until my breathing becomes slower, more regular.

I lie there and spin out an elaborate fantasy about what I would wear if I were thin. I would have my hair cut into a super-trendy shaggy style, and perhaps, if I dared, would have a few blond highlights, just at the front.

I would wear sunglasses a lot of the time. Occasionally they would be big Hollywood film-star tortoiseshell ones, but the rest of the time they would be cool, smart little round glasses, glasses that spelled sophistication, glamour.

I would wear tight cream trousers, lycra crop tops, and the bits of flesh exposed would be taut and tanned. I would, I decide, even look fantastic in a bathrobe. I look at my old white bathrobe hanging on the back of the door, huge, voluminous. I love wrapping it around myself for comfort, trying desperately to ignore the fact that I resemble a balloon with legs.

But when I'm slim I'll keep that bathrobe. It will, being a man's bathrobe, gather in folds of fabric around my athletic new body. The sleeves will hang down, obscuring my hands, and I will look cute and vulnerable.

Even first thing in the morning I will look gorgeous. With no makeup and tousled hair, I imagine meeting Mr. Perfect, and curling up in an armchair with the bathrobe wrapped around me, exposing just my long, glowing legs, my bony knees, and naturally he will be head over heels in love with me.

I think about this for a while, and then I remember my magazine. I draw it out of my bag and once again study the pictures, reaching into my bedside drawer to pull out the scissors and add the latest models to my collection.

And as I put the scissors back I notice, at the very back of the drawer, a box of cookies. My God! I actually forgot about them, I actually forgot about food in the house.

No. I won't. I'm being good now. But then surely it's better to eat them, make them disappear, so there's no more bad food in the house. Surely it's better to finish them in one go than to eat them slowly and steadily over the course of a week. That way there won't be any left after tonight, and then I can really start my diet. The one that's going to work. The one that's going to fulfill my fantasies.

Yes, I'll eat them now and start again tomorrow.

chapter 2

Can somebody turn the sunshine off? It's shining directly in my eyes as I roll over in bed and groan. I can't get up yet, it's so warm, so comfortable, so I just lie here for a few minutes, waiting for the tinny pop music to start playing from my radio alarm clock, and I wish, oh God how I wish, that I could stay in bed forever.

Look, Jemima, see how when you roll over on your back your stomach feels, well, not quite flat, but certainly not fat. See how your breasts roll over to either side, giving the distinct illusion of a vast expanse of flatness in the middle.

Jemima lies there and rubs her stomach, half affectionately, half repellently, for there is something innately comforting in the bulk that is her body. But then she rolls over to her side, and tries to forget her stomach weighing down, sinking into the mattress. She tucks the duvet in tightly around her and wishes she never had to get up.

But today is the class day. Today is the day she is, as the editor put it, going "on the line." And, much as she is looking forward to the class, she cannot help but feel more than a little anxious because she will be breaking her daily routine.

From Monday to Friday Jemima's routine is as follows: she wakes up at 8:45 A.M., lies in bed and listens to Sophie and Lisa getting ready for work. Listens to the door slam as they clatter up the path at 9 A.M., and then hauls herself out of bed.

Avoids the mirror in the bathroom, for it is full length and she really does not want to see herself in all her glory. Starts running a bath, and pours at least five capfuls of bubble bath in to hide her flesh.

While the bath is running, goes to the kitchen and pours herself a bowl of cereal. Healthy cereal. Slimming cereal. (Except you're not supposed to have quite as much as that, Jemima, the bowl is not supposed to be so full the cereal is slopping out over the sides.)

Jemima eats the cereal in a hurry, comes back upstairs for the bath. Heads back to the bedroom and gets dressed, and only then, when she's covered in the comfort of her clothes, does she look in the mirror and quite like what she sees. She likes her intelligent green eyes, and she applies the tiniest bit of eyeliner and mascara, just to accentuate them.

She likes her full pouting lips. But they tend to disappear in the round moon-ness of her face, so she paints them pale pink.

She likes her glossy hair, and she brushes and brushes until it gleams back at her in the glass. She preens in the mirror, pouting her lips, sucking in her cheeks, pushing her neck forward until her chins almost, almost, disappear.

I could be beautiful, she tells herself every morning. If I lost weight I would be beautiful. And as she looks in the mirror she tells herself firmly that today is the start of the rest of her life. Today is the start of her new diet.

And what happens next, Jemima?

Feeling virtuous, positive, excited at the prospect of your new life, you leave your flat at 9:25 A.M. and catch the bus to work. You stand at the bus stop with the same people you see every day and you don't say a word to them, nor they to you.

You find a seat on its own, and sit there, your thighs spreading on to the seat next to you, and you pray that no one will sit beside you, forcing you to hold your breath, squeeze in your thighs, suppress your resentment at their audacity.

And then you alight at the corner of Kilburn High Road, a short walk from your office, and every morning as you walk up the road, just as you pass the shoe shop with its window display of rather nasty shoes, your nostrils start quivering.

There is nothing in the world quite like the smell of bacon frying, I'm sure you will agree. Together with dill, fresh lavender, and Chanel No. 5, it is one of Jemima's favorite smells. If it simply remained a favorite smell then all would be fine, but Jemima's nostrils are stronger than her willpower.

Your steps become slower as you approach the diner, and with each step the picture of a bacon sandwich, rashers of greasy bacon, awash with fat, oozing out of thick white sliced, becomes so vivid you can almost taste it.

Every morning you battle with yourself, Jemima. You tell yourself that today you started your diet, but the smell becomes too much to bear, and every morning you find yourself at the counter requesting two bacon sandwiches.

"He likes his bacon sandwich doesn't he, love?" says the woman behind the counter, a woman called Marge whom Jemima Jones has got to know. Once upon a long time ago Jemima told Marge the bacon sandwiches were for her boss.

Poor lass, thought Marge, *I know* they're for her. But Marge, being a kindhearted soul, pretends to believe her.

"Have a good day," says Marge, handing the sandwiches to Jemima, who tucks them in her bag, continuing the charade, before walking up the street. A few yards away the bacon sandwiches start calling you.

"Jemima," they whisper from the depths of your bag. "We're lovely and greasy, Jemima. Feel us. Taste us. Now." And you plunge your hand in, the craving fast overtaking any anxiety about eating in public, and in one, two, three, four bites the sandwiches have gone.

And then to the office, wiping your mouth with your sleeve and stopping at the newsstand to buy some sugar-free mints to hide the smell of bacon.

Your mornings are spent sorting out letters, and watching the clock until 11:30 A.M., when it is time for tea. "I'm starving," you say to Alison, the secretary who sits opposite you. "I haven't had breakfast," and it is your way of apologizing for the egg and bacon sandwich you bring up from the cafeteria together with a cup of tea and three sweeteners.

And then at 1 P.M., every day, you head back down to the cafeteria for lunch. A salad is what you have, every day, except the salads you choose from the salad bar are as fattening as an eclair.

Coleslaw, rice salad, pasta salad, slabs of cheese, and potato salad swimming in mayonnaise, you pile them on your plate and tell yourself you are being healthy. A whole wheat roll, covered in two slabs of butter, completes your meal, except you are not really full. You are never really full.

The afternoon is spent writing up your Top Tips, before nipping down again at teatime. Sometimes you have a cake, sometimes french fries, sometimes cookies, and occasionally, well, around twice a week, you have another sandwich.

And finally at 6 P.M. your day is over. Waiting for the bus home, you pop into the newsstand and buy a couple of bars of chocolate to sustain you on the journey, and then that familiar feeling of dread pours over you as you approach your house, and your two perfect roommates.

And your evenings blend together into one. Alone again, a blessed relief as Sophie and Lisa are out partying, you eat your evenings into oblivion. You watch television, game shows, sitcoms, documentaries. There are few with such eclectic tastes as you, Jemima, and few with your knowledge.

Or you might read, for you have hundreds of books to quench that thirst for knowledge. And a lot of the time you spend lying on your bed, daydreaming about romance, which is something you have little experience of.

Don't misunderstand me, Jemima isn't a virgin, but her virginity was lost during a quick tumble in the dark with a boy who was so inconsequential he may as well stay anonymous.

And since then she has had the odd fling with men who have a penchant for the larger lady. But she has never really enjoyed sex, has never tasted the pleasures of making love, but that doesn't stop a girl from dreaming does it?

But today, the day of the course, the day of learning how to surf the World Wide Web, is a break from that routine, and Jemima Jones hates breaking her routine. No bacon sandwiches for Jemima this morning, because the class is in the West End, many miles away from her familiar diner.

But at least she will not have to go on her own, because Geraldine, Geraldine of the perfect figure and rich boyfriend, will be picking her up.

"I'm not taking the bloody train," said Geraldine yesterday afternoon, when I asked how she was getting to the class.

"I've got a perfectly good car," she added, fully aware that the entire office was envious of her shining new black BMW, the car paid for partly by her boyfriend and partly by her parents, although she doesn't tell people about the parents' contribution. She only told me because I wouldn't let the subject drop and eventually she had to admit it.

"What about you?" she asked. "Why don't we go together?" I couldn't believe it, going to the class with Geraldine! Walking in with someone else, for once not being on my own. "Are you sure?" I asked. "You wouldn't mind?" Because why would Geraldine want to befriend someone like me? It's not that I dislike her—she, after all, is one of the few to have always treated me like a human being—it's just that I can't help but be intimidated by her perfection.

"'Course not," said Geraldine. "The damn thing doesn't start until ten-thirty, so I'll pick you up at ten. How does that sound?"

It sounded fantastic, and here I am now, sitting in the living room flicking through the pages of a book on container gardening but not really looking at the pictures, just waiting for the hum of Geraldine's car.

There is no hum, there are two short beeps of the horn, and pulling the curtain aside I can just about see Geraldine's elbow resting on the door frame as she taps her fingers to the music I assume she must be playing.

Geraldine and her car go together like apples and honey. They're both sleek, chic, with glossy exteriors and purring engines. Geraldine, as usual, has done herself proud. She's wearing a beautifully cut navy suit, the jacket just skimming her thighs, the lapels showing off a white silk T-shirt. On her head is a pair of large black sunglasses, keeping her highlights off her face, and she's holding a cigarette languorously, sexily, out of the window.

I feel like an ungainly oaf next to Geraldine, so I lumber into her car and just as I put the seat belt on—Geraldine, incidentally, isn't wearing one—she offers me a cigarette, which I take. You didn't know I smoked? Of course I smoke because way back when, in the murky teenage years, all the cool people smoked, and even then I wanted so badly to be cool.

Now admittedly, more often than not it's a pain in the ass because everywhere I go I'm surrounded by virulent anti-smokers, but it still makes me feel, well, not quite cool, but certainly less awkward.

Sitting here in Geraldine's car, when I compare Geraldine's seductive long drags to my short ones, I feel all wrong smoking. I look awkward, awkward fingers grasping the cigarette, exhaling all too quickly. I still, unfortunately, look like a fourteen-year-old trying out her first cigarette.

"So how's everything at work?" says Geraldine, flicking the butt out the window and checking in the rearview mirror that her lipstick is still perfectly applied.

"Same really," I say with a shrug. "I went to see the editor again and surprise surprise, there aren't any vacancies at the moment."

"Oh poor you," says Geraldine, but I think she's probably relieved. Geraldine knows I can write, Geraldine wouldn't be anywhere if it weren't for me because whenever she has a deadline I'm the one she comes running to asking for help. At least once a week I sit in front of my computer reading Geraldine's haphazard copy, before ripping it apart and putting it back together again so it makes sense. If I were promoted, who would help Geraldine?

And I don't mind, really, I don't, and perhaps in a strange way this is why, sitting in her car, I'm feeling less bad, less intimidated by her, and I'm starting genuinely to like her. And perhaps it's also because I know, beyond a shadow of a doubt, that when it comes to words I am infinitely more talented than Geraldine, however slim and beautiful she may be.

"Oh well," she continues, "never mind. Your time will come." She lifts her hand and puts her sunglasses on, groaning. "God, what a hangover."

I look at her in amazement, for Geraldine obviously does not know the meaning of the word. A hangover means bloodshot eyes, pale skin with a hint of gray, lank hair, deep shadows under the eyes. Geraldine, as she always does, looks perfect.

A gurgle of laughter emerges from my mouth. "Do you ever look anything less than perfect, Geraldine?"

Geraldine flicks her hair back and says, "Believe me, I look a mess," but she's pleased because, like all girls who are perfectly groomed, below the perfection is a writhing mass of insecurity, and she likes to hear that she's beautiful. It helps her to believe it.

"So what happened last night?"

"Oh God," Geraldine groans. "Dimitri took me out for dinner and I drank so much champagne I was positively comatose."

"Where did you go?"

"The Collection."

"I haven't been there yet," I say, knowing full bloody well that I'll probably never go there, being, as it is, a restaurant for the rich and the beautiful, but I know all about it. I know about the bright young things from the magazines who go there, and I know about it from Sophie and Lisa, who naturally have been wined, dined, and seduced in both the bar downstairs and the restaurant above.

"I suppose it was filled with the famous and beautiful?"

"Actually," says Geraldine, "actually, it was filled with lots of people who looked as if they ought to be famous, except neither of us knew who anyone was."

"Bloody wannabes," I say with a deep sigh. "They're just everywhere these days," and we both laugh.

Geraldine suddenly turns right and pulls up outside a large mansion block. "Sorry," she says, turning to me. "Ben Williams was bugging me for a lift so I said we'd come and get him. You don't mind do you?"

"No," I say, heart suddenly pounding. "I didn't know he lived here."

"Me neither until he gave me his address yesterday, but even a rat must have a home."

"Who does he live with?"

"Two other guys, apparently. God, can you imagine what their flat is like?"

"Ugh," I say, even though I haven't got a bloody clue. Me? How the hell would I know what a bachelor pad is like, but then again I've watched *Men Behaving Badly* and even I can pretend. "Stinking socks draped over all the radiators."

"Porn mags piled up in the corridor," Geraldine says, grimacing.

"Sheets that haven't seen a washing machine in six months."

"Piles of filthy washing-up overflowing the sink." We both clutch our stomachs and Geraldine makes gagging noises. I laugh, but suddenly I see Ben running out the front door and the laughter stops as my stomach does its usual lurch on sight of this gorgeous man.

"Make him sit in the back," whispers Geraldine. "I don't want to sit next to him."

So Ben walks over to the car and I climb out, trying to be dainty, delicate, feminine. "Morning girls," he says, "both looking particularly lovely today." He doesn't mean me, he's just being polite, so I stand awkwardly on the pavement and Ben looks at me patiently, waiting for me to climb in the back.

"Ben," shouts Geraldine from the driver's seat. "You don't mind getting in the back do you?"

"Oh," says Ben. After a pause, in which I wish more than anything in the world that the ground would open and swallow me up, he says, "Sure." And in a swift and graceful movement he climbs in.

I buckle up my seat belt while Ben leans forward, resting his arms on either seat in front. "So girls," he says, as Geraldine pulls out. "Good night last night?"

"Yes, thanks," says Geraldine, while I stay quiet.

"What did you do?"

Geraldine tells him, and I start playing this little game I play a lot of the time. I do it when I'm in a car and we pull up to traffic lights. If the light stays green until we pass, then I will find true love. Sometimes I add within the next six months. I don't know why I carry on playing it, as it never comes true, but I do it again now. I think, if you ask me what I did last night, then it means that we will end up together. Please ask me, Ben. Please. But then if he does ask me, what will I say? That I stayed at home and ate chocolate cookies? Oh God, how can I make myself sound interesting.

"What about you, Jemima?" Oh Christ. The question's out there before I've formulated an answer.

"Oh, I went to a party."

"Did you?" Ben and Geraldine ask the question simultaneously.

22

"You didn't mention that," says Geraldine. "Whose party?"

Quick, quick. Think, Jemima.

"Just an old friend."

"Wild night, eh Jemima?" says Ben with a wink.

"Yup," I say finally, deciding to throw caution to the wind. "I got very drunk, slightly stoned, and ended up shagging some guy in the toilet."

A silence descends on the car, neither Ben nor Geraldine knows quite what to say, and I feel sick. I know I've said the wrong thing. It doesn't come out as funny as I had intended, it comes out as peculiar, so I take a deep breath and tell the truth. Well. Sort of. "Actually, I'm lying. I stayed in and watched *60 Minutes.*"

Ben and Geraldine get the joke and they laugh. Except unfortunately, at least if you're sitting where Jemima Jones is sitting right now, it really isn't very funny. It's actually rather sad.

chapter 3

I'd heard about the Internet, read about the Internet, talked about the Internet, but I never really understood what it was all about. Of course, this being the *Kilburn* bloody *Herald* we're about four years behind the times technologically and are getting online access for the first time so even Ben's presence doesn't distract me from the computer screen where we're being shown how to use it.

And it's fascinating. Rob, the man who's teaching all of us, is explaining so clearly, so concisely, that I'm beginning to understand exactly what the big deal's all about, and wish I'd had the money to buy a computer so I could have learned about this sooner.

I can see that Geraldine's bored, and to amuse herself she's flirting with Rob, who seems delighted that someone like Geraldine would even look at him, but Ben's my ally in this, Ben's as enthralled as me, and together we're visiting newsgroups, sites, forums.

Rob shows us how to create a page, and explains that this is the Web: that all over the world people are designing pages filled with whatever information and pictures they choose, and from those pages there are links to hundreds, often thousands, of other pages.

He shows us how to search for a topic, and then how to follow those links until we find what we're looking for, and it's like a completely new world opening up for me.

And as the day carries on, the more we learn, the more I start to relax with Ben, the less he seems to intimidate me, maybe because we've got something in common now, I don't have to struggle for something to say.

At 5 P.M. Rob says we're done, and I catch Geraldine's eye as she rolls it to the ceiling. The three of us walk out together, and as soon as we're out the door Geraldine digs into her Prada bag and pulls out her cigarettes.

"God, I needed that," she says, inhaling deeply as we stand on the corner. "That was the most boring thing in the world. I knew most of it, for God's sake. Talk about Internet for idiots."

"I thought it was really interesting, actually," says Ben. "What did you think?" He turns to me and I nod vigorously, because I would agree with Ben no matter what I thought, and it's just a happy coincidence that I happen to feel the same way.

"I loved it," I say.

"I know," echoes Ben, "there's so much it's almost impossible to take it all in."

"Oh shut up you two," says Geraldine, as a little glow lights up inside me because, stupid as it may be, she has linked me with Ben. "Look," she says, gesturing up the road. "There's a really nice bar up here. If you promise not to talk computers all night, why don't we go for a drink?"

Who? Ben? Me? Both of us? She was looking up the road as she said it and I just stand there in silence because she can't mean me, she wouldn't want to have a drink, socialize *after work*, with me. Surely?

"Good idea," says Ben, and they start walking off while I stand there feeling like an idiot, unsure of what to do.

"Jemima?" says Geraldine, turning round. "Come on," and I almost want to kiss her as I race to catch up.

chapter 4

Drug addiction; food addiction; alcohol addiction; cigarette addiction. The funny thing is no one ever talks about Internet addiction.

Internet addiction is the scourge of the new millennium. All over the world men and women are going to bed on their own, curling up miserably while their partners lock themselves away in their studies and tap, tap, tap away into the early hours of the morning.

The Internet is another world, where people can be anyone they want, and, even as you read these words, marriages are disintegrating through lack of communication, thanks to a little colored screen tucked away in a corner of the house.

But of course Jemima Jones knows nothing of this. Jemima Jones doesn't have to worry about partners getting pissed off, or miserable marriages, or even yet another addiction to add to her list.

All Jemima knows, right now as she's on her way home from work, is that the Internet seems like fun, and she can discover all she wants about cleaning silver, fraying curtains, removing cat spray smells, just by tapping a few keys.

And what's even more exciting is that the information she receives could be coming from anywhere in the entire world. She walks along the pavement, lost in thoughts about the Internet, so deeply immersed that before she knows it she's at her front door, and guess what? She completely forgot to buy some chocolate on the way home.

Good girl, Jemima. *Well* done. Today is the day of the first diet that's actually going to work. I'm going to really try this time. No chocolate!

I walk upstairs and can already hear Sophie and Lisa giggling away in Sophie's bedroom as I tentatively push open the door.

Lisa's lying back on the bed, clutching her pillow. "I'm in love," she sighs as I walk in. Oh shut up, I think, but I don't say that. I say, "Let me guess. A new guy started at work and he's devastatingly handsome and he wants to marry you?"

"No, don't be daft. It's the guy we met last week, the new client. He asked Lisa out." Sophie's trying to look pleased, but envy is written all over her face. I don't believe that stuff about blondes being stupid, at least I didn't before I met Sophie, but I know that she believes blondes ought to have more fun, and she can't believe this guy went for Lisa.

"His name's Nick Hanson, he's thirty-three, single, and I love him," sighs Lisa dreamily. "Lisa Hanson. What do you think? Mrs. Nick Hanson, Mrs. Lisa Hanson."

"I think you might be jumping the gun a bit." I'm not bitter, I promise you, it's just that I've seen this so many times before and I know exactly what will happen. At the end of their first date Lisa will come home and will spend the evening sketching wedding dresses and drawing up guest lists.

"So when are you going out?"

"Tomorrow night. Oh God, I love him, he's the most divine man I've met in ages."

I sit down on the bed, something I'd never normally do, but I didn't see Sophie and Lisa last night, and yesterday something actually happened. I have something to talk about. Or perhaps I should say *someone*.

"I did my class yesterday. The Internet one."

"Great," says Lisa.

"Really?" says Sophie. "That's funny, I was just reading an article in one of my magazines about how loads of people are dating on the Internet."

"What did it say?" I ask.

"Honestly, it sounds amazing. You go to these dating places and there are pictures of single people, and you can write to each other, e-mail over the computer. But people are meeting from all over the world. There have even been marriages because of it."

Lisa sits up and looks at Sophie. "Yes, but you wouldn't think of doing it would you?"

"I don't know really," says Sophie. "I mean, I don't think I'd ever be able to work out how to use it, but it sounds quite exciting. You could pick up a gorgeous American hunk and live happily ever after in his mansion in Dallas."

"Sounds a bit sad to me," says Lisa.

"Well," says Sophie, turning to me. "Did you learn how to meet people on the Internet then?"

"Not really, it wasn't that sort of class, but it's amazingly interesting, you can find out pretty much anything. And afterwards I went for a drink, that's why I wasn't home last night."

I'm so desperate to tell someone, anyone, about Ben Williams, I'm practically bursting.

Are you sure you can't hold it in anymore, Jemima? Go on then, tell them all about it.

"Who with?"

I can see I've got them, they want to know and I don't blame them. I mean, it's not often I talk about my social life, probably because I don't exactly have what you'd call a social life, and they can see that something's happened.

"With Geraldine," I pause. "And Ben."

"Who's Ben?" Naturally they don't know, because up until now my crush has been secret, but I have to tell someone, and far better to tell Sophie and Lisa, who would never meet him, than to confide in, say, Geraldine.

"The deputy news editor at work."

"And???"

"And . . ." Should I tell them? Should I keep it secret? Oh, what the hell. "And I think he's completely wonderful." There. A deep breath. It's out there. No going back.

Sophie and Lisa sit in shocked silence. I've never talked about men before, and as I watch them I can see their eyes glaze over as they imagine what this Ben looks like, and I can see they've got it completely wrong.

Jemima Jones is absolutely right, they have got it completely wrong.

Lisa thinks he is probably 5'7", has messy brown hair, thick glasses, and dresses in ill-fitting suits in shades of brown. She thinks he is the type of man who would still live at home, and his idea of an exciting night out is probably going to the movies to see subtitled films.

Sophie thinks he is probably 5'7" tall, and 4'6" wide. She thinks he has to be overweight, incredibly dull, and a complete computer nerd. She suspects that his idea of an exciting night is spent down at the pub drinking pints of lager with his nerdy friends.

If only they knew.

For Ben Williams is the sort of man that both Sophie and Lisa would fall head over heels in love with.

"So come on then, what's he like?"

Now it's my turn to sigh. "He's very funny, he makes me laugh. And he's bright, and charming, and he knows how to treat women."

"But what does he look like?"

"I don't know how to describe him, really. He's about 6'2"." Sophie and Lisa catch one another's eyes and each suppresses a smile, and I know they think I'm lying. So what? I carry on. "He's got brown hair, and beautiful eyes, but I'm not sure what color they are. Green maybe?" Yup, thinks Lisa, looking again at Sophie, she's describing some model she's seen in one of her magazines.

"And he's got these amazing dimples when he smiles," I conclude, smiling happily at the very thought of Ben Williams.

"And does he like you?" asks Sophie, gently, patronizingly, because she doesn't want to hurt me by telling me she knows I'm lying.

"No," I say wearily. "I mean, he likes me, but he doesn't *like* me. He likes Geraldine, but she doesn't like him."

"Well maybe that can grow, him liking you, I mean," says Sophie. "When he gets to know you he'll realize what a lovely person you are." She stops suddenly, aware of what she's just said. "Not that he wouldn't be attracted to you anyway," she stammers. "You've got the most beautiful face."

I can't believe Sophie doesn't see how transparent she is. I know exactly what she thinks of me. She thinks I am huge, vast, the fattest girl she's ever met, and I don't blame her. When I look in the mirror, if I look beyond my face, I see exactly the same thing.

"I haven't," I say, for what else could I say? "He'd *never* fancy me, but I can dream."

"So what about Geraldine?" asks Lisa. "If he's so gorgeous, how come she doesn't fancy him?"

"He's probably not rich enough for her," says Sophie, who has come out with this uncharacteristically bitchy comment because she is jealous of Geraldine. She has never actually met Geraldine, but she has seen her on the rare occasions that Geraldine has come to pick me up or drop me off. She's never said anything directly to me but I know she has seen Geraldine's air of confidence, her BMW, and she is as jealous as hell.

"That's not really fair," I say, although it happens to be true, and I feel guilty at talking about Geraldine, the one person whom I could perhaps call a friend, so I add, "Geraldine's a lovely person when you get to know her."

"Hmm," says Sophie. "Anyway, you never know. Maybe he's sitting in his roommate's bedroom at this very moment telling his roommate all about you."

As it happens, at this very moment Ben Williams is watching the news. He's sitting on his black leather and chrome sofa, feet up on the glass coffee table which is covered with magazines, newspapers, an overflowing ashtray, a few empty cans of Heineken and bits of torn-up rolling paper packages. He's drinking a beer, but not Heineken, those belong to his roommates. He's drinking Beck's, and he's studying the news.

When the reports start he pulls his feet off the coffee table and leans forward, elbows on his knees, dangling the bottle of beer idly between his legs, but his eyes are fixed on the television screen, and as the reporter speaks, so Ben mimics him, over and over again, until Ben's voice is almost indistinguishable from the reporter's.

"Until late last year, this derelict building in one of London's more fashionable districts was ignored by the council, and the surrounding residents in this leafy street," said the reporter. Said Ben.

"This is Jeremy Millston for the *Six O'Clock News*," ends the reporter, as the cameras switch back to the news studio.

"This is Benjamin Williams for the *Six O'Clock News*," echoes Ben, standing up to turn off the television. Perfect. All the inflections in exactly the right places. He checks his watch, and wanders into the kitchen to get another beer, he won't be meeting his roommates at the pub for another half hour.

Ben takes his beer into the bedroom and fishes under the bed, pulling out a large box stuffed with papers. Oh I'm sorry, you want to know what Ben's bedroom is like? Well, not what you expect, for starters. Geraldine and Jemima may have been right about the rest of the flat, the socks draped over radiators and the porn mags piled up in the living room, but Ben's bedroom is his haven, his sanctuary, and a quick look around may tell us exactly what we need to know about Ben Williams.

It may be a rented flat, but Ben and his roommates were given permission to redecorate. Needless to say they haven't done a thing, except for Ben. Ben has painted his bedroom walls a dark bottle-green. His window shade is navy, green and burgundy check, and his duvet cover and pillowcases match.

Dotted around the wall are original cartoons, which Ben collects. A number of the cartoons on his wall have appeared in national newspapers, and all are of a satirical nature. Before you ask, Ben doesn't have the money to afford this, not yet, but he is careful with the small amount he does earn, and half the cartoons were bought from his savings, the rest gifts from his parents.

An old armchair, picked up by Ben for £20 in the junk shop down the road, sits in one corner of the room, facing an old French cherrywood table, also from the junk shop, a bargain at £50. Piled on top of the table are books. Autobiographies, biographies, cookbooks—for Ben loves to cook—fiction, nonfiction. The latest titles, together with some old favorites, are in this corner of the room.

Next to the books is a silver photo frame containing a picture of Ben smiling happily with his parents on graduation day. He is proudly wearing his cap and gown, and a quick glance at his parents shows us where Ben got his looks.

His mother is tall, slim and soignée. She is wearing a slim cream skirt, a navy jacket, and high-heeled cream shoes with a navy toe. On her head is a hat, a designer hat, a hat that most women dream of owning. Ben's father is significantly older than his wife. Tall, handsome, with thick gray hair. All three are beaming into the camera with shining smiles and open faces. They look like a nice family. They are in fact a delightful family.

Ben's father is a wealthy businessman and his mother is a

housewife. Being an only child, Ben has been doted upon, but he has always insisted on making his own way in the world. After university Ben turned down his father's offer to work in the family business, and joined the local paper as a junior reporter on a pittance.

He rented a hovel of a flat, far far worse than this one, and lived with five other boys in similar situations. He allowed his parents to provide the odd treat, such as a beautiful watch on his birthday, or a pair of cuff links, or a suit, but on the whole he paid his own way.

Ben Williams loves his parents and his parents love him. They are a normal, healthy family. The only thing that is slightly abnormal is perhaps how well they all get on. Because Ben's parents have always treated him as an equal. Even when he was a child his parents would stop to listen to what Ben had to say. He was never patronized or ignored, but listened to and related to as an adult. His father now makes the odd offer to come and work in the family business, because his father does not understand the media world at all, but Ben has nearly got where he wanted, and he knows this is the right thing for him to be doing.

Oh Geraldine, if only you knew about Ben's background. You would discover he is, or at least his family is, wealthy enough even for your nouveau riche tastes. But you can't help but judge the superficial, and you will only see as far as Ben's beaten-up Fiat.

So back to Ben's bedroom. In the recesses next to his bed he has put up pine shelves, and stained them to remove that orangey patina that looks so cheap. He sanded down the shelves himself, then bashed them a bit with a hammer to make them look old before rubbing in the stain with wads of cotton wool.

And on the shelves are more books, more photographs. Books piled high, almost overflowing, and photographs of Ben's friends, former girlfriends, lovers.

Look, there's Ben at university with Suzie, the girl he went out with for the best part of his three years there. She's not classically beautiful, not model material, but see how pretty she is, how her skin glows, how white are her teeth, how glossy her long auburn hair.

And there's Ben with Richard, his best friend. The pair of them on holiday, Greece perhaps, suntanned faces, shorts and T-shirts, sunglasses, and arms flung over one another's shoulders, grinning widely into the lens.

And in pride of place is a photograph of a celebrity, a genuine star of one of Britain's most popular soap operas. Cheesy as it may well be, this is the photo Ben is most proud of, for she is Laurie, one of his conquests, but we'll save the story of Laurie until later.

Ben lies back on his bed, crumpling the jacket of his suit, which he flung on the duvet when he got home from work, but this is a good sign, for while we know from his bedroom that Ben isn't a slob we can now assume that neither is he anally retentive.

He lies back holding the piece of paper he dug out of the box he pulled from under his bed. It is a script from the news, a script that Ben painstakingly transcribed in his shorthand, scribbling down everything the newsreader said, and now he lies back and reads the first words in his television voice.

"Good evening."

Practice, practice, practice, Ben. All over the world there are thousands of young men and women, people just like Ben, who dream of being a television presenter. They ache for their fifteen minutes of fame, long to be famous for the sake of being famous.

If they're lucky, if they have the requisite long blond hair, flirtatious nature, and penchant for being wild, the girls may just make it on to the screen as presenters of some wacky new show. The men may, if they have the right contacts, also land on our screens as children's presenters. But few have the dedication to do what Ben's doing.

Ever since Ben was a child Ben has dreamed of reading the

news. At university, studying for his English degree, Ben sat down with Richard and worked out how he was going to do it. He decided his greatest advantage (other than the dimples and white teeth, because Ben, although he is aware of them, doesn't really think about them all that often) would be a background in journalism. He knew he could have got on one of the graduate trainee schemes that all the national newspapers seem so keen on running these days, but he also knew, from speaking to people who had already gone down that route, that most of their time was spent doing gofer work.

And so he decided to look for a local paper. A local paper that wouldn't pay very well, but would give him the required news training. A local paper where the news editor might have the time to take Ben under his wing and show him how to sniff out a news story, how to interview members of the public and celebrities, and win an exclusive interview through charm alone.

A local paper where Ben might have a chance to rise quickly in the ranks, before moving to regional television. And from regional television he would move to network television. He would be an anchorman. He would present the news.

Admittedly, at twenty-nine, Ben's career hasn't progressed quite as quickly as he had planned, but nevertheless he's on course, and changes, he rightly suspects, are afoot.

Naturally he didn't tell the editor of the *Kilburn Herald* any of his plans when he turned up for an interview. He sat there and told the editor he was a newspaper man, he loved newspapers, loved the *Kilburn Herald* (for Ben had moved to Kilburn for the express purpose of working for the *Kilburn Herald*, a paper, he decided, at which he could make changes), had in fact spent years dreaming of working for the *Kilburn Herald*.

He told the editor he was happy to start as a junior reporter, but that at some time, not too far away, he would be news editor. And the editor, being a rather vain and stupid man, was flattered by Ben Williams, and won over by the smile and the dimples.

But he wasn't as stupid as all that. He realized the effect Ben's good looks would have on the people he had to interview. And sure enough, from the very first day Ben and Ben alone was the reporter to land the stories that everyone wanted. His future had started. Ben was on his way.

And now, in this large rented flat in a wide, tree-lined street in Kilburn, Ben puts aside the piece of paper and gets up off the bed. A cursory glance in the mirror tells him he looks fine, not that it matters tonight, it's only the boys at the local pub, but you never know. You just never know.

chapter 5

It may be lunchtime, but Jemima Jones is sitting at her desk wondering how she can find out what to do with terra-cotta pots filled with candles once the candles have burned down. She could, quite easily, telephone a candle shop and ask them, and it would, of course, be easier, not to mention quicker, than logging on to the Internet, but she wants to test the Internet, to find out whether she can do it on her own.

She double-clicks on the sign on her computer and then clicks on CONNECT, listening to the computer dial up the modem and put her through. And here she is, the World Wide Web at her fingertips.

Where should she go first? What should she do?

"Hey, quick work." I turn round and of course it's Ben, jacket off, shirtsleeves rolled up, dimples at the ready.

"Just thought I'd see if I could work it by myself."

"I keep meaning to try it too, but I haven't had the time. Do you mind if I join you?"

Mind? Mind? Is he mad? I would move heaven and earth

for you to join me, Ben. I would cut off my right arm if it meant you would join me.

"Sure, why don't you pull up a chair."

Ben pulls up a swivel chair and sits close to me, and I never thought I'd say this but it's almost too close for comfort, certainly too close to breathe comfortably. I can feel my breath coming out in short, sharp bursts, but Ben doesn't notice a thing. He doesn't even notice how I involuntarily catch my breath as he puts his hand on top of mine on the mouse, and clicks on the Internet.

"What are you looking for?" he says to me, keeping his eyes fixed on the screen.

"Nothing special," I lie. "Just exploring, really."

"Is everyone at lunch?"

I look around at the empty desks, listen to the phones ringing out with no one to answer them, and turn back to Ben. "I think so, it seems pretty dead in here."

"Good." He turns to me with a wink. "Let's explore the sex sites."

I smile broadly to hide my embarrassment. It's not that I don't want to see them, although I'd never dare admit it, I just don't want to see them sitting with Ben, but it will keep him here for a while, so what the hell.

"I just did a story about kids downloading porn from the Internet on to disk, then selling it at St. Ursula's. Let's see what all the fuss is about," Ben says nonchalantly, but I'm sure that's just an excuse to see what it's all about. St. Ursula's is the local public high school with a reputation so bad that on the rare occasions I have to walk past at the time when the children are coming out, I cross the road or, better yet, find an alternative route. It's not quite as bad as the construction sites but nearly. Nearly.

Ben's concentrating hard on the screen, and I have to smile. St. Ursula's indeed! You must think I'm stupid, Ben, but good excuse, though. I have to admit I wouldn't have thought of that one.

"How do you find them?" I ask, ever the innocent.

"God knows, let's try and find out."

Ben clicks until there's a box on his screen saying SEARCH. "Right," he says. "Here goes. What do you think, sex or porn?"

"Try sex first," and Ben leans across me, without realizing that as he does so his right arm brushes my left breast and I think I've died and gone to heaven. There is no expression on his face other than intense concentration as he types in the letters SEX, then presses SEARCH.

Nothing happens for a few seconds and Ben looks at me and grins. "Wouldn't it be a nightmare if the editor came past now?"

I grin back. I would suffer any humiliation just for the pleasure of feeling Ben's arm lightly touching my breasts.

"We'll just tell him we're doing some research," I say with a wicked smile.

Ben laughs. "He'd probably want to pull up a chair himself. One of my friends just got a computer at home and he says that all his friends, even the girls, have been coming over and asking him to show them the Internet. Every time he asks them what they want to see, they all say sex. So there you go, we're not abnormal after all."

You mean you're not abnormal, Ben, because to be completely honest I'm really not that bothered about scouring the sex sites, in fact, I think I'd rather not, but I'm not going to dwell on the potential embarrassment involved in surfing sex sites with the man of my dreams, I'm just going to sit here and enjoy being with you.

Suddenly the computer screen changes, and there's a list on the screen, all of them sexual names, each urging you to click on them, see what they have to offer. I am not going to blush. I am going to be cool, calm, and collected. Even as I sit here reading about oral, anal, sucking, fucking, I am not going to show Ben that I am anything other than a woman of the world.

"Brilliant," says Ben, as I'm concentrating on keeping my face its normal color. "Let's go and see HOTSEX."

Ben clicks on HOTSEX and nothing happens, the screen just goes completely black. Talk about anticlimax. "Do you think it's not working?" Ben says, disappointment written all over his face.

"I think it probably just takes a long time. Look! Something's happening." And sure enough, a series of lines starts appearing on screen. I'm watching Ben out of the corner of my eye, and Ben's watching the screen.

Welcome to the hottest, dirtiest, horniest site on the Internet
We have everything to satisfy your tastes
10 gigabytes of adult GIF files
Download dirty video clips from Amsterdam
Have live interactive sex with the horniest chicks around
Porn, sex, fucking, oral, anal, lesbian, gay
Join Hotsex for just $29.95
If you're a visitor click here to see the special visitor's site

"We did it, we did it!" says Ben in jubilation, clicking on the visitor's site. "We found sex on the Internet!"

"Bearing in mind this is *research*, you're sounding incredibly excited," and I can't help but smile at Ben's reaction.

"Oh yes, sorry, I forgot. Research. Yes, this is research. Of course."

The screen goes black again and then more words of welcome, next to which are three tiny little boxes of a bright blue and green universe, surrounded by a red circle.

And nothing else happens.

"Jesus, what a waste of time," says Ben. "Where are the bloody pictures?"

"Maybe you have to click on a universe?"

Ben tries, but nothing happens. "Shit, shit, shit. Look, I've gotta go for a pee, let's try and sort it out in a sec. Won't be a minute." He walks off and I idly pick up a magazine lying next to the computer while I wait for him to come back.

God, yet another model breaking into the big league and isn't she gorgeous. I study her platinum blond hair and perfect eyebrows, and then make a mental note to add her to my collection when I get home.

"SHIT!" Ben shouts as his footsteps come running up behind me.

"OH MY GOD!" I look up at the screen and clap my hand over my mouth and both of us, just for a split second, seem to freeze in horror. As soon as we've pulled ourselves together, we frantically turn around, breathing sighs of relief that no one else is in the office. Because there on the computer screen, what was a little box containing a universe is now a massive color picture of a naked woman, legs spread, with her mouth wrapped around one man's penis, while another is standing behind and screwing her.

The picture is crystal clear, every detail shines from the screen, and Ben, once he is sure there is no one other than Jemima to see him, is practically salivating. And Jemima? Jemima wants to die.

Jemima has never seen porn before, not proper hard-core porn, and, sitting next to Ben, she blushes furiously, a hot red rising up and covering her face. Don't look round, she thinks, don't look at me, Ben, don't see what I look like.

"What are you two up to?" Geraldine's striding towards us, as immaculate as ever in a crisp camel suit, large gold earrings, and the omnipresent sunglasses on top of her head.

"Research," I bluster, feeling more and more stupid even as the color starts to fade from my face.

"Shit," whispers Ben, but before he can get rid of the picture Geraldine's in front of the screen.

"Oh my God!" she says, almost under her breath. "Where did that come from?"

"Hotsex," I mutter.

"Hot what?"

"Hotsex," repeats Ben. "We found this site on the Internet."

"You'd better not let anyone see what you're doing."

"Really?" says Ben. "Tell me something else I didn't know."

Geraldine muscles between us. "Let me have a go," she says, french manicured nails reaching for the mouse on the table.

"What's this then?" she says, clicking on to DOOR ONE. "What's behind Door One, I wonder?"

None of us has to wonder long, as the picture disappears and more lines start appearing, another picture. This time a man, head arched back in ecstasy as a semi-naked girl, on her knees in front of him, is shown in graphic detail giving him a blow job.

"God," whispers Geraldine. "This is hysterical, it's so, well, so unsexy." I start to laugh because she's absolutely right. There is nothing, but nothing, sexy about looking at a pornographic picture on a computer screen. Then Ben starts to laugh, and soon the three of us are clutching our sides and wiping the tears from our eyes. This stuff is far too clinical to turn anyone on.

"Oh dear," gasps Geraldine, wiping the tears carefully away so as not to smudge her MAC mascara. "What else can we look at?"

"What, more sex?" Even Ben's surprised.

"No, idiot. I mean aren't there any other interesting places?"

"I don't know. I don't know what else to look at."

"Oh Ben, for God's sake. Here, let me." Geraldine gets rid of the sex and clicks a few times, finally coming across HOT SITES ON THIS NETWORK.

"That's probably more sex," I moan, clutching my heart, which I don't think can take the strain of another full-color graphic porn picture on the computer screen at work.

"No, it's not," says Geraldine, "it's just sites that are popular." And sure enough a new list of sites appears onscreen.

"There, that looks good," says Geraldine, gesturing at a site called LA Café. Geraldine reads out loud. "'LA Café. The coolest virtual café on the Internet. Grab a cappuccino, the latest articles from the American magazines, and meet other single people, all looking for that one special person.'"

"LA Café, here we come," says Ben, as Geraldine clicks on the site, and the logo comes on the screen.

LA Café
The coolest site for the seriously single
and the cappuccinos you've been surfing for all your life

"We have to join but it doesn't cost anything," says Geraldine, clicking the JOIN logo. A small box appears saying NAME: KILBURN HERALD.

"Oh forget that," she says, "we won't be picking up anything as the *Kilburn Herald*. What shall we call ourselves?"

"How about the Three Musketeers?" offers Ben, who's now genuinely excited.

"No. Too obvious."

"We're only messing around, let's come up with a name that sounds suitably sexy," I offer, really quite curious to see what's going to happen. I think for a minute. "What about Honey?"

"Brilliant," says Geraldine, deleting KILBURN HERALD and typing in HONEY.

"Hey, that's not fair," says Ben. "If we join as Honey they won't know there's a guy involved. How am I going to pick up women?"

"Be quiet," says Geraldine, "too late now," and so it is. We've joined the LA Café, or rather Honey has joined the LA Café.

"What do we do now?" I ask, after we've sat there for a couple of minutes staring mutely at the logo. "Why don't we click on one of those boxes on the side?"

"Okay," shrugs Geraldine, as she clicks on a picture of three heads together.

Who is Here, it says, as a box flashes up onscreen with a load of names.

Suzie 24
=ˆ··ˆ=Cat
Scott Shearer
Honey

Ben the invincible
Todd
Luscious Lisa:-)
Ricky
Tim@London
Brad (Santa Monica)

Geraldine reads the names. "Well, what the hell's Tim doing at the LA Café if he's in London?" she says.

"Same thing as us, presumably," laughs Ben.

"Let's find out." She clicks on his name and immediately another box appears on screen. The box is divided into two. The top half has Tim@London over the top, and the bottom, smaller half says Honey.

"Hello, fellow Londoner," types Geraldine, the words appearing in the small box at the bottom. "What are you doing at the La Café?" She presses RETURN and the words disappear from the bottom box and reappear at the top, ready for Tim@London to read.

"Picking up luscious Californian babes, of course. Why are you here?"

"Just checking it out. Looking for some Californian hunks. Any recommendations?"

"Lol. I'll have a think."

Geraldine turns to Ben. "What does Lol mean?"

"Dunno," he says. "Ask him."

"What does Lol mean?"

"Laugh out loud. You're new to this then?"

"First time. Any other tips?"

"Sure. :-) means happy. :-(means unhappy. ;-) means a wink, but also <w> means wink. <g> means grin, <s> means smile, and ROFL means rolling on the floor laughing."

"Thanks," types Geraldine. ";-)"

"God, this is amazing." I am truly flabbergasted. "It's a whole other language. Can I have a go?"

Geraldine moves the mouse over to me and I move my

hands quickly over the keyboard. "So, have you found your Californian dream babe yet?"

"Yup, talking to her at the moment. Suzie, she's blond, she's twenty-four, she's a hardbody and a total babe."

"How do you know she's not lying to you?"

"She said she'll e-mail me her photo."

"I hope she's not lying."

"We'll soon find out <s>. So where in London are you?"

I turn to the other two and make a face. "We can't say Kilburn, it's too naff."

"Say West Hampstead," says Geraldine, "it's the next best thing."

So I do as she says and type in West Hampstead.

"Wowowow." Tim@London types back. "I'm in Kilburn!!!"

The three of us start laughing.

"Hi, Honey! So how old are you?" suddenly flashes up on the screen from Todd, and I abandon my conversation with Tim@London.

I type twenty-seven, but Geraldine stops me just as I'm about to press RETURN, to send the words to him.

"Don't say twenty-seven," she urges. "You don't have to tell the truth on this. Tell him you're nineteen." So I do, realizing she's absolutely right. I don't have to tell the truth on the Internet. About anything.

"Just the right age for me!!!"

"How old are you?"

"Thirty-two."

"That's a bit old for me isn't it?"

"You know what they say about older men . . ."

"Yes. That they should know better than to chat up nineteen-year-olds." I press RETURN then add a ":-)" to show that I'm joking. Don't want to annoy him. Not yet, anyway.

"Ouch. Not fair."

"Sorry. But do fill me in, what do they say about older men?"

"Older, wiser, more experienced. In every department."

Geraldine shrieks with laughter. "Go on," says Ben, "see if you can get him talking dirty."

"Oh yes?" I type. "Why not tell me EXACTLY what you're better at."

"I don't believe this," says Ben. "This is sick." But he's grinning.

"Okay, Honey. You want to know what would happen if you went out on a date with me?"

"Darling, I can't wait to hear."

"Well first of all we wouldn't bother going to a restaurant, I'd want you all to myself at home, so I'd cook a gourmet meal, and we'd eat by candlelight on my terrace overlooking the swimming pool to the sounds of soft jazz playing on the stereo."

Geraldine makes gagging noises.

"Go on."

"After dinner I'd lead you into my bedroom and I would give you a massage. I'd unbutton your shirt, and dribble some baby oil on to my palm. I'd warm the oil between my hands and then I'd make you lie on the bed while I slowly rub the baby oil into the smooth, tanned skin of your back."

"How do you know it's tanned?"

"Sssh. You're spoiling the atmosphere. After you're completely relaxed, I'd move my hands lower, pulling down your skirt until I'm rubbing my palms over your bare buttocks. I'd move lower and lower, pulling your panties down as I go, slipping my hand in between your legs, where it's warm, dark, and moist with longing."

"Oh my God! I don't believe this!"

"What a perv!" shrieks Geraldine.

"Let the guy finish!" says Ben.

"Then I'd turn you over, and slowly stroke the oil on to your bare breasts. Your nipples would be erect by now, aching for me to take them between my fingers and rub them gently."

Geraldine and I shriek with laughter, and for the first time in my life I stop feeling intimidated by her, and start to think that actually she's really very nice. Ben doesn't say anything.

He's smiling, but one look at his face and we can tell he wants to hear more. Unfortunately, he won't.

I sit there and cover my face in mock horror. "I can't do this anymore," I say, "this is too horrible," and I quickly type in, "Okay, thanks for the massage. Must do it again some time. Bye."

"Sorry. Did I put you off?" Poor Todd, he's blown it and he's hardly started yet.

"Just ignore him," says Geraldine. "Let's try someone else."

"My turn, my turn," says Ben, reaching for the mouse.

"Hi Suzie," he types. "I'm Ben. I'm with two female friends. Now it's my turn."

"Oh. Okay. How are you, Ben?"

"Good, thank you. But the burning question is, what are you doing with Tim@London, who evidently has no money because he lives in a really grotty area, when you could be with me."

"Ben!" I start laughing. "Like you live in a palace?"

"Sssh," he says. "What difference?"

"Are you rich then, Ben?"

"Richer than Tim@London, and better looking."

"LOL."

":-)"

"How do you know what he looks like?"

"Trust me. I know these things."

"So what do you look like?"

Geraldine groans at me. "God, he's off. Shall we go and get a coffee?"

And they do. They go downstairs to the cafeteria and leave Ben sitting at the computer, chatting animatedly to Suzie, the babe of his dreams. The babe that's as different from Jemima as, well, as a typewriter and a computer linked up to the Internet.

chapter 6

I can't get the bloody Internet out of my head. Truth to be told, I think it's brilliant, everything. The World Wide Web, the chat forums, the possibilities.

Not that I'm looking for anyone, I mean, it's me, for God's sake, the woman who never has any boyfriends, and, although I know what a nice person I am, I'm not the most sociable of creatures. I wish I were, I wish I could be more like my roommates at times, but unfortunately my size dictates my social life, and my size is the one thing I can't control. I know what you're thinking, go on a diet, but it's not as easy as that, I just can't stop the cravings when they come, and somehow living on the Internet seems a far easier option than giving up chocolate.

I mean, this could open up a whole new life for me, a new life that doesn't care about looks, about weight, about expanses of flesh.

Or perhaps I should say, doesn't *know*, because I'm not stupid, if I had described myself accurately to Todd, he would have been off faster than you can say megabyte.

But I really can be anyone I want on the Internet. After all, who could ever find out? What harm could there be? And, let's face it, up until now the only fun thing in my life has been fantasizing first about being thin, and then about Ben Williams, but even those fantasies have been so tame that they're hardly worth repeating.

Are we interested? Okay, let's take a peek into Jemima's daydreams. When Jemima Jones goes to bed and closes her eyes, this is what she sees: she sees herself struck down with gastroenteritis, a bad bout, not so bad as to be seriously threatening, but bad enough for her to lose huge amounts of weight.

She sees herself decked out in little suits, tight fitted jackets, short skirts just skimming her thighs. She sees herself bumping into Ben Williams, who has by now left the *Kilburn Herald*, as in fact has she.

She sees herself going up to Ben at a crowded party, and saying hi, with a cool look in her eyes and a casual flick of her now blond hair. She sees Ben's eyes widen in shock, replaced seconds later by admiration, respect, lust. She sees Ben driving her home, and coming in for coffee. She sees her roommates fall over themselves trying to flirt with him, but she sees that Ben only has eyes for her.

She sees Ben moving closer towards where she sits on the sofa, unable, even for a moment, to take his eyes off her face. She sees his mouth in close-up detail, as he bends forward to kiss her. When they have kissed, and, incidentally, it is a kiss that instantly propels her up to a cloud, Ben looks in her eyes and says, "You're the most beautiful woman I've ever seen. I love you and I want to be with you for the rest of my life."

Ridiculous, isn't it, but Jemima Jones never gets beyond that first kiss and the declaration of love. Occasionally the kiss takes place elsewhere, sometimes at the party, sometimes in the car, sometimes on the street, but his words are always the same, and, as far as Jemima's concerned, those words are the beginning of her happy ever after.

So I think we all agree that right now, at this stage in her life, Jemima Jones deserves a bit of fun.

* * *

The first step in my new life is to stop at the bookshop on the way home from work. Actually it's not really on my way home, it involves a massive detour to Hampstead, but, despite this being a break from my daily routine, I'm beginning to realize that my life is changing, and by the looks of things so far it would appear to be getting infinitely better.

The evidence? Well, as far as I can see, seven important, life-changing things have happened. First, I went on a course to learn the basics about the Internet. Second, after the course I went for a drink, *I actually went out for a drink*, and, not only that, the drink lasted all evening. This, as far as I'm concerned, is the definite beginning of a social life. Third, it wasn't just any old drink, it was a drink with Geraldine and Ben Williams. Geraldine, with whom I had never, until that drink, socialized after work, and Ben, about whom I fantasize every night. Fourth, I was actually able to relax in Ben's company! I wasn't the tongue-tied teenager he occasionally joins for lunch in the canteen, I was almost, almost, myself. Fifth, I had a good time. No, forget that, I had a *great* time! Sixth, Ben joined me on the Internet today, and yes I was embarrassed by the sex, but more importantly I showed Ben I have a sense of humor, at least I hope I did. Seventh, I haven't had any chocolate for two whole weeks.

Is it any wonder that Jemima Jones feels that life is taking a definite turn for the better? Never mind that the drink she shared with Ben Williams and Geraldine was two weeks ago. Never mind that she hasn't seen Ben Williams properly since their brief sojourn on the Internet. Never mind that neither Geraldine nor Ben has suggested a repeat drink. That one evening was enough to set a chain of events in progress. Cause and effect, except Jemima doesn't quite know the full effect just yet. Nor do we.

But nevertheless, two weeks have passed and still Jemima's feeling so happy, so high, so full of excitement at her new life, she treats herself to a taxi to Hampstead. She stands on the corner outside the *Kilburn Herald*, eyes full of hope, hands full of bags, and she hails a black cab.

* * *

"Hampstead, please," I tell the driver, climbing awkwardly into the back.

"Whereabouts, love?" he says, a middle-aged man with a kind face.

"Do you know Waterstone's?"

He nods, and off we go. Up through West Hampstead, passing the hordes of young people on their way home from work, zippy suits, designer briefcases, aspirations in their eyes. Up across the Finchley Road, up Arkwright Road, cut through Church Row as I stare with envy at the houses that once contained bohemian artists and writers, and now contain wealthy businessmen, and right at the tube, down Hampstead High Street, he pulls up, double-parking, for of course there are no spaces in which to park, and clicks his meter.

"Keep the change," I say, handing him £6, for today is the beginning of my new life, and I can afford to be a bit extravagant. I might even do a little shopping, because it's only 5:45 P.M., and the shops will be open for a while yet, tempting me with their glamorous window displays.

But first into Waterstone's, dark, cool, calm, I breathe in the air of reverence and feel a sense of calm wash over me. Books are my special treat, and today I'm going to treat myself. I've decided that I'm going to buy at least three books, and I'm going to browse for hours and soak up the atmosphere, enjoy the anonymity, revel in the fact that no one in here is looking at me or passing judgment on my thighs rubbing together as I walk because they too will be immersed in books.

I start with a table near the front, and gently brush the piles of hardbacks. No, I tell myself, that really would be extravagant, and today is a paperback day, so I walk over to another table. Covers, so many covers, so many different, delectable pictures, and although, metaphorically speaking, it is the thing I hate most, when it comes to literature I always judge books by their covers. First the cover will catch my eye, then I read the back of the book, and then finally the first page. I pick up one, a new novel I've read about in a magazine. "A modern romance that puts all other romances to shame," says the back cover. I open it up to the first page and start reading. Yes. This is the first book I'll buy.

Then I pick up another book. No picture, just a bright yellow cover with large purple letters, the author's name and the title. Hmm, interesting. I read the first page, where I meet Anna, an eighteen-year-old girl about to embark on a university degree. She is going to meet her future lecturer, who will, she suspects, quiz her about her reasons for taking an English degree. It is beautifully written, the sentences so clear, so concise, so vivid, I almost forget about adding it to my pile. I forget I'm in Waterstone's, to be honest I seem to forget about everything, and, as I read on to the fourth page, the fifth, I become Anna's invisible acquaintance, a secret shadowy figure who lurks silently in the background, looking in on Anna's life, holding her hand as she meets the gruff professor.

Jemima is so immersed in Anna's world she doesn't see that on the other side of the room, standing almost exactly parallel to where she is now, is Ben Williams. Ben is also immersed in a book, back to the room, facing the bookshelf; he is reading the first few pages of a thriller, rocking gently on the balls of his feet as he reads.

But before we start assuming this must be fate, I have to point out that although Ben likes Jemima, he doesn't *like* Jemima, so perhaps now is not the time to start jumping to conclusions.

But it is rather strange that both of them should be in Waterstone's at exactly the same time. Ben, it has to be said, comes to Waterstone's once every couple of weeks, but rarely does he take advantage of the fact that Waterstone's is open until 10 P.M., rarely does he venture into this bookstore after work. Ben usually makes his journey on a Saturday, he will pop in on his way to meet some friends for a drink at a sidewalk café.

Tonight, however, Ben is not going out. Nor is he watching the news. Tonight Ben has nothing to do, and this is why he is in the same place as Jemima Jones, at the same time. And because Ben didn't jump in a cab, he got the tube, Ben has only just arrived.

So here they are, Jemima and Ben, these two colleagues, both with their backs towards one another, both lost in their respective handheld worlds of academia and dodgy dealing in the City, both completely unaware of their proximity.

All it will take for Jemima to turn around and see Ben is a tiny twist of fate, a decision to buy the book, to add it to the first, to perhaps turn and look for another one, and, in turning, note that the man of her daydreams is standing opposite her. But fate can be cruel, or possibly in this case understanding, because what, after all, would Jemima do if she saw Ben?

And Ben? Ben would be surprised and pleased to see her, as he would if he bumped into any of his colleagues unexpectedly, but that would be the sum of it.

Luckily we don't have to worry about what either will do, because neither has the slightest idea the other is there. Jemima carries on reading, while Ben closes his book firmly and takes it to the till. He gives the dowdy girl behind the till a winning smile, and she takes the book and places it in a plastic bag, melting while she does so. Please come back in again, she thinks, please come back tomorrow, when perhaps we'll have a conversation, which may lead to coffee, which may lead to . . . anything. Everything.

But Ben just pockets the book and walks out, with not a backward glance. Jemima decides to buy the book, and then looks around for one more. She goes to yet another table and suddenly her eye lands on the perfect book: *The Idiot's Guide to the Internet*.

Well, I may not be an idiot, but flicking through the book I realize that there are hundreds of things I don't know, thousands of sites I might want to visit. Yes, this is the final book. Time to go.

I wander over to the till and hand my pile of three to the dowdy girl looking bored. I try and catch her eye to give her a friendly smile, but she's not interested, she doesn't even look at me when she hands me my books, safely encased in a plastic bag, and when I thank her she just scowls and turns away. Honestly. Some people are just so rude.

I walk back outside, and linger for a moment on the pavement, because I'm not ready to go home and it's such a beautiful evening, and for the first time in ages I don't care that I don't look like the beautiful people milling around me, I want to do something, go somewhere, have a life.

I don't know quite where to go, so I wander down the hill, looking in every window I pass, all the main street chains that line the main street, and even though the windows are filled with garish, high-fashion clothes, size 6 bits of cloth that would normally serve only to emphasize my inadequacies, tonight I don't care, and anyway, a girl can dream, can't she?

On the other side of the road strolls Ben Williams. He too is looking into shop windows, admiring the shirts, the suits, wishing he had a bit more money so he could afford them, but not wishing with quite the same zeal as Jemima, because after all he is a man, and men do not share women's excitement about clothes. Have we ever heard of a male shopaholic? Exactly.

Ben turns round and stops, about to cross the road, and there, standing exactly opposite him on the other side of the road, is Jemima. Ben looks to his left, Jemima looks to her left. Ben starts to cross as a big truck trundles up then stops, sitting slap-bang in the middle of the road, obstructing the view because the road has become too narrow for the truck to pass down due to the early evening shoppers double-parked.

But Jemima doesn't cross, because surely then they would meet in the middle. Jemima sees a crêperie stand on her right, and instead of walking into Ben, of whose presence she is unaware, she turns right and walks down to the crêperie.

And so once again they miss one another. But Jemima's

being a good girl, she decides against the thick crêpe dripping with butter and oozing chocolate sauce. She heads instead for a café, which, to her delight, is almost empty.

She squeezes into a corner table by the window and orders a cappuccino, then pulls out the first of her books and submerges herself, in comfort this time, in Anna's world.

Ben, meanwhile, is dying for a drink. He walks past a café and stops, peering in the window to see what it's like. Nope, he thinks, too empty, I need something busier, buzzier, and of course he is looking too far into the restaurant, well beyond the corner table by the window, the corner table at which Jemima is sitting, head buried, lost in another world.

So close but yet so far, Jemima. I wish we could tell you that Ben Williams is standing but feet away from you, but it's not our place, I'm afraid. Fate will just have to continue taking its course.

And fate, as usual, is shining on Ben Williams. He crosses the road and walks into a bar that's more his scene. Large plate-glass windows on to the street, a smooth polished cherry-wood bar sweeping round the center of the room, with young, good-looking bartenders chatting idly by the glasses. Small round wooden tables with cast-iron legs and twirly iron chairs contain Hampstead's better-looking people, and right at the back is a sofa, a couple of old, beaten-up leather armchairs, and a huge fireplace which is not yet roaring, too early in the year for that, but is alight, casting a golden glow on the people sitting near the back.

Ben pushes open the door, immediately assaulted by noise, heat, animated chatter. Yes, he thinks, this is where I'll have a drink. He goes up to the bartender and orders a bottle of imported beer, then looks around for the most comfortable place to sit, and heads towards the sofa at the back.

He's slightly out of place in his dark navy suit, but he sinks into the sofa, drapes his jacket along the back, and exhales loudly. Good place, he thinks, looking around. He takes a swig of beer, pulls the book from his pocket and settles back, one elbow leaning on the arm of the sofa, his hand resting just above his forehead, pushing his hair back, the other holding the book. The beer rests on the table.

If a photographer from GQ were to walk in now, he would not be able to resist this little tableau. For Ben looks quite amazing, his right ankle resting on his left knee, long legs, well-built body, handsome face. He looks like a set-up, too good to be true, too good for any woman to resist.

So can we blame the tall, slim brunette sitting at one of the tables for taking the initiative? She's with her two girlfriends, all equally stunning, all dressed in the latest fashions, the clothes that Jemima Jones can only dream of wearing. Hip-hugging trousers with tiny bootleg flares at the bottom. Soft leather boots with square toes and center stitching, tiny little tank tops squeezed over perfect, pert breasts.

The brunette and her friends noticed Ben the moment he walked in. Too much of a suit? they asked themselves. "With a face like that," said the brunette, "who cares."

They sit there watching Ben, who is completely unaware of their presence, of their giggles as they try and decide what he does for a living. "Way too handsome for a real estate agent," they decide, "maybe an investment banker?"

The brunette, who is killing time by working in a shop until she finds a husband to sweep her off her feet and carry her into the sunset on his white horse, calls over one of the waiters, whom naturally she knows, because every evening she is in this bar with her friends.

"Do you know that guy?" she whispers, pointing to Ben.

The waiter shrugs. "Never seen him before."

"Look," she says. "Do me a favor. Will you take him over another bottle of beer, I'll pay for it, and tell him I'm buying him a drink."

The waiter smiles. The brunette's girlfriends laugh at her audacity, but with looks like hers, she can afford to be audacious.

The girls watch in silence as the waiter takes a bottle of beer over to Ben on a tray. The waiter bends down in front of Ben and murmurs something, pointing at the brunette, before walking away while Ben, bless him, blushes.

He stares at the bottle, too embarrassed to look around the room, to look at the brunette, and the brunette, much like the dowdy woman in Waterstone's, melts.

"Oh my God," she whispers to her girlfriends. "Did you see that? He blushed! I think I'm in love!"

Ben's face cools down and he looks at the brunette, amazement in his eyes, for she is truly gorgeous, and he smiles and raises the bottle to her, a silent toast.

"Guys," she says to her girlfriends as she stands up, "I'm going in there."

"Good luck," they say, unable to take their eyes off Ben. "Don't do anything we wouldn't do."

She walks, no, sashays over to where Ben's sitting. "Do you mind if I join you?"

"Um, no," says Ben, thinking this doesn't happen in real life, surely? Surely this only happens in the movies. "Please sit down. Thank you for the drink."

"I bet it's not the first time a woman's bought you a drink."

She's wrong. It is. "Um, actually, yes. It is."

"Oh." She shrugs her shoulders and laughs. "Oh well, there's a first time for everything. I'm Sam," she says, extending her hand, using the handshake as an excuse to get closer to him.

"I'm Ben," he says, shaking her hand.

"My favorite name," she laughs, and Ben laughs back.

Jemima Jones finished her cappuccino a long time ago, but she stays in her little café for a while, reading, except she is not comfortable, squeezed into this tiny hard chair, and after a while she thinks she would be far more comfortable at home, lying on her bed.

She pays, walks out of the café, and starts down the hill, feeling ridiculously happy for no reason at all. She goes past the bar and looks in at the beautiful people, thinking that one day she will be slim enough to join them.

And then she sees them. Ben and Sam, sitting on the sofa at the back, and she freezes, her mouth open in a gasp of shock. Ben and Sam are getting on as famously as two people who have nothing in common other than a mutual attraction can get on. Sam is flirting outrageously, and Ben is enjoying having a gorgeous woman flirt with him. Already he knows that he will not be going out with her, because already she has proved to be indescribably stupid, but Jesus does he fancy her.

He realizes he may have to take her out a couple of times before getting her into bed, but he is sure it will be worth it, and so they sit, closer and closer, touching one another more and more, Sam resting her hand on his arm as she talks to him, Ben leaning in towards her to hear more clearly. It is only a matter of time.

How can your moods change so suddenly? I mean, I was feeling so good, so happy, so optimistic, and now I'm rooted to the spot, trying hard to suppress a growing wave of nausea. It's Ben. The love of my life, and he's with a woman, and she's beautiful, and she's skinny, and I hate her, and I love him. I love him, I love him, I love him.

And I can't move, but I have to, because I don't want him to see me, and as I turn and walk away the cloud I've been floating on for the past two weeks disappears into thin air, and in its place it feels like there's a large black rain cloud. I walk slowly down the main street, and call me pathetic, call me a loser, but I can't help it. I can't stop the two fat tears that work their way slowly down my cheeks.

chapter 7

Jemima Jones is not having a good day. The rain cloud followed her home last night, dropping tears into her eyes, removing the hopes from her heart.

She trudged down the street, aware that people were looking at her, and not caring whether they were looking at her size or her tears. Nobody dared ask what was wrong, and Jemima had never felt so alone in her whole life.

She went home, back to an empty flat, lay on her bed and cried, and when the tears had passed she just lay, staring up at the ceiling, wondering why nothing good ever seemed to happen to her.

I know I'm overweight, she thought, but I'm not a bad person. I love animals, and children, and I'm kind to people and why does no one ever fall in love with me, why can't Ben see through the weight and fall in love with me as a person.

Because Jemima knows that Ben is a good person. She knows better than most about judging books by their covers. She knows that people judge her instantly on her appearance, and she knows that people do the same thing with Ben.

Single women of an appropriate age do one of two things when they meet Ben. They either fall instantly in lust with him, or, if they suspect Ben is the kind of man they could never hope to attain, they choose the second option and hate him instead, hate him for being arrogant, vain, self-important.

But we know that's not true because we've got to know Ben a little bit, and Jemima knows it's not true because she looked through his dimples and blue eyes (for she got it wrong when she described him to her flatmates, his eyes are actually the color of the English sky on a hot summer's day) and saw that Ben, like her, was not a bad person.

Ben too makes time for people. Even Jemima. He has the same winning smile and easy charm with everyone he meets, regardless of what they look like. In fact, the only time Ben is awkward is when he meets a woman he fancies, and then he's not entirely sure of how to behave.

Take last night, for example. Ben was wrong about having to take Sam out a couple of times before he would manage to sleep with her. Sam was a sure thing. Sam made this blatantly clear. Too blatant. Too clear. Her aggression, which became more and more apparent as the evening wore on, suddenly started to turn Ben off. He still fancied her, but could he be bothered, he wondered? Did he really want to go through the whole procedure of waking up in bed with a stranger who may or may not become obsessive? Ben got bored, and Ben said goodnight to Sam, although not without a long, slow kiss goodnight.

And he was absolutely right not to have gone home with her, for Sam is exactly the kind of girl to get obsessive. She's the kind of girl who regularly sleeps with men on the night she meets them and then wonders why they don't call afterwards. But she doesn't stop there. She phones them, and phones them, and phones them. She offers them tickets to concerts, dinner invitations, parties.

At first they are flattered, what man, after all, wouldn't be, with a stunning girl like Sam chasing them. But then they become bored. Where is the challenge? Where is the thrill of the chase? And inevitably they start making excuses, and Sam does what she always does. She shouts and screams at them on the phone, calls them bastards, like all the bastards she's ever met. Ends with telling them she thought *they* were different, as if guilt, somehow, will make them come back, and then finally she slams the phone down.

Then she goes out and repeats the whole scenario with someone new.

Ben is perceptive enough to realize the sort of woman Sam is. A "bunny boiler" is how he would describe her to his friends, and they would all groan in recognition.

But because Ben's a nice guy masquerading as a bastard, Ben let her down gently by asking for her number after they kissed and promising he would call. This was perhaps not exactly the right thing to do because Sam wrote down her home number, her work number, and her mobile number. At this very moment Sam is doing what thousands of women in her position have done. She is watching the phone at work and willing him to call. Every now and then she picks it up to check it's still working, and she has been hovering by the phone all day, leaping on it should it dare to ring.

But Ben won't call, not least because girlfriends are not exactly a priority at the moment. The type of women Ben goes for are high-maintenance. They require picking up, being paid for, presents. Ben, at this very moment in time, has neither the funds nor the inclination to think about high-maintenance women in anything other than an abstract way.

So while he fancies Geraldine, he knows that right now she'd never give him a chance, and quite frankly that's okay with Ben. It's enough that she brightens up his days at work. He's happy not to take it further.

Ben is far too busy thinking about his career to think about women. Sure, if someone uncomplicated came along who would be willing to fit in with Ben's life, and just see him occasionally, i.e., on the occasions when he's not working, working out, or seeing his friends, then great. But Ben hasn't met this woman yet.

So Jemima's having a bad day, and Ben's interviewing a local woman whose thirteen-year-old son has just stabbed a schoolteacher. Normally he wouldn't, as the deputy news editor, be writing the stories himself, but this is the *Kilburn Herald* after all, and everyone has to muck in.

Jemima has spent all day hoping for a glimpse of Ben, and each time footsteps come her way she turns, but it would appear that Ben is out of the office. She has spent the day making phone calls. She has discovered the best way of drying your nail polish quickly (dip the nails into a bowl of icy cold water), the best way of keeping lettuce fresh (put the lettuce into a bowl of iced water, add a slice of lemon and put it in the fridge) and the best way of storing tinned foods in the cupboard (buying plastic shelves, £5.99). Jemima is bored. Bored, fat, and unhappy. Not a good combination, I think we all agree.

So it is a welcome relief when her phone distracts her with an internal ring.

"It's me," says Geraldine, which is ridiculous really because she knows full well that her extension number is flashing on my telephone. "Do you want to meet me in the cafeteria for a cup of tea?"

Anything to break the monotony of this work, the pain of Ben not wanting me. Of course I want a cup of tea, just to get away from this desk, from this miserable bloody office.

"Have you lost weight?" is the first thing Geraldine says to me as I walk over to her by the hot water machine, pouring the water over the teabags in two plastic cups.

For the first time today I perk up. I don't know, I haven't weighed myself for the last few weeks, I haven't even thought about it.

"Your face definitely looks slimmer," says Geraldine, picking up the cups and carrying them to the table.

* * *

Jemima could kiss Geraldine, because Geraldine is right, she has lost weight. She hasn't thought about her weight for two weeks, because she actually started to have fun. She discovered the Internet and in Geraldine and Ben she found two people who seem to be real friends, and the minute she stopped thinking about it, stopped worrying about it, stopped feeling guilty about her binges, was the minute she started to lose it.

Until last night, however, because lying on your bed feeling fat and miserable is inevitably the beginning of a binge, and last night, when Jemima had composed herself, she phoned the local pizza delivery company. They brought round a large pizza, although huge might be a more appropriate description, garlic bread, and coleslaw. Jemima opened the front door and pretended she was having a load of friends round. Just to make sure they believed her she also ordered four cans of Diet Coke.

But today is another day, and, although she may have put on a couple of pounds after last night's binge—and yes, it is quite possible for Jemima to put on two or three pounds overnight—in general she has lost weight.

We sit down and Geraldine sighs, running her fingers through her hair.

"Is everything okay?" I say, even though I can see quite clearly that everything is not.

"It's just Dimitri," says Geraldine. "He's getting on my nerves at the moment. I feel a bit funny about things."

Uh oh. I know exactly what this means. This is Geraldine's pattern. This means that Dimitri has fallen head over heels in love with Geraldine, which in turn means that Geraldine is rapidly cooling off, and poor old Dimitri will soon be finding out that she is not the woman of his dreams after all.

"Funny how?"

"I don't know," she sighs. "He's just always *there.*"

"But isn't that how boyfriends are supposed to be?" I mean, for God's sake, Geraldine. "Isn't that what every woman wants?"

"I suppose so." Geraldine shrugs. "But it's all getting a bit on top of me."

Just in case you're interested, here's what will happen next. The more Geraldine backs off, the more keen Dimitri will become. It will probably end with a marriage proposal, which Geraldine will turn down, because by the time the proposal comes around she will be desperate to get away from him. She will, however, keep the ring. As she always does.

"Maybe you should just wait and see what happens."

"Maybe I should start dating other men."

No! Oh God, no! That might mean Ben, she might go out with Ben, and I couldn't stand that. It's bad enough seeing him with a stunning stranger, horrible but just about bearable, but if Ben and Geraldine got together it would kill me. Find out now, find out what she thinks now.

"Who?"

"No one in particular," says Geraldine. "But if I started going out again with the girls I'm sure I'd meet someone soon." She has the confidence of those with unnatural beauty, for who else could be so certain? Other women stay in relationships, miserable, horrible, destructive relationships because the alternative is far too horrendous to even consider. Being on their own.

But of course Geraldine could never begin to understand this. Geraldine has always moved onwards, and upwards. Occasionally sideways.

"What about Ben?" I say in such a casual tone it sounds fake, even to me. "He likes you."

"Ben? Ben? You are joking aren't you?"

Of course I'm not joking, Geraldine, can't you see how I am when he's around? Can't you see the effect he has on me? How could I be joking when I think he is the most perfect male specimen ever to have set foot on the planet?

"No. Why?"

"Well, Ben's just Ben. He's very handsome but what is he? He's a deputy news editor on the *Kilburn Herald*. And Ben isn't exactly the type of guy who's going places is he? I mean, what will he achieve in his life? He'll become the news editor, then the editor, and that's it. He'll stay on a crappy local paper for ever.

"He'll marry some pretty local girl who wants to be a wife and mother, and if they're lucky they'll live in West Hampstead and have 2.4 children and a Volkswagen.

"Ben," she repeats, shaking her head with a laugh. "I don't think so."

Thank you, God. Thank you for being on my side. I don't give a damn what Geraldine thinks of Ben as a person, and anyway I think she's wrong. I don't think he'll be here forever, I think he's far too good for this, but that doesn't matter right now. All that matters is that Geraldine and Ben will never be a "they" or an "us." They will always be Geraldine and Ben, and I suddenly feel so relieved I could cry.

"So," says Geraldine with a sigh. "Enough about me. What's going on in your life?"

She says this regularly, and I do what I always do—I move the conversation straight back to Geraldine because what would I tell her? Would I tell her about my trip to the bookshop perhaps, and turn it into an exaggerated adventure where I tripped over handsome men every step of the way? Would I tell Geraldine about seeing Ben with that girl last night? Would I laugh to cover up the pain and ask Geraldine if she knew anything about her? Or would I perhaps tell Geraldine about ordering a huge pizza and crying all night? No. I think not.

So I stir my tea for a few seconds, then look up, "But what *are* you going to do about Dimitri?"

By the time we venture back upstairs the *Kilburn Herald* has significantly emptied. The news desk is still buzzing, just in case, but features, the area at the back where Geraldine and I sit, is quiet.

"Jemima," whines Geraldine just before walking back to her desk. Here we go. I know exactly what this whine means.

"I need some help."

"Go on," I say with an exasperated smile, although I'm not exasperated, I'm actually delighted at any chance I get to do some proper writing.

"I'm writing this piece about dating again after you get divorced for the woman's page. I'm a bit stuck, could you have a quick look at it?" Which means, if you are as expert at reading between the lines as I am, "Could you rewrite it?"

Geraldine runs back to her desk and picks up a proof then dashes back. "God, you're an angel," she says. "I owe you big time," and she leaves, not turning round but waving just as she walks out the door.

Sometimes I can't believe Geraldine's writing, I can't believe how someone can find it so difficult because it never seems to take me long to rework her copy. I start by rewriting the intro, adding some color, crafting it into something the readers will want to continue reading.

"STANDING at the aisle, reading your wedding vows, you hoped and prayed your marriage would last forever," I tap. "But years later your vows of loving and honoring your husband are as distant a memory as the happiness you once shared.

"Divorce in the nineties is sending thousands of women back to a game they thought they would never see again—the Dating Game.

"And women all over the country are discovering that no matter how wise, how experienced, how old they may be, no matter how much the rules may have changed, when it comes to excitement, disappointment, pain, nothing has really changed at all."

Eyes glued to my computer screen, I type. I lose myself in the writing, and then tidy up Geraldine's "Case Studies"— three women who have agreed to tell their story in the *Kilburn Herald*. When I've finished I send the copy back to Geraldine's basket, so no one will know I had anything to do with it. So that's what friends are for.

It's going home time, but just as I'm about to leave I suddenly remember something. I remember that I haven't taken the books I bought out of my bag, and now would be a perfect time to try out the Internet.

I reach down and pull out *The Idiot's Guide to the Internet*. Right. Time to explore, and turning back to the screen I double-click on the sign on the left that will take me to the Internet. As the machine is connecting, I flick through the little guide.

Now this really is incredible. I learn about Web sites, about art galleries on the Internet where you can post your own pictures or download those of others. I learn of alternative medicine sites, where you can learn how others have fared by trying cures not recognized by traditional medicine. I read about real estate sites, where agents in suits have posted pictures of properties they're trying to sell. I read about museum sites, music sites, dating sites.

I read about newsgroups, bulletin boards for every hobby, interest, and obsession you can think of. Places where people can post a message, a question, a thought, and scores of like-minded people can reply.

And then I read about Tarot, a site where you can have your fortune told, and that's when I stop reading and start clicking. I want my fortune told. I want to know whether I'll find true love. I want to know if Ben is the man for me. Don't worry, though, I promise I'll take it all with a healthy pinch of salt. At least, I'll try to.

The page appears on the screen, with a choice of Tarot card decks, and me being me I click on the Tarot of the Cat People, simply because I've always wanted a cat, and suddenly three small boxes appear asking for my name, gender, and age.

I type them in, and then another box comes up, this time asking for my question. A quick check round the office shows that I'm safe, there's no one around to see what I'm doing, so here goes . . .

"Will Ben Williams fall in love with me?" I type, before clicking the button saying RESULT.

Three cards appear at the top of the screen, with the translations beneath. Card number one represents the past. It is the King of Wands (reversed). "Severity. Austerity. Somewhat excessive and exaggerated ideas. Dogmatic, deliberate person."

Card number two represents the present. It is The Empress (reversed). "Vacillation. Inaction. Lack of interest. Lack of concentration. Indecision. Delay in accomplishment or progress. Anxiety. Frittering away of resources. Loss of material possessions. Infertility. Infidelity. Vanity."

What a load of bollocks! Infidelity? I should be so lucky. Vanity? Please!

But I carry on reading anyway, the final card, the Knight of Wands, representing my future. "Departure. A journey. Advancement into the unknown. Alteration. Flight. Absence. Change of residence."

Well, this *is* a load of rubbish, but I don't want to go home just yet. Maybe I'll go back to the LA Café, at least I know how to find the bloody thing. Ah, who's here today?

Suzie 24
=ˆ··ˆ=Cat
Honey
Candy
Explorer
here4u
Luscious Lisa
Ricky
Tim@London
Brad (Santa Monica)

Who first? Should I talk to Tim@London, given that I sort of already know him, or should I be adventurous and start chatting to someone I don't know? Luckily the decision is taken out of my hands, because the computer suddenly bleeps three times and a box flashes up, with **Brad (Santa Monica)** written at the top.

"Hi, Honey."

"Hi," I type back. Now *this* is more exciting.

"Do you have time to chat?"

"Sure thing."

"So where are you, Honey?"

"London," and then I think, hang on, he's American, he might be a bit thick, so I add "England," just in case.

"Really? I was just there!"

"Oh? Whereabouts?"

"In London. I stayed in the Park Lane Hotel. It was business."

Now this *is* more like it.

"What kind of business?"

"I'm your typical Californian beach bum who's made a living out of what he loves best. I own a gym."

"So you're revoltingly fit then?" Oh God, I'm feeling inadequate again, but this is the Internet, I mean, this guy could never know what I really look like.

"LOL. Revoltingly. I like that. What about you?"

Oh God. This question was bound to come up sooner or later.

"I'm pretty fit but I work too hard to exercise as much as I'd like."

"What do you do?"

"I'm—" I stop. Why be a boring journalist when I could be anything in the world? "I'm a television presenter."

There. Glamorous, exciting, and conveying that I'm probably pretty stunning if I'm on television.

"You must be stunning. You sound like an O:-)."

"What's an O:-)?"

"An angel! Unlike myself. I consider myself more of a }:->. That means a devil."

"LOL. I'm no angel, but I don't do too badly."

"Are you new to this?"

"Yes, I'm new, is it that obvious? Are you here a lot then, if you know I'm not here all the time? You can't be that fit if you're sitting on the Internet all the time <s>."

"Ah ha! Actually, the computer's in my office and I just sit here and mess around if I'm stuck at my desk. It keeps my mind off work!"

"What time is it there?"

"10 A.M. I've been in the office two hours. Before that I went running, and this afternoon I'm going Rollerblading."

"I love Rollerblading." Careful, Jemima, don't get too carried away.

"Yeah. It's a great sport. Good exercise and sociable at the same time."

"You must be meeting hundreds of gorgeous California babes if you're out Rollerblading all the time. What are you doing trying to pick up single women here?"

"Who says I'm trying to pick up single women?"

"Oops. Sorry. Aren't you?"

"Maybe just this single woman. You are, aren't you? Single?"

"Yes."

"How come? You sound way too gorgeous to be on your own."

If only you knew, I think, suddenly deciding to borrow Geraldine's life for a little while.

"I just ended a long relationship," I type. "He wanted to marry me but he wasn't the one."

"How do you know he wasn't the one?"

"Good question. I suppose, naive as it might be, I just think that when I meet the right one I'll know."

"I don't think that's naive. I think that's probably right. I feel the same way and I'm still waiting for that bolt of lightning to strike. But poor guy. He must be devastated. But lucky me <g>."

"Indeed."

"So what kind of show do you work on?"

Think, Jemima. Think.

"It's like a British version of *Entertainment Tonight.*"

"No kidding! Are you like the Leeza Gibbons of British television?"

"No." Even in this world of make-believe I know this would be pushing it. "I'm a senior reporter."

"That's still fantastic."

"So what about you? How did you get into the gym business?"

"Left college, studied business, didn't know what to do, and moved to LA to hang out. Hardly anyone in LA is a native Angeleno, we're all from someplace else."

"Did you want to be in the movie business?" I remember what Geraldine said about people who live in Los Angeles.

"LOL. No way. Too much pressure. I just wanted to find something I loved doing that would make me a lot of money. I started going to a run-down gym every day, and the owner told me it was up for sale. I managed to raise the money, bought it, and haven't looked back."

"So do you make a lot of money then?"

"Put it like this. I'm *very* comfortable."

"What kind of house do you live in?" Now, before we go any further, I think I just have to make it clear that I'm not being a gold-digger here. I just find it incredible that I'm talking to this man in Los Angeles of all places, somewhere I've never been, somewhere I've always dreamed of going, and I want to know everything about his life. I want to know if he really does live in a world of golden sands, palm trees, and open-topped cars blaring rock and roll.

"A nice house! What kind of house do you live in?"

"A not so nice house. I was going to buy last year," Lord, forgive me for stepping into Geraldine's shoes once again, "but then it all fell through, so now I'm renting until I find somewhere nice again. I live with two girls."

"I think I've died and gone to heaven! Any space for a guy?"

"Afraid not."

"So how old are you, Honey?"

"I'm twenty-seven and I have to tell you, Honey's not my real name. My real name is JJ."

"I like JJ. I like twenty-seven even better. I'm thirty-three."

"So how come you're still single, Brad? Or do you have another name too <s>?"

72

"No. Brad's my real name. I date quite a lot, but, as I said, just haven't met the right woman yet."

"What kind of woman would be the right woman?"

"I wish I knew. I keep hoping I'll know when I meet her."

"I know what you mean!" Except, naturally, I don't.

"Oh damn. The phone's ringing. Listen, I have to go now, but I've really enjoyed talking to you, JJ. Can we meet here again?"

Call me cheesy but my heart skips a beat. "I'd love to. How about tomorrow?"

"Same time?"

"Perfect."

"Okay. I'll bring the sunshine, you bring the smiles. Take care."

"Bye." I sit back and turn off the computer, and crazy as it may sound I'm excited about this and it takes the longest time to wipe the smile off my face.

chapter 8

Ben had a hell of a week this week. Really, we wouldn't wish Ben's job on anyone. First of all he had to interview a woman who had the misfortune to have a thirteen-year-old crack addict tearaway as a son, trying to coax the story of his upbringing out of her.

Then he was out on other stories for the rest of the week, he hardly saw anyone at all, didn't have time for chats, just kept his head down and kept working.

But Wednesday night was a bit of a bonus. Ben was home earlier than usual and both roommates were out, so he had the place to himself. He could kick off his shoes, read the *Guardian* he'd saved from Monday *and* watch the news. Just generally chill out.

He was settling back into the sofa, the television on to provide background noise, some early evening quiz show that Ben would never dream of watching, and he was flicking through the *Guardian*.

An ad on page 16 caught his eye but, perhaps more importantly, caught his imagination.

TELEVISION REPORTER

London Nights is a new daily show from London Daytime Television. Entertaining and informative, we need three reporters for on-screen work. A minimum of three years' journalism experience is required, with no television experience necessary. An interest in show business and entertainment, news and politics, or health and beauty is essential.

Screen tests will be held.

Please send your CV, a covering letter, and a demo tape or photograph to . . .

This is it! thought Ben, sitting up with excitement. This is my big break. A reporter specializing in news and politics, this job has my name written all over it. He didn't hesitate, because Ben, after all, is a doer rather than a thinker. He reached for his pen and scribbled down the first draft of a letter.

A photograph, he thought, where can I get a decent photograph? Ben only has decent photographs, but a picture of him in sunglasses and a baseball cap is hardly the right image to project, and, as Ben well knows, a television image is essential.

He pulled a box from under his bed and sifted through the hundreds of photographs. Eventually he found one that was perfect, a photograph he sneaked out from the picture library at work. A photograph of him in a suit standing next to a local celebrity.

Screw the celebrity, Ben, this is your career, and Ben duly whisked the scissors out of the kitchen drawer and snipped the photograph cleanly in half, the celebrity gently floating to the grubby gray carpet.

He finished his letter, attached his CV, and slipped the photograph into the envelope. Now all he can do is hope.

Funny how my appetite seems to have decreased recently. It's lunchtime and I feel no desire to have a huge plate of food.

This salad, a proper salad, is fine, and I'm quite happy sitting in the cafeteria with my nose buried in a magazine.

I bought this magazine this morning. Not my usual glossy fashion mag, I grant you, but one of the cover lines was about Internet dating, and I'm just really curious about this, so I bought it and I'm learning all about Internet cafés.

I didn't even know these places existed. This café, Cyborg, is in the West End. The picture shows metallic surfaces, banks of computers around the walls, and beautiful people sitting at the tables in the center, sipping cappuccinos and eating ciabatta rolls stuffed with sun-dried tomatoes, mozzarella, and fresh basil.

Internet dating, apparently, is the hottest thing since, well, since the Internet. According to this article, and it has to be said I take it with a slight pinch of salt because I know you can't believe everything you read, but according to this people are meeting and falling in love all over the world.

And not only that, Cyborg has become an "in" place, a place to see and be seen, a place where, should you not be lucky enough to find your soulmate on the Internet, you might just meet his eyes gazing at you over the top of your computer.

"That looks interesting," says Ben Williams, towering above me as he puts his tray on the table opposite. "I've heard about that."

My heart starts pounding and already I can feel the faint flush on my neck. Surely this is the perfect opportunity, how can I ask him whether he wants to go, how can I make my voice sound casual when I'm all choked up inside?

"We should go down there one night," says Ben, lifting a forkful of stringy roast beef to his mouth. "The three of us should go. It would be a laugh."

"I'd love to," I gush. "I mean, it sounds really interesting, I'd love to learn more about it." A cooler tone to my voice now, I keep my excitement in check.

"We'll have to find out when Geraldine's free, although it's a bit of a quiet week for me, I could go any time."

"And why is my name being taken in vain?" Geraldine sits

down, a plateful of lettuce, tomatoes, cucumber, and no dressing for lunch.

"Ben was just saying we should go to this place." I gesture to the article. "It sounds like fun." But I'm thinking, why Geraldine too for heaven's sake? Why not just you and me, Ben? Not that I wouldn't want Geraldine there, it's just that I'd die to spend an evening alone with Ben. Die.

"Yup," echoes Ben. "In fact I'm not doing anything tonight. You?" He looks at me and I shake my head. Of course I'm not doing anything tonight. "You?" He looks at Geraldine, who shakes her head, then makes a face. "Sorry, guys, but count me out."

"But why?" asks Ben.

"A computer café? I don't think so. It'll be full of computer nerds and strange men in anoraks."

"That's where you're wrong." The words are out of my mouth before I can stop them because the last thing I'm trying to do is persuade her to come, but my mouth seems to have a life of its own and I push the magazine towards her. "Look at the people in that picture. They're all gorgeous."

"Hmm," says Geraldine, who has to concede that the people are, indeed, better than average-looking. "They're probably models brought in to disguise the computer nerds and anoraks."

"Oh Geraldine," I say, again pretending I want nothing more than for her to join us. "Just come."

"Nope," says Geraldine, picking up a slice of cucumber with her fingers and munching away. "I'm busy washing my hair."

"God, you're pathetic," says Ben, but he doesn't say it nastily, he can't help it, it is so obvious that he wants her to come. "Even if they are computer nerds it won't matter because we'll be there."

"Nope." She's refusing to budge and an involuntary sigh of relief escapes my mouth. Luckily, neither of them notices.

"Well, we're going anyway aren't we, Jemima?" And I beam away as I nod my head.

* * *

They sit and eat, and chatter about work, and in Ben's pocket is the job ad burning a hole, making him itch to tell someone. He's planning on sending off the application today, but he doesn't trust himself, he wants a second opinion before he actually posts it through the mailbox next to the bus stop.

He wants to tell Jemima and Geraldine, he wants to know what they think, whether he stands a chance, whether they could see him on television, but he's not entirely sure Geraldine can be trusted.

Jemima, he knows, wouldn't breathe a word, and Geraldine, he suspects, wouldn't intentionally repeat anything, but it may just come out by mistake, and he doesn't want to risk word getting round the *Kilburn Herald* that he is looking for another job.

Also, Ben, not that it's any of our business but isn't it slightly bad karma to talk about a job before you get it?

So Ben keeps quiet, Jemima keeps quiet, too busy dreaming about tonight, and Geraldine rattles on about Dimitri, the boyfriend that was, although she hasn't quite managed to tell him that yet.

They finish their lunch and walk to the elevator. Please, don't forget, prays Jemima, don't forget that we have a date tonight.

"So, shall we go straight from work?" Ben's looking at me.

Damn. I promised that guy Brad that I'd meet him tonight and I suppose I could go "online" at Cyborg and talk to him from there, but Ben would be with me and I don't want him looking over my shoulder. I have a choice here. Ben or Brad. As if there's any question.

"Fine," I say. "Definitely."

"Great," says Ben, smiling warmly at me, because, I suspect, even though he would prefer to be with Geraldine, he would never be mean enough to cancel me, not when we've made this arrangement.

Later that afternoon Geraldine sends a message to my screen.

"Careful," she says, "word might get out about you and Ben . . ."

"What do you mean?" I send back, knowing exactly what she means, and praying that it does somehow get out, because perhaps if people thought something was going on, something might, in fact, go on.

"You know what people are like round here. If they see you leaving together they might just jump to conclusions!" As if! Geraldine knows this would never happen with me. Yes, the *Kilburn Herald* is a hive of gossip, and anyone seen, ever, with a staff member of the opposite sex is immediately presumed to be having an affair. But nobody in their right mind would ever think I might be having an affair with Ben Williams. In my dreams, perhaps, but that's about it.

"Oh please!" I write, playing along with Geraldine's game. "He's not my type!"

"What, with all those dimples, not to mention the gorgeous hair that always flops in exactly the right place? Are you serious?"

It's not always in exactly the right place, and so what if it's floppy? It's gorgeous. Bitch.

"Absolutely." I type back. "We're just friends."

"Well, have a nice friendly time then, and don't do anything I wouldn't do . . ."

At six o'clock I am so excited I'm practically bursting. I've been to the bathroom, I've put on some makeup, although truth to be told I can't really see any difference, and I'm sitting at my desk trying to stop the urge to jump around the room.

I'm sorry, Brad who?

And then Ben walks over and as soon as I see him at the other end of the room I know he's going to cancel me. How? He hasn't put his jacket on, his sleeves are rolled up, and he looks tense and worried. Shit.

"Are you ready?" I say nervously, knowing full well he's about to say he's not coming.

"I'm really sorry, Jemima," says Ben, and to give him some credit he looks as if he means it. "I've just been given a story to do on edition. I'm going to be here all night."

"Don't worry." False gaiety brightens up my voice. "We can go another time. I've got loads to do at home tonight anyway." Like watch television. Read. Listen to music.

"I'm sorry." I start to feel sorry for him because he really does look as if he doesn't want to be here. "It's fine," I say again. "We'll do it another time."

"Look," he says, and I'm convinced he can see the disappointment in my eyes. "You don't live far from me. If I finish early enough maybe we could meet up later for a quick drink?"

"Great!" I say, too quickly to hide the enthusiasm in my voice, and mentally kicking myself under the desk for not being a bit more cool.

"Okay. What's your phone number?"

I write it down and, idiot that I am, while I'm writing I try to keep the smile from my face. Unsuccessfully.

"I'll give you a ring when I'm finished," says Ben, who is looking more and more pissed off at the prospect of having to work late. "Are you leaving now?"

"In a little while. I've got a few things to clear up first."

He's phoning me! He wants to take me out for a drink! I have a date with Ben Williams! I'm seeing Ben Williams by myself after work! He didn't have to ask me but he wants to see me! Yes! Yes! Yes! Yes! Yes!

But before I go home, before I allow myself completely to give in to the excitement that's taken over my body, I have to meet Brad, and before I meet Brad I have to play my game, remember?

If I connect to the Internet within 45 seconds, then Ben Williams will fall in love with me. Please, please, please connect within 45 seconds.

I watch the little clock on the bottom right of the screen. 33. 34. 35. 36. Still not connected. I can't bear to look. I squeeze my eyes shut, praying that when I open them again I'll be connected. I open my eyes. 42. 43. Connected.

Phew. Thank you, God.

"I thought you weren't going to make it :-(" flashes up on my screen, as soon as I enter the LA Café.

"I'm sorry. I was working on a big story."

"Can you send me a videotape? I'd love to see you in action."

"I'll try," and miracles will happen, "but everything's a bit busy at the moment."

"So how was your day, JJ?"

"Superb." Now at least I'm telling the truth.

":-) That's so English of you! I just came back from a workout which I didn't feel up to at all. I had a late night last night."

"Did you have a hangover?"

"No. Nobody in California gets drunk. Ever. Do you drink?"

"No."

"Smoke?"

"No." Forgive me for I am sinning, but a little white lie never hurt anyone.

"Good! Me neither. I can't stand smoking, it's the one thing I really hate."

"So tell me about your friends." I ask to get him off this line of conversation, and is it just me or does he sound ever so slightly boring? Nah, must be just me, I mean he's a genuine Hollywood hunk, for God's sake, what's boring about that? "What do you do socially?"

"Just kinda hang out, I guess. I have friends from all walks, and a lot in entertainment."

"I'm surprised. I would have thought all your friends would be body-builders."

"LOL. No, I meet all types through the gyms. We have a load of celebrities who work out here, and some of them have become friends."

"Names, names, give me names."

"Okay <s>, but don't hold it against me. I know Jennifer & Brad quite well, and a lot of the cast from *ER*. But a lot of my friends just work in the business, they're the guys behind the scenes. What about you?"

Think Geraldine, think Sophie and Lisa. Think anything but your own life.

"I go out for dinner an awful lot, usually quite smart places, and occasionally to clubs, but not that often, I did that when I was younger."

"I'm trying to get a feel for who you are. What are you wearing right now? (I don't mean underwear <g>, I mean what is your style.)"

Shit. I look down at what I'm wearing. Massive stretchy black leggings and a huge voluminous orange shirt.

"An Armani shirt," I type. "Fitted jacket, short skirt, and cream shoes. I have to look smart for when I'm on screen."

"Mmm. You sound just my type. I'm wearing my oldest pair of Levi's, a faded blue Ralph Lauren polo shirt (it matches my eyes!!) and sneakers. I keep a suit in the office for when I have meetings, but most of the time I'm real casual."

"So what's Los Angeles like?"

"I love it. I love the climate, the buildings, the people. It's unlike anywhere else in America. Have you ever been here?"

No. I've never been anywhere, really. When I was younger, when my parents were still together, we went to a campsite in France a couple of times. I remember the soft sand, the palm trees in Nice, the warm water, but as I grew older, as my mother tried to cope with being a single parent, the foreign holidays stopped, and the French campsite became small hotels in Dorset, Wales, Brighton. What I wouldn't give to go to somewhere like Los Angeles.

"I haven't but I'd love to."

"You should come out here. I bet you'd love it."

"Is that an invitation? <g>."

"Sure! You could come and stay with me."

Blimey, that's a bit quick, thinks Jemima, but then being as naive as she is, Jemima doesn't know that Angelenos have a habit of extending the arm of friendship, before whipping it back again as soon as you try and take hold.

"But we hardly know each other," I type, wondering whether Brad is ever so slightly insane. I mean, who in their right mind would extend this sort of an invitation to someone they don't know?

"We'd get to know each other pretty quick <g>."

"LOL." I'm getting the hang of this.

"So when are you planning your next vacation?"

"I hadn't really thought. Some time soon, though."

"Just don't go anywhere without speaking to me first! What are you up to tonight?"

At least now I can tell the truth. "I'm going out for a drink with a friend."

"A male friend?"

"Yes."

":-("

"Why :-(?"

"I'm jealous."

I know this is ridiculous but reading those words suddenly makes me feel good. Stupid, really, because he's never seen me, but nobody has ever had cause to be jealous before. Of me! Jemima Jones! Going out with another man! This is amazing. New, but nevertheless amazing.

"Don't worry, he really is just a friend."

"Tell me he's fat and forty."

"Okay. He's fat and forty."

"<vbg>. Good. Just remember little old Brad sitting in California thinking about you. Can we meet again tomorrow?"

"I don't know if I can. I think I'm going out."

"Okay. I'll e-mail you instead. How's that?"

"Perfect. I'll look forward to it."

"Will you e-mail me back?"

"Promise."

"Okay, JJ. Take care, and a big hug from me."

"Same here. Bye."

I gather up my stuff and while I'm getting ready to leave I'm trying to picture Brad in California, which is tough bearing in mind I haven't been there, but I have seen it in the movies. I wonder whether he really is a golden-haired, blue-eyed Californian god, or whether he is merely doing what I've been doing, and reinventing himself over the Internet.

Either way, it's going home time, and only a couple of hours, I hope, until I see the love of my life all by myself.

"I had a great day today." God knows why I'm bothering telling them, but I need to talk to someone, so instead of simply hovering in the doorway of Sophie's bedroom, which is what I usually do before disappearing up to my own room, I walk in and sit on the bed, which I know must seem slightly strange to them.

"Oh," says Sophie, and then Lisa. "Great." I can see they're both flummoxed, having never heard me volunteer any sort of information, and never, in the history of our living together, have I walked in and sat on the bed.

"Why?" Sophie, at least, has the decency to be polite.

"No real reason, just a good day. And . . ." I pause for dramatic effect. "And," I continue, "I've got a date tonight."

"A date?" The two girls chorus, looking at me in wide-eyed amazement. "Who with?"

"With the most gorgeous man in the world," I say dreamily, in a tone remarkably similar to theirs. "With Ben Williams."

"Oh," says Sophie.

"Ben," says Lisa. And I know that each of them is simultaneously picturing a fat/ugly/boring/computer nerd in an anorak.

"Where are you going?" says Lisa.

"I don't know. Just out for a drink."

"Well, that's great! Good for you!" Sophie is being patronizingly kind.

"What time is he coming?" says Lisa.

"He's calling me when he's finished work. He's stuck in the office."

"That's brilliant," says Lisa. "We'll be here for a while yet. We're going to a new club tonight so we won't be leaving until later. Maybe we'll meet him?"

"Oh." Shit, no. Not if I can help it. "Maybe."

"Anyway," says Sophie, all smiles, "any chance of a cup of tea, Mimey?"

"Nope." Abso-bloody-lutely not, my slaving days, I have just decided, are over. "Not tonight. I've got to get ready."

I can see Sophie and Lisa look at one another, and from the expression on their faces I suspect they have just realized that the gentle equilibrium of our household could well be about to change.

But Jemima doesn't care, why should she? She's got more important things on her mind, Ben Williams for one. She saunters out of the room, and doesn't let the fact that she can hear Sophie and Lisa whispering about her bother her for a second.

Jemima Jones flings open the doors of her wardrobe and desperately looks for something new. Something exciting, something inviting, something that might make her look slim, or at least slim enough to attract the advances of a certain Mr. Williams.

But it's not easy to hide the flesh of someone as large as Jemima, and in the end she settles on a long black jumper and black trousers.

Jemima lies back in her bath, bubbles stretching to the ceiling, and loses herself in her usual daydreams. This time she sees herself out for a drink with Ben, in a small wine bar in West Hampstead.

Jemima will be on sparkling form, sharp and witty enough to have Ben wiping the tears of laughter from his eyes.

"I never realized you were so funny," he'll say, clutching his stomach with mirth and looking at her in a whole new light, for even Jemima isn't stupid enough to think he'll fall for her beauty.

But perhaps if she is funny enough, charming enough, he

may take a second look at the emerald green of her eyes, or the fullness of her ripe lips, or the shiny swinginess of her mousy but ever so glossy hair.

At the end of the evening he will walk her to the front door, and he will look at her very seriously, then shake his head, shaking away the crazy thought that he might be attracted to her. But the thought will not go away, and he will bend his head and kiss her, a gentle kiss on the lips.

"I'm sorry," he'll say. "I don't know what came over me," but then he'll lose himself in her eyes and kiss her again. That's enough for tonight, a happy ever after would be inevitable after that.

"Jemima?" A gentle knock on the door.

"Yes?"

"I've brought you a cup of tea. I'll just leave it out here shall I?"

"Oh thanks, Sophie. That's lovely." Now *that* really is a first. A smile spreads across my face as I hold my nose and duck my head under the water.

At ten to nine the phone rings.

"Jemima? It's Ben." But of course. Who else could it be?

"Oh, hi." He phoned! He phoned! He phoned! "How was the rest of your day?"

"Fraught. But thank God it's finished now. Listen, I'm just leaving the office so shall I come straight to you?"

There's a silence while I digest what he's just said. He hasn't canceled! He's coming here!

"Hello? Jemima, are you still on for a drink?"

"Yes, yes. Sure. Fine. I'll see you soon."

"Just give me your address again." And I do.

"God, you really do like him don't you?" says Sophie, who's sitting on the sofa manicuring her nails with spiky spongy things sticking up all over her head, wrapping her hair into tight little knots in preparation for this evening.

I nod happily as I suddenly realize what will happen when Ben comes over, that there's no way on earth he could fancy either of them in the state they're in at the moment, and with any luck they'll still be like this when he arrives.

"Well, you look lovely," offers Lisa, sitting there in her dressing gown with curlers in her hair and a face pack looking incredibly like someone who's been dragged through a hedge backwards. Ha!

I can't help myself, I'm so excited I dance round the living room, whirling round and laughing, and Sophie and Lisa actually join me, and the three of us leap up and down in a rare state of happiness and unity. I don't think we've ever felt this before and we probably could carry on for hours except the spell is broken by the doorbell ringing. And me feeling sick.

I freeze. We all freeze. "I'll get it," says Sophie, and I don't even try to stop her as she runs down the stairs and opens the door. I peek my head round the landing. I'm going to enjoy this.

"Hi," says Ben, leaning against the door frame in his beautiful navy suit. "Is Jemima in?" He smiles, and I can see what Sophie's seeing. What I see every time I look at Ben. Dimples, white teeth, and blue eyes.

Ben's face falls. "Have I got the wrong address? Damn, I'm so stupid, I must have written it down wrong."

"No!" Sophie recovers her composure, simultaneously remembering that she looks terrible, that she has spiky spongy sticks in her hair, and no makeup, and is wearing a grotty old dressing gown, and I literally have to hold my hand over my mouth to stifle the laughter that's bubbling up inside.

Sophie doesn't say anything. She can't say anything. She's absolutely, one hundred percent speechless, and she stands aside and gestures upstairs with a look of shock on her face.

Ben smiles his thanks and starts walking upstairs, as I start walking down. We meet in the middle.

"Have a lovely time," shouts Lisa, who at that moment appears at the top of the stairs to see what Ben looks like. She can't see, for she hasn't got her contact lenses in, so she runs downstairs, still caught up in the excitement of dancing round the living room, for a closer look.

"Oh," she breathes, one hand coming up to try and hide her face, the other frantically covering the curlers.

"Oh."

"Oh?" Ben raises an eyebrow, grinning in amusement at the sight of these two strange creatures, and I think I'm going to burst.

Lisa runs back upstairs, followed swiftly by Sophie.

"Bye, girls," I shout as I follow Ben out the door. "Have a good evening."

There's no reply. Sophie and Lisa have collapsed on the sofa, each groaning with embarrassment.

"Oh my God," shouts Sophie.

"Oh my God," groans Lisa. "Did you see him?"

"Did I see him? Did I see him? I've just seen the most gorgeous man I've ever set eyes on in all my life and you're asking me if I saw him? Jesus Christ, look at me."

"Jesus Christ," echoes Lisa. "Look at *me*."

"I'm in love, I'm in love," moans Sophie softly, leaning back against the cushions.

"No, I'm in love," says Lisa, putting her head in her hands at the thought of this gorgeous man seeing her like this.

"Shit," announces Sophie.

"Shit," announces Lisa. "We have to see him again. Where do you think they've gone?"

"You're not thinking what I'm thinking are you?" says Sophie, a sudden glint in her eye.

"We could try."

"Fuck it," says Lisa with a grin. "What have we got to lose."

chapter 9

"You don't mind walking do you?" says Ben Williams, as the front door closes behind them. "I thought we'd go to that bar on the main road."

"No, that's fine," I say quickly, because I'm already struggling to keep up with Ben's large strides, and consequently already trying not to lose my breath.

"Strange roommates you've got there," Ben volunteers after a silence. "I take it they don't always behave like that.

"Or look like that," he adds, as an afterthought.

"No. They're on their way out. That's them looking their best."

Ben laughs. "What are they like?" Not that he's interested, he's just trying to make conversation.

"They're okay," I say, praying he's not interested, praying he couldn't see beyond the face masks and spiky spongy things in their hair. "They're nice girls, really, but I wouldn't say we're friends."

"What do they do?"

"They're receptionists at Curve Advertising Agency."

"What, together?"

I nod.

"Do they ever get any work done?"

"I don't think their job is that stressful." I silently muse on the conversations Sophie and Lisa constantly have about men.

"In fact," I add out loud, "I don't think they ever talk about 'work' at all."

"I bet they're the sort of girls who go out with very rich men, with very fast cars, who have very short relationships."

I laugh in disbelief as I look at Ben. "Very good. How could you tell?"

Ben smiles. "I just can."

Ben can tell because Ben has done that scene. Not as a rich man with a fast car, but as himself, because Ben can intrude on any social scene by virtue of his looks.

Ben had just left Durham University, where he had been hugely in demand, both as a boyfriend and as a friend. He was the golden boy of the campus, and his best friend, Richard, who had been down in London already for two years, had infiltrated the Chelsea set of bright young things, and welcomed Ben home with open arms and lavish parties.

Ben met heiresses, minor aristocracy, Eurotrash, minor celebrities. He went to dinner parties with people he had only ever read about on the rare occasions he had picked up a girlfriend's magazine, and he sat next to them and talked to them as an equal.

Most people wouldn't want to enter these circles. And even if they did, most people wouldn't have a clue how to get in. There was one occasion where Ben found himself spending all evening talking to the star of one of the most popular soap series in the country, a girl who, with her olive skin, long dark hair, and petulant lips, was, at the time, the most adored girl in the country.

When Ben walked into the room—a party held in one of London's smartest restaurants—he spotted her and his heart turned over. Only that morning he had been reading about her in a newspaper, how she had just split from her equally famous boyfriend, a star of a rival soap, and how she was enjoying some time, probably about five minutes, on her own.

Ben was dying to meet her, but how can you approach someone so beautiful and so famous? Not even Ben had the balls to do that.

"Have you met Laurie?" said Richard casually to Ben, after Richard had himself kissed her on both cheeks and been enveloped in a warm hug by the delicious Laurie.

"We haven't met," said Laurie, fixing her gaze on Ben and beaming a smile as she held out a hand to shake his, a smile that spread up through her face and gave her eyes, or so Ben thought at the time, the most amazing warmth.

"I'm Laurie," she said, shaking his hand.

Ben nearly said, "I know," but luckily he didn't, because it's not the done thing in those circles to show you recognize someone, not unless you are equally famous. "I'm Ben," he said, smiling a perfect smile and struggling not to lose himself in her big brown eyes.

They spent the rest of the evening laughing softly together, and after a while Ben forgot she was Laurie, the most lusted-after woman in Britain, and she became Laurie, a gorgeous girl he was talking to at a party.

He didn't ask for her number. Not because he didn't want it, because Ben wanted nothing more, but because he thought she would be so used to being chatted up, she would never be interested in him. Admittedly, they did get on, but no, she couldn't have been interested in him, Ben Williams, trainee news reporter.

But wonder of wonders, Laurie called him. She got his number from Richard, called and invited him to a party. A party where they didn't so much fall in love as consummate their lust for one another, a lust which continued for three months, three months of whirlwind jet-setting and partying.

Ben accompanied Laurie everywhere. They went to film

premieres, to restaurant openings, to exclusive nightclubs, and this in fact was the problem. Towards the end of three months, much as he liked being with Laurie, he was starting to feel that if there was the opening of an envelope, Laurie would insist on going.

With Laurie he mixed with the beautiful people. He even brushed shoulders, on the odd occasion, with Sophie and Lisa, who were never actually invited themselves, but who would be there with their latest glamorous men, not that Ben ever noticed, he was far too busy being Laurie's boyfriend.

And that, you see, was the beginning of the end. "So *you're* Laurie's mystery man," people used to say, instantly forgetting his name. "So *this* is Laurie's boyfriend," they'd say, greeting him distractedly before turning away to someone more famous, and consequently, at least in their eyes, more interesting.

He was bored, and it showed. On the few occasions he tried discussing this with Laurie, she'd smother him with kisses and tell him not to be ridiculous, that he was being silly, that none of these people mattered.

But you see it did matter. It mattered that Laurie had to be the center of attention, wherever she went, and in the end Ben went to her flat one night and told her it wasn't working. He said he wasn't happy, that he really liked her, but he didn't like her lifestyle.

Laurie, being the actress that she is, cried for a while, and tried begging him to stay, promising things would be different, but Ben knew they wouldn't be, and he put his arms around her and kissed her softly on the forehead as he wished her good luck and goodbye.

Ben walked out of Laurie's flat, out of her life, and out of the whirlwind of parties, and truth to be told, although he missed Laurie, particularly at night, he was filled with a huge relief.

Because Ben isn't much good at pretending and, try as he might, he never felt he fitted in with the jet-setters, nor did he want to. It didn't take long for Ben to see beyond the glitz and glamour, to the heart of insecurities, pretensions and inadequacies that people tried to cover up.

He hated the fact that on the rare occasions people asked what he did for a living—and I say rare because most of these people were far too self-absorbed to be interested in anyone else—their faces would cloud over with boredom when he told them he was a reporter on the *Kilburn Herald*.

Ben never tried to disguise his job because he didn't have to. He was, is, secure and confident enough to not care what others think, and this is what he hated most of all, how he was judged by his job, not himself.

So yes, Ben is more than familiar with women like Sophie and Lisa, with the men they go out with, the parties they go to, and he wouldn't touch their lifestyles with a ten-foot pole. But of course Jemima doesn't know this. Nor do Sophie and Lisa, who, at this moment in time, are buzzing round the flat, pulling spiky, spongy things out of their hair, washing off face masks, expertly applying makeup.

They are going out later, but they have decided to do a pre-clubbing pub and bar crawl. They watched Jemima and Ben walk up the road, and they know they won't have gone far, and they will soon be off on a search.

Ben and Jemima reach the bar, slightly incongruous for this part of Kilburn, for it looks like it ought to be in Soho or Notting Hill.

Large picture windows look out on to the street, and a huge bust of a woman, the sort of bust that used to be on the front of ships in pirate movies, stares fondly down from the top of the door frame.

Ben holds the door open for Jemima as they walk in, and Jemima instantly wishes they had gone somewhere else, somewhere less trendy, somewhere where she didn't feel out of place.

For despite being in Kilburn the bar is filled with beautiful, fashionable people. A different sort of fashion to Soho or Notting Hill, more of a street fashion, less a designer label fashion, but nevertheless fashionable. The air is filled with smoke and soft laughter, and Jemima follows Ben to the bar, her shoes clip-clopping on the scrubbed wooden floors as she walks.

Antique mirrors and mismatched paintings cover the wall, and in a small room off the main bar are a couple of beaten-up leather sofas and armchairs. It is to this room that Ben carries their drinks—a pint of lager for him and a bottle of Beck's for Jemima.

Jemima isn't a drinker, has never particularly liked the taste of alcohol, nor has she ever quite known what to order in a bar when asked what she wants to drink. Vodka or gin and tonic sounds too grown up, too much like her parents; Malibu and pineapple, which is the only drink she loves, is too downmarket, and pints or even half pints of beer are too studenty.

Thank God for imported bottled beers, because these days Jemima never has to think. She'll just order a bottle of Beck's, knowing that at least she will fit in.

Ben sits down on a brown leather sofa covered in cracks just under the window, then slides up to allow room for Jemima, who is about to settle herself in the armchair adjacent to the sofa.

Jemima squeezes in next to Ben, feeling more than a touch faint-hearted at such close proximity, and she pours her beer into a glass, because although we all know it's far more cool to drink imported beer straight from the bottle, Jemima can't quite get to grips with it.

"What do you think?" says Ben, looking around the room. "It's nice here isn't it."

"Lovely," I practically choke as I gulp my imported beer through nerves and wonder why places like this always make me feel so awkward.

"So how's work?" Ben opens with the standard question, the question you always ask when you don't know someone very well, but quite frankly I don't care. It's enough that he's here. With me. Tonight.

"Boring as hell," I say, my stock answer. "I keep thinking I should really start looking around but then I still have this ridiculous hope that they're going to promote me."

"They should," said Ben. "I know you rewrite most of Geraldine's stuff and you're very good."

"How did you know that?" I can't believe he knows that!

"Oh come on," says Ben with a smile. "Geraldine's a good operator but she can't write to save her life. I saw that piece you wrote for her today, the one on dating, and there's no way Geraldine would have written an intro like that. I don't think she could write an intro of any sort."

"But she's so nice." I always feel vaguely guilty whenever anyone says anything negative about Geraldine. "We shouldn't really be talking about her like this."

"Like what? As I said, she is very talented, just not at writing. That's your problem, Jemima, you're a very good writer but you haven't got the confidence to be a good journalist. There's a huge difference. Journalism means digging, it means making hundreds of phone calls, standing on people's doorsteps if necessary, to get your story. It means operating on hunches, chasing leads, not stopping until you've got what you want. You haven't got that instinct, but Geraldine has. I know she's not a news reporter, but she could be." He looks at Jemima carefully. "You, Jemima, are a wonderful writer, far too good to be wasted on a newspaper, any newspaper, never mind the *Kilburn Herald*."

"So what could you see me doing?"

"I think you should be going for a job on a woman's magazine."

I look down at the half-empty bottle of beer and idly start picking off the foil around the rim of the bottle. I know Ben is absolutely right, even though I'm not sure I like hearing it from him. I mean, it's one thing recognizing your own weaknesses, but quite another hearing that someone else can see them that clearly, particularly when that someone happens to be Ben Williams. But, having said that, I'd kill to work on one of the glossy magazines I love so much, but I also know the type of women who work there, and I know quite categorically that I'd never fit in.

The type of women who work on glossy magazines are pencil-slim. They have highlighted hair, and hard faces covered in too much makeup. They always wear designer black, and always, like Geraldine, have sunglasses pushing their hair off their faces.

They go out for long liquid lunches, and network every evening in the trendiest bars in town. I could never look like that nor live like that, but of course I can't tell Ben this, so I shrug. "I don't know, maybe you're right. What about you then, Ben? Are you a writer or a journalist?"

"Actually," says Ben with a shy grin, "I think I'm kind of neither." Confusion crosses my face as Ben reaches into his pocket and pulls out a crumpled piece of paper.

"Here," he says, handing it to me. "What do you think of this?"

I skim-read it quickly then double back and read it again more slowly. "What do you mean, what do I think?" Horror suddenly courses through my veins. No! Don't leave! My God, if you left the paper what would I have to look forward to? I would be completely desperate and I would not want to carry on.

"What do you *think*?" Ben repeats, a different emphasis on the words. "Could you see me on television?"

"Yes, of course!" I say, because Ben needs to be reassured, and the truth is I could see him on television. Absolutely. "You'd be brilliant on television, you'd be perfect!"

Ben sighs with relief. "Do you think I'd get it?"

"Well, they'll be nuts if you don't. You'll definitely get an interview, and I'm sure you'll be in with a chance. You've got a background in journalism *and* perfect white teeth, what more would you need?" Listen to me. I'm actually teasing Ben! I, Jemima Jones, am teasing the gorgeous Ben Williams! Ben laughs, showing off those teeth, and I suspect he's surprised at this side of me he's never seen.

Ben bares those beauties in a great big false cheesy smile, and says, "This is Ben Williams on *London Today*." I start laughing, he looks ridiculous, and he raises one eyebrow and says, "There, what do you think of that?"

"Too much white teeth," I laugh. "Even for you."

"Can I read you my application letter?" he says. "I'm sending it tomorrow, but would you tell me what you think?"

"Sure."

"But you mustn't tell anyone. I know I can trust you but I wouldn't want anyone else at work to know about this."

I watch as Ben pulls a copy of the letter out of his briefcase and as he hands it to me I feel totally honored that he's trusting me.

"Dear Diana Macpherson," I read silently. "Re: Vacancy for television reporter as advertised in last Monday's *Guardian*. I am currently working as the deputy news editor on the *Kilburn Herald* but would love to move into television . . ." My eyes glaze over as I finish reading what can only be described as a completely standard letter, and definitely not a letter that would even get him an interview, let alone a job.

I put the letter down and, trying to be as honest as I know how, I say, "It's a great letter. It says everything you need to say, but if you want my honest opinion I don't think it's going to cut it. I think you need something more dynamic, more creative."

"Oh God, do you think so?" Ben's face falls. "I was trying to write something interesting but I was in such a hurry I just wrote down the first thing I could think of. You wouldn't . . ." His eyes light up as he looks at me.

"Of course I would!" I laugh, because I've been dying to since I read the first sentence, and grabbing a pen out of my bag I turn the letter over and start scribbling on the back.

"Health and beauty may not be my strong points," I write,

speaking the words out loud so Ben can hear, "although I do have a bathroom cabinet fully stocked with men's cologne (freebies passed to me by the women feature writers at the *Kilburn Herald*), and my interest in show business and entertainment may be limited—I have a healthy interest because of my work as the deputy news editor, but offer me the chance of a film premiere ticket and I'll run a mile. However, my knowledge of news and politics is exemplary.

"I am, as I briefly mentioned, currently working as the deputy news editor on the *Kilburn Herald*. Not, I'm sure you'll agree, the most prestigious of papers, but nevertheless the perfect place for a solid background in journalism. I started as a trainee reporter and have now been with the paper for five years. Needless to say, it is now time for a change, and I firmly believe that the future for all good journalists lies in television.

"I am, naturally, addicted to news and politics, and am an avid viewer of programs not dissimilar to yours. I'm afraid I do not possess a demo tape, however, I enclose a photograph together with my CV, and look forward to hearing from you."

"There," I say, slapping the pen down as Ben shakes his head in amazement.

"God, Jemima," he says, rereading the words. "You're amazing."

"I know," I sigh. "I just wish someone else would notice."

"That is just so inspired," he says, a wide grin spreading across his face.

"At the end of the day, Ben, they're either going to love it or hate it, but either way they'll definitely notice it."

"Do you really think so?"

"I really think so."

While Ben and Jemima sit there chatting, mostly about work, it has to be said, Sophie and Lisa have got dressed—the pair of them in almost identical black lycra dresses, knee-high boots (Sophie's are suede, Lisa's are leather), with little black Chanel bags over one shoulder. Sophie is wearing a soft black leather jacket with a fur collar, and Lisa is in a cape. These are their pickup outfits—the clothes they wear when they venture to an unknown club to attract potential millionaire husbands.

They do look wonderful. They also look completely out of place in Kilburn, tottering down the street in their smart clothes, leaving bystanders open-mouthed at these two exotic beauties.

They've already been in to the Queen's Arms, a bit of a mistake, they realized as soon as they walked in. They had to wave their arms to see through the smoke, and when they did they saw hundreds of men, all propped up against the bar, who went completely silent, presumably in admiration at the sight of Sophie and Lisa.

"I think I've died and gone to heaven," groaned a builder, clutching his heart while his mates laughed.

"Looking for me, love?" said one to Sophie, as she looked around the pub, wishing fervently she was somewhere else.

"Will you marry me?" said another to Lisa, who kept her nose in the air and kept walking.

Both girls, to their credit, ignored the men, and walked out, heads held high, while the men jeered, and a couple ran to the door to try and jokingly persuade them to come back.

"God, what a nightmare," says Sophie to Lisa as they walk up the road. "Are you sure this is worth it? Shouldn't we just jump in a cab and go into town?"

"Are you mad?" Lisa turns to her in horror. "When we've just met the best-looking man we've seen in ages."

"He is gorgeous," agrees Sophie, "but he works at the *Kilburn Herald*. I mean, he's hardly in our league is he?" Sophie, bless her, has forgotten that she is a receptionist, because in her dreams she is a rich man's wife.

"With looks like that I couldn't give a damn. I don't want to marry him, but I'd kill to have a fling with him," says Lisa, adding, "Phwooargh," with a faraway look in her eyes.

"Okay," says Sophie. "One more try." They walk past the picture windows and into the bar, taking note of the beautiful and fashionable people, and feeling instantly superior. They, after all, are not only fashionable, they are also wearing designer labels, and both make sure the gold intertwined C's on their Chanel bags are facing outward just so that everyone can be sure of this fact.

"They *must* be here," says Lisa, looking slowly at each table.

"I can't see them," says Sophie, walking past the bar and into the room at the back. "Nope," she says as she surveys the room. "Where the hell can they be?"

Doesn't time fly when you're having fun? Both our glasses are empty, so I stand up to get some more drinks, hoping to prolong this evening for as long as possible, praying that Ben won't stand up and say it's time to go. "I'll get this round," I say as nonchalantly as I can. "Same again?"

"Are you sure?" says Ben, who, being the perfect gentleman I think he is, would probably be more than happy to pay for the second round. And the third. But I insist and he agrees to the same again.

But as I stand up I suddenly have a horrifying thought. From the front, I am passable. I can just about hide my size, and hope that people look at my eyes or my hair, but from the back even I admit that I'm huge. Can I back out of the room? Would Ben think I was completely mad? Should I risk turning round and allowing Ben to see me from behind?

As I stand there in this dilemma, Ben starts rereading his application letter, so with a huge sigh of relief I walk, front first, out of the tiny room and into the main bar. BLOODY HELL! WHAT THE HELL ARE THEY DOING HERE?

I don't bloody believe this. Sophie and Lisa never, ever, come to places like this. Drink in Kilburn? Are you mad? Those evil little cows, I know exactly what they're doing. Look at them, tarted up to the nines and standing by the bar looking for something, and don't think I don't know exactly what they're looking for. Me. Or to be more precise, Ben. Bitches.

What am I going to do? I can't let them see me, I can't let

them join us, because look at them now, Ben wouldn't recognize them as the two girls he met earlier this evening, and he might, just might, fancy them. Shit, shit, shit. I turn around and rush back to Ben.

"Ben," I say, thinking, thinking, thinking.

Ben looks up. "Hmm?"

"I just wanted to ask you, before I forget, um. Well, it's just that I wanted to ask you, do you have a demo tape because the ad said send a demo tape." Jesus, I sound like a total idiot but it's the best I could come up with, given the urgency of the situation.

"I'm going to send a photograph. Why, do you think I should send a tape?" Ben is, as I knew he would be, looking at me as if I'm a bit strange.

"Well," I say, sitting down. "There are pros and cons, I suppose. I mean, a photograph doesn't show them exactly what they want to see, i.e., what you'll be like on television, but then a demo is probably bloody expensive to put together."

"Right," says Ben, now looking completely confused as to why I'm sitting down again minus the drinks.

I look over Ben's shoulder and—thank you, God—see Sophie and Lisa walk out of the bar. Highly unusually, bearing in mind this is Kilburn, a black cab with an orange light shining happens to be driving down the road just as they leave, and both girls, on reflex, leap into the road with arms held high.

I can feel Ben watching me as I watch the cab drive off.

"Right," I echo Ben, standing up purposefully. "Drinks," and off I go to the bar.

chapter 10

Jemima really doesn't want to get out of bed, not when she can lie here daydreaming about last night with Ben Williams.

Unfortunately for Jemima, her daydream didn't come true, but it was the next best thing, because, after Ben had insisted on walking her home, he leaned down and kissed her on the cheek.

Jemima blushed bright red, and silently thanked God for being shrouded in darkness so Ben wouldn't see. "I'll see you tomorrow," he shouted as he walked up the road, and Jemima nodded mutely on the doorstep, too happy to speak.

She didn't have time to think about him last night—the three beers had gone straight to her head, and as soon as she touched the pillow she was out like a light, but now, now that it's morning, Jemima has time. Time to go over every word, every sentence, every nuance.

She has time to think about what happened, what could have happened, and what will, she hopes, happen in the future, and in all her fantasies Jemima is thin.

Jemima lies there for too long, and when she looks at the clock she knows that she'll be late for work if she doesn't get a move on. She hurries to the bathroom to run her bath, and completely forgets, yes really, completely forgets about her cereal.

And then, while she's waiting for the bath to run, she decides to do something she hasn't done for months. She stands on the scales. Holding her breath, she balances her weight carefully, not daring to look down until she is perfectly still. And when she does, she starts smiling, because Jemima Jones has lost ten pounds. There's still a long way to go, but Geraldine was right, Jemima has finally managed to lose some weight.

Jemima stands there for a while and then she puts her hand out and holds on to the towel rail. She presses down hard and watches her weight plummet. The harder she presses, the more the weight goes down on the scales. I wish, she thinks. I will, she thinks.

And then, as she is about to get in the bath, she hears voices downstairs and realizes that Sophie and Lisa haven't left for work. She looks at her watch. Nine-ten A.M., and they are never usually here at this time, they will be late.

"Jemima," says Sophie from outside the bathroom door.

I lift my head out of the water. "What are you doing here? You're going to be late for work." Subtext: you're an evil cow and I haven't got anything to say to you.

"I know, we're just leaving but we both overslept."

"Did you have a good time last night? How was the club?" I try my best to be nice, and I don't mention I saw them, that I know what they were up to.

"It was brilliant," says Sophie. "But how was your evening?"

"Lovely." I'm smiling.

"So that was Ben?"

"Yup."

There's a pause.

"He is gorgeous."

My smile widens.

"Why don't you invite him over for dinner one night?" says Sophie, a hint of pleading in her voice.

As if! "Maybe I will." In your bloody dreams. I will keep Ben as far away from Sophie and Lisa as I possibly can.

"Okay, I gotta go. Have a good day." I lie back in the bath and listen to both their high heels clatter down to the front door, the clicking punctuated by whispers and giggles.

Poor Sophie and Lisa. They really think I'm stupid enough to propel Ben into their arms? How wrong they are.

"So how was last night?" Geraldine sashays over, sipping from a cappuccino in a Styrofoam cup she bought on the way to work.

"Fine." I fight to keep the grin off my face, the grin that would give my feelings away.

"Did you go to that computer café?" Geraldine's tongue snakes out to her top lip and licks away the smudge of foamy chocolate that sits there.

"No, Ben had to work late so we just went for a drink."

"Ooh, very cozy." Geraldine looks at me closely. "Jemima? You're not blushing are you?"

"No," I say quickly. Possibly a little too quickly, and I feel a hot flush cover my neck and cheeks.

"Jemima! You are!" She lowers her voice and smiles. "Do you fancy Ben?"

"No!" I say, wishing to Christ I didn't blush half as easily as I do.

"You do!" says Geraldine. "I don't believe it."

The flush starts to fade away. "Geraldine," I say firmly, with a conviction that comes from God knows where. "There would be absolutely no point in me fancying Ben Williams, which, incidentally, I don't, because he would never, ever, be interested in someone like me. I don't particularly enjoy wasting my time, on anything, and certainly not on fancying someone who is so obviously unattainable." I think, in my embarrassment at

Geraldine guessing, I think I have come up with an argument so convincing that Geraldine immediately backs down.

"Okay," she says, "I believe you, but he is good-looking, everyone else seems to fancy him. Except me," she adds with a sigh. "I've got enough bloody problems of my own."

"So how is Dimitri?"

"A nightmare. He's been coming round to the flat every night, begging me to go back to him. I've tried ignoring him but he just stands on the doorstep shouting up at my window, or bangs on the door for hours. The neighbors are going crazy and I don't really know what to do."

"You could move," I say, smiling.

"I think I might have to." Geraldine smiles back, before looking across the room. "Well, well," she says. "Speak of the devil."

"Oh yes?" says Ben Williams. "And what were you saying?"

"Jemima was just telling me you were a lousy shag."

"I thought I was pretty good, actually, Jemima. You certainly seemed to be enjoying yourself."

I laugh, fighting the urge to blush at the very thought. If only. If only.

"I just came over to say thanks for having a drink with me last night. I had a really nice time."

"I've got to get some work done," says Geraldine. "See you guys later," and she walks back to her desk.

"I also wanted to say thank you for looking at the job stuff. I really needed to talk to someone about it, and I know I can trust you."

"Absolutely," I say. "My lips are sealed." With a loving kiss perhaps? In my dreams.

"We must do it again some time," says Ben distractedly, looking over at the newsdesk.

"Great!" Calm down, Jemima, calm down. "What about next week?"

"Sure," he says looking back at me with a smile. "Maybe next week we'll manage to get to that computer café."

* * *

How is a girl supposed to work when she's fallen in love? She's not, that's how. I do practically nothing for the rest of the day, unless you count floating on a large fluffy cloud called number nine, as work. I do manage to get my boring phone calls done, though—soak graying underwear in Biotex before washing to make it sparkling white again; never open the oven door while cooking a soufflé; rinse hair in chamomile tea to bring out blond highlights—and every time I catch a glimpse of Ben I lose myself in a massive fantasy.

At 4:35 P.M. I remember Brad. He said he'd send me an e-mail, and even though there are more important men to think about, it's so boring I log on to the Internet to see what he sent.

Yup, bang on time. As I connect a voice comes out of the speakers. "You have mail," it says in an American accent, and a little box with a picture of an envelope in it says "1." I click on the box, and after a few seconds Brad's e-mail comes up.

Hi. JJ!
I decided to send this just after we spoke—I couldn't wait until tomorrow, so here's a little surprise. If you press view, you'll see a picture of me, it was taken a couple of months ago so it's pretty accurate—I haven't changed all that much, just had a haircut.

I'm on the beach at Santa Monica with my dog, Pepe. She's a schnauzer and the one true love of my life, but I had to send her home to my parents recently because I just don't have the time to look after her. I hope you like what you see, and I can't wait to see a picture of you. Will you e-mail me one by return? You have to get it scanned in to the computer, but I'm sure you'll find a way. If you can, meet me on Friday at the same time to let me know what you think!

I hope you had a good evening last night, and I hope you were good—you have to save yourself for me <g>.
Big hug, Brad. xxx

106

* * *

Now this should be interesting. I move my cursor on to VIEW, and click once. Brad's letter disappears and the outline of a picture comes on to the screen. Just the outline, because the picture takes a while to appear. First, a few lines of sky emerge at the top of the screen then I can just about see the ocean, and suddenly the top of a head of blond hair.

The lines continue, and I'm amazed that I'm actually holding my breath, and when the whole picture is on the screen I exhale loudly. Bloody hell. He's one of the best-looking men I've ever seen in my whole life.

He's crouching, squinting slightly at the lens because the sun is in his eyes. One hand is around his dog, and the other is on the sand. He is very tanned, with blond hair and smiling blue eyes, and his teeth make Ben's look like those of an old hag, so gleaming, so perfect, so capped are they.

He is wearing a green polo shirt and faded Levi's, just as he said, and his arms are muscular and strong, covered with fine blond hair. He looks like an advertisement for the perfect male product of California. In fact, he looks so perfect that for a minute I can't help but wonder whether this is some cut-out from a magazine, but it looks like a photograph, and the dog is exactly as he described. Jemima Jones, your luck is changing.

"Phwooargh," says Geraldine, coming up to stand behind Jemima. "Who's that?"

"That's Brad." I don't even bother looking round, I'm way too busy drinking in his unbelievable looks.

"Who's Brad?"

"The guy I've been chatting to on the Internet."

"I didn't know you'd been chatting to anyone."

"Yeah. I met him at the LA Café, remember the place you found?"

Geraldine nods. "He is absolutely gorgeous. Too gorgeous to be true. How do you know it's him?"

"I don't. I mean, he did describe himself, but I have to agree,

107

he does look too perfect, but on the other hand this is a photograph, it's not a cut-out from a magazine."

"So what happens now?" asks Geraldine, who can't quite believe that of all the people Jemima could have chatted to in the LA Café, she picked one who looks like a god.

"Oh God." My voice is a horrified whisper. "It's awful. He wants to see a picture of me."

"Oh," says Geraldine, who, nice as she is, is still probably thinking that he would never fancy me in a million years if he saw me. She doesn't say anything else. She doesn't have to.

"Exactly," I say with a sigh. "Oh."

"Well, why don't you cut a picture out of a magazine? What's the difference, he'll never know."

I shake my head. "I can't do that. I know I'll probably never meet him but I can't be that dishonest."

"I've got it!" shouts Geraldine, clapping her hands together. "I've got it, I've got it, I've got it."

"What?"

"Right. There is a picture of you in the picture library isn't there?"

"Forget it, Geraldine. That picture is disgusting, it makes me look like a great big blimp."

"Not when I've finished with it," says Geraldine with a smile. "Or rather, when Paul's finished with it."

Paul is the man who works in the graphics department. Young, shy, sweet, the whole office knows he's got the most enormous crush on Geraldine. Paul is one of the few people I really like here. Not that I know him that well, but he's always calm and always takes the time to ask how I am, when people are screaming at him to get pages drawn, titles put into place, pictures put on to his Mac. Paul is the man who always designs farewell cards should anyone at the *Kilburn Herald* be lucky enough to move on. Paul, in other words, as well as being a very nice guy is also a genius.

"Ring the library," says Geraldine, "and tell them to send up your picture."

Ten minutes later a messenger troops towards my desk with a file containing my disgusting picture. I pull it out and feel sick as I survey my double chins and huge fat cheeks.

"No looking yet," says Geraldine, whisking away the picture. "I'll come and show you later."

Geraldine runs off, a woman with a mission, putting her arms around Paul and babytalking to him in a way that turns him to jelly.

"Paaaauuul," she says, arms wrapped around his neck. "I need a favor."

"Sure," says Paul, who at that minute would have given Geraldine the earth.

"Jemima needs to look thin."

Paul looks confused.

"Look. See this picture?" Paul looks and nods. "You're so clever you could make her look thin couldn't you? You could airbrush out her chins and shade her cheeks and make her look thin."

Paul smiles. "As a favor to you, Geraldine, I'll do it. When do you want it?"

"Wellllllllll," she says, looking up at him with huge blue eyes. "You couldn't do it now could you?"

Paul sighs happily, anything to keep Geraldine near, and he sits down and scans the picture of Jemima into the computer. The photograph comes up on screen, and Paul, with a few clicks of his mouse, shades out Jemima's chins.

"That's amazing," gasps Geraldine. "Can you do anything with her cheeks?"

Paul narrows her face, and then chooses the exact same shade of Jemima's skin. With incredible precision, he shades her cheeks in carefully until she has cheekbones. Perfect, beautiful, protruding cheekbones.

"God," he says, staring at the screen.

"God," says Geraldine staring at the screen.

"She would be beautiful if she lost weight. Look at that face, she's absolutely stunning, who would have thought."

Of course we know that Jemima would be beautiful, but Paul and Geraldine have never even dreamed of what Jemima would look like if she were thin.

"Her hair looks a bit dull. I know it's mousy brown but can you put a few blond highlights in, lighten it up a bit?"

"Who do you think I am? God?" laughs Paul, but just a few clicks and Jemima has golden honey blond highlights.

"What about her lipstick? Can you change the shade, that red's too harsh."

"What color do you want?" Paul brings up a color chart on screen and Geraldine points to a natural pinky brown. "There!" she says pointing at the tiny little square. "That's the color."

Jemima, gazing out from the computer screen, looks absolutely stunning, but Geraldine knows it's not enough.

"Just wait there," she says to Paul. "We haven't quite finished. I'll be back in two secs."

Geraldine runs back to her desk and quickly spreads out the pile of glossy magazines threatening to topple over on one side. *Vogue*? No, too posed. *Elle*? No, too fashion victim. *Cosmopolitan*? Perfect.

She grabs *Cosmopolitan* and runs back to Paul, flicking through the pages as she runs.

"That's the one!" she says, stopping at a picture of a girl on a bicycle. Her skin is fresh and glowing, her body is encased in the briefest of lycra cycling shorts and tank top. Her hair is the same color as Jemima's on the computer screen. She is standing astride the bicycle, looking into the camera, with one foot on the pedal. She is leaning forward and laughing. It doesn't look like a model, it looks like an exceptionally pretty girl on a summer's day who's been caught by her boyfriend's camera.

"You know what I'm going to say don't you," says Geraldine smiling.

"I know what you're going to say," says Paul, taking the picture of the girl on the bicycle and scanning it in.

He cuts and pastes. Clicks and shades. And there she is. Slim, stunning Jemima Jones, standing astride a bicycle, with one foot on the pedal, on a hot summer's day. Paul puts it on a floppy disk, and prints out the photograph, handing it to Geraldine. He has to admit he's done an incredible job.

"You are a genius," says Geraldine, giving Paul an impromptu kiss on the cheek.

"And *you* are a persuasive woman," he smiles. "Now go away, I've got work to do."

Geraldine runs over to Jemima, who's on the phone, and without saying a word lays the printed-out photograph in front of her.

"Sorry," I say to the caller on the other end of the phone, because Geraldine's leaping up and down next to my desk and making faces at me. "Can I call you back?" I put the phone down and pick up the piece of paper Geraldine's been flashing in front of my face.

"So?" I say. "I don't want to use a model's picture from a magazine. I told you that."

"It's not a model, you idiot," grins Geraldine. "It's you."

"What do you mean, it's—" And as I look at the photograph I can feel my eyes widen in disbelief as my mouth drops open. "Oh my God," I whisper. "Oh my God."

"I know," says Geraldine. "Aren't you beautiful?"

I nod silently, too shocked to speak as I trace my cheekbones, my heart-shaped chin with my index finger. "How? I mean, when? How . . ."

"Paul did it," says Geraldine, "so it's not really my doing, I just told him to add the blond highlights, change the lipstick, and I found your body. What do you think?"

"I never realized." I didn't, I swear to God, I never realized I could ever look like this. I can't take my eyes off the picture. I want to enlarge the picture and stick it on my face, show people I am beautiful, show them what's underneath the fat.

"Send it, send it," says Geraldine. "This picture is more than a match for Brad's. Send it and see what he thinks."

Geraldine stands behind me as I log on to the computer again and send an e-mail.

"Dear Brad, I got your picture and you look perfect, better than perfect, too good to be true. Are you sure you didn't cut your picture out of a magazine?

"Anyway, I got the boys in graphics to scan in a picture of me taken . . ."

I look at Geraldine. "When shall I say it was taken?"

"Say it was in the summer. Say you were cycling through Hyde Park with friends."

"Okay." I continue, ". . . in Hyde Park when I was with some friends in the summer. I hope you like it, I'm not looking my best."

I grin at Geraldine. Geraldine grins back.

"I'm out again tonight but I'll meet you tomorrow (Friday) same time, same place. Take care, JJ. xx."

"JJ?" asks Geraldine.

"That's what he calls me. Jemima Jones."

"JJ. I like that. I think I might start calling you JJ."

I put the disk in the computer, the disk that's got the picture of me on it, and press the ATTACH button at the bottom of the e-mail. I attach the picture to the letter, and press SEND. When the message comes up saying it's been sent, I breathe a sigh of relief and look guiltily at Geraldine.

"Wouldn't it be a nightmare if he wanted to meet me?"

"Don't be daft. He's thousands of miles away, you're safe as houses. Come on, let's go and get a cup of tea."

"Your mum phoned," shouts Sophie from the confines of her double bedroom when I get home. "She said can you call her when you get in."

"Thanks," I yell up the stairs, grateful that I don't have to make small talk as I head for the living room.

"Hi, Mum," I say, as she picks up the phone in Hertfordshire and says hello in her posh telephone voice. "How are you?"

"Not bad," says my mother. "How are you?"

"Fine. Work's going well. Everything's fine."

"And what about the diet? Lost any more weight?"

Here we go again. "Yes, Mum, I've lost ten pounds in the

last two weeks." For once I'm not lying, and hopefully this will keep her happy for the moment.

I knew this was too much to ask. "Careful," she says. "You don't want to lose it too quickly or it won't stay off. Why don't you join a weight loss club, like me?"

My mother was slim and beautiful when she was young. She was the belle of the ball, or so she always says, and I know from the old black-and-white photographs that she was something special. Before she was married, she looked like Audrey Hepburn, with a beauty and elegance that betrayed her background.

She started putting on weight when my dad left sixteen years ago, and now, since hitting middle age and the boredom that comes with it, she's ballooned, but of course Mum being Mum she doesn't quietly accept it, she turns it into a bloody event. She's joined a weight loss club, made a brand-new circle of friends, all of them larger ladies with shared dreams of taut tummies and firm thighs, and it's now the only thing she has to look forward to in life.

"Honestly, Jemima, it really works. I lost another two pounds this week, and I've made so many new friends. I think it would do you good."

"Okay, Mum," I say wearily. "I'll try and find one in my area." Which of course I won't, because as far as I'm concerned a weight loss club would be a living hell.

Conversations with her mother always seem to go the same way. Her mother never seems to ask about Jemima's work, her friends, her social life. She always asks about her weight, and Jemima immediately jumps to the defensive, suppressing it carefully with a weary sigh.

Her mother, you see, thinks she wants what's best for Jemima. In fact, her mother wants what's best for her mother. Her mother wants a slim, beautiful daughter who will be the envy of all her neighbors.

Her mother wants to take Jemima shopping, and show her off proudly as she squeezes into size 6 leggings. Her mother wants to turn to shop assistants and say smugly, "The things young people wear today. Honestly, I don't know how they do it."

Her mother wants to walk down the street with Jemima and feel immeasurably proud, she wants to soak in the admiring stares, bask in her daughter's beauty. What she doesn't want is what she's got. A daughter she loves, but of whom she's ashamed.

Because at this moment in time Jemima's mother tries her damnedest not to take her daughter shopping. She tries to avoid the pitying stares of shopkeepers, the humiliation of having to shop in plus-size stores, of people staring at them walking down the street.

Jemima's mother loves Jemima, deeply, as only a mother can love her daughter, but she wishes Jemima looked different. If Jemima's mother could have seen the picture Geraldine has just constructed, Jemima's mother would have wept.

"And how's your social life?" my mother finally asks.

Should I tell her I had a drink with the most gorgeous man in the country last night? Should I tell her I've met the most gorgeous man in America on the computer? Should I tell her about the photographs?

"Fine," I say finally. "It's fine."

"So what else is new?" says my mother, who always ends the conversation this way.

"Nothing, Mum." I say what I always say. "I'll call you next week."

"All right, and well done with the diet. Keep up the good work."

I put down the phone and pull the picture of myself out of my bag. Careful not to let Sophie and Lisa see it, I make cups of tea for all of us then go upstairs and lie on my bed, and gaze at my picture for a very long time.

chapter 11

"YOU ARE BEAUTIFUL!!" says the e-mail on my screen. "I couldn't believe it when I got your picture, you said that I was too good to be true but you look like a model! I didn't even know English girls could look that good! I'd really love to hear your voice, how would you feel about chatting on the phone? I understand if you don't want to give me your number, but I'll give you mine. Maybe you can call me later today. 310 266 8787. Hopefully I'll hear from you later, JJ. Take care. Brad. xxx."

"Well," says Geraldine, standing behind Jemima reading the words.

"Well," I echo, feeling incredibly guilty. "That's another fine mess you got me into."

Geraldine laughs. "It's not a mess, it's fun. The only way it could become a mess would be if he wanted to meet you, and he's so far away I'm sure that will never happen. So, are you going to phone him?"

"Why not?" Nothing to lose. "I'll give him a call later."

"I bet he's got a sexy voice," says Geraldine. "As long as he doesn't punctuate every sentence with 'like' and 'really.'"

I laugh. "You are so cynical, Geraldine, I don't understand you sometimes."

"I may be cynical but you, my dear Jemima, are an innocent, and that's why you need fairy godmothers like myself to keep your best interests at heart."

"Ben Williams, please," says a voice at the end of the phone.

"Speaking," says Ben, cradling the phone in one shoulder and looking through a pile of papers on his desk.

"Hello there," says the girl, sounding young, sounding like someone not very important. "This is Jackie from London Daytime Television."

"Oh hello!" says Ben, attention suddenly riveted to the voice on the other end of the phone.

"I'm Diana Macpherson's secretary. We got your application this morning and Diana was wondering when you could come in to meet her." As Jackie says this she's looking at Ben's photograph, and laughing to herself because she made a bet with Diana that his voice wouldn't be nearly as sexy as his face. She's laughing because she is wrong. Boy is she wrong.

"Oh!" says Ben. "That's fantastic!" Calm down, he tells himself, play it cool, this doesn't mean anything. "Well, things are a bit quiet this week, when do you want to see me?"

"We've had thousands of applications and we're trying to see the people on our shortlist as soon as possible. Any chance you could pop in this afternoon?"

Any chance? Any chance? Ben will create the chance. "This afternoon's fine. Would three-ish suit you?"

"Three-ish would be perfect," says Jackie, making a mental note to reapply her makeup after lunch. "Ask for me at the main reception and I'll come and get you."

"Do I need to bring anything?" asks Ben.

"No," she laughs. "Just yourself."

Ben puts down the phone and looks around him. Shabby, he thinks. This room is filled with shabby desks, shabby computers, and people in shabby suits. Soon, he thinks, I will be working in television, where everyone is smart and stylish, where I will never again have to deal with the daily grind of the *Kilburn Herald*.

Careful, Ben, remember that old expression, don't count your chickens before they're hatched, but then again, if you received a picture of Ben you'd interview him too.

If the truth be known, had it not been for Jackie, Ben Williams would not have been seen. It is true that London Daytime Television received thousands of applications, and it is true that most of them went straight to Personnel, where they were sorted out into three piles: Yes, No, and Maybe.

Ben, however, was clever. Ben addressed his envelope directly to Diana Macpherson, so his application bypassed Personnel and ended up on Jackie's desk. Jackie has had a few of these applications, for there are several potential television presenters who possess as much common sense as Ben Williams, but none of the others has caught Jackie's eye in the way Ben did.

Jackie was pushing them all into an internal envelope to send straight up to Personnel when she spotted Ben's photograph, and as soon as she read his letter she went to see Diana.

"Diana," she said, walking through the doorway, for this is television and the formalities normally associated with the hierarchy of blue-chip companies do not exist here. "I think you should look at this."

"Not another bloody job application," said Diana. "Send it up to Personnel."

"Actually," said Jackie, sitting down and drawing her legs up under her, "actually I think you should have a look at this."

"You fancy him then," smiled Diana, reaching first for the photograph. "Mmm," she said, licking her lips. "I see exactly what you mean."

Diana Macpherson is a tough woman, as she would have to be to reach the position of executive producer on a show as big as *London Nights*. She is also single, and happens to have a particular penchant for pretty young boys like Ben. Diana

Macpherson is a rough diamond—brought up on the wrong side of the tracks, she was the only girl from her seedy neighborhood to win a scholarship to a good girls' school, and then go on to university.

She is a bleached blonde, who at forty-one may not be as young as she used to be, but still turns heads by virtue of her micro miniskirts and mane of hair. Everyone is terrified of her, and few have earned her respect, but those who have have also won her undying loyalty.

Jackie, she respects, because Jackie comes from the same side of the street as Diana, and Jackie is bright. Jackie may be working as a secretary now, but when the time is right Diana will make her a researcher, and from there the world will be her oyster.

"So who is he then? Has he got any TV experience?"

"No," says Jackie, "but he's the deputy news editor on some local paper, and he sounds perfect for the news and politics reporter."

"News and politics? Shame to waste that face on news and politics. Nah, he might be better for showbiz. Then again he might be crap on screen." Diana sits in silence for a while, thinking.

"Why don't I get him to come in?" says Jackie. "Then we'll see whether he's as good as he looks."

"Yeah," says Diana, "I could do with a pretty boy round the office again."

Jackie laughs, for the last pretty boy around the office went on to become the presenter of his own chat show, thanks to his affair with Diana.

"Go on," says Diana. "Give him a call and see if he can come in this afternoon."

But Ben of course doesn't know any of this, although it obviously won't be the first time his looks have got him through the door. Ben is far too excited to analyze exactly why he has been chosen to meet the people at London Daytime Television, far too excited to get any work done.

"Jemima," he says on the internal phone when he has said goodbye to Jackie. "It's Ben. Can you meet me for lunch?"

"When? Now?"

"Yup, I'll see you down there. I've got something to tell you."

"I've got an interview," says Ben as we're waiting in line at the cafeteria. "Can you believe it? I'm going in this afternoon!"

"That's amazing!" Of course I'm happy for him, I'm not that bitter, but even as I try to share his excitement I can feel my heart sink. "See," I say brightly, trying to cover it up as I nudge him playfully, "I told you they'd know you were too good to pass up."

"I know," sighs Ben. "But I really didn't think they'd give me a chance." His face falls. "Maybe they won't. Maybe I'll get on really badly with this Diana Macpherson and that will be it."

"Do me a favor. You're being interviewed by a woman? You're in. All you have to do is charm her socks off and boom, you're on television."

"Do you really think so?"

"Yes." I nod. "I really think so."

"Oh God, I hope I get it," he says.

"You will," I say, knowing that I am probably right, that the gods will be shining on Ben Williams because of his good looks and easy charm.

We carry our trays to a table and sit down, me with a plate of salad, real salad as opposed to salads swimming in mayonnaise and calories. I'm with Ben, remember? Ben has invited me to lunch, and anyway these last couple of weeks my appetite doesn't seem to be what it once was.

I know I've only lost ten pounds, but I can see the difference already. My clothes are slightly baggier, my trousers no longer cut into the place where my waist should be, nor are they straining at the seams when I sit down.

I had forgotten how good this feeling was. For the time being, the cravings have subsided, and for the past couple of weeks I've only had a small bowl of cereal for breakfast, and I've bypassed my daily bacon sandwiches completely. The smell still gets me every day, but somehow I've managed to learn to live with it, not to give in to the temptation.

"Can you imagine if I were on television?" Ben says, looking as if he's lost in a world of cameras and fan mail. "It would be amazing."

"I've never understood people who wanted to be on TV." I look at him in astonishment. "I can't think of anything worse."

"Why?"

"Well, for starters think of the lack of privacy. Suddenly everywhere you go people recognize you and want your autograph or your time."

Ben grins. "Fantastic!" he says.

"And then," I continue, rolling my eyes, "there's the press invasion. I mean, you know yourself what it's like. As soon as you're on screen you become public property, and that means newspapers have a license to dig up as much dirt as they can find."

"Are you suggesting I may have sordid secrets?" says Ben with a grin.

"Doesn't everyone?" I look at the ceiling thinking I should be the one on television, because I am probably the only person in the world with no skeletons in her closet. "And anyway, they don't have to be that sordid. Think of the number of times you've opened the Sunday tabloids and seen an ex-girlfriend or boyfriend of someone famous spill the beans on their steamy sex life. I'd hate that. All sorts of awful people would come crawling out of the woodwork."

"I hadn't thought of that," says Ben. "But I don't think any of my exes would do that."

"It's amazing what people will do when there's money in it."

"God, if someone wanted to offer one of my exes money to talk about our sex life together good luck to them. I don't think they'd find anything interesting."

I blush, can you believe it? Ben mentions sex, and I blush. Never mind that it wasn't that long ago I was sitting looking at hard-core porn pictures with him on the Internet. Nope, all he does is say the word and I bloody blush. "Oh well," I say. "That only seems to happen to people who become famous for no reason at all, and I suppose they enjoy all the attention. They probably wouldn't bother with London Daytime Television reporters."

"What about BBC newsreaders?"

"Is that what you want to do?"

Ben groans in mock ecstasy. "I would kill to be a BBC newsreader."

I'm stunned. "Well you are a dark horse. I never realized."

"There are a lot of things about me you don't know," says Ben playfully, as he digs in to his lunch.

"So," says Geraldine, squeezing in next to us. "Is Jemima telling you about her latest boyfriend?"

"Geraldine!" Shut up! I don't want Ben to know about Brad. But, on the other hand, if he thought someone else found me attractive maybe he'd start looking at me in a new light. What do you think, worth a try?

"Well?" says Geraldine. "Are you?"

"What boyfriend?" says Ben.

"The gorgeous Californian hunk on the Internet."

"No," he says, "I don't know anything about this. I don't believe you, Jemima Jones, you've been picking up guys on the Internet?"

"Not exactly. I just went back to the LA Café, I was messing around and I've been chatting to this guy, Brad."

"Brad!" Ben laughs. "God, how typically American."

"But Brad is completely, drop-dead gorgeous. A hunk. No two ways about it," says Geraldine.

"How do *you* know?" Ben's curious.

"He e-mailed me his picture," I say, wishing we'd never brought the subject up because however you look at it dating on the Internet sounds as naff as answering Lonely Hearts ads, and before you ask, no, I've never done that.

"And," adds Geraldine, munching on a mouthful of crisp iceberg lettuce, no dressing, "she's calling him this afternoon."

"Good for you," says Ben distractedly, looking at his watch and jumping up. I look at my watch and see that he's got to make tracks if he's going to be on time for his interview. "Sorry, guys," he says, standing up. "I've gotta run."

"Good luck," I shout, as Ben runs off.

"Good luck?" Geraldine's looking quizzically at me. "What for?"

"Oh, some interview he's doing this afternoon." Good girl, Jemima, that's what I like to see, thinking on your feet.

"So when are you going to call the hunk?"

"I don't know." I sigh dramatically. "This could all end rather nastily, I'm not sure I want to."

"Oh what the hell," says Geraldine, "what have you got to lose?"

She's right. I know she's right.

We walk back upstairs together and Geraldine tells me about a man she met last week, Simon, who drives a top-of-the-line Mercedes, works in investment banking and is taking her out for dinner tonight.

"Right," she says, perching her tiny bottom on the edge of my desk. "Pick up that phone and call Brad."

"I can't," I say, smiling.

"Jemima! Just do it."

"No." I shake my head firmly.

"Honestly, I despair of you sometimes. Why not?"

"Because." I pause for dramatic effect. "Because it's six o'clock in the morning in California and I don't think he'd be very happy."

"Oh," says Geraldine. "In that case I'm going to come back over here at five o'clock, and I expect you to be on that phone. Long distance. Agreed?"

I nod my head. "Agreed."

Sure enough, at five o'clock on the dot Geraldine walks over to my desk. If I didn't know better I'd think she'd set her alarm.

"Okay, okay," I laugh, picking up the phone. "I'm phoning

him." I dial the number without really thinking of what I'm doing, just laughing at Geraldine, who's pulling faces at me as she disappears down the office.

"B-Fit Gym," says the American voice brightly on the other end of the phone. "Good morning, how may we help you?"

"Good morning," I say, suddenly wondering what the hell I'm doing. "May I speak to Brad, please?"

"Certainly, ma'am. May I say who's calling?"

"It's Jemi-" I stop. "It's JJ." Ma'am?

"Please hold the line."

I sit and wait, and I come incredibly close to putting the phone down but just before I do someone else comes on the line.

"Good morning," says another bright female voice. "How may I help you?"

"Oh hello. May I speak to Brad, please?"

"May I say who's calling?"

"It's JJ."

"Please hold the line."

"Hello?" A deep, sexy, male Californian voice. "JJ?"

"Brad? It's me. JJ."

"Oh my God, you called me! I can't believe you called me. It's so good to speak to you."

"Thank you," I say, not knowing what else to say.

"I just got in to the office, what a great surprise."

"Well it's five o'clock here, so I'm wrapping up."

"God, your voice is as sexy as your picture, which, I have to tell you, is now pinned to the wall. In fact, I'm looking at you as we speak."

"I'm really flattered." If only you knew.

"So JJ, did you have a good day?"

"It was fine. I did a bit of filming this morning, which was fun." Don't ask me what it was, please don't ask.

He doesn't. "I can totally understand why you're on television, you look so groomed, I think is the word."

"What, even on my bicycle on a hot summer's day?"

"Absolutely. I had to show your picture to everyone here, and boy, let me tell you, you have a fan club already in California."

"God, that's so embarrassing." I groan audibly.

"Don't be embarrassed. I think it's great that you work out and keep healthy, you're exactly my type of woman."

"Good," I say, recovering my composure. "I aim to please."

Brad laughs. "So listen, Jemima, what I don't understand is how come you don't have a boyfriend. I mean I know you said you just broke up with someone, but you must have men falling at your feet."

"I wouldn't put it quite like that. I do meet a lot of men through work but I suppose I'm picky."

"Well I am honored that you liked my picture enough to call me. So, talk to me some more, I love your accent. Tell me everything about yourself."

"God, where do I start?"

"Okay, tell me about your parents, do you have any brothers or sisters?"

"No brothers or sisters. I'm an only child and my parents are divorced."

"Oh that's tough," says Brad. "Mine are too. Did yours divorce when you were young too?"

"Yup," I say, wondering why on earth I'm telling all this to someone who is practically a stranger, when not even those closest to me, well, Sophie, Lisa, and Geraldine, know anything about my past. "My mother is not a happy woman. She bitterly resents being on her own, and tries to have far more input to my life than is healthy, which is mostly why I moved to London."

"You're not from London then?"

"No, I was brought up in the country. In a small town on the outskirts of London, which I suppose is really suburbia."

"And did you ever get lonely as a child? Did you want brothers and sisters?"

I wasn't just lonely as a child, I was achingly, heartbreakingly lonely. I used to go to bed at night and clasp my hands together, praying to God to deliver a baby brother or sister, not fully understanding that without a father, there was little, if any, chance of that happening. But although I have already revealed more than I planned, this would be too much, so I take a deep breath and say breezily, "Sometimes, but not often. I was fine by myself."

"Look," says Brad after I've filled him in on the finer details of my childhood, the pain-free details. "This might sound crazy, because this is the first time we've actually talked and we hardly know each other, but I have a feeling that we could have something special here." He pauses while I try to digest what he has just said, because truth to be told the only reason I've been doing this is through boredom, not because I thought there could be something special here.

And for God's sake, this man is practically a stranger. Admittedly, a particularly good-looking one, but this seems bizarre. We've never met, this is our first phone conversation and he could be some psychotic killer. And how does he know I'm who I say I am? Oh. Perhaps I'd better get off this train of thought.

"JJ? Are you still there?"

"Yes, sorry."

"Well, it's just that I know it sounds kinda crazy to meet on the Internet, but then people are meeting like this all over the world, and sometimes it does work out. Look. I think you are great. I think you're funny, and honest, and beautiful and I love your accent and I don't want to scare you off but I'd really like to meet you."

Thank God Brad cannot see me, see how my face has paled, how I am thinking seriously about killing Geraldine because I knew, I just bloody knew that this would happen.

"I'm not suggesting you come over here, I mean I know that would be a big step for you and you're probably really busy in your career, but how would you feel if I were to fly over to meet you?"

"Um," I say imaginatively, stalling for time, praying for divine intervention, which of course doesn't come. "Um," I repeat.

"Okay," says Brad. "I can hear that I've thrown you a bit, but would you just think about it?"

"Okay," I lie. "I'll think about it."

Then, as if that isn't enough, I do the unthinkable. I give Brad my telephone numbers, both home and my direct line at work (because I wouldn't want to blow my cover as a top TV presenter), and when we say goodbye I put the phone down and go into the bathroom to look at myself in the mirror.

I look at my chins, my cheeks, my bulk, and as I stand there I make a decision. A huge decision. A decision so momentous that even in this split second I know that it will change my life. I run back to my desk, well, run/lumber, grab my bag, and run down the stairs.

I'm not going far. I'm walking, almost sprinting, up the Kilburn High Road to the brand-new fancy gym that just opened. I pass it every day, barely registering its existence because what, after all, would a gym mean to me.

But today is the day I'm going to change my life. And pushing through the double doors I approach the pert blond receptionist with as much determination as I can muster.

"Hello," I say. "I'd like to join."

chapter 12

"I'll just get you a form," says the blonde behind the reception desk, looking at Jemima Jones with more than a touch of curiosity, because she can't quite understand why someone the size of Jemima would want to join a gym.

Of course she should have realized that she wants to lose weight, but the fact of the matter is that this brand-spanking-new gym isn't just any old gym. The joining fee is £150, and the monthly fee after that is £45. A lot of money, precisely to keep out people like Jemima Jones.

It's a good thing Jemima doesn't wander around before joining, because had she seen the type of people who do frequent this gym, she would have been off faster than you can say Stairmaster.

She would have seen the beautiful people glowing prettily on the treadmills, a hint of sweat showing their suntans off to maximum potential. She would have seen the women in the changing room carefully applying their makeup before they ventured out, just in case the man of their dreams should happen to be cycling beside them.

She would have seen the middle-aged housewives, wives of high-flying businessmen, who drip with gold as they step up and down and up and down and up and down to keep their figures perfect for the round of dinner parties they attend.

She would have seen the muscle-bound men, all young, all fit, all good-looking beyond belief, who go to the gym partly to keep in shape and partly to eye the women.

And Jemima Jones would have been far too intimidated to set foot through the door, but luckily the manager isn't around, and there's no one who can show Jemima all the facilities the gym has to offer, so Jemima just takes the form and sits down in reception to fill it out. She blanches slightly at the price, but then it's a small price to pay for being thin, and this gym is so close she won't have any excuse not to go, so with pen in hand she starts ticking the boxes.

As anyone who is currently spending each night in front of the television eating take-aways will know, the hardest part of an exercise regime is taking the first step. Once you find the motivation to start, exercise can be strangely addictive, much like, in fact, the Internet.

When the form has been filled in and she has written down her bank details for the direct debit, she goes back to the desk.

"Um, I've never actually been to a gym before," I say, feeling faintly ridiculous as the blonde hands me a stack of papers, timetables for classes, information about the gym.

"Don't worry," says the blonde with a bright smile. "Many of the people here haven't been before. We need to get you in for a fitness assessment and they'll work out a regimen for you." My body tenses as I wait for her to look me up and down with a withering glance but she doesn't, she just smiles and opens a large diary on the desk and flicks through the pages. "You normally have to wait around three weeks for a fitness assessment, but we've had a cancellation tomorrow morning. Could you make it at eight A.M.?"

Eight A.M. tomorrow? Is she mad? Eight A.M. is the middle of the night.

"Eight o'clock's fine," I hear myself say, the words hanging in the air before I've had a chance to think about what I've just said.

"Lovely," says the blonde, penciling in my name. "You won't need a leotard, just a T-shirt and shorts . . ." She takes a look at me and sees my face fall at the prospect of wearing a leotard. "Or sweatpants would be fine. And sneakers, you need to wear sneakers."

"That's fine," I say, wondering where the hell I'll get all this equipment, but in for a penny, in for a pound, and looking at my watch I see it's 6:15 P.M., and I know there's a sports shop in a shopping mall in Bayswater that will still be open.

I leave the gym and, crazy as this may sound, I'm convinced that already my step feels lighter, my frame seems somewhat smaller, and in my mind's eye I can already see myself as I'm going to be. Slim. And beautiful. As I once was, I suppose, when I was a child, before my father left, before I discovered that the only thing to ease the pain of being abandoned by an uncaring father was food.

I hop into a taxi—my, my, Jemima, you are being extravagant these days—and instruct the driver to take me to Whiteleys, where I ignore the clothes shops, the shoe shops, even the bookshop, and go straight up the escalator to the sports shop.

Half an hour later my arms are being dragged down to the floor with shopping bags. I've bought a tracksuit, two pairs of lycra leggings, three pairs of socks, and a gleaming pair of Reeboks. I have spent so much money today that there's no way now I can change my mind. That was the idea.

And as I walk out of the shopping mall I stand for a few minutes looking at the bustling crowds, listening to the mix of voices from every part of the world. I could go straight home, that is what I would have done a few weeks ago, but look at this street, look at the last rays of the sun. It's a beautiful evening and I'm not ready to go home and sit watching television, not just yet.

And as I wander down Queensway, pushing through the crowds of tourists, I start to feel like I'm on holiday, and what better to do on holiday than to sit at a sidewalk café and enjoy a drink.

Normally I'd order a cappuccino, and eat the chocolate off the top before adding three sugars, but things are about to change, and I find a small round marble table outside a patisserie, and order a sparkling mineral water.

She doesn't have anything to read, nor does she have anyone to talk to, but Jemima is feeling happier than she has felt in a long time. Happier, perhaps, than she has ever felt in her life. She sits in the fading sunshine and without realizing it she has a huge smile on her face because for the first time she starts to feel that life isn't boring. Life is the most exciting it has ever been.

Jemima Jones's life has been rumbling for a while now, but today is the day it finally turned over.

Ben Williams has just got home to find the answering machine winking three messages at him. Two are for his roommates, and the last one is from Richard, his oldest friend.

Ben picks up the phone and calls Richard because (a) he wants to talk to him as it's been a while, and (b) he has to tell someone about his interview today or he might possibly burst.

"Rich? It's me."

"Ben! How are you, boy?" This is the way they talk to each other.

"I'm fine, Rich, how 'bout you?"

"Rolling along, Ben. Rolling along. I haven't seen you for ages, what have you been up to?"

"Actually, I've got some news."

Richard's voice drops to a whisper. "I know a good doctor."

"What?"

"You've got some bird pregnant."

"Don't be ridiculous." Ben starts laughing. "I haven't got anyone pregnant, chance would be a fine thing! No, I had a job interview today."

"That's great, what for?"

"Come on, Rich, you can do better than that. What's my dream job?"

"No! You had a job interview as a newsreader? No way, that's serious."

"It wasn't for a newsreader, but it is for television. I went for a job interview with London Daytime Television as a reporter on a new show."

"Good work. When d'you hear?"

"I'm not sure. They seemed keen but I have to do a screen test."

"Good luck, I'd like to see my best mate on television. Think of the women you could date then."

Ben just laughs, because Ben wants to tell Richard everything. He wants to tell him about walking in and sitting in the huge domed glass atrium of the TV company. He wants to tell him how it felt sitting surrounded by pictures of the stars of the company, and how a very famous presenter of the morning show came and sat next to him.

He wants to tell Richard about going up in the lift, about stepping out feeling sick with nerves, and waiting just outside for the secretary to come and get him. He wants to tell him how friendly the secretary was, if anything slightly too friendly, but how he assumed that is how they all are in television.

He wants to tell Richard about walking in to meet Diana Macpherson. About her micro miniskirt and high heels, about how she kicked her shoes off after a few minutes and put her feet on the desk.

He wants to tell Richard how Diana fixed him with a cool gaze and said, "Well, fuck me, Jackie was right, you're even prettier in the flesh."

He wants to tell him how he made her laugh, how they

131

ended up talking about the nightmares of being single, about how he pretended to equal her horror stories with stories of his own, because he really felt there was some sort of a bond.

He wants to tell him that they didn't really talk about television, or about work. That she seemed far more interested in him, and that it didn't feel like an interview, that it felt more like having a chat with a friend, and did Richard think that was a good thing or a bad thing.

And he wants to tell Richard how, at the end of their "interviews," Diana shook his hand and said, "All right then, Ben Williams. I won't say you're in 'cuz I don't know what you look like on screen, but our viewers would fucking love those pretty-boy looks of yours, and I want you in on Thursday to have a screen test."

But of course he can't say any of this, because Richard is a bloke, and as well we all know blokes don't *do* detail, they do facts, and Richard would probably fall asleep with boredom.

So they sit and chat, and all the time Ben's mind is far away in the land of London Daytime Studios, and as soon as he says goodbye to Richard, he picks up the phone and dials Jemima, because who better to listen to the details than Jemima Jones, his newfound friend.

"Hello, is Jemima there, please?" Listen to how well spoken he is.

"Sorry, she's out at the moment. Can I take a message?"

"Um, yeah. It's Ben from work. If I leave my number could you get her to call me?"

Sophie nearly drops the phone. "Oh hi, Ben!" she says enthusiastically. "It's Sophie, we met the other night."

"Were you the one with the face pack or the one with strange things in her hair?" Ben's laughing.

Sophie groans. "Please don't remind me. We both looked awful, but for the record I was the one with the strange things in her hair." Lisa looks up from the magazine she's reading on the sofa. Her eyes widen as she mouths, "Is it him?" Sophie nods.

"Ah," says Ben, who can't think of anything else to say.

"But I don't usually look like that," adds Sophie, who wants to keep Ben talking, who wants this conversation to develop into the sort of hour-long conversation women always try to have with men they have only just met, and who they fancy madly.

"I should hope not," says Ben. "I wouldn't have thought Curve would appreciate it."

"Jemima told you where I work?"

"She mentioned it," says Ben, wondering why this message is taking so long to deliver. "Look, can I give you my number?"

"Sure. Sorry. I'll just get a pen," she says, flying back to the phone in an instant. "Okay, shoot."

Ben leaves his number and asks if Jemima could call him back as soon as possible, and they say goodbye.

"Guess what I've got," she says to Lisa, waving the piece of paper in the air then clutching it to her chest.

"You bitch," says Lisa, who sort of does mean it, but sort of doesn't. "You can't keep that, you have to give it to Jemima."

"I will," says Sophie, "but first I'm going to copy it down for myself."

"But what excuse will you use? You can't just phone him, and he wasn't exactly on the phone with you for long," she says triumphantly. "It didn't sound like he was that interested."

"Not yet," says Sophie. "But I think we should invite him somewhere, maybe a party or a club, and if we have to we'll invite Jemima too, but we are going to see him again, and this time we are going to look better than we've ever looked before in our lives."

Lisa grins, happy now that she has been included, and confident that, given the choice, Ben would opt for her tumbling curls.

The girls hear the front door slam, and Jemima comes upstairs, dumping her bags on the living room floor.

"Oooh," say the girls in unison. "You've been shopping. Show us what you've bought."

"It's not very exciting," I say, when in fact I'm very excited, I'm so excited I don't think I'll be able to sleep tonight. "I just bought some gym stuff. I joined a gym today."

"You're kidding," says Sophie, looking completely shocked.

"I kid you not," I say happily.

"But what for?" says Lisa.

"To get fit, what do you think. I am going to lose all this weight and get fit, and in a few months' time you won't recognize me."

"Is this for that guy at work, Ben?" says Sophie slyly.

"No," but of course it's for that Ben at work, although now it's also for Brad in Santa Monica. "It's for myself," I say, and you know what? As I say it I realize it's true. Sure, Ben and Brad are the catalysts, but I'm going to lose weight for me.

"Oh by the way," says Sophie, just as I'm walking upstairs. "Ben called. His number's by the answerphone."

Everything stops, only for a few seconds, but in those few seconds all I can hear is my heartbeat thundering in my ears, and when my world starts again it goes spinning into overdrive. I pick up the phone, and when Ben picks up the receiver at the other end I—ridiculous creature that I am—am almost completely breathless.

"Ben?" I try to calm myself, to take deep breaths. "It's Jemima."

"Hi!" he says, and I start to relax, because I never expected Ben to sound so happy to hear from me. Please let him ask me out, please let him have phoned me because he can't stop thinking about me.

"Aren't you going to ask me?" he says.

Ask him? About what? I remember. "I forgot, oh I'm so sorry, I forgot. How was it, how did it go, did you get the job?"

Ben settles back into his sofa and tells Jemima Jones everything. He tells her all the things he wishes he could have told Richard, and he can hear from her gasps of amazement and

134

sounds of encouragement that she is glued to the phone, one hundred percent completely rapt. *This* is the kind of reaction you only get from women. This is why Ben phoned Jemima.

"I can't believe you're going to be on television!"

"I don't know if I am," says Ben, but of course he does know, he's always known.

"So when's the screen test?"

"Day after tomorrow."

"So soon!"

"Yup," says Ben. "They'd like someone to start in about two weeks, so if I gave in my notice on Monday I'm owed two weeks holiday so that would be it, I could start in two weeks." He pauses. "If I get the job, that is."

"You'll get the job," I say.

"Do you really think so?"

"Yes," I say again. "I really think so."

When my alarm goes off at 7:15 A.M. I groan, roll over, and decide that this is madness. I'll go another time. But no, says a little voice inside my head, if you don't go now you'll never go and think of the money you've spent.

So I crawl out of bed, half asleep, and go to the bathroom, where I splash my face with cold water to try and wake up. I throw my clothes for the day into a bag, and pull on an old T-shirt, my new tracksuit bottoms and the new sneakers.

Stumbling out the door, I walk to the bus stop in a complete daze, amazed at how quiet London is at 7:30 in the morning, so when I reach the gym, I can't believe how many people are already there, puffing and panting through their pre-work workouts.

"Hi," says a big brawny bloke in reception, walking over. "You must be Jemima. I'm Paul, and I'm your fitness instructor."

Paul takes me upstairs, through the gym where I look straight ahead, trying to ignore the bodies beautiful, and into a small room designed specifically for the purposes of fitness assessment.

"Right," he says, putting a form on the table. "You have to fill this out, but first I have to check your blood pressure." He does this, and then I wince as he pulls out what looks suspiciously like a surgical instrument.

"Don't worry," he laughs. "This isn't going to hurt. This," he says, pointing to the pincer-like instrument, "is to measure your fat ratio. That way we can keep track of how much fat is turned into muscle."

Shit! This is a mistake. This is my biggest nightmare. No one's ever measured my fat before, Jesus, no one even knows how much I weigh, and my eyes suddenly fall upon the scales in the corner of the room. Shit, shit, shit.

But what can I do? I can't run away, so I just pretend I've left my body, I'm somewhere else, as Paul measures the fat on my arms, my waist, my stomach, and my hips. He doesn't say anything, just writes the results on the form.

"Okay," he says when he's done. "If you slip your shoes off I'll just weigh you." Shit.

I stand on the scales looking miserably at the wall as Paul juggles with the scales until he has my exact weight. 204 pounds. He writes it on the form, as I try and control my embarrassment, the only relief coming when I remember that had I come a month ago, I would have been nearer 217 pounds, because somehow I have managed to shed almost 13 pounds in the last few weeks.

"So," he says, sitting down and gesturing for me to sit down too. "That wasn't too painful, was it?" I smile at him gratefully, because he didn't shrink with horror at my size, he's being so matter of fact that at last I'm starting to relax.

"What are your aims?"

"You mean apart from getting fit?"

Paul nods.

"I want to be slim. I want to lose all this weight and I want to be fit. And healthy."

Paul nods sagely. "Good. I'm glad you're here, because the biggest mistake people make is to crash diet and do no exercise, which means that yes, in the short term they lose weight, but they inevitably put it back on again, plus you'd be horrified at what serious dieting and no exercise can do."

"What do you mean?" I'm intrigued.

"You wouldn't want to be left with great huge folds of flabby skin would you?"

I shake my head in horror.

"That's why you need to exercise. You have to tone up and firm up, and that's just as important as what you eat. Speaking of which, have you thought about a food plan?"

"I've cut down what I eat, but no, other than that I haven't really thought about it."

"How would you feel about me working out a diet for you?"

I nod enthusiastically as Paul starts explaining about proteins, carbohydrates, fat groups, food combinations.

"Food combining is the best way for you," he says and, pulling a blank piece of paper out from a drawer, he starts writing. For breakfast every day, he writes, I will have fruit, as much as I want, but no melon because it's harder to digest. I will always wait for twenty minutes before eating anything else to allow the fruit to digest.

For lunch I will have salad with only one of the food groups, because I will never mix protein with carbohydrates. For example, he writes, salad with cheese, salad with a baked potato, salad with bread. I could have, he tells me, an avocado and tomato sandwich on whole wheat bread with no butter. Avocado is fine, he says, when it's eaten in the right combination.

For dinner I will have vegetables with grilled fish, or chicken, and again I can have as many vegetables as I want.

"And," he says, looking up, "you will need to drink lots of water every day. At least one liter, preferably more."

"Will I lose weight quickly?"

"You'll be amazed," he says. "But it's better that you don't lose it too quickly because the quicker you lose it the quicker it will climb on again. But this isn't a diet, Jemima, it's a way of life, and once you understand that you'll find that your entire shape starts changing.

"I want you to have regular assessments," he says, standing up and walking towards the gym, "every six weeks or so you should come in to see me to check your progress."

I follow him meekly into the gym and Paul starts by showing me the warm-up exercises. He leads me to the bike, and says, "Five minutes on the bike, I think, just to warm you up."

So I sit and I pedal, and within two minutes sweat is pouring off my brow and dripping on to the floor. "That's it," says Paul. "You're doing great, nearly there." Jesus, I want to stop, I can already feel the muscles, what muscles there are, in my legs cramping up, but if Paul says I can do it, I can do it. And I do.

"Stairmaster next," he says, pressing some buttons on the Stairmaster. Fat burner, he enters, then my weight, then ten minutes. I start climbing.

After two minutes I'm thinking this is really easy, what's all the big fuss about? After five minutes I think I'm going to die.

"I. Don't. Think. I. Can. Carry. On," I manage to get out in spurts of breath.

"'Course you can," says Paul with a smile. "Think of the tiny, pert bottom you'll have." I picture a tiny, pert bottom in my mind, and motivation, inspiration, floods my body and drives me on. I manage nine minutes, and then I really can't do any more.

"Don't worry," says Paul. "Next time you'll do ten, but you have to break the pain barrier. Once you've done that it's easy, and every time you come here you'll find it gets easier and easier."

After the Stairmaster I row 1,500 meters, then finish off with a one-mile powerwalk on the treadmill.

"You've done brilliantly," says Paul, who seems to believe in the power of motivation and isn't letting the fact that he is talking to a bright red, puffing, sodden lump put him off. "I'm not going to give you any weights just yet. First of all we'll concentrate on the cardiovascular stuff to burn some fat, and then we'll work on building muscle."

I stagger down to the changing room, where I shower on shaky legs before going in to work. But you know the strangest thing? The strangest thing is that, tired though I am, walking along the road on my way to the office, stopping briefly to buy a bottle of mineral water, I don't think I've ever felt better in my life.

chapter 13

"I'm going to a farewell party tomorrow night." I type in my e-mail to Brad. "One of my closest friends at work is leaving to work for another television company so I'm pretty sad. I know it will be a good night, but I don't know who I'm going to talk to anymore, other than you, of course, whom I seem to be becoming more and more dependent on.

"Anyway, I won't be able to talk to you later as I'm going straight to the gym, but call me tomorrow when I get home after the party and I'll tell you all about it.

"Big hugs and kisses as usual, JJ. xxxxxxxxxx."

Good heavens, let us just stand here and take a look at Jemima, because the transformation, in just a month, is completely remarkable. Paul, the trainer, is quite frankly amazed, but he is also slightly worried because the weight has dropped off at an alarming rate, and he suspects that Jemima is eating far less than he told her to.

His suspicions are right. Jemima took his diet sheet home with her, put it in a drawer, and promptly ignored all the good advice, and for the last month this has been her daily routine.

Jemima Jones gets up in the morning at 7 A.M., and has a glass of hot water with a slice of lemon in it. She pulls on her tracksuit, shoves her clothes for work into a training bag and is in the gym before 8 A.M. Over the course of the month she has doubled the routine Paul devised for her, and has added some movements of her own. She spends fifteen minutes on the bike, twenty-five minutes on the Stairmaster, fifteen minutes on the rowing machine, and half an hour on the treadmill, mostly powerwalking but with the odd spurt of running.

She then does floor exercises and sit-ups, and gets to the office a little after 10 A.M., completely ignoring bacon sandwiches on the way there.

She sits at her desk and swigs mineral water all morning, and then for lunch she has a side plate of plain lettuce, tomatoes, and cucumber, while Geraldine shakes her head in amazement, still unable to comprehend Jemima's willpower after all this time. Once lunch is finished, Jemima will feel ever so slightly guilty at having eaten anything at all, because Jemima has taken this dieting business to extremes.

She drinks another liter of mineral water during the afternoon, finishes work at around 6 P.M., chats to Brad on the phone usually for at least half an hour, and occasionally an hour, and then goes back to the gym.

She does an exercise class for an hour at the end of the day, and then relaxes in the steam room or the sauna. She still thinks she is huge, although she is infinitely less huge than she was a few months ago, and refuses to watch herself in the mirrors at the gym, except to think that one day all this excess weight will be gone. One day she will have a hard body. One day she will *be* a hardbody.

If Jemima had any choice at all she would eat nothing in the evening, because she has started this new regimen and she is determined to lose the weight, but she knows that if she eats absolutely nothing, she will not have the energy to exercise, and she needs protein, so dinner is a small plate of steamed vegetables and a plain grilled chicken breast.

The food she eats is boring and plain, but for once she doesn't care. She doesn't have cravings, she feels too good at having lost this weight. She likes the feeling of her clothes being large and, although she hasn't as yet bought anything new, she knows that if she carries on being as good as she has been, it won't be long before she will be able to wear whatever she wishes.

Jemima Jones has been losing between five and six pounds of weight a week. Add her weight loss this last month—twenty-two pounds—to the thirteen pounds she lost in the previous month, and we will see that Jemima Jones now weighs 182 pounds.

Paul has told Jemima that, at 5'7", she should aim to get down to 140 pounds, but Jemima Jones has ignored this and has decided that she will weigh 120 pounds, even if it kills her.

Jemima stands in the bathroom, takes off all her clothes and looks at herself in the full-length mirror. She still feels revulsion at the cellulite on her thighs, the bulges on her hips, but even she has to concede that the change is miraculous.

For, despite being 182 pounds, Jemima Jones now has a waist. She has knees. She has a small double chin, rather than a quadruple one, and her face is almost unrecognizable for it has slimmed down so much. JJ is slowly emerging from the fat of Jemima Jones and, although she is not yet the JJ on a bicycle on a hot summer's day, there is no question that she is getting there. She is finally getting there.

And tomorrow night is the night she has been dreading, Ben's farewell party. Everyone has been amazed, because nobody has ever left the *Kilburn Herald* to go on television. Some have left to join national newspapers, regarded as heroes by the colleagues they have left behind, but those are few and far between, and nobody has ever dreamed of knowing someone who started at their crappy local paper and went on to be famous.

"Next thing you know we'll be interviewing *you*," guffawed the editor, clapping Ben on the back after it had sunk in that he was losing his star reporter. "Don't forget us when you're rich and famous, eh?" And Ben just smiled, mentally ticking off the days on his fingers.

For all his diligence and hard work, Ben has been far too excited these last weeks to concentrate on the paper, but he has been forgiven, and his normal daily duties have already been delegated to others, his presence at the office now being a mere formality.

Ben was at the office when he received the call telling him he got the job. He knew the screen test was the best he could have possibly done, but he didn't know whether it was good *enough*, and the days of waiting were some of the worst of his life.

"It's fate," he kept saying to Jemima. "Either it's meant to be or it's not."

"Que sera, sera," she would echo back, hoping that fate would smile upon him, but hoping too that fate would smile upon her, that perhaps it wouldn't mean taking him away from her, because she was absolutely sure that once Ben left the *Kilburn Herald* he wouldn't look back, he wouldn't remember the friends he left behind.

And it is safe to say that Ben and Jemima are friends. They weren't, when we first met them, they were merely colleagues, but as so often happens in times of need friendships are forged, and Ben needed a confidante, more than ever during the week of the long nights, as he dubbed it.

But friendships can be a transient thing, as Jemima well knows, and their friendship, as much as it is based on trust and admiration, is equally based on convenience, and Jemima is certain that once Ben is immersed in the glamorous world of television she will no longer hear from him.

But Jemima wants Ben to be happy, more than she wants him to be at the *Kilburn Herald*, and she was the first person he told when he heard he got the job.

"Ben," said a sharp voice on the phone. "Diana Macpherson here."

Ben's breath caught in the back of his throat, and Diana's laugh cut through the silence. "Well," she said, "I suppose you want to know what I thought of the screen test?"

"Yes," said Ben, not sure what to make of her tone.

"I've just watched it," she said, "and I had to phone to tell you that you. Are. Fucking. Amazing."

Ben gasped. "You're joking!"

"I never joke about things like this. This is one of the best screen tests I have ever seen, and I can't believe you haven't presented before. Are you sure you're telling the truth?"

Ben laughed.

"I've shown it to the head of features and we both agree that you're the right man for the show, but there is one problem."

Ben's heart sank. "A problem?"

"Yeah. It's not a big one, but when we spoke you said you wanted to do news and politics, and I'm afraid that's not what we're offering. We'd like to offer you a year's contract on *London Nights* as the chief show business reporter."

There was a silence while Ben tried to digest what she had said.

"You still there, Ben?"

"Yes, sorry. It just wasn't what I expected."

Diana sighed. "I know, but I've been in this game long enough to know what people's strengths are, and although I know that news and politics are what you really want to do, I also know that you'd be wasted on that. You need to be much more high profile, and quite frankly, Ben, with this as a stepping stone the world's your oyster."

"I know." Ben nodded his head, still not quite sure what to say. Of course it was a wonderful opportunity, but did he want to be seen as a show business reporter? As a fluffy, flim-flam celebrity interviewer?

"Can I just have a few minutes to think about it and then I'll call you right back?" asked Ben, unaware that nobody, no first-time presenter, had ever had to think about an offer from Diana Macpherson before.

"Okay," she agreed. "I'll be in the office for another ten minutes, and if I don't hear from you I'll ring up our second choice. Sorry to be brutal, but that's television for you."

"Don't worry," said Ben. "I understand."

Ben went running round to Jemima's desk, and they sat there, heads huddled together, while Ben told Jemima what had happened and what his reservations were. Don't be ridiculous, said Jemima, it's the chance you've spent years waiting for, you wouldn't be pigeonholed, and all it took in television was to get your foot in the door. "If you screw this up," she said seriously, "you don't know when the next opportunity will arise. Or indeed if," she added ominously, "it will arise."

That was what did it for Ben. He checked his watch, two minutes to go before the ten minutes were up, kissed Jemima on the cheek, picked up her phone and dialed London Daytime Television.

"Diana?" he said in a much firmer voice. "It's Ben Williams. I've thought about it and I'm phoning you to tell you I'd love to work for you, and as soon as we organize the dates, I'll be in the office."

"Phew," said Diana Macpherson, who was smiling. "You gave me a right fucking scare, especially because we didn't even have a bloody second choice!"

And with just one phone call Ben's fate was sealed. It may not be the job he always wanted, but it's certainly a start, and a very good one at that, but before a new beginning must come an ending, and tomorrow night is the last night of his time at the *Kilburn Herald*.

Jemima Jones feels sick at the thought, so sick, in fact, that she commits an unforgivable sin and confides in Sophie and Lisa, only because she has no one else to talk to, and she doesn't mean to say anything, it just comes out by mistake.

"You seem a bit down," says Sophie, as they walk in. "Is everything all right?"

"Fine," I say, and before I can help it a huge sigh has escaped my lips. "I think I'm just overdoing it a bit maybe." I try and cover it up.

"You *are* spending a huge amount of time at the gym," agrees Lisa. "Maybe you should cut it down, I mean, no one needs to exercise as much as you."

Shall we take a look at what's going on here? Lisa is beginning to see that the Jemima Jones of old is well on her way to being the JJ of the future, a JJ that could well be the unthinkable. A threat. Because Lisa, as addicted as she is to the superficialities of life, can see that as the weight is dropping off, a real beauty is emerging, and Lisa doesn't like this. Not one tiny bit.

"Maybe," I say, but actually I'd like to be spending a lot more time in the gym. If I had my way I'd move into the gym, I'd work out all day every day, but I can't expect her to understand this, I can't reasonably expect anyone to understand this. I know what this is, I've seen it on a daytime show. I'm addicted to exercise. Ha! Me! If someone had told me six months ago that I would become addicted to exercise I would have rolled on the floor laughing. But I know about this, I know that this addiction is more or less the same as being addicted to alcohol or drugs. I know my body is now overflowing with endorphins, and I feel fantastic almost all the time.

I once, just once, missed an evening class when I went out for a drink with Ben, and the next morning I felt so damned guilty I doubled my workout, and nearly collapsed with the strain.

"There is another reason, I suppose," I say because I have to say it. I have to tell someone and I can't tell Geraldine. "Ben's leaving tomorrow."

Sophie and Lisa perk up. "What?" says Sophie. "Not the gorgeous Ben that we met?"

I nod miserably.

"Where is he going?" asks Sophie.

"He's going to London Daytime Television. He's going to be a reporter on a new show."

"You mean he's going to be on screen?" Lisa's eyes are wide, and they're so bloody superficial I can see exactly what they're thinking. Finding a handsome man is all well and good, finding a rich man is even better, but finding a famous man almost goes off the Richter scale, and Ben is not only gorgeous, he's about to be famous. They're so impressed they can hardly speak.

"Yes, he's going to be on screen, and I'm just a bit down about it. I mean I'm thrilled for him, really, I am, but I'll miss him. He's become one of my closest friends at work, so maybe that's why I'm feeling a bit low tonight."

"Where's the farewell party?" says Sophie nonchalantly. As if I'm that stupid. As if I'd tell her. Honestly. As if!

"I can't remember," I say, shrugging, standing up and heading out of the room. "Some wine bar somewhere."

Jemima Jones walks upstairs to her room while Sophie looks at Lisa. "Thank you, God," she says with a smile, "for providing me with this golden opportunity." For Sophie has kept Ben's number, just hasn't had the nerve to call him. Until now.

"What are you going to do?"

"Watch me." Sophie digs her Filofax out of her bag, pulls out Ben's number, and picks up the phone.

"Hello, is that Ben? Hi, it's Sophie, Jemima's roommate. Yes, the one with the hair. I just phoned to say good luck, Jemima just told me about your new job and I've never met anyone who's been on television before. You must be really excited."

"Er, yes," says Ben, who can't imagine why this girl he hardly knows is phoning. "I am."

"I just wanted to say well done, because now you're practically famous you probably won't be coming round here too much, so just in case we don't meet again, good luck."

"Thanks," says Ben, with a smile. "Really, that's ever so nice of you."

"Have you had a farewell party then?" says Sophie innocently, winking at Lisa.

"No, it's tomorrow night." There's an awkward silence where neither of them knows what to say, but Ben fills the gap first. "Come along if you like."

"I'd *love* to!" she breathes. "Where is it?" She writes down the address as Lisa jumps around in front of her, pointing at herself and making faces.

"Is it okay if I bring my friend Lisa?" she finally says grudgingly.

"Sure," says Ben, thinking what the hell, he'll be far too out of it to notice.

"Wonderful. We'll see you tomorrow night."

Hi Sweetie

Thanks for your e-mail, it always brightens my day to come in to work and find a message on screen from you. I can't believe how close I feel to you and we've never even met, but as soon as you're less busy you'd better come straight to LA, although I'm not too sure I can wait another three months!

I'm already planning all the things we can do together once you come over here. There are so many things in Los Angeles I want you to see. I'll have to take you to Universal Studios, Rollerblading down Venice Beach, to all my hangouts so you can meet all my friends.

I know this sounds crazy but I've been telling everyone all about you, and I made a copy of your picture which I carry around so everyone's seen you too and they can't wait to meet you.

I'm sorry your friend is leaving, but you seem to have so many friends one less probably won't make that much difference. Wear something beautiful tonight, I'd like to picture you in a black silk dress, cut so it swings around your legs as you walk, and if you have any high-heeled strappy sandals, wear them tonight and think of me.

On second thoughts, if the weather in London's as bad as I think it is you might be better off in a sweater and boots!

Anyways, my darling, take care and don't be too sad. I'm sitting here in the sunshine thinking of you, and I'm still here for you.

Call me when you get home and I'll call you back right away, and have a good time.

Huge hugs and kisses, Brad. xxxxxxx

I'm not sure I like this familiarity, and something about the words might just possibly put me off if I stopped to think about it. It's not that there's anything nasty about them, about his letters, I think it's just that he seems a bit bland, but maybe that's just a cultural difference. Anyway, I'm sure he's completely different in the flesh. He's probably just not very good at writing letters. That's all.

"That was nice of your roommate to call."

"What?" I turn from my screen and look at Ben in horror. "What are you talking about?"

"Your roommate. Sophie. She phoned last night after you told her about the job to wish me luck."

Little cow. I can't believe her! "But I didn't give her your number. Where did she get it from?"

Now it's Ben's turn to look surprised. "I don't know," he says, shrugging. "I assumed you gave it to her."

"Strange." I'm wondering what she's up to.

"Anyway," said Ben, "I said she could come along tonight."

"Oh." So that's what she's up to. "What did you think of her? Is she your type?"

"Jemima!" he admonishes. "The only time I've ever met the girl she looked a complete state, plus you know that she's not the type of girl I'm interested in."

"Sorry," I say, smiling a little inside. "I just thought maybe it was time you had a girlfriend." Careful, Jemima, this is a dangerous game you're playing.

"Girlfriend?" says Ben, laughing. "What would I do with a girlfriend at this time in my life? I'm far too busy being famous. By the way, do you know who I am?"

"Yes," I laugh. "You're Ben Williams, the amazingly large-headed man, whose head is growing by the second." I shake my head in mock disbelief. "God knows what you're going to be like when you're actually on television."

"I will be marvelous," says Ben, throwing up his arms in a dramatic gesture. "I will be a stupendous presenter of rubbish. I will be Ben Williams, panderer to the stars, ass-licker of the famous."

"Ben!" I giggle, thrilled that our friendship has reached this stage of easy teasing. "You won't forget me, will you?"

"But you are lowly Jemima Jones, of the crappy *Kilburn Herald*. I have to forget you, I know no one from anything as downmarket as the *Kilburn Herald!*" Ben is speaking in an extremely exaggerated upper-crust accent, but he stops as he sees a shadow of doubt cross my face. He couldn't be serious. Could he?

" 'Course I won't forget you, Jemima. You're my only real friend here, how could I possibly forget you?"

I smile, and adjust my rapidly shrinking bottom on the chair as I turn to reveal a cheekbone that's only just starting to emerge, but Ben doesn't notice the cheekbone. Ben doesn't seem to notice my weight loss at all, which means only one thing: I'm not thin enough yet.

Perhaps in an abstract way he has noticed I'm looking better, but I suppose when you're with someone for long periods of time it's very difficult to perceive any change in their size. You would instantly notice if they had a drastic haircut, or wore something they never normally wear, but weight is something you rarely notice. Particularly if you're a man. At least that's what I hope.

The only way Ben will notice that Jemima has lost weight is if he doesn't see her for a while, which would be Jemima's idea of living hell, a living hell that, she suddenly realizes, could become a reality.

* * *

"So you will stay in touch?" ventures my insecurity, refusing to let the subject drop.

"Only if you promise to respect and adore me."

"But of course, oh-famous-one," I say, when of course I, unbeknownst to Ben, already do.

chapter 14

At lunchtime Jemima watches Ben walk up the road with his colleagues from the newsdesk. She stands on the corner, holding on to her gym kit, and feels as if her heart is going to burst with sadness.

She had been invited to join them for lunch—the pre-farewell party lunch at which Ben will be forced to drink far more than he should in the middle of the working day—but she had declined because tonight is the party, and since it is starting straight from work Jemima would not have been able to make it to the gym tonight, so she skips lunch and exercises during her lunch break instead.

Who would have thought that exercise would ever be a higher priority than the opportunity of spending time with Ben Williams? Might it be thus assumed that Jemima has become just a touch obsessive . . .

For when she has finished in the gym, when she is certain there is nobody around to walk in on her, she stands gingerly on the scales in the ladies' changing room, squeezes her eyes shut and then looks down. 166 pounds. Jemima steps off and steps on again, just to check, because Jemima Jones has never weighed this little in her entire life.

Cause for celebration, I think we all agree, but on a Friday lunchtime on the Kilburn High Road there is, unfortunately, very little that Jemima can buy to celebrate. She would like a dress, the dress that Brad described last night, but even though she is down to 166 pounds she doesn't want to spend the money just yet.

"When I'm 140 pounds," she tells herself as she walks back to the office after her workout. "When I'm 140 pounds I shall treat myself properly." And as she walks along she stops outside the drugstore and peers through the doorway at the makeup counters. Oh what the hell, she thinks. I may as well give myself a small treat now, and I do want to look the very best I possibly can for tonight, so in she goes.

At 5:15 P.M. I clutch my new makeup and walk into the bathroom, not really surprised that Geraldine's already there, pouting in the mirror as she dusts some bronzer on her already golden cheeks.

"Hello stranger!" says Geraldine. "Getting ready for the party?" She stands back from the mirror and admires her red dress, which makes me think of Brad immediately, because it's just like the black dress he wanted me to wear—a short, flippy soft dress that hugs her curves and shows off her legs, snugly encased in shimmery, sheer natural stockings, with flat red suede pumps on her feet. Bitch. No, sorry, only joking, but to be a bit more serious I look at Geraldine and feel as dowdy as hell.

"I just thought," I start, feeling self-conscious and ridiculous. "I just thought maybe I'd put some . . ." I tail off as Geraldine grabs my makeup bag.

"What have you got here?" She pulls out the makeup, silently, and lays it next to the sink. "Well," she says, looking at me. "Some of this will suit you but some of it won't, but if you borrow some of mine then it will all be fine."

153

"Don't worry," I mumble, trying to keep the dejected tone out of my voice because I'm suddenly rethinking the whole idea. "I'm not sure I can be bothered."

"Jemima!" says Geraldine in exasperation. "You are hopeless sometimes. I've been dying to get my hands on you for days. What you need, now that you're losing all this weight, is a serious makeover, and tah dah!" She holds her arms up in the air. "Guess who's the perfect person to do it."

I can't help it, I start laughing, and I lean back against the counter, careful not to sit on the wet patches around the sinks. "Okay," I say with a smile. "You can start by making me up."

"Jemima Jones!" says the big, booming voice of the editor as I walk into the dark smoky vaults of the Wine Cellar a little after six o'clock. Geraldine is standing next to the editor, and Geraldine smiles with delight when she sees me, not to mention the look of amazement on the editor's face.

"What have you done to yourself, young lady?"

I shrink in horror as a hand comes up to my face. Have I smeared my lipstick? Do I have mascara running down my cheeks? Is there spinach in my teeth?

The editor carries on. "Jemima Jones, you are a shadow of your former self."

Thank God! I suppress the rising giggle and smile with delight, trying to be nonchalant, trying to look as if I'm not thrilled that someone has finally noticed, even if it is just the editor. "I've just lost a bit of weight, that's all."

"Lost a bit of weight?" booms the editor. "Young lady, you are half the size you were. And not only that," he leans forward conspiratorially. "You're also a bit of a looker, aren't you?"

Oh my God, I can feel the blush coming, but luckily I catch Geraldine's eye and I can see that she's also holding back the giggles, and the blush fades away.

Geraldine is trying to suppress the giggles, but she's also smiling broadly at her handiwork, for Jemima Jones does, truly, look like a different person. Admittedly, thinks Geraldine, her clothes aren't great, but she doesn't know that Jemima is waiting to be even slimmer before she buys some new ones.

What she is looking at is Jemima's face. She is looking at the creamy skin, given a hint of gold with the help of Geraldine's supremely expensive foundation. She is looking at Jemima's green eyes, large and sparkling with the help of Geraldine's expert knowledge of eye shadows, eyeliners, and eye drops to turn the whites of her eyes brighter than snow. She is looking at her full pouting lips, made to look even more full with the help of Geraldine's lip liner, lipstick, and lip gloss. And finally she is looking at Jemima's hair, which Geraldine has gathered up in a french twist, soft tendrils falling about her face.

"You look gorgeous," Geraldine mouths to me, as she reaches up and wipes off a tiny smudge of lipstick from my cheek, which, quite frankly, no one other than Geraldine would have noticed.

"Jemima!" My heart skips a beat as Ben comes rushing over and puts an arm around me. "For a minute there I thought you weren't going to come." He thought about me! He actually worried about me, he spent time worrying whether I was going to come. Now this, surely, is a result.

I recover my composure and look Ben in the eye, willing him to notice how I look, to see the new Jemima Jones, to like what he sees and fall in love with me. But Ben just says, "Here, have a glass of champagne," and as he hands it to me he looks over my shoulder and says, "Diana! You made it."

"Couldn't let my new star reporter down could I?" says Diana Macpherson, striding through the room as people part to let her through, because, after all, Diana Macpherson is famous in the media world.

And I can't help it, I watch with a mounting sense of horror as Diana almost gives Ben a kiss on the cheek, but then evidently thinks better of it and straightens up, extending her hand, which Ben shakes warmly. Phew.

"Let me introduce you," he says, turning first to the editor, who is so impressed with Diana Macpherson that his mouth, once open, is captured in a fish pose, the editor having forgotten to close it. Diana shakes hands with him, then with me, but just as Ben's about to introduce her to Geraldine she turns to Ben and says, "Come with me to get a drink," and Ben shrugs at us and allows himself to be propelled by her towards the bar.

"What a bitch!" says Geraldine, who, quite understandably, feels snubbed by the great Diana Macpherson, and only Geraldine would say what everyone else is thinking but would never dare voice out loud.

"Don't worry," I soothe, "I'm sure it wasn't personal," but of course it was personal, I'm not stupid, I saw the way Diana Macpherson's eyes swept over Geraldine with a cold, flinty stare, and from what I've heard Diana Macpherson is not a woman's woman, even more so when the woman happens to be as attractive as Geraldine.

"God, I'm really sorry about that," says a voice next to us. "Diana is a law unto herself, and sometimes she can seem rude." We both turn to look at a young, good-looking guy, dressed in an old pair of Levi's and a brushed cotton shirt. "Sorry," he says again. "I'm Nick. I'm here with Diana." Nick holds out his hand to Geraldine as he says this, and holds her gaze for longer than is altogether necessary, before shaking my hand and making me feel more of a spare part than I do already.

"Here with Diana?" asks Geraldine with a raised eyebrow. "Does that then mean that you are her"—she pauses coolly—"other half?"

"Hardly," laughs Nick. "I'm more like her occasional date."

"And this is where she brings you?" Geraldine's teasing him, but neither Nick nor I misses the flirtatious tone in her voice.

"Yes, but I've promised to take her out for dinner later on."

"Do you, er, work in television?" I venture, trying to be polite but feeling more and more unwanted.

"No," he laughs, shaking his head. "Do you know Cut Glass?"

Everyone knows Cut Glass. Initially a small, funky optician's shop that specialized in hard-to-find trendy glasses that couldn't be bought elsewhere, Cut Glass is now one of the largest, if not in fact *the* largest, optician chains in the country.

"You're an optician." It's a statement, not a question, and Geraldine's eyes instantly dull as she starts thinking of ways to get away from him. I know her so well, I smile to myself. Cute, she thinks, but boring, boring, boring.

"No," laughs Nick. "Not exactly."

Oh God, I can see Geraldine think, this gets worse. He's not even an optician, he's a bloody sales assistant.

"It's my company," he says reluctantly, after a pregnant pause.

"What do you mean it's your company?"

"It's my company," he repeats.

"Oh my God!" Geraldine suddenly pales. "You're Nick!"

Nick's looking at her in confusion. "I told you I was Nick."

"No." She shakes her head. "But you're Nick Maxwell, I know all about you."

"What do you mean, you know all about me?"

"I'm a friend of Suzie."

"What?" he says, his smile growing larger. "Suzie Johnson?"

"Yes," says Geraldine, who cannot believe her luck because Nick Maxwell, all six foot one of him, is not only gorgeous but hugely wealthy, very nice, and enormously eligible, and Geraldine knows all about him already. "Suzie's one of my oldest friends, I've been hearing about you for years."

"Oh my God!" Now it's Nick's turn. "You're Geraldine Turner!"

I've been feeling more and more surplus to requirements, and finally I can see that it really is time to leave these two to get on with it. "Drink?" I say, but they both shake their heads, already lost in the geography of discovering who else they have in common, so I wander off to the bar.

Everyone is having too good a time to remember that they are at this party to bid farewell to their much loved deputy news editor. The lights have got dimmer, the music's been turned up, and Jemima is leaning against the bar sipping her cheap white wine—the champagne finished a long time ago—and surveying the room.

She sees Ben standing with Diana Macpherson and the editor, Diana in mid-flow, pressing her hand on Ben's arm every now and then to emphasize a point. Funny, thinks Jemima, how she isn't touching the editor in the same way. In fact, she doesn't seem to be touching the editor at all.

She's far too old and far too rough for Jemima to feel truly threatened—surely she is not Ben's type in the slightest—but nevertheless every time she places a long manicured finger on Ben's sleeve, Jemima feels her heartstrings tug a little bit more. Leave him alone, she thinks. He's not yours.

Nor, Jemima, is he yours, but Jemima, having rarely, if ever, had a crush on someone before, does not see this. Most women, it must be admitted, spend their teenage years falling in and out of love. They are more than familiar with the pain of going to a party and watching the object of their young desires end up with another girl. They are well versed in talking to their girlfriends about "the bitch" that stole him, and they are equally well aware that, although it might feel it at the time, it is not the end of the world.

But Jemima didn't have an adolescence like most teenage girls. While her classmates were at parties, experimenting with makeup, clothes, and fumbling in darkened bedrooms on beds piled high with coats, Jemima was at home with her mother, eating, watching television, and daydreaming.

Jemima didn't go to any parties until she went to university, and even there she rarely ventured to large social occasions once Freshman Week was over. Jemima Jones found a group of friends who were, she thought, as inadequate as herself. The social misfits they called themselves, pretending to delight in their difference, but each of them wishing they belonged elsewhere.

And up until recently Jemima had shown very little interest in the opposite sex. Yes, she had lost her virginity, but she had never felt what it was like to pine for someone, to lie awake all night praying they will notice you, to wince with pain when you realize they will never reciprocate your feelings.

"Mimey!" My reverie is interrupted by a voice I know well, and I turn slowly, trying to figure out why I am hearing this voice at a work do, and as I turn I know that the cheap, white wine I have been gulping all evening to relieve my nerves has gone straight to my head, and I am, how shall I put it, slightly woozy with alcohol. Oh all right then, I'm slightly drunk.

And when I see them, Sophie and Lisa, standing together, I smile broadly, grin, actually. I'm pretty damn sure I'm doing about as perfect an impression of a Cheshire cat as I know how. "You both look . . ." I pause as I look them up and down, head to toe. "Wonderful!" I exclaim magnanimously, despite the silence that appears to have descended upon the room at their arrival.

For Sophie and Lisa have really gone to town, except they've done it in Kilburn, and somehow what would look magnificent in Tramp looks completely ridiculous in the Wine Cellar just off the Kilburn High Road. They look extraordinary, extraordinarily out of place.

Lisa has obviously been to the hairdresser, who has sent her away with hair so big she almost has to watch her head walking through doorways. She is wearing a tiny piece of black fabric masquerading as a dress, and high, high, strappy sandals.

Sophie has caught her hair in a french twist, much like mine, and has squeezed herself into a sparkly black cocktail dress, which shimmers and shines every time she moves.

They look like a bloody parody of themselves, and I can't, I just can't wipe the grin off my face, and as I say hello to them I see that over their shoulders both Geraldine and Nick Maxwell are also grinning, and just for a second I feel a wicked, wicked glee that they should be so awkward.

Except, of course, Sophie and Lisa don't feel awkward, they feel beautiful, and they have obviously done it for Ben. Bad move. Big, bad move. Ha! Serves them right.

"So where is the clever boy then?" asks Sophie, looking around the room to try and find Ben.

"See that tall blond woman over there?" I point out Diana Macpherson, knowing that Diana, should Sophie or Lisa break in on her territory, will make mincemeat out of them. "He was talking to her a minute ago, he's probably just gone to get her a drink."

"God," says Sophie, smoothing down her dress and giving Diana Macpherson the once-over. "Talk about mutton dressed as lamb. Who is she?" Sophie doesn't turn back to me, just keeps her eyes glued to Diana as Ben walks back and hands Diana a glass of wine.

"Dunno," I shrug, trying desperately to hide an evil grin. "She's not from the paper and I haven't seen her before. Maybe she's a friend of Ben." I stop talking and the three of us watch in silence as Diana brushes a bit of lint off Ben's jacket in a gesture that is way too intimate for simply a boss.

"Maybe she fancies him," I say, wondering exactly what the outcome of this peculiar conversation will be.

"She should be so bloody lucky!" says Sophie indignantly, before she evidently remembers that I, her roommate, have a crush on Ben, and she shouldn't be quite so obvious.

"Tell you what, Mimey," she says in a confiding tone. "Why don't I go over there and get rid of the old bag then you can come over and talk to him. I bet you haven't said a word to him all night."

I can't hide the evil smile any longer, and as the grin spreads across my face I say, "Would you? That's so amazing of you."

"What are friends for?" says Sophie, who's already started striding through the tightly packed people to reach her prey.

"I'd better go with her," says Lisa, tottering behind her.

"What *is* going on?" Geraldine comes to stand next to me. "What are your roommates *doing* here, and, more to the point, why the hell are they dressed like that?"

This is too much for me. I start laughing, and the more I laugh, the harder it is to stop, but I'm not that drunk, okay? Just slightly. Eventually I manage to gasp, "Just watch. I think this is going to be one of those Kodak moments."

"Does your roommate know who Diana Macpherson is?" says Geraldine in confusion.

"No," I splutter. "And nor does she know what she's like, but she fancies Ben and she thinks that Diana is mutton dressed as lamb and Sophie's going to drag him away from her, come what may."

Geraldine looks shocked, but swiftly realizes she's in on a classic moment. "Classic!" she whispers in awe, as she watches Sophie's approach.

Sophie, being the rather silly girl that she is, seems to have decided, in the space of less than a minute, that Ben has obviously been cornered by this overblown, overaged blonde, and as she walks purposefully towards them she is already planning her strategy. Ben, she has decided, is looking as if he doesn't want to be there, so Ben will probably be eternally grateful to anyone who has the presence of mind to take him away from this woman who is, Sophie assumes, ruining his party.

I am, she thinks, as she draws closer and closer, infinitely younger than this blowzy blonde, and far more attractive. Plus, she notes, as she finally walks over, I have better legs. Ben, she decides, now has a girlfriend who will send this woman scarpering. This girlfriend, she thinks, is me. Brilliant! she tells herself. He will never be able to thank me enough!

"Ben!" she shouts, as Ben looks up from his conversation with Diana and stares at her blankly, primarily because he finds it hard to focus on her, she appears to have two, if not three, heads, and secondly because he does not recognize her in the slightest.

His blank stare swiftly becomes mild alarm, because she certainly seems to know him, indeed to know him very well.

"Darling!" she exclaims, grabbing his face between her hands and planting a big wet kiss on his lips. "I'm so sorry I'm late. Have you missed me?" she adds, in a kittenish purr.

"I . . . er . . ." Ben is completely and utterly flummoxed. Who is this strange woman, is she perhaps some PR girl he might have spoken to on the phone?

"Hello," says Sophie, turning coolly to Diana Macpherson, whose face has suddenly turned as hard as steel. "I'm Sophie." She holds out a hand as Diana just looks at her. "Ben's girlfriend."

"My what?" slurs Ben, who has suddenly realized who she is.

"Don't be coy, darling. It's hardly a secret anymore, is it?" Sophie reaches up and affectionately ruffles his hair.

"But . . ." Ben splutters, "but we've only met once. You're Jemima's roommate, aren't you?"

Sophie hesitates, but only for a split second. "Is this a little game, darling? Do you want me to play along? All right then, we've only met once." She turns to Diana and rolls her eyes, while Ben stands there looking flabbergasted.

"Sorry," she says to Diana, who, it has to be said, is far, far brighter than Sophie, and is slowly getting an inkling, thanks to the expression on Ben's face, that this is not quite what it seems. "We just have these little games we play," continues Sophie, blissfully unaware that her plan is not going to, well, to plan.

"Oh?" says Diana, switching on the charm and smiling a smile that her colleagues know means only one thing—she's going in for the kill. "So you're Ben's girlfriend? I've heard so much about you."

Sophie's smile fades for a second before she recovers. "Nice things I hope," she offers, because as far as she knows Ben doesn't have a girlfriend, and, if he does, she might be here, and if she's here then Sophie's in big trouble.

"Oh wonderful things," says Diana. "I was so sorry to hear about your sister," she says, now knowing beyond a shadow of a doubt that Sophie is some stupid tart who fancies Ben, who thought that she could drag him away from her.

"My sister, yes, it was a shame. I'm surprised Ben told you," says Sophie, who's beginning to think that the sooner she gets away from here the better.

Jemima and Geraldine have inched forward until they are feet away, and both are straining their ears to hear what's going on.

"Mmm," says Diana confidently. "Ben tells me a lot of things. I'm his psychiatrist."

"What?" says Sophie, who's completely unsure of what to do next.

"Well, you know," says Diana, leaning forward and lowering her voice. "After the problem last year with *the voices* and the schizophrenic tendencies, Ben and I have been seeing one another three times a week. He didn't tell you?"

"Yes, come to think of it he did mention it, but you know how private Ben is."

"Absolutely," agrees Diana. "Just as long as you keep your kitchen knives well hidden, if you know what I mean." She nudges Sophie. "I shouldn't really say this," Diana says, "but do be careful, I mean we wouldn't want you to end up like his last girlfriend would we."

"Er, no."

"No, exactly. Anyway, Ben tells me you're an osteopath. Come with me to get a drink and tell me all about your work." Before Sophie has a chance to protest, Diana has grabbed her by the arm and propelled her to the bar, while Geraldine and Jemima collapse in tears of laughter.

* * *

"What the fuck?" says Ben, who has temporarily, perhaps due to shock, sobered up somewhat. He turns to me, slurring slightly. "Was that my girlfriend?"

"No, Ben," I smile gently. "You haven't got a girlfriend, remember?"

"That's what I thought," says Ben, looking into his wineglass in confusion. He looks back up at the girls. "Jemima," he says, downing his glass in one. "Geraldine," he says, swaying gently and looking at Geraldine. "What am I going to do without you both?" He flings his arms around both our shoulders while Geraldine, who has not touched a drop all night, rolls her eyes in disgust and disengages herself.

"You'll be fine, Ben," she says. "You'll doubtless find thousands of gorgeous young women at *London Nights* who will fall in love with you. And speaking of love . . ." She looks up until she catches the eye of Nick Maxwell, who has just returned from getting Diana Macpherson's coat. "I have got a date with one of the most eligible men in London."

"Who?" says Ben, who, by the looks of things, is far too drunk to care.

"Never you mind." Geraldine, being sober as a judge, has thankfully realized that Ben is the last person she should be telling, because you never knew how Diana Macpherson would take it.

"Excuse me," she says, checking that Diana isn't around so she can go and say goodbye to Nick. "Back in a sec."

But Ben's arm is still around my shoulders, and I'm so nervous that I seem to have suddenly sobered up, and I can see everything in minute detail, and feel every pressure of Ben's arm on my body.

"You're my only friend," he says to me, turning and burying his face in my shoulder. "I love you, Jemima," he mumbles into my shirt, and I freeze.

And the world stands still.

"What did you say?" I ask haltingly, convinced I misheard.

Ben focuses on me for a few seconds then, much in the

manner that Sophie, who has now left the party, kissed him, kisses me. It is a big, wet, sloppy kiss on my lips, and thank you, God, thank you, thank you, thank you. It lasts a good four seconds, and when it's over Ben stumbles off, leaving me rooted to the floor, shaking like a leaf.

"I love you too," I whisper, watching as he's pulled to one side by the editor, who's just about to make a speech. "I love you too."

chapter 15

Before we take a look at JJ—for Jemima Jones exists now in name alone—we need to know that she has rarely been home since we last saw her. A whole three months has passed and we need to be warned, just so that we recognize her, just so that we don't get carried away and think that Jemima Jones is nowhere to be found.

She has been to work, which has been thoroughly miserable without Ben Williams, and she has been to the gym. She has done her best to avoid her two roommates after the fiasco of Ben's farewell party, and she has buried the pain of Ben not calling her during this time.

She has become increasingly friendly with Geraldine, who, incidentally, is now firmly ensconced with Nick Maxwell, and she is running up enormous phone bills to Brad in California, who, despite being many, many miles away from her, is proving to be the one light in her life.

Jemima feels she knows Brad pretty well by now. She has given him her time, her thoughts and her energy, because she no longer has to save any of the aforementioned for Ben, who has disappeared from her life and reappeared on her television screen.

Brad is investing the same in Jemima, soon to be known full time as JJ, but perhaps it is fair to ask the question, how well can you really know someone whom you've never met? How close can you be to someone whom you talk to via the Internet, fax, and telephone? How do you know they are who they say they are?

It probably doesn't matter. After all, those conversations are the one thing Jemima has to look forward to because food no longer offers the consolation it once did, and Ben phoned three times during the first month he left to say what a great time he was having, and she hasn't heard from him since.

Food. Jemima is eating just about enough to give her the energy to exercise, to watch her skin regain its taut elasticity, to rediscover bones and muscles she didn't think she had. In the first couple of weeks after Ben left Jemima still had cravings, which took all her energy to fight, but fight them she did, and binges are now a thing of the past.

Jemima, when we last saw her at the party, was 166 pounds, but now Jemima Jones weighs 121 pounds. Jemima Jones has lost almost a whole person's worth of weight. Jemima Jones looks exactly like the girl in the picture.

"I can't believe it," says Geraldine, standing in the living room, watching Jemima as she whizzes around looking for her coat. "I just can't bloody believe it." Can any of us, in fact, believe that Jemima, our beloved Jemima Jones, can whizz *anywhere*?

"Believe what?" says Jemima distractedly, spying her huge old black coat lying behind the sofa. She pulls it on and wraps it around herself to keep warm, for Jemima Jones is frequently cold these days, not having the padding to warm her bones.

"I mean look at you," says Geraldine. "You're skinny."

"Don't be ridiculous," says Jemima, "I'm hardly skinny, and I still have this weight here." She grabs what's left of the fat on her thighs, and let me tell you, there isn't a lot.

"What weight there, for God's sake?" says Geraldine. "Trust me, you're skinny. You're the same size as me."

"I wish," says Jemima, who actually is the same size as Geraldine, more or less, only she can't quite get her head round that yet. She knows she *looks* different, she knows she *feels* different, she's just not entirely sure how she should be feeling about it.

"Anyway," she continues. "Where are we off to?"

"An expedition," says Geraldine mysteriously. "You are in my hands today, and all you need to bring with you is a checkbook."

"Oh God," says Jemima nervously. "If you're thinking of taking me shopping you can forget about your designer stores. This trip to LA is wiping me out, I haven't got a penny."

"Don't worry," says Geraldine. "What do you think credit cards are for?"

"I know," sighs Jemima. "But I'm almost up to the limit on mine now, and I don't know how the hell I'm ever going to pay it off."

"Darling," says Geraldine. "Just think about it logically. We're only here for a hundred years or so, which, in the grand scheme of things, is nothing, therefore nothing's really very important, and certainly not money. So you'll pay it off when you get back."

"Geraldine, I don't have rich parents who'll bail me out whenever I get into trouble. How am I going to pay it off on my salary?"

"Jemima, for starters my parents *hardly ever* bail me out. And anyway, what do you spend your money on? Before now you've never really spent anything."

"I know," moans Jemima, thinking about all the restaurants she's never been to, the clothes she's never bought, the holidays she's never had, "but that's no reason to go and spend everything now."

"We're not spending *everything*," says Geraldine. "We're not going to Armani, but if we do happen to see some nice clothes

I'm afraid we might have to have a look. Anyway, you can't go to LA in your old clothes. For starters they're not the sort of things Brad expects JJ to wear, and secondly even if they were they're all swimming on you now. I mean this in a caring, sharing sort of way, Jemima, but quite frankly, darling, you look ridiculous."

Jemima looks down at herself, at the black sweatshirt she is wearing that hangs in folds of fabric on her new body, at the tracksuit bottoms that look like balloon pants, so large are they on her new frame, and she looks up again uncertainly.

"Okay," she concedes. "I suppose you're right." She raises her eyes to the ceiling. "May God and my bank manager forgive me," and they walk out the door.

"First stop is Jeff," says Geraldine, maneuvering her car through the back streets of Kilburn and up into West Hampstead.

"Jeff?"

"My hairdresser."

"Why?" I start to feel ever so slightly nervous, because my long, glossy hair, after all, has always been one of my favorite features, and yes, I trust Geraldine, but do I really trust her this much?

Geraldine pulls a cigarette out and lights it from the car lighter, then offers me one, but I shake my head. "No, thanks. I've given up."

"You've given up?" Geraldine looks as if she's both amazed and impressed.

"Yeah. Brad hates smoking, so I figured I may as well give up before I actually get there."

Geraldine nods.

"Anyway," I continue, "why are we going to your hairdresser?"

"Jemima," says Geraldine with a sigh. "Do you trust me?"

"Yes." Reluctant but true.

"And do you think I have good taste?"

"Unquestionably."

"And do you think I would do anything to you that you wouldn't like?"

"No."

"Exactly. So just sit back, relax, and let me take charge. I promise you this, by the end of the day you will not recognize yourself."

So I sit in silence and look out the window, tapping my foot to the music Geraldine has put on, trying not to feel sick to my stomach at the prospect of some strange man called Jeff being given free rein with my lovely hair.

Eventually we pull up outside a hairdresser's in Hampstead. Peering through the large plate-glass windows, I can see it's a hive of activity, that the hairdressers and their clientele are equally beautiful, and that this is not your ordinary hairdresser. Even through the window I can see it's expensive. The mirrors, in front of which preen the clients, line each wall, but in between are two beautiful round antique tables, on top of which are Chinese vases overflowing with enormous white lilies. There are huge plush sofas facing one another, on which sit nervous people awaiting their appointments, flicking through designer magazines to try and find the perfect haircut before they meet the scissors.

Geraldine marches straight up to a young, slim, dark-haired man, his glossy brown hair slicked back into a ponytail.

"Geraldine!" he says in a rich baritone, turning the hair dryer off and turning away from the client. "How are you?" He kisses her on both cheeks, and it is obvious that Geraldine is a favored client, that she has been coming here for years.

"This is Jemima," she says, as I feel the need to beat a hasty retreat. "Remember our phone conversation?" Phone conversation? What phone conversation?

Jeff nods.

"What do you think? Can you do it for her? Will it look good?"

Jeff stands back and looks at me, then lifts up my hair, feeling it, weighing it, thinking about it. "It's not going to look good." He pauses. "It's going to look unbelievable. You were absolutely right."

Geraldine gives Jeff a warning look. "Just don't tell her what you're doing."

Jeff sighs. "You do realize that is completely unethical, Geraldine. I can only not tell her if she agrees." Eventually he seems to notice me, and he sighs dramatically as he looks at me and says, "Jemima, would you mind if I cut and colored your hair to Geraldine's instructions without telling you what I'm going to do first? God." He shakes his head. "I've never done *this* before."

Oh what the hell. I nod. "It's fine, Jeff. Believe it or not I trust her." But I can't help pleading for a tiny clue.

"Okay," sighs Geraldine. "Not a clue but a question. Do you or do you not want to look like your picture?" I nod. "Do you or do you not like the color of your hair in the picture?" I nod. "Leave it to Jeff then. He's a miracle worker."

"I'm not going to take too much off," says Jeff, lifting my hair again. "Just an inch or so to give you a blunt cut which will take off all these split ends, and I think—" He pulls some hair down over my forehead. "How would you feel about bangs?"

Can you have feelings about bangs? I look at Geraldine, who nods. "Bangs are fine," I say with a grin.

An hour later I'm having severe second thoughts. Surveying my space age-ish head in the mirror—hundreds of tiny bits of silver foil sticking up all over—I turn to Geraldine with a severe tone and say, "You'd better be sure about this."

"Just relax, for God's sake." She turns to Jeff and asks him how much longer it will take.

"Okay," she says. "I'll come back in an hour."

When Geraldine comes back into the salon she actually walks past Jemima, and, when she sees her mistake, she stands rooted to the spot, with a hand clamped over her mouth in amazement.

Remember Jemima's hair, long, glossy, mousy brown?

171

Now look at it, see what Geraldine is staring at, this streaky golden mane which catches the light as Jeff flicks her hair around.

See how cleverly different shades of honey, of ash, of pale, pale copper have been woven together to create a sheath of liquid gold. And see how it spreads behind Jemima's shoulders, bobbing gently as she talks.

Take a closer look. See how the bangs stop just above her green eyes, how the green is accentuated by the gold above it, how the bangs show off her heart-shaped face perfectly.

"Jesus," says Jeff, standing back and surveying his handiwork. "You look absolutely beautiful, if I say so myself."

"Jesus," echoes Geraldine softly, when she finally finds her voice. "Jesus," because she can't seem to think of anything else to say.

"I look disgusting don't I?" I haven't dared look in the mirror, I just buried my head in a magazine, and now I don't want to look. But I can see from their faces that I don't look disgusting, and so reluctantly I raise my eyes to my reflection and I gasp. And I can't help reaching out a hand, corny as it may sound, and touching my face, my hair, in the mirror, and almost without thinking I find myself whispering in agreement. "Oh my God!" I say quietly, turning to Geraldine in amazement. "I'm the woman in the picture."

"No, you're not," says Geraldine in awe. "You're far more beautiful."

Geraldine insists on paying. "It's my treat," she says, and as we leave Geraldine keeps looking at me, and she keeps going on about how beautiful I am.

"Shut up, Geraldine!" I say eventually, after the fourth person we've passed has turned round and given us an odd look. "Everyone will think you're my lesbian lover, for God's sake!"

"Sorry." Geraldine snaps out of it, and we both start laughing as she pulls me into a boutique down a little side alley, but just before we go in I turn to Geraldine.

"Seriously," I say. "I can't believe everything you've done for me. Everything you're doing for me. I honestly don't know how to thank you."

"Jemima!" she sighs, rolling her eyes. "This is the most exciting thing I've ever done. This is like the world's biggest makeover, and trust me, I'm getting as much out of it as you. You," she says in a German scientist-type voice, "are my creation!" And with that we both giggle and step inside.

"Right," she says, sizing up the room. "Step number two is clothes. These," she says, rubbing the fabric of my sweatshirt between her fingers, "have got to go."

What's wrong with my comfortable baggy clothes I wonder, as I start idly flicking through the racks of perfectly coordinated clothes. Although I thought I'd be ready for this, the moment I've always dreamt of, what if I don't look the way I'd envisioned? Because as much as I want to try this new look, I'm terrified that somehow I'll still look like a blob.

But something strange starts to happen to me as I continue breathing in these strange textures and colors, and suddenly I'm dying to try them on and go for it. Suddenly I understand what all the fuss is about. Now I understand why Geraldine dresses so beautifully. You want to know why? Because she can. And for the first time in my life, so can I.

I keep flicking through, loving every texture, every color. Black fades to chocolate brown, fades to camel, fades finally to cream, with a touch of navy thrown in for good measure. I see some beautiful trousers and, ignoring Geraldine, who is piling armfuls of clothes for me into the shop assistant's eager arms, I go to the changing room to try them on.

"What do you think?" I ask Geraldine, wondering why the trousers feel a bit big, and holding them up at the waist so they fall better.

"Too *big* for you, darling. What size are they? I'll get you a smaller size."

"Size 12," I say. Oh my God, I can't be smaller than a size 12. Can I?

"Try these," says the shop assistant, handing me the same trousers in a smaller size. "I think you're more like a size 8."

The trousers fit. The beautifully tailored jacket fits. The short, flippy skirts fit. The little silk T-shirts fit, more importantly, the little black dress fits. The camel suede shoes fit. The soft leather boots fit. And more to the point, I fit. And I cannot believe that the smart, sophisticated woman, grinning like a Cheshire cat in the mirror, is me. Me! Jemima Jones! Once again, I am completely speechless.

"*Now* you're ready to go to LA," says Geraldine triumphantly, as I dig in my bag for my purse, trying not to feel sick at the extraordinary amount of money I'm about to hand over. Oh fuck it. This is a once-in-a-lifetime experience. These clothes will last me forever, and at the end of the day they are what Brad expects me to wear.

"Let's have a coffee. All this shopping and hairdressing is just exhausting!" Geraldine loops an arm through mine and we troop off down the high street, two slim (slim!) blondes, laden down with fabulous goodies.

"Look," whispers Geraldine, as a zippy red sports car joins the end of the traffic jam, just parallel to where we're standing.

"What?" I whisper.

"Look in the sports car." So I do, and sitting in the driver's seat is a dark-haired, blue-eyed, handsome man. He stares coolly at me, holding my gaze then dropping it to take in my new clothes—because, sorry, I couldn't resist, I had to wear those gorgeous trousers right now—then back up to my eyes. And I know what this look means, I've seen this look in countless Hollywood films. This look means he fancies me! He fancies *me*, Jemima Jones!

As the traffic moves off he smiles at her, a small smile of regret that he was not able to talk to her, for she is what he could only describe as a looker and a half. He drives through the lights and stares at her in his rearview mirror. Now she, Richard tells himself as he turns the music up, was gorgeous. He reaches over, picks up his mobile phone and dials his best friend.

"Ben? Rich! I think I've just fallen in love."

"Did you see that? Did you see that?" If she wasn't going out with Nick Maxwell, Geraldine would be green with jealousy, but as it is she's just over the moon. "He fancied you, he fancied you!" she choruses. "And he was gorgeous!"

Jemima's in a daze. Jemima has never had a look like that before from a man who looks like that, from anyone in fact, if the truth be known. Jemima will not forget that look, not for a long time, because that look finally confirmed what she has just discovered this afternoon. Jemima Jones is beautiful. She is slim, she is blond, she is beautiful, and, because of Geraldine's help, she is also chic, stylish, and sophisticated, although admittedly she hasn't quite yet realized it.

"Mimey," calls Lisa, as she opens the front door and dumps the bags in the hallway. "Your mother called."

"Thanks, I'll call her," says Jemima, walking upstairs and pushing open the living room door.

"Fucking hell!" says Lisa.

"Oh my God!" says Sophie. And they both sit on their respective sofas with their mouths hanging open.

"Well?" says Jemima, giving her head a little shake. "What do you think?"

"It's . . ." Lisa stops.

"Just . . ." Sophie stops.

The pair of them are speechless with envy, dysfunctional with disbelief. They had, up until now, vaguely registered that Jemima was losing weight, but so what? Being slim doesn't automatically make you beautiful, and Jemima was never a threat to them, but standing in the doorway of the living room, in her new tailored trousers and understated chocolate brown shoes, Jemima Jones looks exactly like the sort of woman Sophie and Lisa have always tried to be. Except they've never quite made it. They've always got the jewelry wrong, or the shoes wrong, or the makeup wrong. They have always looked glamorous, but neither has ever had an ounce of class. Standing in the doorway in a haze of gold, camel, and cream, Jemima is a vision of loveliness.

"It's fine," says Lisa eventually.

"It suits you," says Sophie eventually, and both bury their heads back in their magazines, while Jemima feels herself slowly coming down off the high. Couldn't they be nice, she thinks, just this once? Couldn't they have told her she looked great, just to make her feel good?

Jemima hovers, then goes back into the kitchen to call her mother, and as she walks out of the room she can already hear the girls whispering. She stops for a second, straining to hear them, and hears the tail end of one of Sophie's whispers. ". . . bound to put the weight back on." And then hears Lisa, ". . . being blond doesn't make up for being a loser."

Back in the old days Jemima would have gone to her room and eaten her way through a box of cookies for consolation, but things have changed, and Jemima can see through the bitchy comments to the jealousy that lurks behind. Bitches, she quickly tells herself, before she can get upset. They don't matter. And she goes into the kitchen to call her mother.

"Mum? Hi, it's me."

"Hello! How are you, darling?"

"I'm fine. I've just got back from the hairdresser's."

"Nothing too drastic I hope?"

"It wasn't really cut, but I've had some highlights." No point in telling her I've gone blond, she'd only disapprove and call me brassy.

"Not blond, Jemima?"

"Not really, Mum. Streaky."

"I hope it's not brassy. I've always thought blond lights can look really cheap."

"No, Mum," I raise my eyes to the ceiling. "It doesn't look cheap."

"Hmm. Anyway, how's the weight?"

I smile, because at least I know she'll be happy with me now, she has to be, I've become the daughter she always wanted. "You won't believe this, Mum. I'm 120 pounds!" There's a silence on the other end of the line.

"Mum?" Surely she can't find something negative to say about this? Surely she'll be happy for me? But that silence is one I've come to know well. She still disapproves.

"That's too thin for you, Jemima," she says finally and belligerently. "You must look like a scarecrow."

"I look fine," I sigh, instantly wishing I'd never bothered to pick up the phone.

"I hope you're eating enough," she says, as I roll my eyes at the ceiling. God knows I've tried. I mean, I've achieved the one thing that I always thought she wanted, but no, it's still not enough, and I suddenly realize that, for whatever reason, I will somehow never be good enough for her. I will never make her happy. I am either too fat or too thin. There is no middle ground. Nothing I ever do is destined to please her.

"Yes, Mum. But what about you? Been out with the girls from the weight loss club again?"

"Oh yes!" she giggles, delighted at the opportunity to talk about herself. "Jacqui, remember I told you about Jacqui? Well, Jacqui's getting married and it was her hen night on Saturday. We went to a nightclub! Can you imagine me in a nightclub? Actually, I did myself proud . . ." I switch off as my mother giggles along to her little story and eventually I say goodbye and go upstairs to my room.

I sit in front of the dressing table and put on my makeup, copying the way Geraldine made me up for Ben's party, and, even though I should be used to it by now, I still can't believe that this is me, that the woman staring back at me in the mirror is Jemima Jones.

And then I brush my long blond hair, watching as the spotlights in the ceiling pick up the golden lights, and eventually I stand up, go to the bathroom and grin widely in the full-length mirror, with one hand seductively pressed on my hip, although it feels completely ridiculous for me to pose in this way.

"Goodbye, Jemima Jones," I say firmly, not giving a damn if either of my roommates should hear. "Hello, JJ," and with that I laugh, flick back my new hair, and go to phone Brad.

chapter 16

Hi, Darling,

I can't believe you're coming, you're actually coming! My friends are even more excited than I am, if that's possible. But seriously, I will come to the airport to pick you up because it's kinda out of the way, so from there we'll go straight back to my house. Don't worry about anything—I've already made up the spare room for you and I think you'll be very happy in there—you have your own TV, VCR, and bathroom, and I've filled the whole house with flowers for you!

If you're not too tired, it would be really nice to take you out for dinner, but let's see how you feel. I'm just looking forward to actually meeting you, and I know I should be worried but I'm not. I really have a good feeling about this, although I probably shouldn't be saying that yet!

Have a great flight, darling, and I'll see you in two weeks' time! (Oh my God—two weeks!)

Huge hugs and kisses, Brad, xxxxxx

* * *

"Well, that's it now," I say, turning to Geraldine, who's reading my e-mail over my shoulder. "Like it or not I'm going."

"What do you mean like it or not? You sound so unhappy about it. Tell you what, I'll go."

I smile, because I *am* excited, but, if you really must know, the only person I desperately want to see looking like this is Ben, but Ben, as you already know, seems to be long gone, and Brad, I suppose, is the next best thing.

"I'm sort of serious," adds Geraldine. "Most women would give their right arm to be flying off to meet a hunk like Brad."

"No, I do want to." And it's true, I do, and I know that I don't have anything to worry about anymore on the looks front, it's just that I'm seriously nervous, I've never done anything this, well, this adventurous in my life. "But what if it's awful?"

"Look at you, Jemima," says Geraldine forcefully. "You're still worried that he's not going to like you aren't you?"

I shrug, because, although I can see that I've changed, that I look like a completely different person, underneath I still feel the same, I still feel fat.

"That's not going to happen," Geraldine continues. "You are *gorgeous*, will you just get used to it and get on with your life?"

"Okay, okay," I say, smiling. Anything to get her off this track, because ridiculous as it may sound I'm getting a bit sick of people telling me how beautiful I am, I just can't take it all that seriously, and I don't feel beautiful. Not yet. Well, maybe I do occasionally, but it only seems to last a few minutes at the most. If anything I feel a bit of a fraud. "I suppose I'd better go and see the editor and ask for the time off."

"You mean you booked your ticket without checking to see if it was okay?" Geraldine is horrified.

"Yes." It wasn't exactly forefront in my mind, what with having to lose about a billion pounds in three months. "I've booked the ticket so now I just have to make the time."

"Talk about flying by the seat of your pants," and Geraldine walks off muttering under her breath.

"Come in, come in," says the editor, leaping out of his seat and coming to open the door for me, which is astounding because he has never, ever done this in the past. "I'm glad you came to see me," he says, except he's not looking into my eyes as he says this, the old lech is eyeing my body up and down. "There are a few things I've been meaning to talk to you about." I just bet there are.

I sit down in the chair he's proffering and try to cross my legs slowly in the way I've seen Sophie and Lisa do so many times before, my right ankle tucked sensually behind my left calf, both legs at an angle, and I suppress a laugh at how I, Jemima Jones, can finally use my looks to further my career. The editor certainly looks as if he approves. In fact, he's so bloody busy approving my legs he seems to have forgotten what it was he wanted to talk to me about. I cough.

"Yes, yes. What was I saying?" He reluctantly drags his eyes up to my face. "Good Lord, Jemima," he says after yet another pause. "I'm sorry, love, I just can't believe it's you."

I smile benignly, now used to getting compliments from men who have known me for years, who before never seemed to notice me in the slightest.

Only this morning the internal phone rang yet again. Yet another news reporter wondering if I could do a story for him, and would I mind meeting for a drink at lunchtime to discuss it further. At first I wondered what the hell was going on, but according to Geraldine I'm now the office "babe," and I know I should be flattered, delighted, but actually I'm slightly pissed off that no one ever bothered with me before. But it's not all bad. At least the work has improved.

For the first time last week I was sent on an interview, and not just a crappy, boring interview, I was sent to interview the new star of a London soap, who conveniently lives around the corner from the *Kilburn Herald*, not having, as yet, earned enough money to move to a better area.

The interview went fantastically. A little too fantastically perhaps, as I ended up trying to maneuver myself out of the way of this admittedly cute man who seemed to have sprouted a thousand hands, all of which were trying to paw me.

Life, I now realize, is certainly different when you're thin. Even the gym has now become a place of excitement, for wonder of wonders, I seem to have been welcomed into the crowd of beautiful people, and even in my leotard—yes, I replaced my huge tracksuits a long time ago with tight black leotards and cycling shorts (even slim I don't quite have the confidence to wear the brightly colored lycra crop tops and thongs I once dreamed of)—with no makeup on at all and my hair scraped back into a ponytail, there's always some bloke who decides he's going to chat me up. Amazing.

"Working hard?" they usually start, as I smile, nod and try to continue my workout, but they still stand there, trying to make conversation, and if Paul, my trainer, happens to be around, he usually steps in and steers them on to another machine. Thank God for Paul.

Thank God indeed, for Paul is the one person who is worried about Jemima. He can't help but smile when he sees these muscular hopefuls chat her up. If only they had seen her before, he thinks, but of course these men had, only they hadn't ever noticed her. Paul has been trying to monitor Jemima's routine, for although she does look amazing, he is worried about how quickly the weight has come off, and he is convinced that under the golden skin—she has been using Clarins fake tan regularly on Geraldine's recommendation—Jemima Jones may not be as healthy as she looks.

He has tried to broach the subject with Jemima, but she is instantly dismissive. "Of course I'm eating enough, Paul!" she keeps saying. "Anorexic? Me? Don't make me laugh." For the record Jemima isn't anorexic, merely obsessed, which is definitely equally unhealthy, and possibly nearly as dangerous. We shall see.

And now, sitting in the editor's office after my lunchtime workout, I watch as he picks up the phone and rings his secretary. "Laura," he barks in his gruff Northern accent, "we'll have two coffees and a plate of cookies." He puts the phone down and says to me, or should that be, leers, "I don't suppose you'll be eating the cookies. Must be hard to maintain that figure."

And more fool me, I blush. "I manage," I say firmly.

"Now then, Jemima. The reason I wanted to talk to you was because I think you are destined for greater things. I always told you your time would come, and now that you've proven yourself with that interview, I think we're ready to move you on to features."

Funny that. Funny how, now that I'm slim and blond, he suddenly wants to promote me. I know I should be grateful, he probably expects me to gush my thanks, but all I can think of as I sit here looking at his expectant face, his chubby cheeks and his little piggy eyes that keep straying down to my legs is, you bastard. You big bloody bastard. You would never have given me this chance if I didn't look like this. If I hadn't lost weight I would have carried on doing the Top Tips page for the rest of my bloody life.

"Well?" says the editor, doubtless expecting me to be overjoyed.

"Well," I say, completely torn, because, bastard though he may be, this is the chance I've been waiting for for years, but then it's also sexist, and really, I'm speechless, and half of me wants to tell him to stuff his offer, while the other half wants to pounce on it. "Why now?" I say eventually, after the editor has started to sweat somewhat.

"It's just a question of timing," he says. "We always knew you were an asset to the paper, and now, with Ben gone, we need another bright young thing to do all the big interviews, and let's face it, Jemima, the fact that you've turned into a stunning young woman doesn't do you any harm."

There. He said it. He actually admitted that he was a sexist bastard. And I sit and look around his office. I look first at the threadbare gray carpet, stained with coffee, the odd cigarette burn. I look at the framed front pages on the wall, big stories that have got into the nationals, and I look at the editor sitting behind his cheap Formica desk in his cheap nylon shirt with his fat fingers and nicotine-stained smile, and my overwhelming feeling is that I want nothing more than to turn on my heel and run. I want to run far, far away from the *Kilburn Herald*. And the mention of my beloved Ben's name is like a knife through my heart because he still hasn't called, and the best thing I can do is get away from here, from him, from all the memories.

But I don't say that. I can't say that. Not just yet.

"I'd love the job," I say finally, forcing a smile. "But on one condition."

"Condition?" The editor wasn't expecting any conditions.

"I need a holiday. I'd like to go away for a couple of weeks."

The editor sighs with relief, and I know exactly what he was thinking during the silence. For a minute there he thought I was going to be telling him I'd only take the job at a massive increase in salary.

"No problem, love," he says. "Geraldine can do your page while you're gone, and while you're away we'll take on someone new to take over the Top Tips. How does that sound?"

"Fine," but shit, Geraldine will go mad. "Oh," I add, getting up to leave. "One more thing. I'm assuming that there will be an increase in my salary commensurate with my new job?"

The editor is almost speechless, probably amazed at the confidence losing weight can bring, for the Jemima Jones of old would never have dared to say anything like that, and, I have to admit, he has a point.

"Naturally," he blusters. "I'll talk to the financial people and we'll work something out. Don't worry, love, leave it to me. Where are you off to anyway?"

"Los Angeles." I smile, closing the door behind me and relishing the look on his face, for the editor's idea of a holiday is

Brighton, or, at the absolute most, a week in Majorca. And as I walk down the corridor I start to feel, for the first time, a small buzz of excitement in the pit of my stomach. "Oh my God. I'm going to Los Angeles!"

"You can't wear that!" Geraldine lies back on my bed and flings her hands dramatically over her eyes. "Jemima! for God's sake, haven't you heard of airplane chic?"

"Airplane what?" I'm being practical, I'm waiting in my tracksuit, a pair of comfortable sneakers, and a T-shirt for my long-haul flight. But I want to look good for Brad, so in my hand luggage I've put a miniskirt, a linen shirt, and knee-high boots which I'm planning to change into just before we land. Just in case you're wondering, the last two weeks have positively flown by, and today's the day, I'm actually going. Geraldine—and what would I now do without Geraldine—is driving me to the airport, as caught up in my adventure as I am myself.

"Airplane chic," she repeats. "You know, the glamorous look that all the celebs and models employ when they fly any-where."

"But, Geraldine," I say, smiling, "I think you're forgetting that, er, I'm not a celeb or a model. I'm a journalist on the *Kilburn* bloody *Herald*. And anyway"—I open my bag and show her the contents—"I've packed clothes to change into, I don't want to be uncomfortable on the flight."

"First, Brad doesn't know you work on the *Kilburn* bloody *Herald*," she reminds me. "He thinks you're Miss Snazzy Televi-sion Presenter, and while I'm not suggesting you wear a suit or knee-high boots on the flight, at the very least employ a bit of glamour." She clicks her teeth. "Those clothes," she gestures to my overnight bag, "are completely wrong for a flight. Even if they are only to change into at the end."

I shrug as she opens my suitcase and starts rifling around. "This," she mutters, pulling out a crisp white T-shirt. "This," she says, holding up a pair of black stretchy trousers and nodding approvingly. "And this," she says, digging out an oversized black sweater, "to loop casually over your shoulders. Now all you need are the accessories to complete your look."

"Accessories?"

"I knew it!" she says. "After all my lessons you still haven't learned about the importance of accessories. Jemima, my darling, accessories are everything. But Auntie Geraldine came prepared so you don't have to worry. Be back in a sec."

I get changed into the clothes Geraldine chose as she runs to the car. A minute later she runs back holding a Louis Vuitton vanity case, which even I, Jemima Jones, know costs an absolute fortune.

"Now Jemima," she says, looking at me very seriously. "This vanity case was a present from Dimitri, and although Dimitri and I are no longer, this is my pride and joy. I am lending it to you now, but guard it with your life."

"Geraldine, I'm speechless. But what do I need it for?"

"To look the part. Everyone carries a Louis Vuitton vanity case when they're traveling. And now," she says, "for the pièce, or pièces, de résistance." She opens the vanity case and pulls out a pair of large tortoiseshell Cutler & Gross sunglasses. "These were used in a fashion shoot a couple of weeks ago and I lost them. I feel terrible, I phoned the PR and she's just about forgiven me. I can't think where they've got to." She grins wickedly as she hands them to me. "You don't actually need to wear them on the flight. Wear them at the airport, and when you're not wearing them on your eyes, wear them on top of your head." She shows me how to loop my hair back perfectly with the glasses, which, it has to be said, do seem to add a touch of instant glamour.

"Hmm," she says, rifling around in the vanity case. "What else have I got here?" She pulls out two bottles of Evian water and a can of what looks like hair spray, followed by a selection of exotic-looking jars. "The water is obviously for you to drink on the plane. Whatever you do, avoid any alcohol, it will only make you retain even more water than you already will. The can is a spray of Evian water, which you have to use as follows." She flicks back her hair and, with a flourish of her hand, sprays the mist finely over her face, breathing a sigh of relief when she's done. "There," she says. "It's what all the models do, as it stops your skin drying out. These," she adds, gesturing to the pots, "are also freebies. I phoned the company and told them I was writing a piece about their products so they sent me the whole range. They're super-duper moisturizing products, and I would suggest you use them every couple of hours. Darling, you have no idea how flying dries out your skin. And finally," she says, pulling out a tiny little white plastic bottle, "eye drops to give you those bright, white, sparkling eyes, even after an eleven-hour flight. God," she adds, almost to herself, "someone should pay me for this."

"Geraldine," I say, shaking my head but unable to stop smiling, "you, are a godsend. What would I do without you?"

"What you'd do, Jemima, is look like every other wannabe flying to Los Angeles with stars in her eyes. Now you look like a there."

"A what?"

"A there. A made-it, whatever you want to call it." She looks at her watch. "Jesus, we'd better leave if we're going to make it. Are you all set?"

"Nearly. I've just got to write a note for Sophie and Lisa." Geraldine rolls her eyes. "I have to, Geraldine. Just in case there's an emergency."

"I bet you're glad to see the back of them."

"I don't mind. They don't bother me much, they're quite amusing in a sad sort of way."

"Yup, an ugly sisters sort of way."

"Exactly," I laugh.

"So how do you feel?" Geraldine asks, as we lug my cases to the front door.

"Nervous as hell?"

"Don't be. I wish it was me. You're going to have a blast."

Jemima Jones is getting a lot of attention at the airport, although she hasn't really noticed, too caught up in the excitement of her trip to take in the admiring glances. Perhaps it's the fact that she does indeed look like a made-it, particularly when she puts the sunglasses on to hide her exhilaration, perhaps it is simply that, with the help of her fairy godmother Geraldine, she seems to have perfected the art of looking impossibly cool, not to mention beautiful. Whatever the reason, the package-tour people are nudging one another and whispering, "Who do you think it is?" "I'm sure she's famous." "Isn't she the girl from that film?"

"I'm going to miss you," says Geraldine, putting her arms around me and giving me a huge hug. "Who's going to make my days bearable for the next two weeks?"

"Who's going to rewrite your copy, you mean." I grin, hugging her back and completely forgetting to mention that Geraldine has the joy of writing the Top Tips column in store for her.

"That too," says Geraldine, "but seriously, I really am going to miss you. Have the most fantastic time. Will you call me?"

"Of course I will."

"As soon as you get there? I'm dying to know what he's like. God, he might be short, fat, and balding."

"Don't!" I admonish, because I'm nervous enough as it is. "That would be awful," and then I remember that although I've never been short and balding, I was once fat, and in a split second I remember how people judged me, how they misjudged me, more like. "But it would be okay if he was a nice person," I add, although I'm crossing my fingers and praying he has a full head of hair. "Anyway, we've seen his picture, I'm sure it really is him."

"If you're sure, I'm sure," says Geraldine, "but whatever he's like you've got a ticket to Los Angeles. Are you absolutely certain you can't fit me in your suitcase?"

We both look down at my suitcase, so full all the sides are positively bulging. "Quite certain," I laugh, "although what I wouldn't give to have you come with."

* * *

"Take care," says Geraldine, giving her another hug, and as Geraldine leaves Jemima she realizes that she really will miss her, that Jemima has become very important in her life, that Jemima has helped her to rediscover the joys of female friendship, for, up until recently, Geraldine always considered herself a man's woman, a woman with no time for female friends. Isn't it strange how things change . . .

And that's it. I'm on my own. I walk up to the Virgin check-in, a bottle of mineral water in one hand, the Louis Vuitton vanity case in the other, and a pile of glossy magazines, "to keep you from getting bored," from Geraldine under my arm. I hand my economy ticket over the counter, and someone, somewhere, must be smiling upon me today, or perhaps Geraldine's ploy is working, but whatever it is the check-in girl seems to think I might be a made-it as well, and although she tells me it's not airline policy to upgrade those who simply look the part, the economy class is full, and Virgin would like to upgrade me to first class.

What a result!

"Gosh! Really? That's fantastic!" I say, forgetting to act like a famous film star, like someone who would naturally be upgraded. "Actually, I've never even flown before! And now I'm flying first class! Thank you, thank you so much."

Needless to say the check-in girl looks shocked, she realizes her mistake, but lucky me, it's too late, and I don't even care that I've been desperately uncool because I'm the one with the upgrade! I'm the one flying first class!

And then I have two hours to kill in the airport, and I buy books at the airport bookstore, splash myself with perfume in Duty Free, and look longingly at the jewelry shops, picking out what I would buy if I had the money.

I also spend far too much time looking longingly at the Silk Cut cigarettes, but no, I do not smoke any more. Not even when I'm so nervous I could be sick. No. I'm fit and healthy. I do not need to smoke. So, when a voice comes over the loudspeaker telling me my flight is boarding, I bounce down to the departure gate, trying to control the urge to shout with excitement and joy.

Eleven hours is a hell of a long time to spend on a flight, but eleven hours can pass incredibly quickly when you're Jemima Jones and you've never flown before. Eleven hours can pass incredibly quickly when you are sunk in the height of luxury, when you are fed and watered at the drop of a hat, when you have your own personal video screen and can choose any film that catches your fancy. Jemima Jones is far too excited to sleep, and when the stewardesses pull down the shutters on the airplane windows and the rest of the people in first class pull on their sleeping masks and gently snooze, Jemima Jones watches videos, reads her magazines, and spends a disproportionately long time with her head leaned back, thinking about her life.

She thinks about the way her life has changed. She thinks about Brad, about what he's going to look like, what he's going to think of her, what she will do in Los Angeles. And she thinks about Ben, but she tries not to think about him too much, for every time she does she cannot help but feel a physical pull, a pang perhaps. Try as she might to get on with her life, the fact remains that she misses him, that she suspects she'll never feel quite the same way about anyone ever again, and this is something that she doesn't think she'll get over for a very long time.

So she sits in first class and sprays her can of Evian on her face, drinks her mineral water, and religiously rubs moisturizer in to stop her skin dehydrating. An hour before they arrive she goes to the lavatory to put on her makeup, and as she stands there, as she brushes her mascara on, the butterflies suddenly start flying around her stomach and she looks at herself in the mirror and says disbelievingly, "Jemima Jones, what the hell are you doing?"

chapter 17

They always say that you're supposed to feel tired after a long-haul flight. I don't feel tired, I feel excited, and happy, and nervous. It's almost as if up until now it's been a big game. There I was, playing around on the Internet, having this make-believe romance with someone I'd never met, and it was fun, it gave me something to look forward to, but now, now that I'm actually here, I'm so frightened.

Not because he could be *anyone*, he could be an axe murderer, a pedophile, a rapist, although that had crossed my mind, but more because I've come all this way and what if he doesn't like me. I know what Geraldine would say, what if I don't like him, but that's kind of irrelevant, I mean, I've never been in a situation where I've had a choice. And I know things are different now, I know I don't look like I used to, but it still seems ridiculous that I might not like someone who likes me.

What if I'm not what he expected? What if he sees through the illusion and sees the fat unhappy girl lurking beneath? After all, it wasn't that long ago that I was a laughingstock. It hurts me to even say that, but I know it's true. I know that despite the few people who saw through, who were kind to me anyway—people like Geraldine and Ben—most of the people I knew simply felt sorry for me.

And although I look in the mirror and I don't recognize myself, in a weird sort of way this feels like a game too. It feels like it can't be real, that I'm playing at being thin, and that at some point I will be fat again. I know I'm thin because I'm buying size 8 clothes (even they are slightly big on me) but I still feel the same, and I'm so scared that Brad will see that. And, more to the point, where the hell is he anyway?

I've got my suitcases, I've walked through customs, and I can't see Brad, or even anyone who looks remotely like him, anywhere. I thought he'd be standing right at the front, I suppose, if I'm honest, I had stupid daydreams about this gorgeous hunk running over to me and scooping me up in his arms, but although there are many, many people here, none of them looks like Brad.

What if he doesn't turn up? What if he's not in? Where will I go? What will I do? As the panic starts to set in I realize that now I really do want a cigarette more than I've ever wanted one before in my life, but even as the thought crosses my mind I notice that all around are signs saying that it is a no-smoking airport, implying that anyone caught smoking will be hanged, drawn, and quartered, so I just sigh deeply and try to look like a woman who knows what she's doing.

"Excuse me?" I turn, breath catching in my throat as I see a short, fat, balding man standing in front of me.

"Brad?" Sorry, sorry, sorry, but I haven't got a hope in hell of hiding the disappointment in my voice. Oh my God, I'm thinking. You lied to me, you lied about your picture. I conveniently forget that I also lied about mine because that is hardly relevant now. Shit, I think next, I've got to spend two whole weeks with this revolting man, and then I think no! I'm not going to judge him, he might be really nice, but even as I stand here thinking that, I'm looking at him and wishing I hadn't come. Wishing I'd left it as a game.

"No." He shakes his head as I exhale loudly in a sigh of relief. "I'm Paul Springer. I'm a film producer."

"Oh?" I say uninterestedly, wondering what on earth he wants.

"I hope you don't mind me asking, but you're very beautiful, I assumed you had to be an actress."

"Thank you," I say, with a genuine smile this time, because when compliments have always been things that other people get, you do feel ridiculously thrilled when you start getting your own. "But I'm not," I add, and I start to turn away, because at first I thought he might have been Brad's driver, or someone he sent to pick me up, but he quite obviously doesn't know him, or me either.

"A model then?" He grabs my arm.

"No. Afraid not." I try and shake off his arm.

"Well you should be. Are you new in town?"

"Yes." I'm now wondering how to get away from this man without seeming rude but I'm not entirely sure how to do it because his hand appears to be stuck to my arm.

"I'd be very happy to show you the sights."

"Thank you, but I'm here staying with a friend."

"Here's my card." He stands there holding out a business card with a chubby hand, and as I reluctantly take it he comes up with what is obviously his number one pick-up line. "I know you don't act, but I have a part in my next movie that I think you'd be perfect for." I'm amazed that Geraldine was so right, I'm actually speechless, and I look at him open-mouthed because it is so obviously a line, but what is most bizarre is that this line must work, but not, obviously, on me.

"Thank you," I say uncertainly. "I'll be in touch," and with that he licks his lips slowly and repeats, "Perfect, just perfect," and this time I forget my British reserve and politeness, pick up my bags, and move to the other end of the hall.

I'm looking at my watch when a voice says in my ear, "JJ?"

and this time my heart starts pounding as I turn around and look into the eyes of the most beautiful man I've ever seen.

Oh my God, oh my God, oh my God! His picture didn't do him justice, nothing could do this man justice. Can a man be beautiful? Can anyone be as perfect as this man standing before me, looking at me hopefully, doubtfully, for I still haven't said anything.

"Brad?" I say eventually, when I've got my breath back, and he doesn't say anything, just nods before sweeping me up in his arms and giving me a hug, a huge, enveloping hug, and, in those few seconds that I'm in his arms, I feel like this is the moment I've been waiting for all my life.

"I can't believe you're here!" he says finally, when he releases me, and we stand there trying to take one another in, remembering our pictures, trying to work out whether we are the respective people we thought we were. I look at him and think, you could not like me, you could not be with me, you are far too beautiful to be with me, but he hasn't backed away as I thought he might, there is nothing on his face that is showing disappointment, and I am the first one to tell him he is not what I expected.

"Your picture doesn't do you justice," I say nervously, so scared he'll see through me to the fat girl I've fought so hard to hide.

He smiles, perfect white teeth which I look at with amazement, because I have never seen teeth more perfect, nor lips more sculpted, nor eyes so blue. "Neither does yours," he says, and I feel a familiar heat rise up my face, the blush that Jemima Jones so hated, the blush that JJ is supposed to have banished forever. I stand and I blush, and all the while I cannot take my eyes from his face, and I cannot believe my luck.

Brad laughs and pushes his hair, his sun-streaked blond hair, out of his eyes and he shakes his head. "You are so much better than I expected. You're gorgeous, JJ, you really are." He reaches down with a suntanned arm, an arm covered in fine blond hair, and my stomach twists in an unfamiliar feeling, a feeling which, it slowly dawns on me, must be lust, pure and simple lust, and he stands tall, taller than me, and says, "C'mon, let's get out of here."

And as we walk out of the airport to his car, I allow myself to exhale with relief, because I am good enough, and as I lower myself into the tan leather seats of his sleek black convertible Porsche, I cannot wipe the smile off my face and I surreptitiously pinch myself, just to confirm this isn't all a dream.

He turns the ignition on and looks over at me with a grin, and I still cannot wipe the smile off my face, and I still cannot quite believe this is reality. Thank you, God, I pray silently, closing my eyes for a brief second. Thank you for making me slim. Thank you for delivering me this perfect man.

What a couple they make, Brad and JJ. Even before they've hit the highway everyone is staring at them, drinking in their beauty, this vision of the Californian dream. Two beautiful people, in a beautiful car, on a beautiful day. They drive on to the Santa Monica Freeway, the wind whipping their hair back, sunglasses protecting their eyes, and Jemima Jones tips her head back in her seat and gazes at the sky, at the tips of the palm trees that rush past her, and she thinks that for the first time she understands about being happy. She keeps sneaking a peek at the vision sitting next to her, still unable to believe that she will be spending the next two weeks with him. They don't talk, the noise of the engine and the cars rushing past make it too difficult to hear each other speak, so the music is turned up, and every now and then these two beautiful people look at one another and smile. When something looks this good, how could it possibly go wrong?

"This is Santa Monica Boulevard," says Brad, pulling off the freeway. We stop at a traffic light and a sports car I don't recognize pulls up next to us. I turn to look at the driver and it's a young, good-looking guy, who, much to my astonishment, gives me an appreciative glance before shouting to Brad, "Nice car, man. Nice babe."

Brad smiles and puts his foot down as we drive down this huge, wide road lined by huge shops that are far bigger, far brighter than any at home. Right at the end I can see palm trees, and beyond a hazy blue, and just as I'm about to ask him where this leads, he turns to me and says, "This road takes us all the way down to the ocean. We'll drive down there, then take Ocean Boulevard to my place. I think you'll like it a lot, it overlooks the water."

Like it a lot? I'm already in love with the air here, the sunshine, the beautiful people, although to be perfectly honest I haven't seen that many yet, but this is, after all, the mecca of the rich and famous, and I'm already trying to celebrity spot as we drive along this road that seems to have no pedestrians whatsoever.

"How are you feeling?" Brad turns to me, raising perfect eyebrows.

"Fine, great, this is fantastic."

"Are you tired?"

"Not really, although I'm waiting for it to hit me."

"How about stopping for some coffee?"

"That would be great."

We turn right past more shops, but this time there are hundreds of people milling around, then left into a picture-perfect road, palm trees on either side *and* down the middle. I sit there marveling at how clean everything is, how wide the roads, how perfectly pastel the tiny boutiques, how different from Santa Monica Boulevard, because this is obviously where the smart people live. Brad pulls up outside a Starbucks, and as he's parking I sneak another look at him, still unable to believe how incredibly blond, and gorgeous, and perfect this man is.

He jumps out the door, and runs over to my side to let me out.

Being a weekday the place is quiet, the green iron tables and chairs scattered on the street outside are almost all empty; at the one exception sits a lone blond man in a baseball cap and sunglasses sipping a cup of what looks like coffee and reading a copy of *Variety*. His dog lies disconsolately under his chair, nose on paws, eyes closed, doubtless dreaming of dog-food commercials.

We walk in and up to the counter. "Hi," says the man behind the counter, "what can I get you?"

"JJ?" Brad turns to me.

"Um. I'll have a cappuccino." Both Brad and the man behind the counter look at me strangely.

"Would that be decaf or regular?"

"Um, regular, please."

"How many shots?"

"I'm sorry?"

"How many shots?" The man looks pleadingly at Brad, who evidently decides to take the matter in hand. "Don't worry," he says to him, "she just got here from England. We'll have two tall skinny lattes with a shot of almond."

"We will?" I look at Brad with a raised eyebrow. "Skinny?"

"Don't worry about it," he says with a laugh. "It means fat-free with a shot of almond syrup. You'll like it."

Our coffee comes in paper cups which we take outside, and we sit down at one of the tables and Brad smiles at me. "You're really here," he says, while I think, yes, I'm really here, and yes, you've already said that. On several occasions, but that thought doesn't last very long, it's pushed aside almost instantly by the thought that Brad is most definitely the best-looking man I have ever had the pleasure of being with.

"This is so weird," he says. "Meeting someone like you on the Internet, then actually meeting, and most of all seeing that you absolutely fulfill my expectations. More than fulfill. For a minute there"—he laughs at whatever he's about to say—"for a minute there I was worried that you'd cut the picture out of a magazine and you'd turn out to be really fat or something."

I laugh politely with him, thanking God I lost the weight, that I didn't have to put up with the humiliation of turning up looking like the Jemima of old, but a part of me wishes he hadn't said that, wishes he hadn't sounded so superficial, so like a person I would have hated had we met six months before. But I manage to push the feelings aside and I merely smile and say, "I know.

"I thought the same thing about you," I continue, "and this guy started talking to me at the airport and I thought it was you." I tell Brad the story and he listens attentively before saying, "That's what everyone in LA is like, trust me, you'll get used to it."

"You mean everyone just hands out business cards to complete strangers?"

"Well yes, there is that, but more that men have no problem approaching women they find beautiful."

"But he was revolting!" I counter.

"That doesn't matter," says Brad. "Some of the most beautiful women in Los Angeles are with some of the ugliest men."

"But why?"

"You have to understand that nobody actually comes from Los Angeles. Everybody flocks here hoping to fulfill a dream. The men all want to be film producers, and the women all want to marry film producers. It's not like New York, where the women are successful in their own right. Here the women want to marry success, and for the men, the ultimate status symbol is having a beautiful, hardbodied woman on their arm."

"But don't these women feel sick at the thought?"

"You are naive aren't you?" Brad looks amazed before smiling to himself. "That's so refreshing. No, these women don't feel sick because power is a tremendous aphrodisiac."

"But surely anyone could go around picking up women and saying they were a film producer?"

"Sure. That's exactly what happens."

"You mean this guy could have been a floor sweeper."

"In this case it's unlikely because he gave you a card with a company name on it that's well known, so you could easily check up on him. But I've heard a lot of stories where guys get business cards printed, and anyone could set themselves up as a freelance film producer or director."

"How extraordinary."

Brad laughs. "So I take it you won't be following this up?"

Now it's my turn to laugh. "Not bloody likely."

"I love hearing you talk," he says. "I know I've heard your voice on the phone, but it's a completely different experience being here with you, watching you, watching the way your hands move."

"Thank you." I'm suddenly embarrassed, and I keep thinking he's made a mistake. He shouldn't be with me, he should be with one of these beautiful models, or actresses. Not me, dull Jemima Jones from the *Kilburn Herald*.

"So were they okay about letting you have time off work?" he says, moving the conversation back on to more neutral, comfortable ground.

"Fine, and they're going to promote me when I get back."

"Promote you? What can they promote you to?"

Shit! Nearly gave the game away. Remember, Jemima, you're now JJ, a television presenter.

"They're giving me a much bigger slot on the show."

"I can really see you on television," he says. "Maybe you should talk to some people over here, that British accent would drive them wild."

"Maybe I should," I say, feeling a warm glow spread inside, already enjoying the fact that Brad is thinking I might be staying, that already he likes me enough to think we may have a future.

I know you're probably thinking I'm mad, but trust me, if you were here, if you were sitting opposite this earthly version of a god, you would have thought the same thing too.

Would we, Jemima? Would we really? Well, maybe Jemima Jones is right, because it is oh so very easy to be blinded by what people look like, and yes, she's right, Brad is the ultimate specimen of the perfect man. But let's be honest here, they hardly know each other, and although they like the look of each other, which is, as we all know, a good start, looks—and

Jemima of all people should be remembering this—aren't everything.

We finish our Starbucks coffee—and incidentally, it *is* delicious—and then we climb back in his car and drive home, and what a home! Brad lives in a gorgeous house overlooking the beach. A modern, box-like house; inside the rooms are enormous, bleached wood floors stretch as far as the eye can see, and french windows open out on to a large wooden deck.

"I bought it because the space reminds me of a loft," says Brad, as I just stand in the center of this room that's about ten times the size of my whole flat, completely blown away by the beauty of the light, the sound of the ocean, the sparkling, fresh *Californianness* of it all.

He shows me around, shows me the modern, stainless steel and beech kitchen, points out the huge modern canvases on the walls, makes me sit in an oversized white linen sofa that's so deep it practically swallows me whole.

"I thought I'd cook dinner here tonight," says Brad. "I figured you'd be too tired to go out." I nod my assent, saying that would be lovely, and Brad takes my things up to the spare room, and shows me the bathroom. "I'll be in the kitchen when you're ready," he says, as he closes the door and I breathe out a sigh of relief.

Everything is perfect. Not only is he perfect, but he didn't assume we'd be sharing a room, and although I hope, oh God how I hope, this becomes more than just friends, I'm not ready for that yet.

So I stretch my arms behind my head as I lie on the white damask bedcover and watch the ceiling fan circle overhead. The last of the day's light is filtering through the wooden slatted blinds, and I can't help it, I'm smiling a huge, self-satisfied smile. And after a while I get up to go into the en suite bathroom, and as I do I pass an old gilt mirror on the wall. I know you probably think I have a thing about mirrors, and you're probably throwing up with my vanity, but it's not that. It's just that if you looked the way I used to and then lost all the weight too, you'd need some sort of affirmation of who you are. You'd also need to keep checking that you're still here, it's still you.

So I walk up to the mirror and look at myself, watch my face as it breaks into a big smile.

"I've made it," I say quietly, and yes, okay, slightly gleefully. "JJ, you've bloody well made it."

chapter 18

There's a brief knock on the bathroom door which I don't hear for a few seconds, being, as I am, submerged under the water.

"JJ?"

I sit up with a start, and frantically look around the room for a towel before remembering that I have locked the door.

"Yes?"

"I just wanted to check that everything was okay. Do you need anything?"

"No, I'm fine. Thank you, though."

"Oh. Okay. I'll go and start preparing dinner."

"Brad?"

"Yes?" I hear his footsteps come back to the door.

"There is one thing?"

"Sure."

"Would you mind if I made a phone call to England?"

"Of course not. That's fine. There's a phone in your room next to the bed. Do you know the dialing code?"

"Don't worry, I've got all these instructions on my AT&T

card." Once again Geraldine came to the rescue, insisting I apply for this card so my progress reports to her would be cheaper.

"Okay. Fine. See you in a little while."

I walk out of the bathroom enveloped in a fluffy white robe which Brad had thoughtfully hung on the back of the door, another huge white fluffy towel wrapped around my wet hair, and I dig into my bag and pull out a little booklet of instructions from AT&T. I read the instructions then sit on the bed and pick up the receiver.

1 800 225 5288. "Hello and welcome to AT&T. To place a call, press 1." I follow the instructions and wait with bated breath as a phone starts to ring.

"Hello?" The voice is half asleep.

"Geraldine?"

"Oh my God, it's you! Hang on, let me wake up."

"What time is it there?"

"Two o'clock in the morning."

"Oh I'm really sorry, I didn't realize. Look, why don't I call you tomorrow . . ."

Geraldine interrupts. "Are you crazy? I've spent all day thinking about you and hell, it's only sleep. I want to hear everything. What's he like, how's it going, is he gorgeous?"

I laugh and lower my voice to a whisper. "Geraldine, you would not believe what he's like."

"Uh oh. You mean he's awful, he's not like his picture, he's short, fat, and balding."

"No way. He is, and I mean this absolutely seriously, he is the most beautiful man I've ever seen."

"You're joking!"

"I swear. He is about a million times more perfect than his picture. I just can't take my eyes off him."

"And what did he think of you? Were you what he expected?"

"That's the amazing thing. He said that the picture I sent him didn't do me justice either. I mean, I don't want to sound big-headed or anything but I think he likes me, I really do."

"Jemima, that's not being big-headed, that's being honest. That's fantastic. So, have you decided what to name your children?"

I laugh. "Not yet, but wait until the end of the evening."

"What are you doing tonight? Let me guess, he's taking you somewhere really snazzy like Spago, or that other place, Eclipse, and your dinner guests are Tom Cruise and Nicole Kidman."

"Somehow I don't think so. No, we're staying in and he's cooking me dinner."

"He cooks too! Jemima, whatever you do don't let this one get away."

"I'm not going to, if I can possibly help it, but every time I look at him I wonder what he's doing with someone like me."

"Don't be ridiculous, Jemima. He's lucky to have someone like you."

"Hmm. Maybe," I say, even though I don't really believe it.

"So, do you think tonight's going to be the big seduction?"

"Christ! I hadn't even thought about that. It's almost as if he's too perfect to even imagine touching, let alone sleeping with."

"Sounds too good to be true."

"I think he probably is."

Geraldine stifles a yawn. "Sorry, Jemima, I'm getting sleepy."

"Don't worry, I'll let you go back to bed. Thanks for waking up."

"Don't mention it, darling. I'm delighted to hear everything's going well. Give me a call in a few days and let me know what's happening."

"Okay. Take care."

"Yeah." Geraldine yawns again. "You too."

I put the phone down and pull my suitcase on to the bed and start to unpack, in a funny sort of way feeling much more secure now that I've spoken to Geraldine, now that I have her approval.

Brad, very quietly, puts the phone down in the kitchen, careful not to bang the receiver, careful not to be heard. He stands back and slowly a perfect smile spreads over his face as he hits the air in an imaginary high five. Yes, he says to himself. Yes.

What should I wear? What should I wear? I've pulled all the clothes out and hung them up, and now I'm having a major clothes crisis. I don't want to look too sexy, but nor do I want to look as if I've made no effort at all. I need Geraldine now, not on the end of the phone but here, in this room, smoking a low-tar cigarette and pulling out the perfect outfit with her perfectly manicured nails, although I don't need her encouraging me to spend any more money than I already have.

I just don't know. I try on a little black dress, and, although I stand for a while marveling at how it hugs my flat stomach and tiny waist, I know it's far too dressy, and I pull it off and carefully hang it back up. I try on a pair of cream silk trousers and a white T-shirt, and it looks great, but then I think, what if he does try to seduce me, trousers aren't exactly sexy.

In the end I settle on a white T-shirt and a short, A-line, tan suede skirt. Suede. I know, I know, I must be crazy bringing anything suede to Los Angeles, after all, it's so hot here, but it's my newest acquisition and I love it, I love the sensuality of the butter-soft suede. Yes. I look in the mirror. This is it. Perfect. I clip on some chunky silver earrings and slip my feet into flat white sneakers. Casual, sexy, perfect. Maybe, by osmosis, some of Geraldine's style has rubbed off on me after all.

"Wow," says Brad after I eventually emerge, having spent what felt like hours perfecting my makeup, blow-drying my hair into a glossy, gold mane. "Wow."

"You like it?" I do a little twirl and Brad grins as he hands me a glass of champagne.

"You look great. Really, I love that skirt." He gently strokes the fabric and smiles his appreciation, while, I have to say, my stomach does a mini flip, but I calmly sip the champagne as if I'm the kind of girl who drinks champagne every night of the week, a girl, in fact, much like Geraldine.

"Come into the kitchen and talk to me while I finish up," says Brad, and as I follow him through I can't help but notice that the lights have suddenly become far, far dimmer than they were when I arrived, and in the huge stone fireplace there's now a fire crackling away, which, even though it's probably seventy degrees outside, does give a cozy glow to the room.

I pass the dining table, wrought iron and glass, and see that Brad has already set the table, fresh flowers in the middle and two tall candles on either side, waiting to be lit.

Naive as I am, even I can see that Brad has aimed for romance, and just to confirm this he flicks on the music by remote control, and soft, sexy, soulful sounds emerge from every corner of the room.

"Quadrophonic speakers," he explains, seeing me look around, trying to work out exactly where the music is coming from. "It cost a heck of a lot, but it's worth it for the effect."

I bet, I think, but of course I don't say that, and I can't help but wonder, as we walk into the kitchen, how many times he's done this before, but as soon as I think it I try and banish it, because at the end of the day it's here and now that matters, that I'm here and he's doing it for me now.

"How's the champagne?" he asks.

"Delicious." I take another sip, before realizing that my glass is empty. Damn. Must be my nerves, I obviously gulped it down without even tasting it.

"Here." He laughs, proffering the bottle and filling up my glass. "I don't usually drink, but this is a special occasion." He laughs again, and I watch him over the rim of my champagne glass, still unable to get over how incredible-looking this man is.

The effect? Jemima is absolutely right. Brad is well used to creating effects, and well versed in creating seduction scenes. Jemima may think he's a superb cook, that he's doing all this for her, but Brad has done this many times before. And what is he cooking? He is starting with goat cheese, placed perfectly on a round slice of walnut bread that has been lightly toasted, warmed in the oven, and drizzled with walnut oil and a hint of lemon juice, all resting on a bed of lettuce. For the main course he is preparing chicken breasts marinaded in rosemary and garlic, served with butternut squash and a selection of fresh vegetables, and for dessert he has created an exotic fruit salad with fat-free ice cream to go with it. Not perhaps the most adventurous menu, it's true, but remember that this is a man obsessed with keeping the calories down, and truth to be told it's a wonder the goat cheese got in there at all.

Brad isn't a marvelous cook, but he has six marvelous recipes that he brings out over and over again. He carefully notes which he has served to whom, just in case he makes the terrible mistake of serving the goat cheese twice in a row. Luckily, he hasn't had to worry about this with Jemima.

Admittedly, he hasn't gone out of his way like this for a while, and we shall discover the reasons why later on, but for now let us see whether the effect is working . . .

"You know what I can't believe?" says Brad, chopping carrots and courgettes—or zucchini as he calls them—into julienne.

"Hmm?" I'm feeling more than a little bit woozy, the champagne combined with jet lag is having a complete knockout effect, but I can't seem to stop drinking it, anything to calm my nerves.

"I can't believe that someone like you doesn't have a boyfriend."

"Well." I sway ever so slightly on my stool. "I can't believe that someone like you doesn't have a girlfriend."

Brad smiles. "How did I know you were going to say that?"

"Kismet?" I say sarcastically, instantly regretting it, because I didn't mean to be sarcastic, it just kind of came out. I mean, what was I supposed to have said? But Brad, thankfully, seems to have missed the sarcasm.

"Yeah!" he says enthusiastically. "Kismet! I'm a big believer in fate, what about you?"

Okay, we can talk about this. This is something we have in common. This is good. Maybe we'll find hundreds more things we have in common, maybe there is a foundation there on which to build something different and special. God, I hope so.

"Absolutely," I say. "I do believe in fate, but I also believe that we control our own destinies, and I'm not sure which I believe in more. I think that mostly I believe that life is a bit like a tree, and that there are several branches we could take. I think that's where the controlling our own destiny bit comes in. If we choose a certain branch then our life will go one way, and fate will throw things at us from then on."

Brad nods his head sagely. "So," he ventures after a pause. "Do you think that this is fate?" He puts his glass down and looks at me very intently.

"I certainly believe there's a reason for us meeting." God, can you believe how cool I sound? "And I'm sure that everyone comes into our life because they have something to teach us."

"So what lessons do you think you could learn from me?" A hint of a raised eyebrow, a touch of flirtation in his voice?

"How about I tell you tomorrow morning?" Well *done*, Jemima, finally I've had enough champagne to give me the confidence to flirt.

"How about I give you your first lesson now?" Brad starts moving towards me, and, stupid cow that I am, I jump up in a panic.

"Let's eat first," I say brightly. "I'm sure I'll be in far more of a learning mood once I've had some food. Anyway I'm starving, mmm, this looks delicious. I never realized you could cook too, you kept that very quiet. So, is the food ready?" Shut *up*, Jemima. You're making a fool of yourself. I shut up.

Brad laughs and reaches over to ruffle my hair. "You're funny, JJ, did you know that?"

"It has, er, been mentioned in the past." What? Does he think that all blonds are brain dead? I resist the urge to say something even more sarcastic, but I suppose I can't hold this against him. I mean, he hardly knows me, and I can't blame him for jumping to conclusions, for not knowing what I'm like, whether I'm funny or not. "Well, the food is ready," he says. "Why don't you light the candles while I bring it out."

So I duly do what I've been told, and when Brad walks in, holding two plates, he flicks a switch by the door with his elbow and plunges the room into darkness, all except for the two candles on the table and the flickering light of the log fire.

"That's better," he says, sitting down.

"Much," I agree.

"Now I can hardly see you," I add. It's a joke, that old sarcasm just won't stay down tonight, and once again I thank my lucky stars that for Brad, being (a) American, and (b) Californian, sarcasm is as alien to him as Marks & Sparks knickers.

"Oh," he says, sounding wounded. "I'm sorry if I disappoint you."

"No, Brad," I appease him, daring to place a hand on his, "I'm joking. British humor. Sorry."

"Right," he says, attempting to laugh but failing. Never mind, a man this beautiful could never believe that someone wasn't interested in him for long, and he's almost instantly back to his usual self.

We make small talk during the goat cheese salad. We start laughing together in the interval between the hors d'oeuvres and the main course, and by the time the chicken's on the table we're starting to relax, and I can't speak for Brad, but I'm definitely beginning to feel that we might well have something here.

"So what are you looking for in a relationship?" I venture eventually, numerous glasses of champagne having given me more than a hint of Dutch courage.

"What am I looking for? I'm looking for someone who's honest, sensitive, feminine. Someone who isn't necessarily into having a career, who'd be a great wife and mother." He pauses at this point and gazes into my eyes, and it feels really, I don't know, really intense, and after a few seconds which feel like a few hours I start to feel *really* uncomfortable, so I look away.

"I want someone who makes me laugh, who enjoys the good things in life, who has integrity and depth.

"I want someone . . ." Oh God, just how long is his list going to be? I mean, I expected a couple of pointers, not an hour-long monologue about his expectations. Stop it, Jemima, stop being so negative.

". . . who's self-aware, who is open to loving and being loved. And I need someone who looks great; who looks after herself, who doesn't drink or do drugs, who is slim, and fit, and healthy."

Strange, that, or am I just being difficult? How come he kept telling me what he wanted and then finally told me what he needed? Is there a difference? Maybe, maybe not. Is this important? Maybe, maybe not. Whatever, right at this moment I'm too damn busy trying not to fall asleep at the table to worry about it anymore. I am soooo tired and, exciting as this is, as gorgeous as he is, I really don't think I can keep my eyes open for too much longer.

Brad finishes his litany, and finally, thankfully, he notices my drooping eyelids.

"Oh you poor baby," he says gently, "you're tired."

I nod, because quite frankly I don't think I can speak. The combination of alcohol and tiredness would definitely make my words come out all wrong.

"Why don't I put some decaf coffee on, we can sit by the fire while you drink it, then you can go to bed." I nod again,

gratefully this time, and on surprisingly (or perhaps not) un-
steady feet I walk over to the fire and pretty much collapse in
front of it.

Brad goes to make the coffee, and when it's ready he sets it
on the coffee table behind me. He sits on the floor next to me,
and strokes the hair out of my eyes. I know I should feel nervous, in any other circumstances I'd probably be throwing up,
but I'm way too far gone to feel nervous, to worry about what
to do, what to say. I just sit there and find myself concentrating
on his hand, his big, strong hand softly brushing the hair out of
my eyes, then stroking my cheek, and finally resting on my
chin.

"C'mere," he says softly, and I don't have the energy or, to
be honest, the inclination to resist. I mean, please, here I am in
this unbelievable house in Los Angeles, LOS ANGELES! with
this stunning man and I'm supposed to say no? I don't think so.
And anyway, I'm curious, I want to know how it would feel to
lie next to someone this beautiful. I want to know what his
skin would feel like, taste like, what it would *be* like. Let's face
it, the brief interludes I've had in the past haven't exactly been
anything to write home about. But this would be more than
something to write home about, this is moviemaking time, this
is so unreal I almost feel as if I'm in a film. Even the way he
gently cups my chin as his face moves closer and closer to mine
feels as if it's happening in slow motion.

And finally those perfect lips are on mine, and he's kissing
me, and I would go into more detail but I'm, quite frankly,
slightly embarrassed. I mean, it's never happened like this before, it's never been this slow, or gentle, or lovely, if you want
to know the truth.

And I don't feel the way I've felt before. I don't want to do
it with the lights off, or lying flat on my back so my stomach's
almost flat, because now it *is* flat, and I don't have to feel self-
conscious, or worry that he's not going to be able to do it because my size will turn him off.

Now, wonder of wonders, I'm semi-naked with a man who's

bigger than me! His chest is bigger than mine! His arms are bigger than mine! And, more to the point, what a chest! What arms! Oh my word, I thought bodies like this only existed in the pages of magazines. Look at these pecs, look at these biceps and triceps and everythingceps.

And then all our clothes come off (and I don't even mind!), and I'm watching him as he does things to me that no one has ever done to me before, and after a while I have to close my eyes because I'm seriously embarrassed, but a little while after that I stop being embarrassed because this unbelievable feeling suddenly starts spreading throughout my whole body, and the next thing I know he's lying on his back, inside me while I rock on top of him, and I'm screaming the whole house down. I don't even know where this scream is coming from, all I know is that it sounds guttural, animal, and I couldn't stop it even if I wanted to. Which I don't, because this is so gooooood. Mmm-mmmmmm, this is so gooooood.

"That was incredible." Brad rolls on to his side and gazes at me, planting soft butterfly kisses down my cheek.

"That. Was. Incredible!" I murmur, still trying to come to terms with what just happened. I think I just had an orgasm! For the first time in my life I know what all those magazines have been writing about, and, while I'm feeling wonderful, I also feel a bit shellshocked by the whole thing, it was just so amazing, and so unexpected.

"No, I mean, that was seriously unlike anything I've experienced," says Brad.

You think? What about me? I've never experienced anything so completely deliciously mind-blowing in my entire life.

"I know," I say, before I suddenly get hit with this irrational thought that he's going to think I'm cheap, I hardly know the guy, after all. "You don't think I'm cheap do you?" I say, before I can help myself. "I mean I don't usually do this, I never usually do this. This isn't like me at all . . ."

"For someone who never usually does this," he says, taking

212

my hand and curling it up inside his masculine palm, "you're awfully good at it."

I laugh, for he's put me at my ease. "That's not what I meant."

"I know," he says. "And I also know that you're not the kind of girl to take lightly. This was one of the best nights of my entire life."

"Mmm," I say, really falling asleep now. "Me too," I just about manage to murmur, and that's as far as I can remember.

Brad very gently picks her up—can you imagine *anyone* picking up Jemima Jones a few months ago—and carries her to bed. He bypasses the spare room completely, and tucks her up on the left side of his huge king-sized bed. He pulls the bed-covers up and tucks them under her chin in case she gets cold from the air-conditioning, and Jemima murmurs and turns over, still fast asleep.

"Thank you, God," Brad whispers as he kisses her softly on the nape of her neck. "Thank you for making her so perfect," and with that he goes to the bathroom to take a shower.

chapter 19

"Morning, sleepyhead."

I peel open my eyes, which is a hell of an effort, I can tell you, and for a split second I'm completely disoriented. Where am I, who's talking to me? And then I remember and as I shield my eyes from the sunlight streaming in through the blinds I remember that this beautiful man standing at the side of the bed is Brad, and that last night we made love, and that it was the greatest experience of my life to date.

He sits on the bed and I drink in his looks, the fact that even in a T-shirt and running shorts and sneakers he looks positively delicious, and he leans over to kiss me good morning, and I keep my lips sealed tightly shut because I'm so worried about having morning mouth when he smells so clean, so masculine, so sexy.

"What time is it?" I venture when he leans back, out of breath shot, as it were.

"Nine o'clock. I didn't want to wake you so I just went out for a run."

"Jesus, nine o'clock? I never sleep till nine o'clock."

"That's because you're never jet lagged."

I want to get out of bed and brush my teeth, wash my face, make sure my makeup isn't all over the place because I can feel already that my skin is gritty, that I definitely didn't wash it off last night, but I can't get out of bed because I don't appear to be wearing any clothes, and, slim as I may now be, walking around naked in front of someone I hardly know—despite the fact we have been as intimate as any two people can be—is not an experience I think I can deal with right now.

I wipe my fingers under my eyes, hoping to remove any stray mascara or eyeliner that may have worked its way down there during the night, and smile at Brad in a way that I hope he'll find sexy.

"So what are you in the mood for this morning?" he says, and I think about my morning mouth and then I think, screw it, and I pull him down towards me and kiss him. Properly. Tongues and everything.

I didn't think it could get better than last night. Really, I thought I'd hit the height of orgasmic experiences, but today, this morning, in the bright sunlight of day, it was even better. Warmer, softer, funnier. I never thought you were supposed to talk during sex, at least, I've never said anything before because it always brought me back to where I was, and made me feel almost shameful. But Brad and I talked to each other this morning, very gently. Before, during, and after. And we laughed, which was a complete revelation, because before today I've never thought sex was supposed to be funny. Not that it was ha, ha, funny, just intimate I suppose, and maybe that's what was such a revelation for me.

"Jesus," says Brad, lying back on the bed, breathing heavily. "You really are something, JJ."

I lean over him, my hair trailing over his face as I kiss him softly on the lips, slowly coming to terms with the idea that this man is mine. At least for the time being.

"So now what?" I say, wondering how we're going to spend the rest of the day.

"What do you mean?" says Brad, with a panicked look on his face, and I start to laugh because I realize he thinks I'm asking "now what" about the relationship.

"What are we going to do today?" I say.

"Oh. Right. Well, I have to check in to the gym later on this afternoon, but how about this morning we go for breakfast then maybe Rollerblading?"

"That sounds fantastic," I say, trying not to let on that I lied about Rollerblading and that I'll probably make a complete fool of myself. But then again, Rollerblading is the perfect exercise to keep my thighs slim and toned. "But can I work out at the gym later on?" Rollerblading, I'm afraid, isn't enough to keep the guilt at bay.

"Sure you can," says Brad. "In fact, this afternoon there's a spinning class which you might enjoy."

"Spinning?"

"Yeah," he laughs, seeing I haven't a clue what he's talking about. "It's cycling on the spot, but real fast. It's kind of a killer but you feel great afterwards."

"Maybe," I say, because, although it does sound great, I think at this stage I'd rather stick to what I know.

We get up, shower, and climb in Brad's car, and he takes me for a short drive around Santa Monica, just to give me a feel for the place, and, driving along, with his right hand resting on my left leg, I am truly in heaven.

There seem to be hundreds of people milling around, and, although some of them are beautiful, quite honestly I'm surprised at how ordinary most of them are. I somehow expected all of Los Angeles to look like something out of a film, but for every gorgeous person there seem to be ten more who aren't.

"That's Third Street Promenade," says Brad, pointing to a cobbled street lined with shops and restaurants. "It's famous in Los Angeles for the street performers, especially on the weekends." As we stop at the lights I can hear Frank Sinatra playing, very loudly, and I can't figure out where it's coming from.

"Hang on," says Brad. "You gotta hear this," and he parks the car round the corner and takes my hand as we walk down to where the music's coming from.

In the middle of the street is a man in his sixties. He's wearing a fedora, a black jacket, and a bow tie. He's holding on to a microphone and swaying slightly while crooning along to the huge Karaoke machine that sits behind him. It's all Frank Sinatra, and what I can't believe is that this man sounds more like Frank than Frank himself. Everyone milling past seems to stop, at least for a few seconds, before leaving with smiles on their faces, and the bucket resting on the ground in front of him is slowly filling up with dollar bills.

"Isn't he great?" says Brad, putting his arm around me as we stand next to one of the benches that line each side of the street. I nod, because it is great, and as I turn to look at Brad I notice that sitting on the bench is an old homeless woman. You can tell she's homeless, her gray hair is long and matted, her raincoat is ripped and torn, and strewn around her feet are a dozen plastic bags. Her eyes are closed, and she's humming along, and suddenly she opens her eyes and sees me.

She stands up, collects her bags, and as she walks off she touches my arm and says, "You gotta hear 'New York, New York.' He does it last. It's wonderful," and with that she disappears.

"Now that," I say, looking at Brad, "is bizarre."

"Not really," says Brad. "This guy's an institution. He's here practically every week."

"But that woman . . ."

"Right. Santa Monica seems to be a mecca for the homeless. Listening to this guy is probably the highlight of her week."

"But how did she get here?"

"Who knows," he says, shrugging. "How did any of us get here?" and with that he leads me to the bucket, throws in a couple of dollar bills, and we go back to the car.

We drive through wide residential streets, huge roads lined with grassy verges and large houses, and eventually we hit Montana, a quiet road that reeks of money, simply because the small boutiques and restaurants on either side are so quaint, and Brad pulls up outside a small coffee shop which looks packed. Outside, on the street, there's one spare table, and Brad tells me to grab it while he gets breakfast.

Don't think I'm being egotistical, please, but I can't help but notice that three—three!—men put down their papers, stop their conversations, and turn to stare at me, and although my initial thought is that it must be because I have something on my face, I soon realize that it's because I look good.

Tutored by Geraldine, I'm in my new secondhand Levi's, 26 waist, a white shirt, and brown suede loafers, and when I put them on this morning I thought that, perhaps for the first time, I really do look like the woman I wanted to become.

"One coffee," says Brad, placing the cup in front of me as the men look away, because one look at Brad and they know they couldn't compete, "and one fat-free blueberry muffin."

It's delicious. He's delicious. This life is delicious. I think I could stay here for the rest of my life.

I suppose this is the time when we ought to be talking, getting to know each other, but we did so much of that last night, and now that we've slept together all we seem to be doing is staring at one another and grinning. Brad holds my hand, only allowing me to have it back to pick up my muffin and take the occasional bite, and even as I'm eating he strokes my leg, or my arm, or something. It's as if we have to have permanent contact with each other, and everyone seems to be staring at us, or perhaps that's my imagination.

But in my imagination I imagine that they're staring because they wish they had what we had. I have no idea what it really feels like to be in love. I loved Ben, it's true, but I never *had* Ben, and, as I sit here with this man I've just made love to, I wonder whether perhaps it wasn't love with Ben, it was merely infatuation.

Not that I love Brad, not yet, of course not. But I feel so high, I can't stop smiling, and I'm sure that my glow is lighting up the whole of America.

"You're so beautiful," Brad says to me again, and I bask in the glory of his admiration. He checks his watch and says we should go blading because he'll have to do some work when we get to the gym.

And so we stop at the rental shop and pick up some blades for me then we drop the car home, Brad picks up his blades, and we walk, in sock-clad feet, down to the promenade.

"Um, there's something I have to tell you," I start nervously, as Brad looks concerned. "I lied about Rollerblading. I've never done it before in my life."

Brad throws his head back and laughs. "Why on earth bother lying about that? Don't worry, you'll be fine." He continues chuckling as I shakily put the boots on and stand still, too terrified to move.

"Here," he says, taking my hand, "This is how you blade," and he shows me how to start with my feet at right angles to one another, how to push off with the right and glide forward with the left, and wonder of wonders, me, clumsy, oafish Jemima Jones, can do it. I'm not very good, admittedly, but Brad keeps hold of my hand, and with those strong arms he balances me every time I threaten to tip over.

It takes a while, but soon we're blading side by side, on this wide tarmac boardwalk that runs alongside the beach. I don't even care that every few minutes these gorgeous women pass, headphones on, perfect figures gyrating to the music that's filling their ears. And I don't even care that these women all eye Brad up and down as they approach, because he's not looking at them, he's looking at me. And I don't even care when one of the blond bombshells turns to her friend skating alongside her, also with a headset on, and mouths "gay," gesturing at Brad, who doesn't see. I don't care. Actually, I think it's funny, and in a way I know what she means. It's almost as if Brad is too damn perfect to be straight. It's not something I would ever have thought in England, but here, where the gay culture seems to be so much bigger, here I can understand why she would have said that.

I laugh to myself, especially when I picture what Brad was doing to me at ten past nine this morning, and then I stop laughing to myself and I start shivering with pleasure at the memory.

"This is so much fun," I shout, as we pick up speed and head down towards the Santa Monica pier.

"I thought you'd never done this before," he says, and with a grin I shoot off in front of him, amazed that I'm so confident on these wheels.

"I lied," I shout back and he grins and blows me a kiss as he races to catch up with me.

Jemima and Brad look like the perfect couple, like they've just stepped out of a romantic love story, and even though they're not really talking, they're giggling together and teasing one another in a way that is increasingly like two people falling in love with each other. Or could that be two people falling in love with love itself?

Two hours of Rollerblading has completely done me in, and when we've finished we stop at a deli and help ourselves to salad, which we put in a container and take to Brad's gym to eat in his office. Just in case you're wondering, I'm even more conscious of keeping my figure here, so I bypass the salads of rice and pasta, which, delicious looking as they are, are not what I need to maintain my figure. I opt, instead, for mounds of exotic salad leaves, piled high with roasted vegetables and sesame seeds, not, according to the woman in the deli, roasted in oil. Completely fat free. Aren't I good? Aren't you proud of me?

The gym, just off 2nd Avenue, when we get there, is much like I expected. A sun-filled reception houses a huge desk, behind which sit two gorgeous women in perfectly coordinated aerobic gear. One is wearing a pink bodysuit with tight, tiny orange Lycra shorts, and the other is in an orange bodysuit with pink shorts, both with tiny thongs at the back. They are extremely tanned, extremely fit, and extremely friendly, which surprises me somewhat, because back at home, when women look like this, they usually turn out to be class-A bitches.

"Hey, Brad!" says one enthusiastically as they walk in.

"Hey, Brad!" says the other, looking up in her wake.

"Hey, Cindy, Charlene. I'd like you to meet JJ."

"Hey, JJ," they both say at the same time. "It's so great to meet you."

"And you." I suppress a laugh, because what could be so great about meeting me?

"You're JJ!" says Cindy suddenly. "Oh my God, we've heard so much about you. We've even seen your picture. Wow, you're here."

"Yup." Is anybody over here ever going to say something that makes sense? "I'm here."

"And you're from England?" It's Charlene's turn.

"Uh huh."

"That's so great. I had a boyfriend from England once. He was from Surrey. Gary Tompkins?" She's looking at me expectantly, as if I might know him. As if. I shake my head and shrug my shoulders. "Sorry," I apologize. "It's a big place."

"Don't worry," says Charlene, "he wasn't so hot anyway. But welcome to Los Angeles. Do you think you'll stay?"

"I'm here for two weeks," I say. "Then I have to get back to work."

"That's too bad," says Cindy. "It's a great place. Maybe you could come back."

"Maybe," I say, wondering if everyone here is so friendly. I mean, I've heard Americans are like this, but I never really thought it would be true.

"They're really nice," I say to Brad, as we pass through the reception area and through the actual gym, and then I stop because I have never in my life seen a gym so well equipped, nor people so perfect. The gym is buzzing. Heavy hip-hop music, a song I vaguely recognize, is bursting out of every corner, and although everyone in here is sweating up a storm, they all look fantastic, the sweat only seems to set off their glistening tans and perfect bodies.

"God," I whisper in bewilderment, because it's worlds away from my gym, where most of the people are either there because they're at the before stage and they look terrible, or because it's a place to see and be seen, and they'd never let something as mucky as sweat mess up their makeup or hairdo.

"You like it?" asks Brad, obviously proud of this thriving business. "Meet Jimmy, one of the personal trainers here."

Tall, bronzed, and buff, Jimmy shakes my hand. "It's so great to finally meet you, JJ. Welcome to Los Angeles, and if you need any help here, *anything* at all"—looks at me meaningfully—"don't hesitate to ask."

"Hands off, Jimmy," says Brad, pushing him playfully.

"Whoa, Brad," says Jimmy, holding up his hands with a cheeky grin on his face, "you can't blame a guy for trying."

"Hello?" I say. "I'm here."

"Sorry, JJ," says Brad. "But boys will be boys. C'mon, we'll go to my office and eat lunch."

So we do, and ridiculous as this may be—seeing as it's the middle of the day and we're eating salad out of plastic containers—we start feeding one another, and soon food is everywhere but in our mouths and we're kissing furiously when the door bursts open and we leap apart.

Brad, for the record, leaps farthest, but then it is understandable, after all, he is the boss, and we both look up to see a large girl standing in the doorway.

"Oh," says the girl. "I didn't realize you were here."

"I just got here," says Brad, dusting the food off himself and trying to straighten himself out, while I take a good, long look at the girl, partly to try and work out who she is, and partly because, and it's a hell of a shock to see it, partly because the girl standing in the doorway looks an awful lot like the girl I used to be. She's small with dark, glossy hair, and I can see that she would be pretty, she could be pretty, all she has to do is lose weight. Because this girl is huge, she has two, no, three chins. She is wearing a smock-type shirt to hide the huge bulk of her breasts, she has her arms crossed to hide as much of her body as she can, and she has that slightly wounded look in her eye. She could be me, I think as I carry on staring at her. I could be her.

"This is JJ," says Brad. "And this is Jenny. My personal assistant."

"Hi, Jenny," I'm determined to be friendly, to make an effort, to show Jenny that her size doesn't bother me, it doesn't make me think Jenny's any less a person just because there's more of her. I stand up from my sitting position on the desk and walk over to Jenny with arm outstretched to shake her hand, but as I get closer I feel instinctively that she won't be shaking my hand, that, for some strange reason, there's a strong air of hostility in the room. And I'm right. I come to a standstill because Jenny doesn't move. Jenny just nods hello. Jenny doesn't say anything, and Jesus Christ, how I remember what it was like to be Jenny.

I remember how I felt when someone skinny and beautiful was introduced to me, how inadequate I felt, how I couldn't look them in the eye, and I try desperately to think of a way to make Jenny feel at ease.

"That's a beautiful shirt," I say finally. "Did you buy it here?"

"No," says Jenny, forced to speak, and then she turns to Brad. "I have some files here for you. Shall I just leave them on your desk?" Her voice is as cold as ice, and I recoil, but then I think how much worse it would be, how magnified those feelings of inadequacy would be if you worked somewhere where you were surrounded by bodies beautiful all day, so I try again.

223

"Have you worked here long?" I say, trying to offer her my friendship.

"Yes," says Jenny, refusing, this time, to look at me, and with that she turns and walks out of the office.

"I'm sorry," says Brad, running his fingers through his hair. "She can be difficult sometimes."

"Don't worry about it, I suspect I understand far better than you know," I say without thinking.

"What on earth do you mean?" Brad's voice sounds slightly harsh, and I wonder what he would think if he knew I used to be the same size as Jenny. I'm tempted, just for a second, to tell Brad how I used to be, but then I decide against it. Too soon.

"It's just that I imagine it's very hard for her, working some-where like this, being surrounded by skinny people all the time. What I don't understand is why she does work here. Surely it would be easier for her to work somewhere less . . ." I pause, wondering how to put it. "Less body-conscious."

"I think you're probably right," says Brad, "but you see Jenny's been with me for years, she's like my right arm, and to be honest I think that's the only reason she stays here, out of loyalty to me."

"You're sure she hasn't got an eensy weensy crush on you?" I tease, too taken with Brad to remember that it's no laughing matter being the fattest girl in the office and having a crush on the most beautiful man in the building.

"Jenny?" Brad snorts with derision. "No. She's more like my sister."

Hmm. Once upon a time that was what Ben would have said about me. "Well, I know someone who definitely does have a crush on you." I reach out my hand and place it on Brad's thigh.

"If I lock the door will you promise to tell all?" Brad's mov-ing over to the door and shutting it gently.

God forgive me for acting like a brazen hussy, but I can't

help it, he's just too irresistible. I cross my hands over my chest and slide my shirt off my shoulders revealing nothing underneath except bare flesh. I push Brad into a chair and straddle his lap while slinking my arms around his neck. "Promise," I purr, "swear, and cross my heart."

chapter 20

I stretch luxuriously in bed and fall back against the mound of pillows, thinking about my life. I think about Brad making love to me this very morning before going to the office and arranging to meet me later. I think about the life I've left behind, the sheer drudgery of working at the Kilburn Herald, and I think about what my friends would say if they could see me now, because, even though it's only been just under a week, I know already that I could get used to this.

How can I go back there? Back to dreary old London, when Los Angeles is so warm, so exciting, so inviting.

And then, I can't help myself, I start thinking about Ben. Funny how he crops up at the strangest moments. I can go for ages without giving him a thought, and suddenly he'll pop into my head. And when he does, of course I still miss him, but these days only when I remember him, which thankfully isn't all that much of the time because I'm having far too good a time.

Another thought creeps in, one I don't want to think about, one I'm hoping I'll be able to forget about, but no, the harder I try not to think about it the more I can't help it. Okay. I give in. Last night we were at the Mondrian Hotel, a huge, minimalist designer haven on Sunset Boulevard. A place that Brad insisted I see, even though I'm really not that bothered about "in" places, it's not as if I frequent them at home.

But it was spectacular. I've never been anywhere like it. The vast, minimalist lobby, stark glass doors leading on to a wooden deck lit by candles. I loved it. I loved the oversized terra-cotta pots, the large Indian mattresses strewn with cushions scattered by the side of the pool. And I'm trying not to think about what happened after that, about what Brad said, because every time I think about it, all sorts of negative thoughts start flooding in, and I don't want anything to go wrong, I don't want to shatter this perfection. Not now.

But it was bizarre. Okay, here goes. I'll tell you. There we were, sitting at a table in the bar of the Mondrian, the candlelight throwing flattering shadows on the faces of the beautiful people, but none more beautiful than Brad, in my opinion anyway. We sat, and we kissed, and we talked, and the more we talked the more we revealed about our lives, our loves, our hopes, our dreams, and the more we revealed the more I thought that this was it. Sorry. This is it.

"I'd like to live in a house on the beach," I said, pictures fresh in my mind because earlier that evening I'd sat scanning the property section of the *Los Angeles Times*, escaping into a fantasy world of swimming pools, sand between my toes, crashing waves.

"I think I'd be happy anywhere," said Brad, "as long as I was with you."

Jemima, oh, Jemima. Didn't you think it just a little strange that Brad was being quite so forward in just under a week? Were there no warning bells going off in your head? Would it not perhaps have been sensible to sit back and wonder whether he might just perhaps have an ulterior motive?

But no. It seems that Jemima Jones wasn't ready to spoil her perfect world just at that moment. Instead she sighed with happiness, and the conversation moved on, twisting and turning, until finally they were left only with the practicalities of her stay.

"Are there any bookstores around here?" I asked, knowing that is the one thing that would really make me feel at home, to have the luxury of browsing among my beloved books.

"The best ones are probably the Barnes & Noble or the Borders on Third Street Promenade," said Brad. "If you'd have told me earlier we could have gone in there before. You really do like reading don't you?"

I nodded.

"So what kind of stuff do you read?"

"Everything." I smiled mysteriously. "I have completely eclectic tastes and I'll read pretty much anything. What about you?" I asked, realizing I had no idea of his literary tastes, and, although it might not be important to you, I think it says a hell of a lot about a person.

"I don't really have the time," he admitted, taking another sip of champagne. "I kind of like science fiction when I do read." He paused for a while before adding, "I read more when I was at high school. I remember reading a book by that guy, oh, you know, what's his name." He looked at me for help while I shrugged my shoulders and shook my head. "You *do* know, the one that shot himself in the head. He wrote that book about the old man on the ocean—on that boat."

Did I hear that? Was he joking? My eyes widened in disbelief, but then I thought, he must be joking, he's going to laugh any second now. "Hemingway?" I said slowly, expecting him to crack up.

"Yeah." He nodded vigorously. "That's the guy. Great book."

He didn't laugh. He didn't even smile. What could I say? I wouldn't mind if his taste ran only as far as trashy cops and robbers books, but to forget the name of one of the most famous writers ever—and an American writer nonetheless! I was completely, utterly speechless, and it suddenly became blindingly obvious what was wrong with Brad, and that it is absolutely true that nobody is perfect. Brad, gorgeous, beautiful, kind, sweet Brad, I thought, with more than a hint of dismay, is thick. Thick as pig shit. Oh my God, why did he have to say that.

But no, I tried to tell myself. Just because he doesn't have the same interests as you doesn't mean he's necessarily stupid, just . . . different. And that doesn't mean he's a bad person, or he's not going to treat you well.

I'll try and forget it, I decided, put it out of my head. And I did try, really I did, but somehow it sounds a lot easier than it is.

And my dismay, concern, pissed-offness, whatever you want to call it, must have shown on my face, because Brad suddenly said, "Is everything okay?"

"Yes." I smiled. "Fine," and he leaned forward and gave me a long, sumptuous kiss on the lips, and I relaxed a bit, and then I decided that I really didn't care about the other stuff because this kiss made it all worthwhile. That this was what I had been waiting for. This man was who I had been waiting for. And this stuff, this feeling of being cared for, being looked after, being protected, is surely what it's all about.

But now, lying in bed this morning, I can't help but wonder if that *is* enough. Don't be ridiculous, of course it's enough. It has to be enough, but, just to be completely reassured, I pick up the phone and dial.

"*Kilburn Herald* features."

"Geraldine? It's me."

"Jemima? Hi! I miss you, and, you nasty old bitch, guess who's got to do your bloody column while you're away. Thanks a lot." She doesn't mean it, although she finally understands why I've been so unhappy writing the Top Tips.

"I miss you too."

"You can't be missing me. You're probably having a fantastic time. I want to hear everything. How's the gorgeous Brad? Are you in love? Have you done it yet?"

"Fine, not sure, yes."

"Yes?"

"Yes."

"Oh my God! How was it, how was it? Tell me everything! I want all the gory details."

"It was unbelievable, Geraldine. Seriously, truly, unbelievable. I have never had such amazing sex in my life. He is just so gorgeous. Every time I look at him I can't believe I've got him."

"So is he completely voracious?"

"Completely. We even ended up having sex on his desk in his office."

"Oh," sighs Geraldine. "I'm so jealous."

"Why? Don't tell me it's all gone horribly wrong with that guy you met at Ben's farewell party, Nick Maxwell?"

"No, it hasn't gone wrong at all. In fact, it's probably more right than ever before. But we haven't slept together yet."

"You're joking?" This is most unlike Geraldine, who regularly uses her body to control her relationships.

"I wish I was. It's not that I don't want to, or that he hasn't tried to get me into bed, but this is different, Jemima. I really like him. I mean *really* like him, and I don't want to blow it by jumping into bed with him too soon."

"Oh." Shit. Does that mean I've blown it with Brad? "Does that always blow it?"

"According to *The Rules* it does."

"What's *The Rules*?"

"It's all about how to play hard to get to hook the man of your dreams."

"And you believe it?"

Geraldine sighs. "I never did, but I decided to give it a whirl just to see, and I think it really works. And," she continues, "the cardinal sin is to sleep with them. At least, you're not supposed to until they're madly in love with you and you know they're definitely not going to disappear the next morning."

"But it's been ages, Geraldine."

"I know." She sighs again. "I'm practically climbing the

walls. I even passed a sex shop yesterday and seriously thought about going in and buying a vibrator."

"Geraldine!" I don't want to hear about vibrators, for God's sake, I've only just had an orgasm, and it's hard enough to talk about that, let alone vibrators. I love Geraldine for this, though. I love the fact that she's never embarrassed, but the only thing I'd change is her self-centeredness. Although I know she's probably the only true friend I've ever had, she always, always, brings the conversation back round to herself as soon as she can. Still, that's not such a bad thing, and at least I know I can rely on her. Even if I don't want to talk about vibrators with her.

"Don't worry," Geraldine says. "I didn't, but only because I didn't have the nerve to go in there by myself. I wish you were here, Jemima."

"I don't."

"Well, you know what I mean. It just kills me hearing you're having sex all over the place and I'm being Miss Born-Again Celibate."

"It's not all perfect, you know," I admit. Finally.

"How can it not be perfect?"

"Well, I don't know how to put this . . ."

"Just say it."

And I do. I tell Geraldine about the conversation last night, about the Hemingway situation, and Geraldine hoots with laughter.

"So what?" she says, when she's recovered her composure. "So he's not Mr. Intelligent. Darling, he's rich, he's gorgeous, and he's crazy about you. Who gives a stuff about anything else."

"Maybe you're right." I'm starting to feel better about it.

"When," says Geraldine dramatically, "have I ever been wrong?"

"So I should just ignore the fact that—"

"That he's stupid? Yes. And anyway, just because he doesn't read Hemingway hardly means he's stupid does it? He does, after all, appear to have a thriving business."

"Yes, that's certainly true." I'm feeling much better now.

"So. No problems. Right?"

"Right. Thanks, Geraldine. What would I do without you? Have you spoken to Ben recently?" Where did that question come from, Jemima?

"No. Why? Have you?"

"No, I just wondered how he's doing."

"I've seen him on TV if that's any consolation and he seems to be doing fine. If the truth be known, he's turning into a bit of a heartthrob as far as the public are concerned."

"Hmm." Why does this piece of knowledge make me feel uncomfortable?

"Anyway, my darling, this must be costing you a fortune, and I've got to file the copy on those bloody Top Tips. I'll call you in a couple of days, how does that sound?"

"That sounds wonderful."

"Okay, I'm out with Nick tonight. God knows if I can hold off much longer. I'll let you know next time we speak."

We say goodbye and I put down the phone. Geraldine's absolutely right, I'm being ridiculous. I go into the kitchen and open the fridge. A few fat-free yogurts, some fruit and several bottles of mineral water, and I examine the aforementioned while shaking my head in amazement. Open any bloke's fridge at home and you're likely to find a six-pack of beer, some leftover Indian take-away and, if they're extremely lazy, a pile of pre-packaged meals for one from a gourmet food store.

Right, I decide, closing the fridge door with a bang. Gym first then supermarket, because tonight I will be cooking dinner for Brad. I put on my gear and get ready to leave when the phone rings.

"Hi, sweetie." Brad has taken to calling me sweetie. "I miss you. Are you coming in?"

"Yes, I'm just about to leave. Listen, how would you feel if I cooked you dinner tonight?"

"I'd love that. Do you want to go shopping this afternoon?"

"No, don't worry, I'll go by myself. I want to surprise you."

"I can't believe how much work there is to do, and while you're here. I feel so bad, I really wanted to show you Los Angeles, all the fun stuff like Universal Studios and Disneyland."

"Brad, I'm not interested in all that touristy stuff." Which isn't quite true, but, as much as I would like to see it, I'm also quite happy in my role as Los Angeles wife. "I'm just really happy to do what you do, it gives me a better sense of who you are, what your life is like."

"Are you sure?" The relief in his voice is obvious.

"Yes, I'm sure."

"Okay. Leave now, I can't wait to see you."

"I'm leaving, I'm leaving!" I laugh, blowing him a kiss before skipping out the door.

"Jenny!" What a coincidence, to bump into Jenny in this juice bar, but then again, it is just down the road. I will make her like me, I will make this girl my friend, even if it kills me, and it looks like it might, because Jenny just eyes me up and down in a seriously unfriendly fashion before giving a grudging "Hello."

"How funny seeing you here!" No one could say I wasn't trying. "I just finished my workout. Let me get you something to drink."

"No, that's okay. I have to get back to the gym."

"So why did you come in here then?" I gesture round the little coffee shop down the road from the B-Fit Gym.

"Okay," sighs Jenny. "I'll have a mineral water."

Poor thing, I know exactly what she's up to. She'll probably have a mineral water here then go home later and eat a box of cookies. "Why don't you sit down?" I pull out a chair for her. "I'll bring the drinks over."

I pay for both mineral waters, and carry them over to the corner table where Jenny's sitting glumly, chin resting on her hand.

"Thanks," says Jenny.

"It's my pleasure," I say warmly, honestly, trying so hard. "Brad says you've worked for him a long time?"

"Yes." Her answers are still monosyllabic and I can tell this is really going to be hard work.

"Do you enjoy it?"

"I guess." Jenny shrugs her shoulders.

"You must know Brad very well by now." I'm trying to keep it light, but the strangest thing happens. Jenny blushes, and it's so like how I used to be with Ben that I suddenly see that she obviously has the most enormous crush on Brad and I've just put my foot in it big time. "I didn't mean . . ." I say lamely.

"That's okay," says Jenny, as the blush starts to die down. "It's fine."

"Look." Let's try and start all over again, Jemima. "There's obviously some kind of tension between us which I don't understand, because I'd really like us to be friends."

Jenny looks at me in horror. "I can't be friends with you."

"Why ever not?"

Jenny shrugs. "It just wouldn't work."

"I think you'd be surprised, Jenny," I say gently. "I think you'd find we have a lot more in common than you think."

"I don't think I'd be surprised at all," says Jenny bitterly.

"No, I'm serious," and it dawns on me that the only way I'm ever going to make this girl like me, or trust me, is to be completely honest with her and tell her the truth. "Can I tell you a secret?"

Jenny looks up without interest and shrugs her shoulders.

"Okay. You see me now and I'm slim, I'm fit. A few months ago I was seriously overweight. Far, far bigger than you."

"Yeah, really," says Jenny, getting up to leave. "Don't bother. Number one, I don't appreciate being patronized. Number two, I don't believe you. And number three, even if I did, it wouldn't make any difference to me. As far as I'm concerned you're my boss's new girlfriend and that doesn't mean *we* have to be friends. Thanks for the drink. I'll be seeing ya."

"But Jenny—" It's too late, Jenny has picked up her bag and

walked out. What did I say? What did I do? I probably shouldn't let this bother me, but it does, I can't help it. I know people used to feel sorry for me, but no one ever disliked me. I'm the girl who gets on with everyone, and I hate the fact that Jenny doesn't like me. Maybe if I knew why, I could deal with it, but she just seems to have taken an instant dislike to me, and I so want us to be, if not friends, at least on pleasant terms.

I constantly go over this conversation and wonder what exactly I have said to upset her. I act like a paranoid idiot, peering round corners before walking anywhere so I don't bump into her again, and when I get back to the gym Jenny, luckily, is nowhere to be seen, and Brad's in his office.

"The weirdest thing just happened," I tell him, after he's kissed me hello, and not just a peck on the cheek, a long, passionate kiss, and I physically have to push him away, because although it seems I can never resist him, at this very moment in time I have to get this Jenny business off my mind. So I tell him, only missing out the bit about the size I used to be, and it does cool Brad down. Completely.

"I'm sorry," he says, sitting back down behind his desk. "You mustn't let it upset you, she's just very protective about me."

"But it's crazy." I'm beginning to get slightly annoyed about this now. "I'm really trying to befriend the girl, and if I didn't know better I'd say she absolutely hated me."

"She doesn't hate you," sighs Brad.

"How do you know?"

"I just know. She's threatened by you."

"But surely you've had other girlfriends before. Is she like this with all of them?"

Brad shrugs. "I haven't really had serious girlfriends before. Look," he says, standing up and coming round to massage my shoulders, "it really doesn't matter. It's not important, but I'll talk to her, okay?"

He won't discuss it anymore, so I reluctantly agree and, as I do, I feel that Brad's massaging hands are going AWOL, and they've left my shoulders and they're moving down, past my collarbone, down to my bra.

"Brad," I plead, because I'm really not in the mood, but somehow I haven't got the strength to resist him, or the way he makes me feel, and it's a good job his phone rings a few seconds later, or there would have been a repeat performance of a week ago, which is all well and good, but I'm still trying to prove to myself that there's more to this budding relationship than simply a great sex life.

"Can I borrow your car?" I mouth to Brad as he talks on the phone, and he nods and throws his car keys on the desk, not thinking about insurance, or whether I can even drive. I can, luckily, drive, despite not owning a car in London, but never, in my wildest dreams, did I think I'd be driving a convertible Porsche.

Now I really have died and gone to heaven, this car isn't a car, it's sex on four wheels.

"Hey, babe," yell two young guys pulling up alongside me. "Where are you going?"

"Shopping," I yell back with a huge grin.

"Can we come?" one shouts, hand over his heart to show he's fallen in love.

"Sorry," I yell. "Only room for me and my bags."

I press my foot down to the floor and zoom off, and, presumably to demonstrate this love at first sight, they try and follow me, but the car is way too fast for them and within seconds they've disappeared.

"Hel-lo," says a good-looking man crossing the road at the traffic light. "Now this is what I like to see in Los Angeles. A beautiful single blonde driving a Porsche."

"How do you know I'm single?"

"A man can dream can't he?"

I smile and shoot off. I pull in to the first place that looks like a supermarket, park in the lot and grab a shopping cart. In a tight T-shirt, leggings, and Reeboks, with my sunglasses on top of my head and my hair in a sleek ponytail, I'm delighted to note that I look like every other hip, young Santa Monica housewife doing the weekly shopping, except of course that I'm walking down every aisle shaking my head with disbelief.

Never in my life have I seen such a choice of low-fat, non-fat, fat-free, cholesterol-free food. There are fat-free healthy scones, caramel popcorn rice cakes, low-cholesterol lemon snaps, reduced-fat gingersnaps, fat-free cholesterol-free chocolate fudge brownies, the list goes on and on and on, and despite saying goodbye to my binges a long time ago, I have to seriously resist the urge to sweep everything off the shelves and into my shopping cart.

"Excuse me?" says a masculine voice, and I turn with a raised eyebrow.

"I hope you don't mind me bothering you but I was wondering whether you knew the best way of cooking zucchini."

Now this, I don't believe. I mean, I'd heard about people being picked up in supermarkets, I'd even helped Geraldine write about people being picked up in supermarkets, but I never *really* thought it happened, and certainly not to me, but perhaps I'm wrong, perhaps this is a genuine query.

"You could try steaming it, I suppose. Or go Italian and coat it in egg and flour and fry it."

"You're English!" he says, his pose relaxing. "Where are you from?"

"London."

"Welcome to Los Angeles. Say, you wouldn't want to *show* me how to cook this would you?" Now it's his turn to raise an eyebrow.

"I'd love to." It is a pass! "But my boyfriend would hate it."

"Oh I'm sorry," he says. "I knew someone that pretty would have to have a boyfriend."

I shrug and carry on down the aisle, taking the most ridiculous amount of time to get my shopping done, first because the layout is somewhat different from my local Sainsbury's, and second because I have never seen such choice.

And when I've finished and I've loaded up the car, I sit for a minute, unable to believe quite how forward everyone here is, and how easy it seems to be to meet men if you're in Los Angeles and on your own. Sophie and Lisa would have a field day. Maybe I should phone them and tell them to come out. Then again, maybe not.

chapter 21

Jemima may well wonder about the divine Ben Williams every now and then, but she would never dream he's as famous as he now is. Sure, she's heard about it, she even saw his first foray on television when she was back in London, but she can have no idea of how Ben fever seems to have gripped the nation.

It doesn't happen all that often, but sometimes a new television presenter will appear, more often than not a woman, and soon every newspaper in the country is writing about them, every person in the country is wishing to be them, and their career takes off in leaps and bounds until you can barely leave your house without seeing huge billboards advertising their presence.

This is how it is for Ben Williams. Those first days on *London Nights* left him breathless with excitement, not only because of his immediate increase in salary but also because, even then, even after a handful of appearances on television, he was recognized.

The very first time he was asked for his autograph he was in a supermarket. He'd had a great day but he was tired, and all he could think of was getting home, putting his feet up and having a nice, cool beer.

But, walking down one of the aisles, lost in a world of his own, he gradually became aware that he was being followed. At first he thought he was going mad, that his senses were deceiving him, and he kept turning round to find no one there. But eventually he spotted two women standing staring at him, whispering to one another behind their hands.

"It *is*!" he heard one say, as the other gave her a shove and propelled her in Ben's general direction. Ben didn't know what was going on, so he ignored them and carried on shopping, until he had no choice.

"Excuse me," she said, a browbeaten housewife in her mid-forties. "I hope you don't mind, but aren't you that man on television?"

"I'm not sure," said Ben, not quite knowing what to say. "Which man?"

"Oooh you are! I recognize your voice. You're the new bloke on *London Nights* aren't you?"

Ben, to his credit, blushed slightly, and although part of him wished she would keep her voice down because he didn't want everyone to hear, part of him wished she'd shout a bit louder, so everyone *would* hear.

"Um, yes," he mumbled, smiling the bashful Ben smile that would soon ensure his already burgeoning heartthrob status.

"My friend and I think you're fantastic!" The words came out in a rush, and as she said it she started rummaging around in her bag, producing a pen and a torn-up scrap of paper.

"Honestly," she continued. "You brighten up our house every night. Doesn't he, Jean?" she shouted over to her friend, who looked as if she were trying to work up the nerve to come over.

"Would you mind?" She offered him the pen and paper, which Ben looked at for a moment wondering what he was supposed to do with it. The woman sidled up next to him and said, "I'm Sheila. Could you just put 'To Sheila, with lots of love.'" She tailed off, trying to remember Ben's name. "Is it Tom?" she asked, as Ben felt a fit of nervous giggles coming on.

"No," he managed to contain himself. "It's Ben. Ben Williams."

"That's it!" she said. "Ben Williams."

Ben balanced the piece of paper on the handle of his shopping cart, aware that passing shoppers had stopped to see what was going on, were looking at him in a way, he realized, that meant they too had recognized him, but thankfully no one else was going to do what Sheila was now doing.

"Oh thank you," she breathed heavily, tucking the paper very carefully into the front pocket of her bag. "We'll be watching you tomorrow."

"No, no," said Ben, recovering his composure. "Thank *you*, and enjoy the show."

As Sheila and Jean wandered off, heads together like a couple of lovesick teenagers, Ben understood, for perhaps the first time, how his life was about to change.

He went home and phoned Richard to tell him what had happened, and Richard nearly wet himself with laughter.

"You know what this means don't you, Ben?" he said, when he finally stopped.

"What?"

"You can't go anywhere without your full makeup on now," and with that he started laughing so hard he had to put down the phone.

Richard thought it was funny that night, but six weeks later, when they decided to go out for a few drinks, he thought it was fantastic.

"Let's just go to a local pub," suggested Ben.

"Not on your life, mate," said Richard. "You're famous, you don't go to local pubs, you go to bars and restaurants where the women are gorgeous."

And so it was that they ended up at Fifth Floor, on the top of Harvey Nichols, one Friday night, and Richard was right, the women were gorgeous. They bought champagne, and within minutes found themselves surrounded by stunning women, model figures encased in the latest fashions. Nobody actually asked for Ben's autograph, nobody would be that uncool, but it was blindingly obvious from the stares, the whispers, the flirtatious looks, that everyone knew exactly who Ben was.

"Fantastic!" said Richard at one point. "I must remember to bring you out with me more often."

"Yeah," laughed Ben, who was enjoying himself, but still wasn't completely comfortable with his newfound fame.

"What about the redhead?" Richard nudged Ben, and they both watched her perfect undulating backside as she went to the ladies' room to apply more lipstick.

"What about her?" said Ben, admiring the way she carried off a skirt that short, that clingy.

"She's up for it, Ben. What about you?"

Of course Ben was up for it, what red-blooded young man wouldn't have been? But Ben, remember, is not just a dizzy television presenter. Ben's a journalist, and Ben has met many women like this, and he knows perfectly well how they operate.

"Rich, do you really think I want to wake up next Sunday and read all about my bedroom exploits in the *News of the World*?"

"She wouldn't!" said Richard.

"She bloody well would."

"How do you know?"

"Trust me." He almost added, "I'm a journalist," but he restrained himself at the last minute. "I just know."

So Richard went home with a blonde, and Ben went home alone, and the next day Richard phoned him with tales of the blond, all related in a very bad Monty Python pastiche. "Did she go, eh? Did she go?"

And that was merely the beginning of Ben's journey into celebritydom, a small stepping stone. For now, just a few months down the line, Ben is well and truly established. No longer is he a mere reporter, he's now a presenter. *The* presenter. The public knows he's single, they know he lives with two roommates (although with his new large income he's started looking for a flat of his own), they know his likes and dislikes. But to be fair, none of them *really* knows him. They don't know what his sense of humor's like, they don't know what makes him tick, what he thinks about when he lies in bed at night, because Ben, being the journalist that he is, has perfected that art of putting on a face for the press, and, charming as he is to the other journalists who now clamor to interview him, he never shows them who he really is.

Only his close friends know that. Only people like Geraldine. Richard. And Jemima Jones. But Ben hasn't had too much time on his hands to think about his former work colleagues. He tried to keep in touch, really he did, but he was swept up in such a whirlwind it was difficult for him to find the time, and the longer he prevaricated, the harder it was to pick up the phone. And now his life is work, parties, launches, interviews. Never has he been so busy.

And never has London Daytime Television had such a bright star. Everywhere she goes Diana Macpherson is patted on the back, congratulated on her brilliant discovery.

Diana, as far as she's concerned, made Ben, and that means one thing in Diana's book. He owes her. Big time. And she's simply waiting for that day when she can call in her debt, because Diana Macpherson always wants what she can't have. And she wants Ben Williams, not only because he's gorgeous, but because he's shown no interest in her whatsoever.

Diana Macpherson is well used to bedding rising stars, wannabe celebrities who hang on her every word, feed the aura of power that surrounds her. What she's not used to are men like Ben, men who are polite, charming, friendly, but make no response whatsoever to her overt flirtations.

Just last week she called him in and told him they ought to have a drink, just to discuss how the program was going, to see whether they could come up with any other ideas.

Ben thought it was a bit strange, but, television being television, he'd already heard all the gossip about Diana and her boy toys, that her nickname was the Piranha, and he could tell from the way she looked at him that the last thing on her mind was the program.

"Rich," he whispered into the phone, checking there was no one around to overhear.

"What's the problem?"

"It's Diana. I don't think I can hold her off much longer."

"How many times, Ben? How often have I told you not to shit on your own doorstep?"

"*I* don't want to," Ben said emphatically, "but we're going out tonight for a drink and I'm running out of excuses."

"Whoa," Richard laughed. "Better put your chastity belt on."

"For God's sake, Rich. I need advice."

"Tell her you've got a girlfriend." Richard was already sounding bored.

"She knows I haven't."

"Well, I don't know. Just say you've got a headache." He laughed at his joke.

"Forget it," said Ben. "I suppose I'll cope."

Diana turned a business drink into dinner at a small French bistro in Chelsea, a dark, cozy, candlelit restaurant, perfect for romantic trysts.

"It's my local," she told Ben, who tried to ignore the fact that she had completely transformed herself between the last time he saw her in the office and the time she reappeared to tell him she was ready to go. She was wearing a plunging, see-through, fitted shirt, a black Wonderbra more than visible underneath, with a very tight skirt and very high heels.

"You look nice," Ben said, aware that she was his boss, that he had to flatter her, but trying to keep things as professional as he could.

"Oh thanks," she said, preening like a schoolgirl and trying to sound surprised. "This old thing?" she said, brushing her shirt, the shirt she'd bought at lunchtime with the express purpose of finally seducing Ben.

They sat down and Ben did his damnedest to talk about work. The wine was flowing, and he tried to drink as slowly as possible, to stretch out every drop, while Diana kept topping up their glasses—his always half full, hers always completely empty.

So they made small talk about work through the appetizers, while Ben tried, unsuccessfully, not to get too drunk, and to give him his credit he did manage to stretch work talk until halfway through the main course, when Diana put down her knife and fork, and leaned forward.

"Ben," she said in what she hoped was a husky voice. "I don't often meet men as charismatic as you."

"Thanks, Diana. Shall we get some more mineral water?"

"Ben," she said again. "What I'm trying to say is—"

"Waiter?" Ben looked around frantically for the waiter while Diana sighed and sat back in her chair, for Ben had spoiled the moment. Her moment.

Ben declined dessert, at which Diana was delighted, for she had already decided that Ben would be coming back to her place for a nightcap. Then the timing would be right. The timing would be perfect.

"My house is just round the corner," she said as they walked out, her having paid, for Diana Macpherson probably has the largest expense account in the country.

"Okay, fine. Thanks for a lovely evening," said Ben, backing off.

"You don't mean you'd let me walk home by myself?" said Diana, mock indignantly. "A girl on her own at night?"

Girl? thought Ben. In your dreams. "Sorry, sorry," he apologized, now not knowing what the hell to do, because, much as he didn't want to sleep with her, he didn't want her to fire him either, and, despite being famous and sought after, Ben knows exactly how transient the television world is, and he knows perfectly well that today's fame could be tomorrow's unemployment.

They walked along, side by side, and when Diana took Ben's

arm he resisted the urge to flinch. Oh fuck, he just kept think-ing. Oh fuck.

And when they reached the door, Diana turned to him, a playful smile on her lips. "Now how about that nightcap?" she said.

Ben silently prayed. If you help me now, God, I promise I'll go to church, and he heard the sound of an engine, and as he turned round he glimpsed the orange light of a black cab that was free. "Taxi," he yelled, sticking out his arm, while Diana looked crestfallen.

But the taxi driver had been working all day, and he was off home to his wife and kids. He shook his head at Ben as Diana smirked. "Why don't you come in and I'll call you a cab?" she said.

But she didn't pick up the phone, and Ben was so impressed with the minimalist grandeur of her flat and, by this stage, so drunk that he forgot to ask why not. She placed a large whiskey in his hand, and a firm hand on his thigh.

Oh fuck, Ben thought again, but before he had a chance to think up a strategy Diana was kissing him, and, although he knew he shouldn't, in a funny sort of way he was quite enjoy-ing it. This was Diana Macpherson! Oh what the hell, thought Ben in his drunken state, why not?

And so Ben and Diana finally consummated their profes-sional relationship. Ben, drunk though he was, ensured he gave the performance of his life, which probably wasn't such a good thing, because Diana, having experienced the most over-whelming orgasm of *her* life thanks to Ben's proficiency at oral sex, thinks she has fallen in love.

The oral sex was Ben's way of proving to Diana that he was a good lover, for the sex, at least in Ben's eyes, was pretty damn average. Sure, he made all the right moves and did all the right things, but, as far as he was concerned, he could have been fucking a shopwindow dummy, and yes, he managed to do it, but no, it wasn't good for him. And, perhaps most importantly,

Ben has remembered why he doesn't have meaningless sex with faceless women. Because it's not worth it.

There's only one problem. The sex may have been meaningless but the woman has a face. And a name. Diana Macpherson. His boss. Oh shit.

And after this night of passion, when Diana took the lead and Ben just thanked God he didn't suffer from Whiskey Dick, Diana has decided that Ben is the best thing that's ever happened to her. Her constant gazes at Ben have not, unsurprisingly, gone unnoticed in the office, and rumors of a suspected affair have already started flying around.

But Diana would never confirm them. No one would ever dare ask her to her face. And anyway, one night of passion hardly constitutes an affair, except Diana doesn't plan on leaving it at one night. No siree.

"I just knew he had that star quality the minute he walked in the door," she tells Jo Hartley, a freelance journalist who's writing a huge piece about the rise and rise of Ben Williams for an upmarket tabloid. "Presenters like Ben are few and far between, and it's my job to spot them then develop them and realize their full potential."

"Was it a conscious move, to employ someone who was single, because so many of the other presenters are married? And presumably with Ben and his obvious sex appeal you're attracting a much younger audience."

"Mmm," nodded Diana, thinking about Ben's obvious sex appeal. "I'd say you'd just about hit the nail on the head."

The piece runs over a double-page spread, with several pictures of Ben as a child, as a teenager, and finally in all his current glory.

"Un. Be. Lievable," says Geraldine as she sips the cappuccino she picked up on the way to work and reads the paper. One of the news reporters walks past her desk.

"I see you're finding out all about our old deputy news editor," he says as he passes.

"Who would have thought?" she says, eyes hardly able to leave the page, and then she shrieks with laughter as she reads the next quote.

"Even Diana Macpherson, the feisty head of programming at London Daytime Television, seems won over by this man's charm. At the very mention of his name her eyes glaze over like the rest of the female population.

" 'I love his obvious sex appeal,' she says. 'I chose him, initially as a reporter, and even then I knew that I could develop that.' "

When Geraldine finishes the piece, she sits back and lights a cigarette, trying to postpone that bloody Top Tips column. But then her eyes sparkle as she grabs the paper again, pulls out the two pages covered in Ben Williams and carefully folds them up and slips them into a manila envelope.

"Darling Jemima," she writes on a compliments slip. "If I had time I'd write a letter, but I wanted you to see this. Can you believe it?!! Ben Williams splashed all over two pages!! Wish I'd known then what I know now . . . maybe I would have taken him up on his offer after all!! Hope you're having a spectacularly marvelous time, and give Brad's pecs a lick from me. Speak to you very, very soon, all my love, Geraldine."

Smacking her lips, she seals the envelope and addresses it to Jemima, and on her way to the post office she smiles with delight at the thought of Jemima's surprised face when she gets it.

Ben's sitting at the breakfast table about to dig into a bowl of cereal when he hears the thud of the paper on the mat. Shit, he thinks. Today's the day the interview goes in. He hates doing publicity, but Diana, in her professional mode, has told him he has to do everything, because everything depends on the ratings and good PR means better ratings.

For the last few weeks Ben has had daily conversations with

the head of publicity at the TV station, who's constantly arranging for Ben to see journalists, or to take part in one of those rent-a-celeb pieces in which Ben's opinion on complete crap sits alongside other celebrities' opinions on the selfsame complete crap. But never has he had a profile this big. He agreed to the interview, under duress, and it was only afterwards that he discovered they were doing more than just talking to him, they were ringing up all his friends as well.

So with heavy heart he opened the paper, immediately cringing with embarrassment as he saw the pictures. Now where in the hell did they get *those* from?

I can't believe I said that, he thinks, starting to read the piece, before realizing that he didn't say it, that Jo Hartley had taken what he *had* said and paraphrased it into more tabloid-friendly language.

He carries on reading, shocked at what they'd found out about him. Nothing spectacularly juicy, just stuff that he'd forgotten about. They'd dug up people he'd vaguely known at university, and there are several paragraphs devoted to his life as a rugby fanatic, but luckily no real kiss and tells, just mentions of previous girlfriends.

"Jemima was right," he murmurs, scanning the rest of the page. "Being famous isn't quite what it's cracked up to be." Bloody hell, he thinks. Jemima Jones! Now why the hell didn't I think of Jemima. She'll give me advice about Diana, he thinks. She'll tell me what to do. And then he thinks of how long it's been since he last called her, and how she had always known just what to do.

Jesus, Ben, he thinks to himself, you've been a real bastard not calling Jemima. Geraldine, he thinks, he could live without. Yes, he fancied her, but there was never the connection that he had with Jemima. You should never have left it this long, he thinks, and with that he picks up the phone and dials her home number.

"Hello. Is Jemima there, please?"

"No, she's on holiday in Los Angeles for a couple of weeks."

"She's what? What's she doing there?"

"Who *is* this?" Lisa vaguely recognizes the voice.

"This is Ben Williams. Is that Sophie?"

"No," says Lisa, mentally rubbing her hands together with glee because Sophie's popped out to get some cigarettes and she'll go ballistic when she finds out Ben Williams phoned. "This is Lisa," she laughs. "The brunette."

"Oh hi. How are you?"

"Just fine," she says. "And I don't need to ask how you are, all I have to do is switch on my television."

"Yes," Ben laughs, because what is he supposed to say? There's a silence while Lisa tries to think of something clever to say next, but she can't think of anything at all, and the silence stretches on.

"Sorry," says Ben, finally. "I thought you were going to say something."

"Oh. No."

"What's Jemima doing in LA?"

"She's staying with her new boyfriend."

"You're joking!" Ben's flabbergasted. "Not that Internet guy?"

"Yes, that's the one."

"You haven't got her number by any chance have you?"

"Hang on," says Lisa, reaching for the pad by the phone. She reads the number out to Ben, and then says, "Um, you should pop in some time. Have a drink with us." Which of course means have a drink with me.

"Yeah, sure. I'll do that," says Ben, which of course means he'll forget about her the instant he puts down the phone. Which he does. He also neglects to phone Jemima in LA, because Diana Macpherson is next on the line, presumably hoping to soothe his furrowed brow. But he will phone Jemima, he honestly will. As soon as he remembers again.

chapter 22

A week can pass incredibly quickly when you're having fun. A week can also pass incredibly slowly when you find that you're actually quite lonely, you're not surrounded by the safety network of your friends, your home, familiar surroundings.

Not that Jemima Jones isn't having a good time, how could she not? Her evenings are a riot of new sounds, tastes, smells, and naturally the whirlwind of passion that she's having with Brad.

But her days aren't quite what they could be, and even after a week Jemima Jones is discovering that being on your own, in a strange city, albeit a city where the strangers treat you like old friends, is not quite the same as being on your own at home. Particularly when you're as strapped for cash as poor Jemima is now. The *Kilburn Herald*, as we already know, pays her a pittance, and all the money she saved by not having a life has almost trickled away. For now she's just about okay with Brad paying for everything, so let's just hope he *continues* to treat her as well as he has been . . .

Her daily routine here has changed enormously. She and Brad wake up at 8 A.M., and thus far they have had wild, wanton sex before both getting up and going for a run along the beach, which is sheer bliss for Jemima, so unused to living near the water, to the warm, early morning sun, to the friendly smiles of passing people.

They stop for breakfast on the way back, a glass of vegetable juice, a fat-free, sugar-free blueberry muffin or cranberry scone, and then Brad climbs in the shower at home. He kisses her goodbye, and Jemima showers, makes herself some coffee and climbs back into bed, poring over the magazines that are scattered all over Brad's coffee table, but no longer does she tear out the pictures of models. She doesn't need to, she's fulfilled that dream, and, while she's still interested, that degree of desperation has disappeared.

At around 11 A.M. she puts on her tiny Lycra leotard, her leggings, her sneakers, and she goes to do her workout at the gym. If Brad's not too busy, he'll take her out for lunch, or she may go wandering by herself, although it's hard for her to get around, because Brad needs his car, and Los Angeles, even Santa Monica, is not a place to be without a car.

But Jemima is slowly running out of places to wander. She has been up and down Third Street Promenade more times than she cares to mention. She has been into the bookstores, and has emerged with nothing, because all of the titles seem to be geared to those working in the film world, and Jemima, frankly, has no interest in books telling you how to write a film script, which director did which work, and why the film industry is so wonderful.

She has been into all of the shops lining Third Street Promenade. Repeatedly. She has been into the Santa Monica mall, into the eating section, and stood for a while, completely flabbergasted at all the stalls offering every type of food you could imagine. Chinese, Japanese, Italian, gourmet coffee, croissants, Ethiopian, Thai, and in the hundreds of tables planted in the middle of the mall were hundreds of people, all tucking into oversized portions in Styrofoam containers. She stood there, and she thought how six months ago, had she walked in here, she would have worked her way round all the stalls, but now, despite enjoying all the exotic smells mingling together, the thought of actually eating anything slightly repels her.

She has been up and down Montana, into all the smart, expensive boutiques and coffee shops. She was even extremely tempted to buy a cream designer suit that looked like a dream on her newly skinny body—which, incidentally, much to her delight is getting skinnier by the day thanks to a completely fat-free diet and an exercise regime that would make Cher jealous—but she didn't buy the suit, because where, after all, would she wear it? How, after all, could she afford it?

She has discovered that people don't dress up in Los Angeles, that anyone wearing a suit with anything other than sneakers on their feet is regarded as somehow strange, an outsider, someone not to be trusted. So she is living in her jeans, and if she and Brad go out in the evening, she teams the jeans with a cream bodysuit, a brown crocodile belt, and a jacket.

She has sat by herself at a long wooden trestle table in Marmalade, and flicked through the *Outlook*—the local Santa Monica paper—while eating a selection of three salads, and trying not to look as if she is desperate to talk to someone.

She has been to every Starbucks that she can find, and she has perfected the art of ordering coffee, American style, be it latte, mocha, or frappuccino.

She has walked up and down Main Street, past the New Age bookstore, which she is sorely tempted to try, but hasn't, as yet, had the nerve to go into. She has, however, been into the designer aerobic shops and has finally succumbed to outfitting herself in the very latest exercise wear. Now Jemima looks more like an Angeleno than most Angelenos.

She is constantly meeting people, or should we say, people, men, are constantly meeting *her*. Wherever she goes she is accosted by someone offering to buy her coffee, take her out, show her around, and although there have been times when she has been tempted, she has never said yes, because that, as far as she's concerned, would be tantamount to infidelity. So she smiles sweetly and tells them she has a boyfriend, before wishing them a nice day and walking off.

She has discovered American television, and, although she feels slightly guilty, a large part of her afternoon, when not Rollerblading by herself with Brad's Walkman attached to her waist, is spent watching shows that she's never heard of. She thinks she has just about got the plot of *The Bold and the Beautiful*. She is addicted to *Days of our Lives*. She adores *Rosie O'Donnell*, and the *Seinfeld* reruns, as far as Jemima Jones is concerned, are a positive gift from heaven.

Yesterday she found that the best place to have lunch, on those occasions when Brad could not make it out of the office, is a large, bustling restaurant called the Broadway Deli. She hit upon the deli by accident, and, while she was standing there, scouring the restaurant area, wondering if she had the nerve actually to sit at a table by herself when everyone around her was in couples, threesomes, foursomes, and moresomes, she noticed a lunch bar on the right.

And not only that, there was a spare stool, and she squeezed in next to a man who was just leaving, and picked up the paper he'd left behind.

"Coffee?" said the man behind the bar, as I nodded vigorously. As he placed a huge white cup and saucer in front of me and poured the coffee, I smelled a smell I hadn't smelled in what felt like years, a smell that instantly propelled me back to London, back to Geraldine, back to Ben, back to the *Kilburn Herald*.

Bizarre as it may be, I suddenly realized that the Broadway Deli was the first restaurant I had been into that allowed smoking, albeit only at the bar, and as I sat there sniffing I have never wanted a cigarette more badly in my life.

And as if the gods were listening, there, just in front of me, a little to my right, was a pack of cigarettes, calling me, tempting me. Nothing strange about that, I know, but they weren't just any old cigarettes, they were Silk Cut. King Size. Ultra Low. My brand.

"Excuse me," I said to the girl sitting next to me, "but are those your cigarettes?"

"Yes, help yourself." The girl watched as I greedily pulled a cigarette out of the pack and gratefully bent my head as she held out a light. I closed my eyes and inhaled deeply, feeling the smoke hit my lungs, and, partly because it was so forbidden, so naughty, the acrid taste was at that moment in time possibly one of the greatest tastes of my life.

"You look like you really needed that," said the girl in amusement.

"God, yes. You'd never believe this is now my only vice would you?"

"Sounds boring."

"I have a horrible feeling you might be right." I stuck out my hand. "I'm JJ."

"I'm Lauren. You're English too aren't you?"

I nodded. "Where are you from?"

"London."

"Me too. Whereabouts?"

"Kilburn."

"You're joking! What road?"

"Mapesbury. Do you know it?"

"Know it? That's unbelievable, I'm in the Avenue."

"God, what a small world."

"Wouldn't want to paint it."

"What?"

"Nothing," I mumbled, feeling a bit stupid. "Just something I heard someone say once, but I can't believe we're from the same place."

"I know," echoed Lauren. "Bloody incredible."

As we sit there smiling I suddenly breathe a sigh of relief because for the first time in Los Angeles I think that I may have found a friend. You know how sometimes you just know that you're going to be friends, sometimes within seconds of meeting someone? That's kind of what it was like with Lauren. She was just so natural that she put me at ease instantly.

We ordered our food, a plain salad, no dressing, for me, and Lauren ordered the Chinese chicken salad, and as soon as the waiter behind the bar disappeared we turned to one another in amazement.

"So what are *you* doing here?" I asked, assuming Lauren must live in Los Angeles because she looked so tanned, so fit, so healthy, so LA. But then I took a closer look and saw—this is Geraldine's influence on me—that her trousers and belted cardigan were, if I'm not mistaken, definitely designer, that her shoes were definitely expensive, and that her bag was definitely a Prada. Just how much more stylish can you get?

"I came out here about a month ago to be with this man, and now it's all gone horribly wrong and I can't face going home again because I told everyone this time I'd met The One, so I'm stuck here in this grotty little apartment, and every night I dream of curling up in one of the sofas at the Groucho, or drinks at the Westbourne, or dinner at the Cobden, and I miss home but I just have to sit it out. What about you?"

"This is more and more weird," I laughed, shaking my head. "I mean, I came out here to meet a man too, but I've only been here just over a week, and so far it's going fine. I think. He is gorgeous, and he's being lovely to me, but . . ." I tailed off and shrugged my shoulders. Do I want to reveal my doubts to this stranger? Not just yet, I have to see whether I can trust her.

"So where is he now?" asked Lauren.

"At work."

"Didn't he take time off to show you the sights?"

"He wanted to, he just has too much going on at the moment."

"What does he do?"

"He owns a gym. B-Fit Gym, I don't know whether you know it?"

"Oh my God!" Lauren's eyes opened wide, filled with admiration. "You're the one who came out to meet the hunk. I know exactly who you are. I can't remember his name. Damn," she said, almost to herself.

"Brad?" I was feeling slightly nervous, did she really know all about me, and if she did know, how did she know?

"Yes! Exactly. The most perfect specimen of manhood I'd ever seen. Bloody hell. Congratulations!"

"I don't understand how you know all this." Still feeling a bit bemused.

"Oh don't worry," said Lauren breezily. "Nothing sinister. I go to the B-Fit Gym, I've been going every day since I got here, and you get to know the people. Not that I know your gorgeous Brad, he's never even looked at me, but I overheard someone saying he was flying out an English girl that he met on the Internet or something."

"That's me, I'm afraid." I cringe as I admit it.

"Why sound so embarrassed about it?"

"It's just it sounds so naff, meeting on the Internet."

"Nah, not at all. Us single girls have to go wherever the opportunities are. So what's he like then? I've got to be honest with you, I really am impressed. He's just so perfect."

Do you know what's weird? If Lauren wasn't so open, so friendly, so natural, I probably would have been intimidated by her and I would almost certainly have taken offense at this candidness, but just then I was so relieved to have found an ally. To have found someone who, despite the long dark hair and slight cockney lilt, was somehow reminding me more and more of Geraldine with every word she spoke.

"He *is* gorgeous isn't he," I said, smiling like the cat that got the cream at the thought of his gleaming white teeth, the softness of his hair, the hardness of his muscles.

"Phwooargh, is he ever."

And then I couldn't stop this sigh escaping. "I know, I know. I just think that everything should be perfect, and I suppose I had this vision of us spending all this time together and doing all these things together, and although I see him in the evenings I'm starting to feel a little bit lonely."

You might think it strange that I'm being so open with a girl who's practically a stranger, but then isn't it sometimes easier to pour out your heart to someone you hardly know, who doesn't matter, who won't judge you?

"Don't worry about that," said Lauren, giving me a friendly shove. "You've got me now. I'll be your friend. God knows I could do with a reminder of home right now." She looked dreamily into space. "Keep talking. I'll close my eyes and pretend we're at the K bar."

I laughed.

"So," she carried on. "Friends? How about it?"

For a moment there I was so happy I could have hugged her.

"Tell me about your man then," I asked. "How did it all go wrong?"

Lauren sighed and handed me another cigarette before lighting one for herself. "Okay. Here goes. Are you sure you want to hear the full story?"

I nodded. "Sure as I'll ever be."

"Okay. I met Charlie in London about six months ago. Actually I wasn't supposed to be meeting him, I was supposed to be meeting one of his associates to try and set up an interview with some woman they look after."

"Hang on." I put a hand on Lauren's arm, trying not to start laughing. "Sorry to interrupt but what do you do for a living?"

"I'm a journalist. Anyway, so there I was—"

"No!" I said. "You're not going to believe this."

Lauren looked at me and her mouth dropped open. "Don't even think about telling me—"

"I bloody am!" I laughed out loud.

"No fucking way. Who do you work for?"

"Don't ask," I groaned. "The *Kilburn Herald*."

"Hey, it's a starting point," she said. "I used to work for the *Solent Advertiser*."

And then I started laughing even harder.

"What's so funny about that?" said Lauren.

"Don't worry. It would take too long to explain. So where do you work anyway?"

Lauren named one of the top glossy magazines, a magazine I would have killed to work for, a magazine of which several cut-out pages, even as we speak, are nestling in the top drawer of my bedside table at home.

"Now it's my turn to be impressed. Don't tell me you're something really important like editor," I said.

"I bloody wish!" said Lauren. "But actually I am the style editor."

"So how come they let you come here?"

"I've taken a three-month sabbatical. The plan was to come here, realize that this was true love, get married so I can get American citizenship and then move husband and myself, and naturally by that time at least three babies, back home to Blighty."

"But I take it your plans have changed?"

"Too bloody right. So where was I? Ah, yes. Charlie. So Charlie turned up instead of this guy I was supposed to be meeting, and sat in on the interview."

"Was this in London?" I interrupted, trying to get the full picture.

"Yup. They'd flown over for a ten-day publicity tour, and this was right at the beginning. So Charlie walked in, and I thought he was nice. Nothing spectacular, but nice, you could tell he was a good person, and he is attractive. He wears these little round tortoiseshell glasses which I completely adore, and he was really sweet after the interview. Anyway, the interview was fine, and the next day he phoned me to check everything was okay, and he asked me out.

"We went out that night, and he was so nice to me I suppose I started to fall for him, and we spent pretty much every night together."

I raised an eyebrow.

"Not like that," Lauren grinned, before grimacing. "Although now I wish we bloody had, I wouldn't be sitting here if we had."

"Uh oh, is that the problem?"

"It sounds so shallow doesn't it? I mean, here's this wonderful man whom I did find attractive, and he was convinced he'd met the woman he was going to marry."

"So why on earth didn't you sleep with him?"

"I was reading this book about how to play hard to get . . ."

I shook my head and sighed. "Not *The Rules* by any chance?"

"Yes! You've read it?"

"No," I laugh, "but a friend of mine is doing it at home."

"Well, all I can tell you is it bloody well works. On the day he left Charlie told me he'd never felt this way about anyone before, and he wanted me to come out to California. So basically we spent the next few months with him phoning me every day, and I suppose I convinced myself that this time it really was going to work, and I completely fell in love with the idea of being in love." She paused to take a bite of salad.

"And?" I prompted, dying to hear the end.

"And, I finally got the time off work, came out here, he picked me up at the airport, he was exactly as I remembered him, and we spent all afternoon kissing and cuddling and it was fantastic.

"And then," she exhaled loudly, "and then, we went to bed."

"Do I want to hear this?"

"No. You don't. It was a bloody nightmare."

"Just no chemistry or was he just awful?"

"Well this is the weird thing. Up until then I had this theory that there was no such thing as being bad in bed. I always thought that it was just a question of having the right chemistry, and if the chemistry wasn't there then it would be awful."

"Tell me about it." I nodded, remembering the terrible sex I'd had before I met Brad.

"Christ, was I wrong. I now believe that there is such a thing as being completely crap in bed, and Charlie was completely crap in bed."

"But what do you mean, how can anyone be that bad?"

"I know. I wouldn't have believed it myself. But," she said leaning forward confidingly, "his dick was about this big!" She held out her little finger.

"Uh oh," I said. "A no-hoper then?"

"A no-hoper. I mean, he really should have come with a warning. You get to know someone, you think they're perfect, and then boom! You discover they have the dick of a ten-year-old."

"So what did you do?"

"I put up with it for about two weeks, because I kept hoping that it would get better, and I tried not to think about it. Also—" She paused. "Also, it wasn't just that. He was bloody crap at going down on me."

"Oh." What was I supposed to say? Hardly the sort of thing you discuss with strangers, is it, no matter how friendly they seem.

"Yeah," she nodded. "You know how it is, he couldn't find my clit if it had a big red arrow showing him the way." I blushed, and I'm still blushing at the memory of the language she used, but she didn't seem to notice.

"Then I started coming up with excuses, I was really tired, I had my period."

"And he believed them?"

"Nah." Lauren shook her head and laughed. "Eventually, the last time we had sex I just knew as an absolute certainty that this was the most pointless experience of my life. I could hardly feel anything for God's sake, and if it wasn't for his balls banging against my—"

"I get the picture," I interrupted, not wanting to hear any more.

"Sorry." She paused and shrugged her shoulders. "So anyway, the next day I told him I was moving out."

"How did he take it?"

"Nightmare." Lauren raised her eyes to the ceiling. "He was so upset he didn't speak. I sat there for three hours talking at him and he didn't say one single word. He just sat and looked at the floor."

"God. Nightmare. Did you tell him why?"

"What? Tell him his dick wasn't big enough? No, I couldn't do that. I just came out with all this shit about how I wasn't ready for a relationship, we lived too far apart from each other to ever really make it work, and eventually I sealed it by telling him I thought I had a problem with commitment." She drifted into silence, obviously lost in memories.

"And now you're here, picking up strange women in the Broadway Deli," I said, breaking the silence.

"Exactly," laughed Lauren. "So please tell me the sex with Brad is out of this world, because I've forgotten, I really have."

"You will be delighted to hear it's out of this world."

"Really?"

"Really."

"Give me the details, go on."

I shook my head, because nice as she is, I'm not the sort of person who finds it easy to talk about sex, and certainly not in the sort of language she's used to. As you've probably noticed.

"So is this true love? God, how I need to hear a story with a happy ending."

"I don't know. I'm not sure I'd even know what true love is."

"What? You've never been in love?"

"Well . . . There was this guy in London I was crazy about, I'd never felt that way about anyone before, and I always thought I was madly in love with him. Not that anything ever happened, we were just friends."

"Why? Is he blind?"

I love this woman! "No. I didn't look like this when I was in London." I thought for a moment, wondering whether to tell Lauren, and what the hell. I'd been so honest up until then, why stop? "If you want to know the truth I was the size of a house."

"No way." Lauren looked me up and down in disbelief. "No way."

"I swear," I swore.

"So how the hell did you get to look like this?"

"Lots of hard work. Tons of exercise and no food."

"It was obviously worth it. You look fantastic."

"Thank you."

Lauren looked at me curiously. "So has your life changed, now that you're thin?"

I shrugged, thinking about how invisible I felt before I lost weight, and how much that had changed. "In some ways of course," I said slowly. "You can't even begin to imagine what it was like being . . ." I paused, wondering whether I could now say the F word out loud, and after a deep breath I managed it, "fat. It colors your whole life. Nobody wants to be seen with you, nobody notices you, or if they do it's because they think you're worthless."

"Why were you that size?"

A good question, and one I'd thought about many times since losing the weight. "I suppose in a way I wanted to hide from everyone. Even though I hated it, it was my protection, it kept people away and a part of me was very frightened of people, especially of men, and my size made me feel safe."

Lauren nodded. "I can understand that. But what about men?"

"What about them?" I laughed. "I never really had any boyfriends, just the odd fling which makes your Charlie look like an Adonis. Men were never really an issue."

"So what about this guy in London?"

"You might know who he is actually. When I knew him he was the deputy news editor of my paper, but now he's moved into TV. Ben Williams. He's a reporter on—"

"Fucking hell! Gorgeous Ben Williams! I know exactly who he is, I was completely hooked on the show before I left. I've been trying to get a bloody interview with him for weeks."

"But you're the style editor, surely you don't do interviews?"

"Not usually, no, but pass up the opportunity of meeting

263

Ben Williams? Not bloody likely! God," she said, shaking her head. "You're something, JJ. All these gorgeous men!"

"Yeah, but Ben was never interested in me."

"But you know him! He's your friend! What's he like, tell me everything."

So I did, and before we knew it, four hours had passed, and by the time we left, we were firm friends. Lauren gave me her phone number and said if there was anything I needed, just give her a call, and I gave Lauren my phone number, saying there was no reason why either of us should be lonely anymore. Corny isn't it, but not so corny if you think how lonely I've been. We walked out together and said goodbye, and spontaneously both of us reached over at the same time and gave one another a hug. A hug that said thank God we've found each other, thank God we've finally found a friend.

chapter 23

The phone rings as I walk through the door.

"Sweetie, where have you been?" Bless Brad for sounding so worried.

"I met the most amazing girl today." The excitement is still in my voice, the thrill of having someone to talk to when Brad's not here. "And we just sat and talked for hours."

"Where did you meet her?" Brad sounds a bit, well, a bit perturbed. It crosses my mind that maybe he thinks I'm lying, so I tell him the whole story, just leaving out the bit about the small dick because men don't appreciate that kind of thing.

"That's great," he says, although if I'm honest he doesn't sound all that interested. "Honey," a slight digression from his usual pet name, "I'm coming home early tonight. Wanna try a yoga class?"

"That sounds . . . interesting," I say cautiously, because let's face it, yoga doesn't mean losing weight, and if it doesn't help me maintain my new slim figure then what is the point? Really?

"Okay. I'll be home soon, and then maybe tonight we'll go out for dinner. I thought we'd try this restaurant on La Cienega."

"You mean, we're actually leaving Santa Monica?"

Brad laughs. "Don't make it sound such a big deal, you're making me feel guilty."

"I didn't mean to. Sorry."

"Hey, don't worry about it. It'll be nice. I want to make a fuss of you tonight, and I think you'll enjoy this restaurant, it's French, so it should remind you of home."

"Darling, I'm English."

"I *know* that," he laughs, "but France, England, Italy, they're all Europe."

"I know *that*," I laugh back, and we say goodbye.

We don't really need to join Brad and Jemima at yoga, just a quick peek perhaps. Suffice to say Jemima finds it strange, and more strange is the fact that there are equal numbers of men and women, all decked out in the latest lycra, all deep breathing and contorting their bodies into strange positions.

"I'm not sure whether I can keep this up," puffs Jemima, lying on the floor with her legs over her head, straining to make her toes touch the floor just above her hair.

"You're doing great," Brad says smoothly, lying next to her, looking as if he does this every day of the week. "You'll feel great afterwards. Now ssshhh. Breathe." And Jemima does, trying to forget that she, like everyone else in the packed room, looks completely ridiculous.

"There," Brad says when the group has finished and are standing round talking to one another. "How do you feel now?"

"Fantastic," lies Jemima, who feels pretty much the same, has been bored throughout, and finally understands why she has never been to a yoga class before.

"Told you so," he says, kissing her on the nose. "Let's get out of here."

* * *

We go home, and, as Brad is showering, as I'm brushing my teeth, he opens the glass door and pulls me in the shower.

"See?" he says, rubbing the soap gently all over my body and setting every nerve I have on fire, "never say I don't look after you," and before I have a chance to reply he bends his head and kisses me.

Quickies, I think ten minutes later, can be just as exciting as long, luscious, languorous sex.

"Mmm," says Brad, enfolding me in a towel. "Maybe we should cancel tonight and just spend the evening in bed."

"Haven't you had enough yet?" Does this man never stop?

"I could never get enough of you," he says, looking deeply into my eyes until finally I break away with a kiss and go to get dressed.

We go to Le Petit Bistro, a busy, bustling restaurant, and I spend the whole evening marveling at the mix of weird and wonderful people surrounding us. Opposite us is a table of six of the best-looking men I've ever seen, presumably gay, because each of them stops talking when we walk in, and, instead of looking at me, which I'm slowly getting used to, they all, one by one, look Brad slowly up and down from head to toe.

At the far end is a woman like no woman I have ever seen, and for a moment I think she might be a man in drag. Throughout dinner she keeps her white fur coat on, which matches her white stetson and the enormous diamonds glittering in her ears and around her throat.

"Is she someone famous?" I whisper to Brad, pointing her out. "Nope," Brad says, shaking his head. "Just some rich old woman with no fashion sense at all, darling!" and we both laugh. But I can't believe what this woman looks like. She must be seventy if she's a day, and she obviously doesn't give a damn that she looks ridiculous. Part of me thinks, good for her, but the other part thinks, does she honestly look in the mirror before she goes out and say, yes! I look good.

And then I look over to the right, and I nearly squeal with excitement. Finally, I finally see what I've been waiting to see since I arrived. A real-life celebrity. And not just any old celebrity, George Clooney! The man I used to sit and fantasize about, when, that is, I wasn't fantasizing about Ben.

"Oh my God," I whisper, "that's George Clooney."

"Where?" Brad doesn't seem very interested, but I gesture slightly with my head and Brad turns to look.

"Oh yes," he says uninterestedly and immediately looks away and goes back to eating his endive and heart of palm salad.

"Now he," I say, trying to look, but trying to look as if I'm not looking, "is gorgeous."

"Why don't you talk to him?"

"And say what? I love you?"

"You could just tell him you admire his work. People don't generally bother celebrities here, you see them all over the place, but if you are going to talk it's better to be cool and just say something flattering. I love you probably wouldn't go down too well."

"I couldn't say anything," I say, which is true. I'd be far too embarrassed to approach him, but think what Geraldine will say! Think how jealous Sophie and Lisa will be!

"Speaking of love . . ." Brad finally puts down his knife and fork while I start shaking because, inexperienced though I may be, I know what's coming next. I know because Brad suddenly has a very serious look on his face, serious but soppy at the same time. He reaches over and takes my hand, which he holds very gently, stroking my fingers with his thumb, and I watch him doing this and I wonder why I'm not feeling completely and utterly happy.

"JJ," he says, and I look up, into his eyes. "I never thought I'd say this. I never thought this would happen, but you do know I love you."

Well I didn't know, actually. I mean, I know that Brad certainly says and does all the right things, and that most women probably would have thought, even after just over a week, that he really is in love, but I can't get rid of this feeling that something isn't completely right.

And I still can't put my finger on it, and I want it to be right, I want it so badly to be right, so most of the time I try not to think about it. I know I said those things about him being stupid, but, as Geraldine said, that's not it. I just have this feeling that this can't be real, this is like a play, like a couple of actors, but maybe that's my insecurity kicking in. Maybe it's just that I can't believe someone this gorgeous could love me. Plain old Jemima Jones.

But you see, every now and then I catch Brad sitting, staring at nothing, and he looks as if he's in another world, miles away, thinking about someone else, and even though when I interrupt these reveries of his he's all over me, covering me with kisses which usually end in us making love, I can't help but wonder where he's been when he's gone. Mentally, that is, because physically I know he's either at the gym or with me, he definitely wouldn't have the time to actually be with another woman. I just sometimes think his thoughts are. That's all.

And so when he sits here and tells me he loves me, I try to push that feeling away, because no one's ever told me before that they loved me, unless you count Ben's drunken mumblings at his farewell party, which I don't, and therefore nor should you.

And surely when someone like Brad is in love with you, you have to love them back? So what if he's Californian, so what if he's not as intellectually capable as some of my friends back home, that doesn't mean he's not my soulmate. And he loves me. *Me!* Jemima Jones!

But my other concern, if you can call it that, is what are you supposed to say when someone tells you they love you? Are you supposed to be ultra-cool and say "I know" or are you supposed to say "I love you too"? I can't decide, so I don't say anything at all.

"I know this must seem very quick." Brad looks at me earnestly. "But they always say you know when you know, and I know. I really do. I feel like I've found my soulmate." I know I just thought the same thing, but it sounds so ridiculous spoken out loud, so naff, and for a minute I look at him wondering if he is on another planet after all. I don't really know what to say, and, although the silence probably isn't very long, it feels very long. It feels like hours.

"I think I feel the same way," I say eventually and, much as I hate to admit it, I think I say it partly to make Brad feel better, and partly to fill the silence. I mean, someone has to say *something*, don't they?

"You are just what I've been looking for," he continues. "You're just so perfect. *We're* so perfect together."

"But I'm going home in a few days," I say. "What are we going to do?" And I think about Lauren, and wonder whether I could cope with a long-distance relationship, but then I stop comparing myself to Lauren because, after all, I know the sex with Brad is fantastic. Probably the best thing about the whole relationship.

"That's what I wanted to talk to you about," he says slowly.

"What, you mean stay?"

"Not forever." He obviously sees the panic in my eyes. "But maybe you could change your ticket and stay for, say, three months. It would give us a chance to see if this really would work."

"But what about my job at home? What would I do here? What about all my *stuff*?" Thoughts start whirling round my head, how would I do this, how could I do this?

"Okay," says Brad. "Let's work this out. First of all you'd need to phone your work and see if they would let you have the time off. The worst thing that could happen is they say no, in which case you'd have to make a choice. Do you just leave and try for another job when you get back home, or do you go straight back home?"

I nod, thinking, again, about Lauren, and wondering whether she might just possibly consider finding me some work, or at the very least putting me in touch with people who could. I mean, hell, it's not as if I'd be leaving some fantastic job, some fantastic magazine, it's only the *Kilburn* bloody *Herald*.

"Second," continues Brad, "you don't have to worry about what to do out here. I know hundreds of people in the television industry, so if you decided to stay I'm sure we could find you something. In the meantime you don't have to worry about working, or about money. God knows I've got enough for both of us, so that shouldn't be a problem."

"But Brad, I need to work. Much as I love being here, I'd get so bored with nothing to do all day." I don't bother mentioning that I'm bored already.

"I know it's not a long-term solution, but in the short term, if you were bored, you could always work at the gym."

"Doing what?" I have this ridiculous vision of myself teaching an aerobics class.

"What about PR? I don't have anyone except Jenny, and I know she has a hard job coping all by herself."

Yeah, really, I think. Jenny would love that. But of course I don't tell Brad that working with me would be Jenny's idea of hell because she hates me, because I know he'd tell me she doesn't and I am being ridiculous, so I don't say anything, I just sit and wait for what he's going to say next.

"And third, what *stuff* do you mean?"

"I'm still paying rent on my flat at home, and all my stuff is there, my things."

"Don't you have a friend who could look after it for you?"

"But I'm not sure I want to give it up. If," and I kiss the palm of his hand as I say this, "if things don't work out, and I'm not saying they won't, I think it's far more likely that they will, but if they don't I don't want to have to go back to London with nowhere to live."

"So sublet your room." Brad leans back as if it's all so easy, and, as I watch him watching me, I realize that it is easy. He is absolutely right. Life should be an adventure, and this is the biggest adventure of my life. I've started it, so I may as well go with it and see where it takes me.

"Okay," I say, smile, and take a deep breath. "Let's do it."

"You'll stay?"

"I'll stay."

"Jemima Jones," he says, leaning forward, taking my face in his hands and giving me the hugest kiss on the lips, "have I told you how much I love you?"

A few minutes later we're rudely interrupted by the sound of applause. I blush furiously as the table of six men all hoot and cheer, and even our bloody waiter joins in. "Would you like to see the menu," he asks, one eyebrow raised, "or are you covered for dessert?"

I phone Geraldine the next morning, and she's over the moon.

"You lucky cow!" she keeps saying. "I hope you've got a spare room because I'm coming to visit."

"I wish you would," I say, realizing how much I miss her, how much more fun this would be if Geraldine were here.

"I'm serious," she says. "I'll be packing my stuff before you know it. The only thing is you've got my bloody Louis Vuitton vanity case."

"I'm sorry," I groan. "Do you want me to send it back?"

"Don't worry," she laughs. "I'm sure I can live without it. Anyway, I can get Nick to buy me another one."

"Ah. Nick. So?"

"So?" And I can tell instantly that she's not doing *The Rules* anymore.

"So I take it you're no longer a *Rules* girl?"

"I most certainly am a *Rules* girl," she says indignantly. "Just because I slept with him doesn't mean I'm going to stop."

"You slept with him!"

"I figured it was about time, and, bless him, he really went to town. Flowers, champagne, everything."

"And did it warrant fireworks as well?"

"Mmm. It was absolutely, one hundred percent delicious."

"I don't believe this, Geraldine. You're in love!"

There's a long pause. "You know what, my darling Jemima? I think I bloody well am!"

And I know I shouldn't be, but I'm jealous. I'm supposed to be in love too, so why can't I muster the same enthusiasm, the same dreamy tone in my voice?

"I'm really happy for you," I say. "I hope you get everything you wish for."

"Mmm," she says. "An eight-carat diamond engagement ring *and* Nick Maxwell. My life is perfect."

I'm shocked. "You mean he's given you an engagement ring?"

"Don't be silly. I'm just planning my future."

I laugh. "Listen, this is costing me a fortune and I need to speak to the editor. Can you put me through?"

"Good luck," she says, blowing me kisses. "With everything."

"And how's the land of Hollyweird?" booms the editor down the phone.

"It's weird," I laugh, "but actually I'm in Santa Monica, which is not quite the Los Angeles you see in films. It's a bit more down to earth."

"Never been myself," says the editor, "but wouldn't mind taking the wife and kids. Life's too short to be taken slowly," he adds, yet another one of his boring clichés. "So you're back in next Monday then, Jemima?"

"Er, well, actually. That's why I was phoning."

"And I thought it was because you were missing me," he says with a sigh. "Go on then, love. This is going to be bad news, I knew it the minute they told me you were on the phone."

"The thing is that I'd like to stay for a bit."

"Not found a job on the *Hollywood Reporter* have we?"

"No, nothing like that."

"Must be love then."

"I think it might be."

"Look, Jemima," he says, and from the tone of his voice I know he's going to agree, he's actually going to agree! "I wouldn't normally agree to this, but, seeing as you're one of our best reporters, I'm going to have to say yes. How long are you proposing to stay?"

"Three months?" I can't help it, it comes out as a question.

"All right, Jemima, but there is a condition."

"Yes?" I'm doubtful.

"The *Kilburn Herald*, great as it is, needs a touch of glamour. I'll agree to you staying out there if you agree to do a weekly page on Los Angeles. I want our readers to get some Hollywood gossip firsthand. I want to know who's doing what, where, with whom. And, more to the point, I want to know it first."

"I'd love that!" I gasp, because this is my dream job. A column! All of my own! "But I have a condition of my own."

"Yes?" says the editor warily.

"I want a picture byline."

"No problem there, love. Have we got a decent picture of you?"

God, no. The only picture of me in the office is a fat picture. "I'll send you one from here," I say, thinking on my feet.

"Okay, Jemima. Let's see how you do."

"Thank you so much," I gush. "It's going to be great."

"I'll expect your copy every Wednesday morning, first thing. And Jemima, love?"

"Yes?"

"I hope he's worth it." And chuckling to himself, he puts the phone down.

Jemima Jones used to believe that she was born with a wooden spoon in her mouth. Jemima Jones used to believe that there was such a thing as an exciting, glamorous life, only that it would never happen to her.

But what Jemima Jones never understood was that sometimes, in life, you have to make things happen. That you can change your life if you're willing to let go of the old and actively look for the new. That even if you're on the right track you'll get run over if you just sit there. And heaven knows Jemima Jones hasn't been sitting anywhere for a long time now. Jemima Jones is now running with the winds, and suddenly, for the first time in her life, everything seems to be going right.

In fact, at this very moment in time I would say that Jemima Jones is an inspiration to us all.

chapter 24

" I'm sorry, JJ," says Cindy, coming back on the line, "but I'm afraid Brad's in a meeting and can't be disturbed. Just hold the line and I'll put you through to Jenny." Before I can yell no, I'm put on hold and I can't put the phone down because that would be childish, and anyway, why can't Brad be disturbed? Since when has he been too busy to talk to me? I've been here for four and a half weeks, and I've never had a problem getting through before.

"Hello?" Jenny comes on the line and even in one word I can hear the exasperation in her voice.

"Jenny? It's JJ. How are you?"

"Fine."

"Look, I know Brad's in a meeting but can you just let him know I'm coming in about three o'clock."

"Certainly. Oh by the way, he said that in case you called I should let you know that he has another meeting tonight and won't be home as planned."

"Fine. Thank you, Jenny."

"You're welcome," she says, sounding as if she means the

very opposite, as if I've once again pissed her off royally. Call me crazy, call me paranoid, but don't I detect the tiniest hint of triumph in her voice? Must be my imagination.

And now I'm the one who's pissed off. Not only will I be on my own all day, it looks like I'll be on my own tonight as well, and the thought fills me with dread. Oh God, have I made a terrible mistake, should I have just got on that flight home and gone back to where I belong?

No. I'm determined to be positive, to make the best of the time I have here, to make the best of the relationship I have with Brad. Damn it, I think, as I pick up the phone and rifle through my address book to find Lauren's number. I'm going to go out tonight and have some fun.

"Lauren? It's JJ."

"Hi!" She sounds extraordinarily pleased to hear from me. "I was just thinking about you!"

"That's lucky," I say, "because I was just thinking about you."

"So what's the plan, Stan?" she says.

"What are you doing tonight?"

"I was looking forward to yet another miserable bloody take-out from the local deli, and stuffing my face in front of the TV."

"Does that mean I can't tempt you with a girlie night out?"

"Tempt me, tempt me," she laughs.

"It's just that Brad's got a meeting so I'm on my own, and I thought maybe we could check out that new restaurant on Main Street."

"Cool, schmool in the pool," she says, in a perfect Californian accent as I laugh, wondering where on earth she gets her expressions from. "I'm there. Listen, what are you doing now?"

I look at my watch. "I'm off to the gym."

"Me too. Why don't we meet at the gym, grab some lunch after the workout, and then we can arrange what to do later?"

"Perfect," I say. "Oh, by the way. Lots to tell you."

"I can't wait," she says, and we put down the phone.

It's only when I arrive at the gym that I realize that I'm actually excited about seeing Lauren again. For the first time since I arrived, I'm starting to feel more at home. I've got a home, a boyfriend, and now, finally, I'm starting to find friends. Lauren may be the only friend I have out here right now, but it's a start, and it's starting to compensate for missing Geraldine. I'm even missing Sophie and Lisa—although they can be bitches, at the end of the day I'm probably closer to them than to anyone. I mean, I live with them. They're practically family.

But Lauren's someone who could become a real soulmate. Isn't it funny how sometimes you can instantly connect with people? How, despite being almost strangers, you can feel that you have known someone all your life? The ideal is for this to happen with a man, a potential soulmate, life-partner, but it can, honestly, be just as gratifying when it happens with a friend, someone like Lauren.

And thank God I've found her, because the more I think about it the more I realize that it really wouldn't have been much fun, spending so much time on my own, particularly as Brad seems to be starting to take me slightly for granted. I mean, think about it. I've flown all this way to be with him, I've even changed my flight for him, and he hasn't had the decency to take time off work.

Admittedly, he's busy, but he seems to be getting busier and busier with every passing day, which doesn't seem to be exactly fair on me, but before I get too pissed off he is the greatest lover ever, and he is sweet to me. Hell, he loves me, for heaven's sake. What could be better than that?

So I meet Lauren at the gym, and we work out together, which is much more fun than working out alone, and truth to be told I'm starting to get the eensiest, weensiest bit bored with the gym, and on the way out we bump into Jenny, who, it seems, is starting to make an effort.

"This is my friend Lauren," I say to Jenny, partly to be friendly and partly to goad Jenny, to see whether she'd still be rude to a friend of mine. "And this is Jenny."

"Hi," says Lauren with a friendly smile.

"Hi," says Jenny warmly, or at least warmly for her. "Nice to meet you."

"Working hard?" I try, still stuck for conversation with this difficult woman.

"God, it's gone crazy in here," says Jenny, rolling her eyes to the ceiling. "Your poor boyfriend's run off his feet."

Now that is a result. It's the first time Jenny has referred to Brad as my boyfriend, and is this just because Lauren's here or is some of the frostiness disappearing?

"Poor you." I say warmly. "Don't let him work you too hard."

"Don't worry," says Jenny. "It's all part of the job. Anyway, have a good day." She smiles as she disappears, and I turn to Lauren with my jaw practically on the floor.

"Was it my imagination or was she reasonably friendly?"

Lauren shrugs. "She seemed fine to me. Why? Isn't she normally?"

"Maybe it's just me, but the last couple of times we've met she's been the bitch from hell."

"She's probably just jealous of you," says Lauren as we walk to the changing room. "She's not exactly a goddess is she?"

"Yeah, but neither was I, and I know what it's like."

"Have you told her that you used to be like her?"

"I tried, but she didn't want to know."

"It's tough isn't it? Looking at you now, I have a problem believing you used to be fat."

I sigh and run my fingers through my hair. "Me too," I say with an uncomfortable laugh. "But I was, and I know how un-happy it makes you, and I can see so much of me in Jenny."

"What if you tried to help her?"

"I don't think she'd accept it."

"Maybe she's one of those people who's happy the size she is."

"Next you'll be telling me she's got a gland problem."

"Maybe she has."

"Bollocks. The only reason anyone's that size is because they eat too much. Trust me. I know."

"Look," says Lauren. "Why are you getting so worked up about her? She's only Brad's bloody PA isn't she?"

I nod.

"Exactly. She doesn't have anything to do with your life, and, while I admit that it's always a good idea to get their secretaries of PAs or whatever on your side, she seems perfectly fine now, so just relax about it."

"Maybe you're right." And I should relax and I should forget about it, but during lunch, even as I'm laughing with Lauren, and Lauren whoops with joy, I can't quite get Jenny out of my head, and I can't quite figure out why.

"So come over to me at seven tonight, okay?" I scribble down my address.

"Bloody hell," says Lauren, simultaneously taking the piece of paper and looking at her watch. "It's four o'clock! Where on earth did the afternoon go?"

"Who cares," I laugh and kiss her on the cheek. "At least it went. See you later," and I wave as we walk off in opposite directions.

When I get home there's a message from Brad on the answerphone. I call him back, miraculously he's not in a meeting, and he apologizes profusely for not being around in the evening. "What will you do?" he asks.

"I think I'll just pop out for a quick drink with Lauren. What time will you be home?"

"Not late," he says. "Around nine?" It's a question, and I say that's fine.

"I love you, baby," he says, his voice as smooth as honey. "I'll make it up to you."

"That's okay," I say.

"I love you too," I add. As an afterthought.

So I glue myself to the television set for the rest of the afternoon, and finally at six o'clock, I start getting ready to go out, and I know this must sound crazy but I feel more excited than I've felt in ages. I shower, dry my hair, take an incredible amount of time putting on my makeup, and choose a little black number for tonight. "What the hell," I say out loud, modeling in front of the mirror. "Why not?"

At seven on the dot the doorbell rings, and there, on the doorstep, is Lauren, equally done up, and we both laugh.

"Thank God," says Lauren. "I thought I'd gone a bit over the top, but you obviously had the same idea. Now we can go clacking off to take this town by storm."

"Do you think everyone can tell we're English?" We're standing side by side in front of the mirror in the hall.

"Dunno really," says Lauren. "I'd say from the neck up we look like two Californian babes, but from the neck down, tarted up like this, we're as English as tea and scones, which can only be a good thing."

"What do you mean?"

"The Americans love our quaint accent. How posh can you be?"

I put on my best Queen's English accent. "The rain in Spain stays mainly on the plain."

"In Hertford, Hereford, and Hampshire, hurricanes hardly ever happen," says Lauren, and we both give each other high fives in the classic American style.

"Before we go you've got to show me round," says Lauren, already peering round doorways, so I naturally give her the full guided tour.

"I'm not surprised you're staying," says Lauren, when she's inspected every room, every gadget, every appliance. "It's bloody gorgeous."

"You're right," I smile. "It is bloody gorgeous. And I'm bloody lucky."

"That you are," says Lauren, and linking arms we leave the house.

The restaurant's so well hidden from the paparazzi we almost miss the bloody place. Eventually, after trooping up and down the road, Lauren spies a lone doorman standing outside a huge pair of cast-iron doors.

"Maybe that's it?" she says doubtfully, because there are no signs, no windows, nothing.

"Let's go and ask." Where did this new-found confidence come from? We troop up to the doorman, but before we can even open our mouths he has said good evening to us, and swung open the door.

"Are we in the right place?" I whisper, as Lauren strides down the hallway through to the double doors at the end.

"I bloody well hope so," she whispers back. "I haven't got the nerve to ask, it sounds so naff. We'll soon find out," she says, pushing open the next set of doors, and, sure enough, we step into the restaurant. At least I hope it's *the* restaurant. It could be any restaurant, except when we look at the other side of the room we see a huge, stainless-steel bar running along the whole length of one wall, and we know this must be it. Even this early in the evening there are scores of people crowded around, all busy talking to one another and scouring the room at the same time, just to check that someone more interesting hasn't arrived.

"Thank God," says Lauren with a sigh. "This, finally, feels like home. In fact, if I close my eyes I could almost pretend I'm in Saint."

"Saint?"

"You must know Saint. The bar?"

"Oh of course," I lie. "Saint."

"Please allow me to buy you a drink," says a smooth, swarthy man with chiseled cheekbones and come-to-bed eyes.

"No, thank you." I drag Lauren away before she gets the chance to completely melt away. "We're fine," and I pull her to the other end of the bar.

"What did you do that for?" pouts Lauren. "He was delicious."

"He was disgusting! Lauren, for God's sake, talk about being in love with himself."

"With those cheekbones I'd be in love with myself too," she says, looking over my shoulder and trying to find the guy, trying to give him meaningful eye signals.

"You can do much better than that," I say purposefully, leaning over the bar and trying to catch the bartender's attention, which doesn't take long at all because he's staring at Lauren like it's his birthday, Christmas, and Thanksgiving all rolled into one. "Ladies," he says, with a well-practiced smile. "What can I get you?"

"Phwooargh," whispers Lauren, eyes glued to his well-muscled torso as he pours us cocktails, and, I have to say, she has a point. "Now he's much more my type."

"You are incorrigible!" I laugh, but if I didn't have my gorgeous Brad I'd be thinking the same thing.

"It's all right for you," says Lauren, reading my mind. "You've got a man. And he's divine. I've only had the crap-in-bed Charlie, and I'm still on the lookout."

"Can you just try and make it a bit less obvious?" I whisper. "Nothing puts a man off more than a woman who's desperate." I'm interrupted by the bartender, who places the drinks in front of us and holds Lauren's eye for about twenty seconds longer than is altogether necessary.

"What were you saying about men being put off?" smirks Lauren, sipping from her cocktail and checking out the bartender's bottom.

"Oh shut up! Cheers."

"Here's to men!" says Lauren, clinking her glass to mine.

"Here's to friendship!" I say.

"Here's to both!" And we take a good, long swig.

The cocktails are a lot stronger than Jemima and Lauren realized, and two hours later they're both rip-roaringly drunk. Men surround them all evening, and Jemima, despite despairing of Lauren's hunting earlier on, is having the time of her life.

Never has she felt more beautiful, more desirable, and she's flirting and laughing as if she's looked this way, had this much attention, all her life.

"I've gotta have a piss," says Lauren, half falling off her stool and stumbling off into the distance. Funny, she thinks, as she holds the door open for a girl who looks very familiar as she scuttles off with her head down. "Isn't that girl that Jenny?" But no, she thinks. It can't be. What would someone like that be doing among all these beautiful people here?

At 10:30 Jemima looks at her watch. "Shit!" she shouts. "I'm supposed to be home."

"Don't worry about it," giggles Lauren. "Play the *Rules*! Be hard to get for a little while!"

"I've got to go," says Jemima, who's slightly more sober than Lauren, "and you'd better go too."

"No!" says Lauren, banging her fist on the table to emphasize her point, except she misses the table and ends up banging her thigh. "We're staying," except it comes out "shtaying."

"Nope." Jemima gets up and pulls Lauren to her feet. "I'm putting you in a taxi."

"Just give me one sec. Oh shit. Shit." She turns to Jemima. "What's my phone number?"

"I don't know," says Jemima. "Can we just go?"

"Not until you've looked up my phone number."

Jemima digs out her address book and shows Lauren her phone number, and as Lauren tries to focus on it she shouts the number out to the bartender, who's hovering nearby with pen and paper in hand.

"Got it," he mouths. "I'll call you."

"All right," says Lauren, as the pair stagger out. "Well would you bloody believe it? Now *that's* what I call a result."

Amazing how quickly you can sober up when there's a crisis. Not that Jemima's having a crisis exactly, it's just that she expected Brad to be home waiting for her. She didn't expect to come home to an empty house.

"Brad?" she calls, after fumbling at the door with the key for what feels like hours. She manages to get in, dumps her bag, and slowly climbs up the stairs. "Sweetie?" she says softly, pushing open the bedroom door. "Oh," she says, seeing the bed's empty. She checks every room in the house, but he's not there, and she's not feeling good about this. Not feeling good at all.

Why does everyone else seem to have a hangover the next day, whereas I get the headache, the nausea, later on that very same evening? There's only one thing for it, coffee, and, trying very hard to focus on everything in the kitchen, I make myself a strong black coffee, which, fifteen minutes after drinking, seems to have the desired effect and I feel a lot more sober than when I first walked in.

But where the hell is Brad? Didn't he say he'd be home around nine? Why isn't he here? The more I think about it, the more I start worrying that something terrible's happened, because for all his busyness, he's not unreliable, he wouldn't just turn up late, not when he knows I'm waiting. Surely.

Car crash? Accident? What? Where is Brad and why isn't he home? I check my watch again. It's 11 P.M., two hours after he said he'd be home. Maybe he came home, realized I wasn't here and went out again. He'll be home any minute. I'll wait up for him.

But by midnight there's still no sign of him and now I'm starting to feel sick with worry. If I were at home I'd know what to do, but here I don't even know what the hospitals are called, and anyway I'm probably being silly, maybe something came up.

I get into bed and watch television to try and take my mind off things, but every time I hear something, some little noise, my ears prick up and I expect to hear his key in the lock. Except I don't. So I keep flicking, and suddenly I find myself watching a travel program, the featured destination today being London, and this huge wave of homesickness washes over me as the camera pans over Big Ben, the Thames, the Houses of Parliament.

Ben works near there, near the Thames, near the South Bank. I wonder what Ben's doing now? And that's my very last thought before falling fast asleep.

chapter 25

I thought my hangover would be over by this morning, I thought the headache and nausea of last night was it. Jesus, was I wrong. It takes me a few seconds to orient myself, to re-member where I am, why my head's pounding, and then, when I roll over and see the other half of the bed hasn't been slept in, I start to feel even more sick and I remember that Brad didn't come home last night, and by the looks of things he hasn't been home at all.

My heart starts to pound, and a wave of nausea washes over me as I shake my head, trying to clear it, to work out what is going on. And then I hear noises from the kitchen, plates clash-ing together, the scrape of cutlery.

I pull on a dressing gown, and, with hand to my head to protect my hangover from any more of the brutal noise from the other end of the house, I slowly make my way to the kitchen and stand quietly in the doorway, watching Brad, won-dering what to do next, what to say.

He's humming to himself as he stirs scrambled eggs on the stove, and on the counter next to him is a wooden breakfast tray, immaculately laid for breakfast for one. There's a basket of muffins, a glass of orange juice, coffee, and a vase filled with huge, dewy red roses.

What is all this about? I don't say anything for a while. Just lean against the door frame watching him, and after a few seconds Brad turns round and jumps as he sees me.

"Hi, baby," he says, coming over to kiss me on the lips, and I can't do this, I can't pretend that everything's okay when it quite obviously isn't. I feel as if he's broken my trust so I turn my head away, leaving Brad to skim my cheek.

"I'm sorry," he says. "I am so sorry about last night."

"What happened?" Even I'm surprised at how cold my voice is. How stern. "Where were you?"

"The meeting just went on and on, and it was so late I ended up sleeping at the office."

"Where in the office?"

"I swear," says Brad, seeing that I don't believe him. "I slept on the couch in the lobby. The maids couldn't believe it when they walked in this morning."

"Why didn't you phone, at least let me know where you were?" It comes out like a whine and I have to remember to be more angry, less pleading.

"I knew you were going out, and by the time the meeting finished it was so late I didn't want to worry you."

"So you just let me think you'd been in a car crash or something?"

"Oh I'm sorry, baby, I didn't think for a moment you'd be that worried. I figured you'd be fast asleep and by the time you woke up in the morning I'd be home."

"I can't believe you've been this selfish." Careful, careful. I don't really want to be angry, because this is the first time I've ever had a proper boyfriend, and look how gorgeous he is, and if I really do lose my temper I might scare him away, and if that happened what would happen to me?

"JJ, I'm sorry. You're right, I was selfish, but it won't happen again, I promise you." Brad looks sorry, he looks like he means it, and with his head hung low he looks so contrite, so like a little boy, so completely vulnerable and gorgeous, I have to forgive him. What else can I do?

I know you probably think I shouldn't forgive him, I should make him feel guilty a bit longer, but the story is plausible enough as long as you don't look too deeply, and I don't want to look too deeply, I want to believe him. Despite the fact that more and more problems with this relationship seem to be emerging every day, I want to at least pretend that everything's rosy, because look at us. We look so good together. We're the perfect couple.

"Okay," I say, shrugging.

"Okay?" His face lights up. "Does that mean I'm forgiven?"

"I suppose so."

"God, I love you, JJ," he says, putting his arms around me and kissing me on the nape of the neck, the one place he knows is guaranteed to send shivers shooting down my spine.

I lean into him, smelling his smell, feeling the light stubble on his face with my cheek, and slowly I allow myself to feel better. Brad circles my back lightly, moving his hand slowly down until it's sliding in between my legs, and I can't help the small gasp that comes out of my mouth, and then the pair of us are sliding down the wall to the kitchen floor, and soon the breakfast has been forgotten, and the only sounds emerging from the kitchen are our soft whispers and groans of pleasure.

"I do love you," I say to him afterwards, after possibly the best sex we've ever had, when I'm feeling guilty at making him feel guilty, when he obviously loves me so much. "And I'm sorry for being a bitch."

Oh Jemima, stop being such a wimp, you weren't a bitch in the slightest. Perhaps you should have been, but more importantly you offered Brad the information that you love him, and you said it first, it wasn't a reply to him. Do you really, Jemima? Do you really love him?

Lying on that floor, feeling the muscles in his back, for the first time Jemima starts to believe that she might love him, that everything may well work out after all.

"I'm taking the day off today," says Brad, as he goes in to take his shower. "I want to spend the whole day with you, with no interruptions." He kisses my shoulder blade as I walk past him, naked, to the bedroom, with, and you'll be very glad to hear this, no inhibitions whatsoever.

"Really? The whole day?"

"Really," he says, turning away. "I thought we could have lunch, maybe go blading later. Whatever you'd like."

"I'd love that. I don't mind where we go, as long as I'm with you. The only thing I have to do is get started on the column I was telling you about. Maybe we could go star-spotting? I've got to work out exactly what I'm going to write about."

"Celebrity gossip is the last thing you should be worrying about in this town," Brad says with a smile. "All you have to do is pick up a copy of *Daily Variety* and the *Hollywood Reporter* and you've got everything you need."

"Well." I'm doubtful. "Maybe if we got back in the afternoon I could do some work later on."

"Good," he says, closing the bathroom door. "That sounds perfect. I'm just going to take a shower. Won't be long."

The phone rings as I'm lying dreamily on the bed, going over every inch of Brad's body in my mind. I don't normally pick up the phone here, it still feels a bit strange, answering the phone in a house that isn't yours, but Brad's in the shower, and there seems little point in letting the machine pick up. It might be important.

All I hear is a long groan then, "JJ, it's me, Lauren. Just tell me, are you feeling as disgusting as me?"

I laugh. "No, not even a fraction as disgusting as you. You had far more than me to drink, remember?"

Lauren groans again. "I wish I *could* remember. I can't remember a bloody thing. How did we get home?"

I tell her about our ride home in the taxi, about her leaning out of the window and singing old Abba songs at the top of her voice, about her very nearly throwing up in the backseat.

"I really disgraced myself didn't I?" she says.

"Absolutely!"

"Really?" Lauren's voice picks up. "Tell me, tell me. Did I give out my phone number to any gorgeous men?"

"Actually, you did. You screamed it from one side of the restaurant to the other for the bartender, but I think every man in the place was writing it down."

"Oh my God! It's coming back to me. The bartender, I remember the bartender! Was he as handsome as I think he was?"

"You are a complete nightmare!" I laugh. "Yes, he was as handsome as you remember. You scored better than me."

"You weren't out to score. You've got the gorgeous Brad. So was he tucked up in bed wondering what you were up to?"

"No, he wasn't." I don't know whether to tell Lauren or not, because I've got a sneaky feeling I know what she'd say, which would, in fact, probably be the same thing Geraldine would say. In other words, they'd both tell me to be careful, not to accept things at face value, not to believe him, and, stupid as this may sound, I don't want to hear this right now, I want to believe everything's fine, that he was telling the truth.

I listen to check the water's still running, Brad's in the shower so he won't be able to hear, and then I tell a tiny white lie. "He wasn't in when I got back, his meeting ran on, but he came home when I was in bed." Not quite a lie, I just omitted the fact that it happened to be this morning.

"Hmm," says Lauren. "How late was he?"

"Not very. Everything's fine. I'm not worried so why should you be?"

"Okay. If everything's fine with you then it's fine with me. So what are you up to today? How about lunch?"

"I can't today, Brad's taken the day off work and we're going out."

"Sounds like a guilty man to me." Now that's exactly what I didn't want to hear.

"Sounds like a man in love to me," I say with a false ring of confidence, hoping to convince her, hoping to convince myself.

"Well, have a good day," says Lauren. "Don't worry about me, all by myself."

"Come with!" I say, trying to sound as if I mean it, because even though I think Lauren's fantastic, I'm so looking forward to spending a whole day with Brad, just the two of us, on our own, I don't mean it at all. "I'd love you to come with and Brad won't mind, he'd love to meet you!" Which isn't exactly true, because Brad has shown surprisingly little interest in what I do or who I meet when I'm not with him.

"Yes," says Lauren, with a hint of sarcasm in her voice. "Because I really love playing third wheel."

"You wouldn't be." Even I can hear that I don't sound sincere. "Brad and I aren't like that."

"Brad and I. There you go. That's a sure sign if ever there was one."

"So you're not coming?" I think I've just about managed to hide the relief.

"Nope. But thanks, JJ, it's really nice of you to ask me."

"Will you be okay? What are you going to do?"

"I might catch a movie this afternoon. Oh, hang on, my call waiting's going."

I sit on the phone and wait. And wait. And wait. I hate this, I hate people who leave you hanging on the line for hours. Just as I'm about to put the phone down Lauren comes back.

"JJ? Oh my God! I'm so sorry, but that was him! He called!"

"Who?"

"Bill! The bartender!"

"And?"

"And I now have plans for today. We're meeting for lunch."

"Just behave yourself," I laugh. "We don't want you getting into trouble."

"I will. Behave, that is. I don't plan on getting into trouble just yet."

We both laugh and say goodbye as Brad walks out of the bathroom.

"Who was that?"

"Lauren."

"Who's Lauren?" Typical. That's how much attention Brad has been paying to my life.

"Brad!" I hit him playfully. "You know exactly who Lauren is. She's my new friend, the one I met at the Broadway Deli, the one I was out with last night."

"I totally forgot you went out with her last night. Where did you go?" Brad's toweling his hair as he talks.

"We went to that new restaurant on Main Street."

Brad stops toweling for a second then starts again, but slower, more thoughtfully. "Which restaurant?" he asks, his voice sounding slightly strained.

"The Pepper," I tell him. "It was fantastic."

"Oh," says Brad, picking up speed.

"Have you been there?" I ask.

"Is this a trick question?" Brad asks, putting down the towel, and maybe I'm going crazy but I could swear he's paled underneath his golden tan.

"What on earth do you mean?" I ask, trying to work out whether he has gone pale, and if he has, why.

"You know I've been there," he says carefully.

"No, I don't," I say, completely bewildered, I mean, what is going on here?

"I thought I told you I went there."

"No, silly," I laugh, relieved that I must have been imagining it, that there's nothing sinister going on. "You didn't."

"Oh, I thought I did," Brad says, adding, "I went on the opening night."

"Nope, you didn't tell me that. Fabulous isn't it?" I say, sitting down at the dressing table and picking up a hairbrush.

"Mmmm," says Brad, as he crosses the room, takes the hairbrush from my hand and stands behind me, watching me in the mirror as he brushes my hair.

"That feels so nice," I murmur, as I close my eyes.

"It's supposed to," says Brad, as a thump down the hall makes us both start.

"Mail," he says, putting down the brush, and a few seconds later he calls out, "JJ, there's something here for you."

"For me?" What could have come for me? I feel a buzz of excitement as I run down the hall to the front door, where Brad hands me a letter addressed in Geraldine's distinctive handwriting.

"It's from my friend Geraldine in London," I tell Brad, who's not really listening, and I smile as I rip open the envelope and draw out these newspaper pages. I read the compliments slip and laugh, thinking that Geraldine never changes, and wondering how she's getting on with the Top Tips column, and then I open the pages that are clipped on to the slip, wondering what they are.

"Jesus Christ!" My hand starts shaking and I have to put my hand over my heart to stop it pounding.

"What's the matter?" Brad looks at me in alarm.

"Nothing, nothing."

Brad walks over and looks at what's written on the pages. "Who's Ben Williams?" he says.

"Just someone I used to work with." I can't take my eyes off the page, I scan all the pictures, read the headlines, go back to the pictures. It's Ben. My beloved Ben. Oh my God, I'm not supposed to feel like this. I look at Brad in alarm, but his back's turned to me, he doesn't see the expression on my face. So I stand there and I start to read, with my heart tumbling around at the sight of the man I thought I'd forgotten about or, at the very least, put firmly in my past.

"Sure he's not some old boyfriend of yours?" Brad's smiling, but I don't return the smile, I can't look up from the pictures of Ben, and I don't say anything at all, I just walk into the bedroom and collapse on to the bed, trying to stop the pages trembling as I devour every single word.

I'm not entirely sure how I manage to calm down, but I do, and I even resist the urge to pick up the phone and call Geraldine. I'm not sure how I feel. Confused might be the best description. I really thought I was over Ben, I really thought that I'd finally found happiness with Brad, and that I'd always think Ben was good-looking but that it would be in an objective way, that it wouldn't actually affect me personally.

And I'm confused because I can't believe that the mere sight of him, simply reading about a man whom I know, a man I thought I once loved, can make me feel like the Jemima Jones of old, the Jemima Jones I thought I'd said goodbye to.

But Ben's not here, I tell myself, and even if he were there would be no guarantees. Okay, so I look completely different, but he was never interested in the past, he probably wouldn't be interested now.

And I look at Brad, at this huge, golden lion of a man, and I know that he could have his pick of women, but he has chosen me, which must mean I'm very lucky. And okay, sometimes I worry that maybe we don't have as much in common as perhaps we should, and occasionally I do find myself comparing him to Ben and, apart from the looks front, he seems to fail pretty miserably, which is why I try not to do it all that often, and we may not have the same sort of teasing friendship I had with Ben, but then Ben never wanted me and Brad does.

And he is good to me, he treats me well. Okay, so last night he slipped up, but work is work, and I have to try and understand that side of his life. I am lucky. I must be. I mean, look at him.

Oh yes. One more thing. The sex, of course, is amazing.

And we do have a blissful day. We go for a long, leisurely walk right up to the end of the Santa Monica pier, where we sit on a bench facing the ocean, and Brad tries to persuade me to ride on the Ferris wheel, but I decline because I'd feel too much like a tourist and right now I'm trying to feel like a native, like Brad's wife, and, considering it's only been four and a half weeks, I think I'm doing a pretty good job.

We walk back along the pier, hand in hand, and I smile to myself as I watch the other women watching Brad, and Brad makes me laugh when he points out one bizarrely dressed woman and whispers, "Would you look at that? What *is* she wearing? God, cowboy boots with those awful legs and that dreadful miniskirt."

And I try very hard to shove Ben to the very back of my mind, I try to keep reminding myself how lucky I am to have a man like Brad.

We kick around in the ocean like a couple of kids, yelling and screaming as we splash one another with water, and then, after smooching in the sand to yells of encouragement from a group of boys sitting around a boom box, we continue walking until we hit Shutters on the Beach, according to Brad the best hotel in the area.

We walk through the lobby and it is beautiful. The polished wooden floors, the overstuffed white damask sofas, the beautiful bowls of fresh roses that sit on the antique furniture, and we walk through to sit on the terrace overlooking the water, feasting on delicious food, feasting on one another.

And after lunch we go back home, pick up the car, and Brad drives me up to the Pacific Palisades, where we park the car and take a two-hour hike into the mountains. Now this, breathing in the clean, fresh air and striding alongside my gorgeous man, is what life should be about.

And when we get back we share a bath, and naturally one thing leads to another and we end up having frantic wet, soapy foreplay in the bathtub, when the phone rings.

"Leave it," I murmur, just on the brink of orgasm.

"I can't," moans Brad, standing up and going to the phone in the bedroom, as I groan and roll over. "Hello?" I hear him say. "Oh, hi." There's a silence for a bit, while I assume he's listening to someone and I pull a towel off the rail and wrap it around myself, still basking in the delicious glow of afterlove, and wondering how on earth I could have missed out on this incredible feeling for so many years. And then, I know this is crazy, but I'm sure I hear Brad whispering.

Eventually he puts the phone down, but he doesn't come back to the bathroom, he goes to the kitchen, so I follow him in there wondering whether I'm going mad.

"Who was on the phone?" I say, trying to make it sound like a casual inquiry.

"The phone? Oh, just work."

"Why were you whispering?"

He looks at me as if I *am* crazy. "What are you talking about?" he says. "I wasn't whispering." And I believe him.

We would have thought this strange. Actually, we probably would have thought it a hell of a lot more than strange, but Jemima doesn't think like this. Jemima refuses to think like this, and when Brad leaves, half an hour later, to sort out a problem at work, he tells her he loves her and she believes it.

And when she eventually sits down at Brad's desk to do some work of her own, she reads the piece about Ben Williams again. Ben was a fantasy, she thinks. Brad's a reality. I'm much happier with Brad than I could ever have been with Ben, and with that she opens the *Hollywood Reporter* and starts scouring the page for stories.

chapter 26

Ben meant to call Jemima, really he did, but when you're a celebrity and you have a work schedule that means you're working pretty much all the time, and when you're not working you're going to launches or opening supermarkets or giving interviews to the press, it's very easy to forget to do things like call old friends.

It's even easier to forget to call them when you're good-looking and single and you've slept with your boss, which seems to have caused the two of you to have entirely different reactions. You think it's the biggest mistake of your life and you're trying to forget about it, but your boss is spending all her time trying to figure out how to orchestrate a repeat experience.

For the last three months one of the producers on the show, Simon, has been trying to arrange an interview with Alexia Aldridge, the hottest actress in Hollywood. The producer and his team of researchers have made hundreds of phone calls to her agent, her publicist, her assistant. They've sent hundreds of faxes, promising her huge amounts of airtime, promising to pay for her flight, her accommodation, if only they can have an exclusive interview when her new film opens in London.

The agent said yes, it was a good idea, could they put it on a fax, which they did. They never heard from him again, despite sending numerous additional faxes. The publicist for the film said yes, it was a good idea, could they put it on a fax, which they did. They never heard from her again. The assistant said yes, it was a good idea, the best person to talk to was the publicist. The publicist, when they finally managed to get hold of her, apologized for not getting back and said she'd spoken to Alexia, who would love to do it, it's just that things were a bit busy at the moment, and perhaps they should talk to the film publicist nearer the time. This time the film publicist said yes, it was a good idea, and thousands of faxes later they had agreed a time, a date, and a place, not mutually convenient, merely convenient for Ms. Aldridge.

There was just one problem, and this problem was becoming Diana Macpherson's problem. Alexia had been in London recently, and she happened to have watched *London Nights*. There was only one person she'd allow to interview her. Ben Williams. Who else?

Under normal circumstances, the production team at *London Nights* would have told Alexia Aldridge that the interview was going to be done by their showbiz reporter—funnily enough, the job that Ben was doing when she spotted him—and that it would be impossible for the main presenter to do it.

But Alexia Aldridge rarely gives interviews. Not quite in the same league, or the same age, as Streisand, nevertheless she is something of an enigma, and that she has agreed to talk at all makes it something of a worldwide scoop, irrespective of what she may or may not actually reveal.

And Diana Macpherson, who should be over the moon at this brilliant coup, is actually not very happy. Not happy at all. Usually she would be buying champagne for the whole crew, but just recently she has started to think more about her personal life. She's started watching mothers in the park, and once or twice she's even stopped to coo at particularly attractive babies. Diana Macpherson has never thought of herself as a woman, more of a working machine, but for some strange reason she's started fantasizing of late about relationships, marriage, babies.

Not sex. That's always available when you're as powerful as her, but Diana wants more than just sex now, and, despite initially targeting Ben as a new shag, Diana now sees him in a completely different light. Diana now thinks that Ben might just be the man she's been looking for. And think what beautiful babies he'd make. She does. Frequently.

And she was convinced that she pulled it off the other night. Ben may have been trying to avoid her ever since—or is that her imagination—but it must have meant something to him, and anyway, she forgives him because after all, he is young, he doesn't yet know what's good for him. And Diana Macpherson would be very good for him. In every way.

The last thing she wants is to send Ben to Los Angeles, but it looks as if, this time, she really has no other choice.

So now we can understand why she's not happy. Plus, of course, there's the additional problem of finding someone to replace Ben while he spends the better part of a week in America. Plus there is the cost of sending an entire film crew to the other side of the world. Plus she could be left with egg all over her face if Alexia Aldridge changes her mind, or decides to clam up on film. And Alexia Aldridge is young, single, and tremendously beautiful. But no, Diana tells herself, she might want Ben to interview her, but she'd never bother getting involved with someone as lowly as a television presenter from England.

Allow me to let you into a little secret here to help you fully understand why Diana is allowing Ben to slip from her grasp. Diana Macpherson is scared of one thing. Ratings. Diana Macpherson has reached her position of power by being clever, by making good moves, and securing an exclusive interview with Alexia Aldridge, albeit a very expensive one, is a good move, and she's not about to let her get away, even if it means letting Ben Williams get away. Temporarily.

So Diana calls Ben into her office to tell him the news, and ignores the fact that Ben walks in looking as if he's been called into a torture chamber.

"We've got the interview with Alexia Aldridge," she tells him.

"Great," says Ben, looking at the door and wondering how quickly he can get out of there.

"But she'll only do it on one condition."

"Hmm?"

"That you do the interview."

"Okay. Fine," says Ben, standing up and getting ready to go. "Is that all?"

"No, Ben. Sit down. She can't fly over here because she's getting ready to start her next film, which means we have to fly you over there."

"Over where?" Now Ben's interested.

"Los Angeles."

His face lights up. "I've never been to Los Angeles! God, how exciting."

"It's not going to be fun, Ben," Diana says sternly. "I'm sending you out in two weeks' time with Simon and a film crew. You're there to work, and it will be hard work. And"—she pauses—"I want the best fucking interview I've ever seen. Got that?" Diana, hackles raised at Ben's rejection, is being more professional than Ben has ever seen her.

"Yes, Diana," he says meekly. "I'll deliver the goods."

"I bet that's what you say to all the girls," she says, smiling, unable to resist the temptation to flirt just a little.

Shit, thinks Ben, who just smiles sweetly, laughs at her little joke, and backs out of the office.

He runs over to Simon. "Have you heard?" he says, enthusiasm and excitement written all over his face.

"Yeah. Bloody brilliant isn't it?"

"But we're there to work, Simon, and it will be fucking hard work." Ben does an impersonation of Diana that's frighteningly accurate, and Simon falls about laughing.

"Fuck that, mate," he says. "It's gonna be interview in a day, then birds and booze the rest of the week."

"Simon," says Ben, in a serious tone. "You're a man after my own heart."

Ben spends the rest of the day trying to keep his excitement in check. "Lucky bastard," says each researcher as they pass his desk, for Ben is not a celebrity to them, he is merely a work colleague, someone to have a laugh with. By mid-afternoon he's calm enough to get some work done, and he spends the rest of the day plowing through press cuttings about Alexia Aldridge. If he weren't such an avid video-watcher he'd have to start watching her films, but luckily for Ben he's seen them all, and the only thing he has to do tonight is phone Richard to make him green with envy.

The two weeks have flown by for Ben. The night before he's due to leave, while he's throwing clothes into a suitcase, he suddenly remembers Jemima. Should he call her now? Will she still be in Los Angeles? Should he tell her he's coming? No, he decides, he'll take a chance and surprise her when he gets there.

Coincidence perhaps? This mini-excursion of Ben's might seem little more than another coincidence, particularly given that, thanks to Geraldine, Ben has stomped back into Jemima's consciousness with a bang, but maybe it is more than that. Maybe fate is finally working to give Ben and Jemima the happiness for which they've both longed, the happiness they each thought they'd found, Ben in his dream job, Jemima in her dream man.

Perhaps neither of them has been quite as fulfilled as they'd hoped, and perhaps fate will sort that out once and for all. On the other hand, that could be quite wrong. Ben and Jemima might miss each other completely. After all, Ben's going to be doing all that hard work, and he's only there for a few days. And Jemima may make it work with Brad, because on the face of it he certainly looks like her dream man, but at this precise moment in time Jemima Jones isn't having a particularly good day. Admittedly, these things are relative, and perhaps it is just because yesterday, the day she spent with Brad, was so perfect that she was bound to be on a bit of a downer today.

At least she's found some stories. She's just putting the finishing touches to her column, for which she's managed to cobble together stuff from the local papers, together with a review of the Pepper, and as she finishes reading it she decides that actually it's quite good after all. If you didn't know, you'd never dream that Jemima was spending most of the time on her own, because Jemima has painted Los Angeles as the epitome of glamour and excitement. Which I suppose it can be. It's just that it isn't like that for her.

When she finishes she puts her head in her hands and sighs, thinking about what happened earlier today, when she went to the gym, wondering why on earth Jenny seems to blow so hot and cold.

"Hi, Jenny," I said, when I passed her in the hallway. Jenny ignored me.

"Jenny?" That's it. I'm not taking this shit anymore, and I stopped feeling sorry for her a long time ago. Well, this morning, anyway. Jenny turned round with a sigh.

"What?" Jenny said, sounding bored.

"What exactly is your problem?" I'd had enough and I was determined not to let her get away with this.

"I'm really likely to share my problems with *you*," Jenny said sarcastically.

"Look, I'm really trying to be friendly, and you're just—"—I was practically spluttering with rage—"bloody rude."

"Bloody rude am I? Well I don't remember anyone saying I had to be nice to you."

"I'm your boss's girlfriend, for God's sake, it's not that you have to, it's just that I've never done anything to hurt you and it would be nice if you were nice."

"Being Brad's *girlfriend*," Jenny said, putting a nasty emphasis on the word, "means shit, as far as I'm concerned. You think you can fly over here, with your blond hair and your skinny legs, and just take over. Well you can't."

"What the hell are you talking about? I'm not trying to take over, I'm only in here once a day."

"Forget it," said Jenny, shaking her head. "I don't like you, and I'm never gonna like you. Let's just leave it at that." And she started walking away.

"No." I couldn't help myself, I grabbed her arm. "I won't just leave it at that."

Jenny looked with disdain at my hand on her arm before shaking it off, marching back up to me and saying very slowly, "Why don't you just go screw yourself." She stood for a few seconds, evidently enjoying the shock on my face, and then she walked off, leaving me standing there shaking like a leaf.

If I'd been able to find Brad I would have told him what had happened, told him to sort it out, fire her, something, but Brad wasn't around, and Lauren wasn't at home, and I've just had to live with this all day, and yes, I'm upset. I'm hurt and upset that someone should hate me for no reason at all, and even though I've chucked all those plans for befriending Jenny out the window, I hate confrontation. However, I can only be pushed so far, and this, as far as I'm now concerned, means war.

I go to the kitchen, where I pour myself a Diet Coke, and then I walk back into the bedroom, climb on the bed and reach for the remote control, but, as I reach across, the glass tips over and spills Diet Coke all over the white linen sheets.

Shit! I run to the kitchen for the cloth, but no amount of wiping seems to get rid of the stain and I know Brad will go mad because he likes everything to be perfect, but do I know where the sheets are? Do I hell. In a total panic I desperately search the hall cupboards, the bathroom cupboards, the bedroom armoire for spare sheets, but I can't find anything, so eventually, feeling faintly ridiculous, I pick up the phone and dial the gym.

"Charlene? It's JJ. I'm fine. You? Is Brad there? Oh? He's in a meeting? Can you do me a favor, can you just ask him where the clean sheets are, it's an emergency." I wait for a few minutes, watching the stain, mentally urging Charlene to hurry up.

"In the cupboard at the top of the wardrobe?" I look around the bedroom and see where she means. "That's great, Charlene. Thanks. Yes, you have a good day too," and I put the phone down, and just as I'm about to get up the bloody phone rings again and it's Lauren.

"I've just spilled Diet Coke everywhere, can I call you back? I've got to change the sheets."

"Bugger the sheets," says Lauren. "I've got to tell you about my day from heaven. I'm in love." She starts to tell me all about "Bill the horny bartender" and screw the sheets, this is much more important, this is my friend for God's sake and the sheets will have to wait.

"You know those times when you meet someone and everything is absolutely perfect?" Lauren asks me.

"You mean, like it was with Charlie?"

"No," laughs Lauren. "I mean like when you're a teenager and you have these incredibly romantic experiences which feel like something out of a film, and sex is never really an issue because neither of you is doing it yet."

"Yes." And I sort of understand what she's trying to say, even though I never experienced anything of the sort when I was a teenager. My teenage experiences were confined to comfort eating and not being invited to the parties that all the cool people were invited to.

"I swear, that's what it was like with Bill. We just had the most perfect day," sighs Lauren. "We met up for a coffee first at that place on, I think it's Second Street, the Interactive Café?"

"Yes," I nod. "I know the one."

"And then we went for a walk along the beach, and I felt like a teenager again, we were splashing around in the sea like a couple of kids."

I smile, because Brad and I were doing exactly the same thing, probably at exactly the same time.

"And then we went for lunch."

"Don't tell me you went to Shutters on the Beach."

"No," says Lauren, bemused. "Why would we go there?"

"Don't worry about it. So where did you go?"

Lauren continues telling me, and, trying hard not to worry about the stain, I encourage her with snorts of laughter and approval, and then after a few seconds I vaguely become aware that those bleeps that have been bleeping for the last few seconds don't mean the phone is faulty, they mean call waiting.

"Hang on," I interrupt Lauren. "I've got another call coming through. How do I work this bloody thing?"

Lauren explains, and I do as she says and press the buttons she tells me to.

"Hello?"

"Still me," says Lauren.

"Shit. Hang on, let me try again."

"Hello?"

"Nope, still me."

"Oh, I give up. It's probably someone really boring for Brad anyway. I'll just ignore it, carry on telling me what happened." And Lauren does.

What Jemima could never know is that the person trying to get through is Brad. Brad who has lost all his cool, calm, Californian composure. Brad who at this moment is in a blind panic, and is frantically redialing his number, only to be told the person is on the other line and his call will be answered shortly. Which it isn't. "For fuck's sake, pick up the goddamned phone!" he screams, drawing worried glances from the staff who are milling around outside his office.

"Oh shit!" he shouts, grabbing his car keys and running for the door.

"Brad?" says Jenny, who's been having a meeting with him about new marketing plans. "Brad? What's the matter?" She stands up, obviously worried, and puts a hand on his arm, but Brad ignores her and just keeps running.

He tears out of the building, jumps in his car and puts his foot down. Ignoring the pedestrians, ignoring his fellow drivers, ignoring the speed limits, Brad shoots off, looking suspiciously like he's about to have a heart attack.

"All right, darling," says Lauren. "I'll see you tomorrow."

"Do you know where he's taking you tonight?"

"No, and I don't care. Can you believe he's changed his shift for me? Thank you, Lord, for finally introducing me to a decent man."

"I don't want to put a damper on things," I say, putting a damper on things, "but doesn't this sound vaguely familiar? I mean, what if he's crap in bed?"

"He won't be," says Lauren. "You can always tell what a man's going to be like by the way he kisses, and he's the best kisser in the world."

"I thought Charlie was a good kisser."

"Yeuch, eurgh, yeuch." Lauren makes choking, vomiting noises down the phone as I start laughing. "I was lying. Charlie was a crap kisser."

"Brad's a great kisser."

"Yeah, well. He would be."

"What do you mean?"

"Someone that good-looking must have had loads of practice."

"He's not the promiscuous type," I say indignantly.

"I didn't mean that. I just meant he probably spent all his time at school making out behind the bike sheds. Do you think they have bike sheds here?"

"Nah. I think they probably did it under those things you watch baseball on."

"What? Oh, you mean those bench things."

"Mmm. I think they're called bleachers or something."

"You're probably right. So what are you up to tonight?"

"Don't know. But whatever it is it won't be nearly as exciting as your night."

"I hope you're right," says Lauren, laughing. "Listen, I've gotta go. I've got legs to wax, facials to prepare, mustaches to bleach."

"You haven't got a mustache!"

"Ah ha! It works then?"

"You're going to do it aren't you?"

"You bet your damn life I am. I'm fed up with playing hard to get and then discovering they can't satisfy you when it's too late. This time round I'm going to make sure he's good at sex right from the beginning."

"Just make sure you use a condom."

"Condom? This is California, babe. I'm cutting the fingers off Marigold gloves and using those instead!"

I snort with laughter at the thought. "Have a good time."

"I will! I'll call you first thing." And we both say goodbye, and I look at the stain again, which, much to my horror, looks as if it may well have seeped through to the mattress. I go over to the cupboard in a panic and reach up to try and open the door, but I can't quite reach it, so I drag the chair by the dressing table over, and, balancing precariously on the chair, I just about manage to get the door open.

I reach into the cupboard then cover my head with my arms because a pile of stuff comes out, just missing me, to land on the floor.

"Ouch," I shout, because it didn't quite miss me, a magazine caught me on my forehead and it bloody well hurts. Right, sheets. I can see them at the bottom and I carefully pull one out before climbing off the chair to gather up the stuff that's now on the floor.

What is all this shit anyway? I start picking up the papers, and then something catches my eye and I kick some papers aside with my foot to see what it is. And I freeze.

No. This cannot be happening. For a few moments the whole world seems to stand still, and I have to close my eyes because maybe, maybe, this is a bad dream and when I open them again this *stuff* will have disappeared and I won't have to deal with it because I'm not sure whether I can, I'm not sure whether I'm experienced enough, or strong enough, and even if I were I don't know whether I could, and oh fuck. Why me. Why is this happening to me?

And I open my eyes and it's not a dream, it's real, and I think I'm going to throw up, but somehow curiosity kicks in and instead of running to the bathroom I put my hand on my heart, which is beating about a million beats to every second, and I sink down on to the floor without even thinking about it and I start looking through the pile.

chapter 27

"Now this," says Ben, turning to Simon and raising a glass of champagne, "is the life."

"Better buckle up," says Simon with a grin. "We're about to land."

"I don't want to land," groans Ben. "I want to stay on this plane for ever and ever." The stewardess walks past and smiles at Ben, who gives her his most charming smile and turns back to Simon. "See what I mean? Beautiful women, free champagne, delicious food."

"You can afford to fly first class," grunts Simon. "On my measly pay I'd end up in cattle class with crappy seats and crappy food."

"I didn't pay for this," says Ben.

"Yeah, but you got upgraded because you're famous. I don't somehow think that they'd automatically upgrade overworked producer Simon Molloy just because I have a nice smile."

"But they did," grins Ben.

"Only 'cuz I'm with you."

They do up their seat belts and prepare to land.

"Where are we staying again?" asks Ben.

"Ah," says Simon, reaching into his briefcase. "Now here, I really have done us proud. London Daytime Television wanted to put us up in some grotty hotel, but I managed to wangle this place called Shutters on the Beach." He pulls a brochure out of the case and hands it to Ben. "Nice isn't it?"

"Nice?" says Ben, as the plane starts to descend through the sky. "It's bloody gorgeous."

"Bloody gorgeous," he says again, as they walk through the reception area, the very same reception area Jemima has only recently walked through herself. Ben, being a man, doesn't notice the details in the way Jemima did, but nevertheless he can appreciate the quiet beauty of the place.

"I've got to make some calls, and then I've got to meet the publicist," says Simon, as they follow the bellboy up in the elevator. "How about we meet a bit later on?"

"Let's speak," says Ben, looking at his watch. "I'm not sure I'm up for a night out tonight, I can feel a serious bout of jet lag coming on."

"Okay," agrees Simon, who's not feeling so hot himself. "If you bail out on me tonight then tomorrow, after we've done the interview, we have to do some heavy drinking."

"You're on," says Ben with a grin.

"Good."

Ben is tired, but he's also excited, and he hasn't got any calls to make, any people to meet, and after half an hour of flicking through hundreds of television stations, he decides to go for a walk.

He has no idea where he's going, but he doesn't care. Just the fact that he's able to walk around in nothing more than a pair of jeans and a T-shirt is enough, the fact that within minutes of leaving the hotel he passes three of the most beautiful women he's ever seen is enough, the fact that he's actually here, in Los Angeles, is enough.

Ben doesn't know about jaywalking. He doesn't know that

in California, should you be stupid enough to cross at the lights before the sign changes to a green pedestrian, you can be fined. So here he is, standing at the street corner with a crowd of people, wondering why no one's crossing the empty road. He strides across as a black convertible Porsche screeches past him, missing him by centimeters, and as the car roars off the driver, an impossibly handsome blond man, screams, "Asshole!" Ben stands for a few seconds, shaking, as a young man with long hair and baggy clothes walks up to him.

"Don't cross until it says so, man," he drawls, walking off.

"Oh," says Ben, recovering his composure. "Thanks."

I don't know what to feel. I don't know whether to be horrified or whether to be fascinated, whether to laugh with relief because it wasn't my imagination that something was very wrong, I wasn't mad, or whether to throw up.

Everything seems to be standing still. The only thing I'm aware of at this very moment in time is the pile of photographs and magazines in front of me. I feel as if I'm in a daze, but somehow I can't stop myself from looking, it's as if I need to see this because if I don't look at everything it may not be real.

I reach across and pull over one of the many magazines from the pile. "Big and Bouncy!" it proclaims on the cover, a lurid headline over a picture of a woman who's not so much a woman, more a mountain of flesh. She's completely naked, grinning into the camera and spreading her legs, presumably to help the viewer see what they would otherwise miss due to the rolls of skin, the acres of fat that would otherwise completely obliterate her genitalia.

Jesus Christ. Who buys these things? What are they doing *here*? In Brad's apartment.

I turn the first page and read the note from the editor, addressed to those men who like larger ladies. I turn every page, and you know what I can't believe? I can't believe that someone like Brad could get turned on by these enormous women, so what the hell are they doing in his apartment?

The horrified part of me doesn't want to look, wants to run crying into her mother's skirt and hope the big, bad, nasty world will go away, but that other part of me, the fascinated part, can't stop turning the pages because these women are me. They're what I used to be, except I never knew what I looked like then because I never dared look in the mirror properly. I used to pretend that if I couldn't see the fat then no one else could either.

Except looking closely I can see that these women aren't really me. They have pouting, glossy smiles, they lick their lips seductively as they look into the camera, they seem proud of their size, their bulk, their excess weight, but they shouldn't be proud. Or should they?

Am I going mad? Is it possible that men would have found me attractive then, despite being hugely overweight? I love the attention I get now that I'm slim and blond, but has my life changed all that much? Yes, I feel better, more confident, but I'm still the same person inside, and if I'm being really honest with myself I wouldn't say I'm that much happier now, and all the insecurities I had when I was fat are still there, they haven't gone away, even though that sounds ridiculous.

The weird thing is that people judge me by my looks as much as they did before, only now they just come up with a completely different conclusion, and yes, I have a boyfriend, but my life certainly isn't the fairy tale I thought it would be. Most of the time, even though I'm in Los Angeles, with Brad, most of the time, I suddenly realize, I'm desperately lonely. Far, far lonelier than I ever was back home in Kilburn.

And the more I think about it, the more I realize that I really haven't felt myself since arriving in Los Angeles. I feel almost as if I'm playing a role, that I've become so immersed in being Brad's girlfriend I've forgotten who I really am. In fact, it's not even since I arrived in LA. If I'm totally honest about it, I haven't felt myself since I lost weight and I never understood before how much I used the excess weight to protect myself.

I finish reading the magazines and then I pick up the stack of photographs, and slowly, methodically, I go through them. Each of them features a huge woman, and, just as I think I've had enough shocks to last a lifetime, I see the one thing that suddenly explains everything, and I can't help it. Clichéd as it sounds, I cover my mouth with my hand and gasp.

Because there, in all her naked glory, is Jenny. Jenny, lying on Brad's bed, smiling seductively into the camera. On the bed where Brad and I make love so often. Lying there as if it's hers. No wonder. No wonder she hates me. And everything becomes horribly clear.

And as everything starts falling into place, I'm left with one overwhelming thought. What the hell is Brad doing with me? Why did he tell me he loved me? Why does he want me to stay? Why me?

I sort of feel as if the connections are there, in my mind, they're just not quite fitting together. But I don't have to think about this for very long, because suddenly the bedroom door opens, and Brad's standing in the doorway.

I know it's him, I don't even bother looking up, I don't need to, and I wait for him to say something but he doesn't, all I can hear is the sound of his heavy breathing. He's out of breath, he's been running, he's rushed to get here, and eventually, after this long silence, I do turn to look at him except I don't look him in the eyes, I just look at the trickles of sweat which are just beginning to slide down his forehead.

"They're not mine," is the first thing he says. I don't say anything, I just start shaking. It's almost like a freeze-frame in a film, nobody moves, and finally I find my voice.

"I suppose you're looking after them for a friend."

"It's a long story," he says. "But they're not mine."

"Brad," I say quietly. "I'm not stupid."

Brad runs his fingers through his hair and sits down on the bed, head in his hands, and all I can think is that he looks guilty. Guilty. Guilty. Guilty.

"Perhaps you ought to tell me what this is all about," I say, only my voice doesn't sound like mine, it's far too collected, far too calm, and this situation doesn't feel like my own, it feels like an out-of-body experience, like something I'm watching in a cinema.

Brad's silent for a long time, and I don't bother pushing him. I just sit and wait, still flicking through the magazines, as if I'm in a dream.

"I don't know what to say," he says.

"Okay." My voice is as cold as ice. "I'll help you. Am I right in assuming these pictures are yours?"

Brad nods.

"So presumably you have them because you find these women attractive."

Brad shrugs.

"Do you?"

He shrugs again.

"Do you?"

"I guess."

"So now would you like to explain this?" I pull out the picture of Jenny and put it in front of Brad, who groans and drops his head in his hands, like I did before, like that child, like everything will disappear if he closes his eyes, that if he can't see me or the incriminating evidence, perhaps I won't be able to see him either. I know how he feels.

"At least I understand why she hates me," I continue. "No wonder she bloody well felt threatened, she couldn't pose for your sick porn collection while I was here, could she."

"It's not like that," says a voice from the doorway. Jesus Christ. It's not my day. There, in the doorway, is Jenny. Brad groans again and covers his eyes.

"Oh really," I say. "Seeing as Brad seems to have lost the power of speech, perhaps you'd better tell me what it *is* like."

"I'm sorry, Brad," says Jenny, walking over to stand next to him and putting her hand on his shoulder. "I came over because I knew something was wrong when you ran out of the office. Are you okay?"

"Is he okay?" This is unbelievable. "Excuse me? Hello? Never mind about him, for Christ's sake. I want you to tell me what these are."

Jenny gives a cursory glance at the pictures. "Okay," she says to me, not even having the decency to show the slightest hint of embarrassment. "You really want to know what's going on?"

"Yes." Although suddenly I'm not so sure.

Jenny looks at Brad. "I'm going to tell her," she says, but Brad doesn't say anything, he doesn't even bother looking up, he just carries on sitting there with his head in his hands.

"Brad and I were at high school together—"

"You what?" I say. "I don't believe this."

"Well believe it," says Jenny. "We weren't together," she pauses. "Then." She shrugs. "I looked pretty much the same as I do now. I was the overweight kid that everyone laughed at. Sure, I had my friends, the social misfits, the geeks, the nerds that no one else wanted to know." Her voice softens as she looks at Brad.

"Brad was the high school hero. He was the golden boy, the star of the football team. He went out with the head cheer-leader, and I fell in love with him the moment I saw him.

"He never noticed me, of course, not in that way, but I remember how he was always nice, he never made cruel comments about my size, or laughed and shouted Big Bird when I walked into the room. He used to tell the others to shut up, not to go on about my size, he'd tell them to leave me alone, which only made me love him more.

"It wasn't until we left school that I understood why he stuck up for me. He'd long gone by then, left for college, while I stayed and took a secretarial job. There was a woman I worked with, Judy, whom I became very close to. She used to say I was just like her when she was a girl, and Judy certainly looked like me, we were the same size.

"We were at work one day when I mentioned what school I'd been to. 'You must know my son,' she said, and she pulled a picture of Brad out of her wallet. I remember staring at his photo in disbelief, and, although I admitted I knew him, I never told her how I felt about him.

"Even when I left that job I kept in touch with Judy, and she'd always tell me how he was getting on. I never really had boyfriends, I never felt that anyone would be interested in me, but I never let go of the dream that Brad and I would somehow, someday, be together."

I've stopped looking at the pictures. I can't take my eyes off Jenny, and I know I should hate her, she's ruined my life, but I can't hate her because sitting here listening to her voice I'm hearing the story of my life.

"Judy used to tell me about his girlfriends," she continues. "But they never seemed to last, and then a few years ago she told me he was in LA, he'd started this gym, and he was looking for an assistant. I thought about it and thought about it, and I knew I had to come out here, I had to be with him.

"Even if nothing ever happened, I knew the only way I'd be happy was if I was near Brad, so I left my hometown and caught a Greyhound bus to Los Angeles.

"I didn't think Brad would even remember who I was, but I went to the gym, and his mouth dropped open when he saw me"—a small smile plays on her face at the memory—"and I started working for him that day.

"Two months later we had an office party, and Brad drove me home. He came in, and that was that. We fell in love."

Jenny pauses, and I stop her from continuing, I don't think I want to hear any more, I don't want to hear about them being in love. I just want to hear the answers to the questions that haven't been answered, but it's finally beginning to sink in, this whole sordid thing, and my voice comes out in a whisper. "So why am I here?"

Jenny's voice hardens again. "You think it's easy to look the way I do in a town like this?" she says. "You think I don't know what people think of me, what people would think of Brad if they knew he and I were together?" You know, strange as it seems, I start to feel sorry for her. I start to understand, because, even though I haven't been here long, already I know how superficial Los Angeles is, how people will only accept you if you're beautiful. And slim.

"So that's why you're here," Jenny sighs. "Because Brad needed a trophy girlfriend. He needed someone who's blond and skinny." The disdain in her voice hits me like a slap in the face. "He needed someone like you to prove that he'd made it."

"But why do you put up with this?" I'm still whispering, and I'm not sure why. Maybe because I can't believe what I've just heard, or maybe because I can't believe the pain this is causing. Not just for me, but for Brad. And Jenny.

"Because I love him," says Jenny simply, as a tear starts rolling down her cheek. "I love him, and I know what this town is like, and I understand why he needs someone like you. I have to understand. I have no choice."

"I'm sorry." Brad's words come out in a whisper and he looks up, up into Jenny's eyes. "I'm sorry, Jenny." He looks at me. "And I'm sorry, JJ. I never meant to hurt you, I never meant for you to find out."

"What?" I really don't believe this. "You thought you could spend the rest of your life with both of us?"

He shrugs. "I didn't know what else to do."

"I can't believe I'm here," I say, the words out before I can even think about them. "I can't believe I'm hearing this." I look up at the ceiling. "Why me?" I ask softly. "Why did this have to happen to me?" I look at Brad. "This is true isn't it?" I say, because for a moment there I thought that maybe Jenny had made it all up, maybe she found a way of hurting me beyond belief, of winning the war. But I don't really have to wait for an answer from Brad. I can see in his eyes that it's true, and I can see from the way Jenny takes his hand and he doesn't pull away that it's true.

I stand up and walk to the wardrobe, ignoring them both, and, as I start pulling my clothes off the hangers and flinging them on the bed, I'm vaguely aware that Brad and Jenny leave the room. Brad and Jenny. Even the words, their names, make me feel sick.

But other than the sickness, there really isn't any other feeling. No rage, no grief, not even much pain. Numbness. I just feel numb. I pull out my suitcase and start piling in clothes, throwing things on top of one another, not bothering to fold, or smooth, or press. Suddenly I have this overwhelming urge to get out of here. Fast.

Brad comes back into the bedroom. "Jenny's gone," he says softly.

"I'll be gone too," I say curtly. "As soon as I've packed I'll be out of here."

"You don't have to go," he says.

What? Did I just hear what I think I heard? "Are you completely out of your mind?"

"I mean, I do have a spare room. You can stay there."

"Don't be ridiculous."

"Where will you go?"

"I don't know." And even though I'm planning to phone Lauren as soon as possible, I don't intend to share that with him. "Look," I say to Brad. "I'd like to be on my own if that's okay."

"Okay," he says. "Will I see you again?"

"I very much doubt it." And as I look at him I realize that actually this is the first time I'm really seeing him. Despite the pain, the deception, the lies, he is still the best-looking man I've ever seen. But looks mean nothing. So he's good-looking. So what? And I suddenly see that that's all Brad ever was to me. A handsome man. I fell for his looks, not for who he is.

And, most importantly, I fell for him because he wanted me. He was the first man to show any interest in me, and I was flattered, and I think, oh God why didn't I realize this before, I think I felt I had to love him back.

Brad leaves and I pick up the phone to ring the airline.

"I'd like to change my flight to London," I tell the reservation girl on the other end of the phone.

"Certainly, ma'am. Just tell me which flight it is and when you were thinking of flying."

"LAX to London Heathrow. As soon as possible. Can you get me on the flight tonight?" I give her the flight number and hold my breath.

"I think that flight is full, ma'am. Can you hold the line while I just check my computer?"

I hold, and my foot taps the floor impatiently as I wait for what feels like hours for the woman to come back on the line. "I'm sorry, the flight is full, but we do have a seat on the flight tomorrow."

"Thank God." I breathe a sigh of relief.

"You do realize that will be full fare."

"What?" She's got it wrong, she must have got it wrong. "But I changed my flight a few weeks ago for $100 and I understood that that was the cost."

"I'm afraid that the inventory is now full, we are unable to do that anymore."

"So how much is full fare?"

"That will be $954 plus tax."

I can't have heard right. I clutch the phone and whisper, "What?"

"Nine hundred fifty-four dollars plus tax."

"But I can't afford that!" In my head I'm mentally calculating how much that is in pounds, that's about £700! No way, I haven't got that sort of money.

"I'm sorry, ma'am, that's the best we can do."

"So you mean I have to wait here until I'm booked to go home? I can't change my flight again for $100?" I can't believe this is happening to me, I really can't.

"I'm afraid not."

"Forget it," I sigh. "I'll just have to stay in this godforsaken place then, won't I? Thanks." And I put down the phone, feeling as if I'm going to cry.

Lauren, I'll have to call Lauren, and surprise, surprise, she's not there. Probably out with her bartender, I think, and that's when it hits me. I'm on my own. Again. I came out here to be with Brad and now he's left me and that's it, I'm in a strange town, with one friend who isn't home, and I'm all by myself.

I can't help it, I can't stop the tears that start rolling down my cheeks and within seconds I'm gulping huge pockets of air, sobbing like a baby. I pull my knees up to my chest and cradle them with my arms, crying as if my heart is going to break. Stop it, I try and tell myself. He's not worth it, but even as I think that I know that this isn't about Brad. This is about me. This is about finally thinking you've found someone to share the rest of your life with, and not being good enough for them. It's about thinking that being blond and slim and perfect will automatically bring you happiness, and then discovering that life is full of as many disappointments as there were before.

It takes about an hour to cry myself dry, and when I've finished I leave a message on Lauren's machine. "It's JJ," I say, hiccuping a little. "Something terrible's happened, I need a place to stay. Whatever you do, don't call me at Brad's. I'm going out and I'll keep ringing you until I get you. Speak to you soon." And I put the phone down.

chapter 28

I lug my suitcase down the hall, thanking God that Brad didn't change his mind and decide to see me off. It's so heavy I'll probably do my back in, but I'd rather be laid up than accept any help from him now.

I take the case to the front door, and the taxi driver runs out and picks it up for me.

"Where to?" he asks, when I'm settled in the backseat.

"I haven't got a clue."

He turns round and looks at me quizzically. "You don't know where you're going?"

I shake my head, and as I do the first tears come, but not in a torrent, just a single tear rolling down my cheek.

"Are you okay?" he says gently.

"Yes." I try to smile. "I'll be fine." And we sit there for a bit as he waits for me to compose myself, and as I wipe my eyes I remember the Santa Monica mall, the food hall, and my nostrils are filled with the mingling smells and I know as an absolute certainty that the only thing that will make me feel better right now is food. Lots of it. As much as I can eat.

Cravings. I'd forgotten about cravings, but now I'm getting the strongest craving of my life, and for your information I'm not sitting here thinking about lettuce, or rice cakes, or even, gasp, a loaf of bread. I'm sitting here thinking about spare ribs. About Singapore noodles. About pasta. About cookies. About cakes dripping with sugar and cream.

And the more I think about it, the more vivid the pictures become until I can almost smell the food, taste the food, hear it beckoning me from afar.

"Santa Monica mall," I instruct the driver, not caring about my fat-free, cholesterol-free, obsessive diet. I don't give a damn, I just need to stuff my face.

"Are you sure you'll be okay?" he says, as I start to lug the suitcase up the steps of the mall. "I'm sure," I tell him, and push open the doors.

Where do you start when you're about to have the biggest binge of your life and you have a choice of practically every type of food from around the world? It doesn't matter really, because I plan to sample everything, and I start with a sandwich from the deli.

I don't bother sitting at one of the tables, I stand just next to the deli counter cramming a pastrami on rye sandwich into my mouth, barely tasting it.

Next I hit the hamburger stall, where I bypass the burgers and go for the fries instead.

I stop at the Chinese and order Singapore noodles and spare ribs, at which point I do sit down because it's far easier to tear the flesh off the bone with your teeth when you're sitting down.

Sweet things, sweet things, sweet things. I go to the bakery and buy a bag of six hot, fresh cinnamon rolls, and I stuff them into my mouth within minutes.

Now what? I look around, stomach full, but I know I haven't even started if I'm hoping to fill the huge, gaping hole in my heart. The candy store. I fill a huge paper bag with sweets, every kind imaginable, and even before I've left the shop I'm cramming handfuls into my mouth without even tasting them.

I leave the mall and lug the suitcase to a phone booth outside, undoing the top two buttons on my tiny denim shorts, which are now painfully pressing into my flesh, and as I dial I rub my stomach to try and dispel the ache from so much food, and I curse myself for wearing a short white crop top instead of a voluminous shirt to hide my sins.

"Lauren?"

"I've been so worried!" shouts Lauren down the phone. "Don't tell me now, just get your ass over here."

"Oh thank you, thank you, thank you."

"Don't be stupid," says Lauren. "What are friends for?"

Ben has been walking around Santa Monica for what seems like hours. He's discovered that the busiest street seems to be the Third Street Promenade, and he's still trying to get over the fact that there's a Virtual Supermarket, a computer shop where you go in, log on, and order whatever you need from the computer.

He stops for coffee at the Barnes & Noble café, and sits for a while, enjoying the cappuccino and the people. He was going to buy a book, but he couldn't find anything other than film books, so he picks up the local paper that someone left on the table next to him, and idly flicks through.

After a while he decides to get back to the hotel. He turns the corner and passes a phone booth, and, being the boy that he is, he keeps his eyes glued to the perfect rear view of the woman on the phone. Why don't they make women like that in England, he thinks, taking in the curve of her well-toned buttocks and tanned, muscular thighs, the golden skin set off by faded denim shorts and a white crop top. Ben walks past and turns back, hoping to see the face behind the mane of streaky blond hair, but the girl has turned away, and Ben smiles to himself and walks back to the hotel.

*   *   *

"Christ, you look awful," says Lauren, opening the door.

I feel awful, and, as I push past Lauren, clutching my hand to my mouth, I catch a glimpse of myself in the mirror and my golden skin is no longer golden, it's a rather peculiar shade of green.

"Through there," says Lauren, pointing down the hallway. "Quick."

I stumble past her and collapse on my knees in front of the toilet. Up comes the pastrami on rye. Up come the Singapore noodles and spare ribs. Up come the fries. Up come the cinnamon rolls. And finally, up come the sweets.

And when it's all finished, when there's nothing left, I rest my head on the toilet seat while my eyes and nose continue streaming, and I'm aware that Lauren's standing behind me, gently rubbing my back.

"Here," says Lauren, handing me some tissues. "I'll just get you a glass of water."

She comes back and helps me to my feet. "Oh you poor thing," she says. "You're shivering." She leads me to the sofa, then runs back to her bedroom and comes back with a blanket, which she tucks around me.

Lauren doesn't say anything, she just sits beside me and puts her arm around me, and I lean my head into her shoulder as the pain and the shock finally hit, and this is what I need, to be looked after, to be treated like a child, to feel safe and secure for the first time in ages.

"How about a cup of hot, sweet tea?" she says eventually, and I nod.

"You're so English," I manage with a small smile when Lauren comes back with two steaming mugs.

"I'm not *that* English. You won't find any milk or sugar in there. It's fat-free dairy substitute and sweetener. So," she says sitting down, "what happened?"

I tell her. Everything. Lauren sits there open-mouthed, and when I've finished I look for her reaction, but she can't speak.

"Say something," I plead.

"I can't," says Lauren. "Fucking hell."

"I know."

"Fucking hell," she says again.

"Yeah."

"Fucking hell."

"Lauren!"

"I'm sorry, I just don't know what to say. I can't believe it. This doesn't happen in real life, surely?"

"That's what I thought, but I'm afraid it does."

"What a bastard," sighs Lauren.

"Yes."

"And what a bitch."

"I don't know." I shrug. "You'll probably think I'm completely out of my head, but you know what? I actually feel sorry for them. I mean, I feel completely sick that I got caught up in it . . ."

"I noticed," says Lauren, with a smile.

"Yeah, well. But think how awful it must be for her."

"You *are* out of your head," says Lauren in disbelief.

"Maybe, but I know what it's like to be her. The only thing I can't believe is that he treats her like that."

"Hello? JJ? What about the way he treated you?"

"That too."

"Well. Good riddance to bad rubbish is all I can say."

"You're right. You're right. I know you're right."

"Shall I come out with some more clichés?"

I nod.

"Plenty more fish in the sea."

"Men are like buses."

"You can lead a horse to water."

"What's that got to do with anything?"

Lauren shrugs. "Dunno, but just bear in mind that too many cooks . . ."

"Oh Lauren." I shove her and she grins, because she knows I'm feeling a little bit better already.

"See," says Lauren. "There is some light at the end of the tunnel," and we both start laughing.

"That's better," says Lauren. "You can stay here for as long as you like."

"That's the other thing," I say disconsolately. "I tried to change my flight today but I can't get back any earlier without paying full fare."

"So how long are you staying?"

"About two months." Now this really does scare me. "I can find somewhere to stay, an apartment maybe, or a cheap hotel." Which of course I can't, because I don't have the money.

"What? When I've got a perfectly comfortable sofa bed? You're staying here, for free, because I've got more than enough room for both of us. End of story."

Thank God. That's exactly what I hoped she'd say. "Lauren, what would I do without you?"

"More to the point, what would I do without you?" Lauren says with a smile.

"But what am I going to do for money? I mean, I've got the column on the *Kilburn Herald* and my paltry salary from them but that's hardly enough."

"You're a journalist, JJ. Money is the least of your worries. First of all, I can get the features editor at the magazine to commission you."

"What?"

"Yup. You can write a piece for the magazine on good-looking bastards."

"You mean, tell my story?"

"Not exactly. You can mention the basics, but we'll save the full story for an in-depth feature, which, unfortunately, wouldn't be right for us. For this piece you can write a bit of first-person stuff, but expand on the theme, how we're taken in by looks, how we're blinded by lust, how easy it is to fall for what someone looks like, not who they are."

"For your magazine?"

Lauren nods.

"Are you sure they'll want it?" She nods again and already I'm thinking about opening the magazine and seeing my by-line, my name in big letters, and the thought has the desired effect because I'm starting to feel that there is something to look forward to after all.

"No worries. I know you can do it. Next," she says, picking up her phone book, "I'm going to ring *Cosmopolitan* in London and you're going to offer them a story on Internet romances, and that's when you tell your full story. Warts and all."

"Can't they sue me?"

"Like bastard-features and bitch-face are likely to read English *Cosmopolitan*? Anyway, all you have to do is change the names and you're sorted. JJ, you don't have to worry about money. There are thousands of pieces you could be writing out here and filing back to magazines and newspapers in London. Think about it, you're in Los Angeles. You're in the place where all the stars live, so just get on the phone and set up some interviews. It's as easy as that."

I really am starting to feel better. A whole lot better.

"And meanwhile, when we're not working, which will be most of the time, you and I are going to have a blast. Screw them. We're two gorgeous single English girls, and the world is our oyster."

"Yes." I raise my mug. "The world is our oyster. I'll drink to that."

"So," Lauren says, "how about starting tonight?"

"Starting what?"

"Starting to have a good time."

"You mean you're not seeing Bill the horny bartender?"

"I'm going to cancel him. You and I are going out."

"Lauren." I shake my head, still unable to believe that any-one can be so kind. "I don't want you to cancel him. To tell you the truth this has really taken it out of me. All I want to do tonight is curl up and watch TV."

"Okay," says Lauren. "So we'll curl up and watch TV."

"No." My voice is firm. "I know how you feel about Bill and there's no way you're canceling him. In the nicest possible way, Lauren, I want to be on my own tonight." A total lie, but I know I'll cope and there's no reason why I should spoil Lauren's evening as well.

"Are you sure?" Lauren's doubtful, but pleased.

"I'm so sure," I say.

"Okay. I've got plenty of food in the fridge so just make yourself at home. I'm going to jump in the shower, and then how about I run you a nice hot bath?"

"That sounds lovely," and it does, except I have to really force myself not to think about the last time I had a bath, with Brad, and what we ended up doing.

Before she leaves Lauren lines up an assortment of pots, jars, and tubes.

"These," she says in a serious tone, "are my babies. Use them well," and she blows me a kiss and disappears.

I unscrew each pot, each jar, each tube, and sniff deeply. I examine the packaging, read how each one will give you younger skin, thicker hair, firmer flesh. I pour half a bottle of almond-scented bubble bath in the water and lie back, cucumber slices on my eyes, a hot damp towel wrapped around my deeply conditioning hair.

And when I've toweled myself dry with one of Lauren's huge fluffy towels, I walk into the kitchen and open the door of the fridge. Hooray. For someone as skinny as Lauren, there's an extraordinary amount of food. Without thinking, I pull out a tray of sushi, a carton of yogurt, a cellophane package of pre-cooked chicken.

But I don't stop there, even though I know I should. I pull out packets of ready-made salads, cheese, fat-free cookies. I spy the bread box and dig down to where half a loaf of whole grain bread is temporarily residing.

And then I sit at the kitchen table and I eat. And eat. And eat. And eat.

"Oh hello," says Ben, hoping he's got the right number because there's a male voice on the answering machine, and he doesn't exactly trust those roommates of Jemima, even though Lisa, the one he spoke to, sounded more normal than that blond nutcase. "I hope I've got the right number. I'm trying to get in touch with Jemima Jones. This is Ben Williams, an old friend of hers from London. I'm in Los Angeles for a couple of days, and I'd love to meet up with you, er, with her, so if this is the right number and Jemima's there, could she please call me at Shutters on the Beach. Thanks," and he puts down the phone.

I lie in bed and I know I should feel guilty at the amount I've eaten today, but I don't. The food at the Santa Monica mall doesn't count because as far as I'm concerned I threw it up before it had a chance to convert into fat, and tonight, well, tonight. Yes, I'll admit I was tempted to throw it up again, to stick my fingers down my throat and get rid of all the food, but that's not the answer. And eating isn't the answer either.

And anyway, the throwing up earlier wasn't just about the food, I think it was about the shock today, the combination of both, and I do feel better. I still feel alone, but I've got Lauren, thank God, and I believe her, I believe that everything will be fine.

I rub my hands over my stomach, feeling how it's bulging slightly, and thanking God that I've exercised as much as I have, that I don't have folds of flabby skin anywhere on my body, and then I remember a time at home, back in London, when my stomach was huge. When it used to take about ten minutes to rub from one side to the other. Well, not exactly, but you know what I mean. I remember how I used my size and my flesh to hide away from the world, to hide my sexuality, to hide who I was, and I know that, despite in a strange way feeling comforted by my size, I won't get that way again, I don't *need* to be that size again.

My stomach is nothing like it used to be, but as I stroke I can feel that neither is it concave, the way it's been since I arrived in Los Angeles, and actually, if I'm being completely honest here, I quite like the fact that it curves slightly. Okay, I know that with a triple workout for the next couple of days it will soon be back to its flat self, and that this bulge is just the temporary result of tonight's binge, but the more I stroke it the more I like it. It feels rounded, feminine, womanly.

I get up in a while, curious to see what it looks like in the mirror, and I go into Lauren's bedroom and pull the full-length mirror around to face me. I lift my T-shirt up over my head and stand there, naked, just looking at myself.

I look at my taut, muscular figure, so lean now that I look more like a boy than a woman. I run my hand over my flat breasts and remember how pendulous they used to be, how like the women I saw in the pictures today. How like Jenny. No. I'm not going to think about that.

I skim my waist, marveling at how tiny it is, and I try to pinch an inch, except I can't, all I can manage is a few millimeters of skin.

So I get into bed and I decide that I'm not going to binge anymore, but I'm not going to stay obsessed with being as skinny as I can be. I think it's high time I just relaxed and lived a little. And I suppose my weight will just settle at whatever it's supposed to settle at. How's that for a revelation?

chapter 29

"Who *are* all these people?" Ben whispers to Simon, as they're led into a room that is apparently known as the den.

"The film publicist, the assistant, the agent. God knows."

"But why are they all here?" whispers Ben. "I mean, this is only a bloody TV interview."

"I know," Simon whispers back. "Anyone would think we were out to murder her."

"Where is she anyway?"

"The assistant said she'd be down in a minute."

"Jesus. Can you imagine how much money she must make? Look at this place!" Ben is gazing around the building in awe, at the huge, Mexican-style villa set high up in the hills above Santa Monica.

"This is the *den*?" says Ben, laughing, because he'd pictured a small, cozy room, a bit like a library, the very opposite of the enormous white room in which he and Simon are now standing. Simon creeps across the flagstone floors to the french windows at the far end.

"Get a load of this, Ben," he says, looking out at a heart-shaped swimming pool cut into the side of the hill, complete with rocks, statues, and fountains.

"I think I'm in the wrong business," says Ben, walking over to join him.

"I think you are," says Simon. "I think I am too."

"Can I get you something to drink?" The boys turn round as Alexia Aldridge's assistant walks in the room.

Simon nudges Ben and says under his breath, "Double scotch on the rocks?"

"That would be lovely," says Ben.

"Iced tea?" she says.

"Perfect," he says.

"Iced tea?" says Simon, looking at Ben in disgust. "Iced tea? No bloody alcohol in iced tea is there?"

"Somehow I don't think alcohol would be appropriate," Ben laughs.

Simon checks his watch. "I'd better go down to the front door, the crew should be arriving any minute."

Ben walks over to the bookcase, looking for clues to some inner life of Alexia Aldridge that the public might not know, although he thinks it's unlikely. Ben is sure that there's very little chance of him finding out some fantastic fact about her, something guaranteed to make the front page of every tabloid.

Ben reread his cuts last night, and the more he read the more he started to read between the lines. He suspects that Alexia Aldridge hates playing the Hollywood game. That she's actually fiercely bright, and very few men are strong enough to match her. He suspects that she's extremely private, and that were it not for the publicity value of the occasional hand-picked interview, she would lock herself away in her beautiful house and never come out, unless she were making a film. And he suspects that she's fantastically insecure, which is surprising for one so young, so beautiful and so talented, and that she hides those insecurities with the arrogance for which she's so famed.

Finally he suspects that he's going to leave this house having fallen deeply in love with Alexia Aldridge.

The bookcase is an eclectic collection of art books, psychology books, contemporary literary fiction. Ben's not surprised, it's the standard stuff of everyone he's ever interviewed. What does surprise him, as he pulls out a book on the artist Egon Schiele, is that it's been read. That the pages are dog-eared and slightly bent, and that someone has obviously pored over it, cover to cover.

Ben turns as he hears someone walk into the room.

"Sorry I took so long," says Simon, leading the cameraman and soundman into the room.

"God." Ben puts a hand on his heart. "For a minute there I thought it was her."

"I could pretend," says Simon, pouting and fluttering his eyelashes.

"Where is she anyway?" says Ben. "What's taking so long?"

"Hollywood luvvies," says Simon, sitting down and pouring himself some iced tea, "are even worse than theatrical luvvies." He drinks it down in one gulp before adding, "Darling. Mmm," he says, looking at the glass. "That's bloody nice, that is."

An hour later the crew have set up their equipment and they're standing around, looking at their watches. The door opens. It's the assistant again.

"I don't want to trouble you, but any chance we could get to see Miss Aldridge soon?" says Ben politely.

"Like, this year," mutters Simon, softly so she can't hear.

"Oh, I'm sorry," says the assistant. "She should be with you shortly. She's just finishing getting dressed."

Half an hour later they're still sitting there.

"This is definitely happening isn't it?" says Ben.

"Of course it is," says Simon, except he's not sounding half as cocky as he did earlier on.

And then twenty minutes later, just as they're giving up hope, the assistant rushes in and clears the glasses and jug away. "She's on her way," she says, and they stand up to greet her.

Nothing could have prepared Ben for the sheer magnetism of Alexia Aldridge. She is beautiful but not classically so. Her mouth is slightly crooked, her nose has a bump on it, but the aura around her is such that none of the men can take their eyes off her.

She's wearing tight lime green trousers, a white sloppy sweater, a huge amount of makeup that makes her look as if she's wearing no makeup at all, and her hair is perfect. *She's* perfect, thinks Ben, who, for a few seconds, is so mesmerized by meeting a real-life Hollywood star he can't move, can't speak, can't do anything at all other than stare at her.

"Miss Aldridge?" Simon is first to recover his composure. "It's a pleasure to meet you. I'm Simon Molloy, the producer and director. And this," he says, "is Ben Williams, our presenter."

"I'm delighted to meet you," says Ben, shaking her hand.

"And I, you," she says coyly, looking up at him from under her eyelashes as Simon looks at the crew and raises his eyes to the ceiling.

And so they start running the tape, and Ben starts asking her questions. He sits in a large white armchair opposite Alexia, who curls up on the sofa, one hand resting on the arm, the other protectively curled round her knees.

"So tell us about your latest film," he starts, keeping it professional, trying to put her at ease before he starts asking her any personal questions, because she has to trust him, and Ben knows that it may take some time to build up this trust, but he's finding it hard to concentrate on anything, she's just so beautiful.

Alexia starts talking, in her famous throaty voice, and Ben sits there and nods his head, but he's not listening to a word she's saying, he's losing himself in her big, brown eyes.

They talk about the film—why she decided to do a low-budget film and waive her usual multi-million-dollar fee; what she felt when she first saw the script—the story of a single girl who's trying to find love, but can't tell the difference between passion and love, and nearly loses out when she doesn't realize what she's found, and how she feels at the superb reviews; the film, like all other American-made films, has opened in the States already and is not due to open in England for months.

"I know you're very private about your own love life," Ben ventures, as Alexia nods encouragingly, "but would you say you related to the character?"

"You mean, do I go for passion rather than love?"

Ben nods.

"I think relationships are very difficult, especially in this industry," she starts. "And I think it's very easy to get swept away with glamour, excitement, passion. But look at Hollywood marriages, they so rarely last, and I think the trick is, just as my character in the film does, the trick is to look for friendship rather than passion."

"So are you attracted to your male friends?"

Alexia laughs. "Now there's the tricky bit. Unfortunately I've yet to have a friendship with a man which turns into something more, but I'm still looking."

"So you're not in a relationship with anyone now?" Ben almost blushes as he says this, because it sounds so personal, and the question isn't for the benefit of the viewers, it's for him.

"No." She shakes her head and leans forward, giving him a flirtatious smile. "And to be honest I'm happy with that. I'm very busy with work, and I have a lot of close friends, and I really feel, for the first time in my life, that I don't need a man to fulfill me."

"So obviously you related to your character quite a lot." That's it, Ben, bring it on to more comfortable territory.

"Absolutely." She nods. "I suppose when I was younger I did go for that initial passion, but you change as you get older, and now I'd like to think I look for something more substantial."

"How do you think you've changed?" I love her, Ben's thinking, still mesmerized by her beauty, she is my perfect woman.

"I'm much more aware as a person. I think I've finally found self-fulfillment. I'm more relaxed with who I am, I do yoga, I meditate, I believe in the power of visualization and I use it. Frequently." She pauses and looks at the ceiling for a few seconds. "But I think the main thing is I've learned how to nurture my inner child, and that's the thing that's really made a difference."

"Your inner child?" says Ben, feeling slightly stupid, for he doesn't have a clue what she's talking about.

"Absolutely." She nods again. "My inner child. The lonely, scared, insecure child that lives inside all of us."

"Er, yes," says Ben, with typical British reserve. "Quite. So how did you come to find your, er, inner child?"

"I did these fabulous rebirthing classes," she says earnestly, "and taking me back to the trauma of birth, actually being able to feel the shock and terror of emerging from the womb into this world, completely changed my life."

Ben's just sitting looking at her, not quite open-mouthed, but the look of love that had been in his eyes since the beginning of the interview is rapidly disappearing. There's always a bloody catch, he thinks. She's beautiful, she's single, and she's full of psychobabble bullshit. Damn.

"But surely someone like you doesn't have to go through something like, um, rebirthing?" he ventures.

"This is all image," she says, "and actually I'm very ordinary. I go to the supermarket, I go shopping, I go for walks. I'm just like everybody else."

Yup, thinks Ben, and that's why it's taken us months to set up an interview with you. That's why, in fact, we're bothering to interview you at all. Because you're just so ordinary.

"Do you get recognized when you go out?"

"Occasionally," she says, "but, believe me, when I'm walking around with no makeup on and a baseball cap I look very different. It's lovely when people come up to you and tell you they admire your work, but sometimes it can be bothersome if they just want to touch you and get close to you."

"Has it ever worried you?"

"There was a recent incident, which I haven't talked about

before. A guy started following me," she says slowly. "He knew where I lived and started sending me letters. First of all he told me he liked me, then he loved me, and eventually they got more and more bizarre and he thought he was married to me."

Thank you, God, thinks Ben, knowing that this is the story that will make the papers, that Alexia Aldridge has her very own stalker.

"Were you frightened?"

"Yes." She nods. "And finally he started sending packages and saying that he knew where I was, who I was with, and what I was doing, and he was going insane with jealousy. In the last note I got he said if he couldn't have me, no one would, and he was going to kill me."

"What happened to him?"

"He's being held for questioning, and it's the first time I've slept in months. But it'll take a long time to get over that feeling of always looking over your shoulder. I guess"—she shrugs her shoulders and smiles—"it's kind of an occupational hazard."

Ben catches Simon's eye, who winks and gives him the thumbs-up.

"I think it's time to wrap it up," says the assistant, standing up. "Miss Aldridge has a meeting."

"It's okay, Sandy," says Alexia Aldridge, waving her away. "I have a few more minutes. Do you want to carry on?"

Ben looks at Simon, who shakes his head. "I think we've got enough," says Ben. "If we could just finish by wishing you luck." And they do, and Alexia smiles her famous smile and thanks them, and they get ready to pack up.

"It's been a pleasure," she says, shaking Ben's hand for rather a long time when the interview is over and the crew have walked out of the room. "I wish I had more time."

"You were wonderful," says Ben, still trying to figure out whether she's flirting with him, but suddenly not really caring. Although it would be an ego trip, all this rebirthing talk has changed his view of her completely.

"Maybe we'll meet again in London?" she says.

"Oh absolutely. That would be great."

"Here," she says, handing him a card. "These are my numbers. You should call me."

"Oh." Ben's shocked. "Okay."

"In fact," she continues, "I was wondering whether you were free tonight. I'd love it if you stayed for dinner."

"You mean the crew?" says Ben, who's just checking.

"No." She smiles her pussycat smile and taps him on the nose. "Don't be silly. Just us. You and me."

A million thoughts seem to go through Ben's mind at once. She's Alexia Aldridge! She fancies me! What a story! I could dine out on this for years! But I promised the crew I'd go out with them! They wouldn't mind! She's full of shit! But she's Alexia Aldridge! But what would be the point?

"Um, I'd love to," he says finally. "But I'm taking the crew out, and they've worked so hard I can't let them down."

Her smile hardens. "Okay. Never mind. But look, you should call me, I'm spending more and more time in London and I'd love to see you. I know a great healer in London who I think would really help you learn to love yourself. I must introduce you."

Alexia, unknowingly, has banged the final nail in her own coffin.

"That would be so great," he says, and he kisses her on the cheek, pockets her card, turns away, and rolls his eyes at Simon as she walks out of the room.

"Are you fucking crazy?" says Simon in disbelief, who had been surreptitiously listening to the entire conversation. "She wanted you, mate. You turned down Alexia Aldridge. You're fucking nuts."

"Simon!" admonishes Ben in a whisper. "You heard her, all that rebirthing, healing shit. She may be Alexia Aldridge but she's a woman from another planet."

"So fucking what? I can't believe it." Simon shakes his head. "Alexia Aldridge and you turned her down."

"Okay," says Ben, gathering up his stuff. "She's gorgeous.

She's beautiful. But she's full of crap. Even if I did stay for dinner, what would we talk about? Past-life regression therapy? I don't think so. All she would have been is a great story to tell your friends, and I'm not interested in that."

"You're not interested in a shag?"

"Not with someone I can't even talk to."

Simon frowns at Ben. "You know what? You're weird, you are. Anyway, that stalking story was the business. Well done." He claps Ben on the back. "I think, after that, we all need to go and get very drunk indeed. Sandy?" He walks over to the assistant, who's still hovering in the room. "Do you have any suggestions for bars or restaurants where we could go tonight?"

"Surely. What kind of thing are you looking for?"

"Somewhere fun, somewhere laid back."

"Where are you staying?"

"Santa Monica."

"Why don't you try Schatzi on Main? It's Arnold Schwarzenegger's restaurant and it's really fun, and I hear the food's great."

"Great. Thanks." And with that they thank her for her trouble and leave Alexia Aldridge's house.

"I still don't understand you," says Simon, driving back to the hotel.

"What's to understand? At first I thought she was gorgeous, but as soon as she started talking that drivel I went right off her."

"Still." Simon thinks for a minute. "She is supremely shaggable."

"If you're into that whole celebrity shagging bit."

"Which I am."

"In your dreams."

"That's about the only place," Simon admits, as Ben laughs. "And tonight we're going to get very drunk and try and shag some celebrities."

"You mean *you*'re going to get very drunk and shag some celebrities."

"Yup. Female, though. Before you get worried I'm not interested in you."

"Bloody glad to hear it."

"How are you feeling now?" We just got back home after a heavy dose of retail therapy. For Lauren, that is. I, needless to say, couldn't even afford a baseball cap at this precise moment in time, and, even though Lauren offered to buy me a sweater I fell in love with, I declined. She's been far too good to me already.

"Lauren, will you stop asking me how I'm feeling every five minutes!"

"I'm just worried about you, that's all."

"I'm fine. Really, I'm fine."

"So you're up for going out tonight?"

"Definitely."

"Okay. You know where I thought might be fun? Schatzi on Main. It's Arnold Schwarzenegger's restaurant, and apparently it's a good place for single women."

"But you've got Bill."

"Which still leaves you. And anyway, just because I slept with him last night." She stops talking, closes her eyes and licks her lips. "Mmm, but just because of that it doesn't mean I'm attached."

"You mean you haven't planned your wedding day yet?"

"No, but after all, tomorrow is another day."

The crew have opted out of Schatzi on Main. "Too posh," they moaned, when Simon told them where they were headed, so the cameraman and soundman have discovered an authentic British pub, and they're jumping for joy at the prospect of authentic British ale.

Simon's not happy. He doesn't want to let his crew down, but on the other hand he goes to authentic British pubs every night of the week at home, and he just can't see what the big deal is.

"Don't worry," says Ben, when Simon knocks on his door to tell him they're leaving. "We can always go to the other place later. I'm nearly ready," he says. "I just have to make a phone call," and he picks up the phone and leaves another message for Jemima.

"Who's the bird?" asks Simon.

"You wouldn't be interested," says Ben with a smile. "She's just an old friend who's out here," and as he puts down the phone he suddenly has a very clear picture of Jemima in his head, and he realizes just how much he wants to see her.

They leave the car behind and walk to the pub, and within minutes they're hugging their pint glasses and sitting in a cluster around a chipped round oak table in the corner.

"This isn't so bad," says Ben, who's beginning to like it here.

"It's fine," says Simon, who knows he doesn't have a hope in hell of spotting any stars, let alone shagging them, in a place like this.

So, four men together, they sit and talk about Alexia Aldridge, and then fill in the rest of the time with TV gossip. They talk about Ben's copresenter, fellow researchers, producers, even Diana Macpherson, and, although they tease Ben about the rumors, he keeps his mouth very firmly shut.

And every twenty minutes or so one of them gets up, goes to the bar, and gets another round for the boys.

At ten o'clock the cameraman starts yawning. "Bloody jet lag," he says, rubbing his eyes. "I'm heading back."

"How about it?" Simon asks Ben. "Still up for Schwarzenegger's place?"

"I don't think so," says Ben, who's caught the cameraman's yawn. "I think I'm about ready for bed too."

"Oh come on, Ben," says Simon. "You can't let me down now."

"Okay," says Ben reluctantly. "But just for a quick drink."

It is a quick drink, because truth to be told Simon's not feeling so hot either. They stand at the bar, unable to get bar stools, and have a quick whiskey.

"God," says Ben, looking round the room. "The women here are amazing." Simon follows his glance as it rests on two women sitting in the corner of the room. Both have their heads down, deep in conversation, and then the blond, this gorgeous, tanned, smiling blond, throws back her head and laughs.

Funny, thinks Ben. I'm sure I've heard that laugh somewhere before. He shakes his head, trying to remember what's so familiar about the laugh, but he doesn't remember, and there's no way he knows this woman. Unfortunately. He keeps glancing back at her anyway, because she is truly lovely, but she doesn't look up at him, not once, far too immersed in the conversation with her friend. Probably got a boyfriend waiting at home, thinks Ben, because she is so obviously not there to pick up men.

"Right," he says, finishing his drink. "Shall we make a move?"

I'm not as fine as I say I am, but I'm not that bad either. Amazing how spending some money, especially when you haven't got it, can perk you up. And being with Lauren is fun, actually, it's a hell of a lot more fun than being with Brad, and every time I think about the way he held me, the way he kissed me, I then have to think about how one-dimensional he actually was, how he never felt like a real person.

And tonight, sitting here at a corner table in the bar of Schatzi on Main, is perfect. Exactly what I needed. I know Lauren planned to get as drunk as we were the other night at the Pepper, but it's turned out to be a far more mellow evening. Yes, we've had some stares, but I suppose two single women in a busy bar will always get attention, but no one's bothered us, and it's nice to just sit, have a few drinks and chill out, as they say.

And the more time I spend with Lauren, the more I like her. She's so open, so warm, so loyal, and I honestly feel as if I've known her for years. She seems to understand exactly what I'm thinking, as if she picks up my mood before I've even opened my mouth, and she always seems to know exactly the right thing to say and do.

Take tonight, for example. Given her drunken debauchery the other night, I was worried she'd spend the night flirting, but to be honest she's hardly looked at any of the men in here, and there have been some gorgeous ones. I know, I'm facing into the room. Not that I'm paying that much attention, I'm too busy laughing at her stories and telling her stories of my own.

But then the weirdest thing happens. I've just finished telling her about the Sophie story, the night of Ben's farewell party and how Sophie pretended to be Ben's girlfriend, when I look up and see two men, just walking out of the restaurant.

My heart completely stops because one of them, the taller of the two, looks exactly like Ben.

"What is it?" Lauren asks me. "You look like you've seen a ghost."

"No, it can't be." I stand up and try and see him more clearly, but there are so many people, and by the time I manage to get a good viewpoint all I can see is his back disappearing through the door. Same build, same hair, but of course it's not Ben. Ben's busy being a television star at home. "It's nothing," I sigh, sitting down again and wishing with all my heart it *was* him. "I just thought I saw someone I knew, but I was wrong."

chapter 30

Ben Williams slept like a baby last night, and this morning he wakes up feeling fantastic. The only vague blot on his horizon is that Jemima hasn't called him back. He knows he's been remiss in their friendship, he knows he should have kept in touch, and, although part of him worries he's got the wrong number, the other part worries that perhaps she hasn't forgiven him for just walking out of her life.

But he's not *that* worried, it just would be nice to see her, and he's leaving tomorrow. He wonders whether to call again, but three phone calls, he decides, would be just a touch excessive.

So today is his free day in Los Angeles, and he knows what he should be doing, he should be doing something incredibly touristy like Disneyland or the Universal Studios tour, but when he asked at the front desk they said he'd definitely need a car to get there, and Simon's taken the car to an edit suite, so he's a bit stuck on his own.

This is ridiculous, he thinks, when he's had his shower. He's in the most glamorous city in the world and he doesn't know what to do, so in the end he decides to go down to the beach.

The Rollerbladers are out in full force, and Ben wonders whether to hire blades and try it out for himself, but making a fool of yourself in Hyde Park on a Sunday morning when everyone else is also an amateur is one thing; making a fool of yourself in Los Angeles when everyone on skates looks as if they've been born on them is another. So he just walks along the beach, and goes down to the pier.

On the way back he walks past a bookstore, and, despite his bad luck the other day, something about this bookstore says it's much more his kind of place, that there is likely to be decent fiction, and Ben walks in and within the first three minutes he has found two books—two first-time novels by young American writers that he cannot wait to get stuck into.

And, as he walks over to the desk and waits for the cashier to check his Visa card, he does a double-take. Surely not, it can't be. . . . But of course, it is. The very same beautiful blond he saw last night, this time on her own, just leaving the bookstore. He almost wouldn't have recognized her, but he saw her smile, and it's a smile that, even after a brief glimpse last night, he can't seem to get out of his head.

Hurry up, hurry up, come on, come on, he thinks, as the cashier dawdles behind the desk. Ben looks impatiently at her, then back at the blond, who's stopped just by the door to pick up a book on display. This is fate, he thinks. Of all the bookstores in all of Los Angeles she has to be in this one. And more to the point, a bookstore! She likes books! She could be brainy as well as beautiful! He looks up again. She's gone.

Ben grabs his books, grabs his card, and runs out the door. There she is, those gorgeous thighs striding along the street. He dodges the people meandering along, just in time to see her climb into a car, and in a way it's probably not a bad thing because why is he following her so frantically, what would he say to her if he stopped her, caught her? Damn, he curses. That's it. I'm never going to see her again.

"Thanks for lending me your car," I shout, tossing the car keys on the table in the living room.

"No problem. Did you get what you wanted?"

"I just went browsing in the bookstore, bought a couple of new novels."

"Hey, JJ?"

"Yup?" I walk in to Lauren's bedroom and sit on the bed as Lauren tries on the new outfits she bought yesterday.

"Remember that scarf you were wearing when I first met you?" Her voice has a pleading tone in it already.

"Which one? The green silk one?"

"Yes . . ." Lauren whines hopefully.

"You want to borrow it tonight?"

"Yes . . ." Another whine, with a cheeky smile.

"Okay, but guard it with your life, it's one of my favorite possessions. I suppose you want me to get it for you now so you can see what it looks like?"

"Would you mind?"

I open my suitcase and dig through the pile of clothes. It's not there. I open the drawer I'm using for my underwear. It's not there. I look in the bathroom, the bedroom, and the kitchen. I look under the sofa, over the sofa, and behind the sofa. It's not there.

"Oh shit." With a sinking feeling, I realize I know exactly where it is. It's hanging behind Brad's bedroom door.

"Have you lost it?" Lauren walks in from the bedroom.

"No. The bloody thing's at Brad's."

"Don't worry." Lauren's face falls. "I don't really need it."

"Never mind about you! That's my favorite scarf."

"Do you want me to call him?"

"Oh my God, you're such an angel. Would you?"

Even knowing that Lauren's going to be talking to him makes me feel slightly sick, and as I watch her walking over to the phone I start shaking. She has a brief cool conversation with him in which he says he does have the scarf and he'll leave it at the gym for her. I hear her say, "Uh huh. Uh huh. Uh huh. Okay. I'll tell her. Bye."

"What did he say? What did he say?"

Lauren has a huge smile on her face. "Jemima Jones, this must be your lucky day."

"Why?" I'm still shaking.

"You've had a message, you've had a message," Lauren starts singing, getting up and dancing round the living room in time with her odd little tune.

"Who from?"

Lauren stops and pauses for dramatic effect before announcing in her best Johnny Carson impersonation, "From . . . Ben WILLIAMS."

My mouth drops open.

"And not just that. HE'S IN LOS ANGELES! And not just that, HE'S AT SHUTTERS ON THE BEACH!"

"I knew it," I scream. "I bloody knew it. I'd know that haircut and that back anywhere. He's here. He's round the corner. Give me that phone. NOW!"

The shakes, if anything, have got worse, but Ben's here! My Ben! My love! I wait for the hotel to put me through, praying that he's still there, that he won't have gone back home, because I have never wanted anything more in my life than I want to see Ben Williams right this second.

And the phone rings, and rings, and rings. And just as I'm about to give up hope the receiver's picked up and a breathless voice, a voice I used to know as well as my own, says, "Hello?"

I swallow, feeling my heart pounding, wondering why I'm so out of breath when I haven't been anywhere, and I try to speak slowly, calmly.

"Ben? It's Jemima."

"Jemima! You're still here!" And is it my imagination or does he truly sound delighted to hear from me?

"I can't believe you're here!" I say, for want of something better.

"I can't believe I haven't spoken to you for so long," he says, for want of something better.

And then we both start talking at once, I'm so excited, he's here! He's here! He's round the corner.

"What are you *doing* here?" we both say in unison, before stopping and laughing.

"I'm not telling you on the phone," says Ben. "Look, are you around this afternoon?"

"Yes." I'm around for you anytime, Ben.

"How about meeting up?"

"I'd love to."

"How about meeting up now? We could spend the rest of the day together."

"I'd love to."

"Where shall we meet?"

I think for a minute, then suggest a café round the corner from his hotel. "See you there in fifteen minutes?" I say.

"Done."

Oh my God, I'm whirling round Lauren's tiny apartment like a dervish. What to wear, what to wear? I pull on some skintight black trousers, a crisp white linen shirt, and a pair of white sneakers. I loop a crocodile belt around my waist and tip my head upside down to give my hair that sexy, tousled, just-got-out-of-bed look.

"I'm seeing Ben!" I keep shrieking to Lauren, who seems to have caught my enthusiasm, and at this very second is bouncing up and down on the bed and clapping her hands.

"Has he seen you like this?" Lauren suddenly says, while I apply the finishing touches of lipstick.

"Like what?"

"Thin."

No. Oh God. He has no idea. I'm so nervous, what will he think, what will he say? I just shake my head.

"He'll be speechless," she laughs. "I'll drop you off. Come on. You'll be fine. Remember, it's only Ben, he's your friend."

"Exactly. It's Ben!"

We jump in the car and Lauren puts her foot down, and three minutes later I climb out of the car, seriously worried that the butterflies in my stomach are making me feel nearly as sick as my binge the other night.

Ben's not there. I sit at a corner table for a while and look at my watch, putting my sunglasses on to hide the nerves, to stop Ben seeing right through to the churning emotions inside, and eventually, after I'm bored of sitting with nothing to do, I walk over to the counter to order a cappuccino. I'm standing there as I hear the creak of the door opening and I turn my head slowly to see who it is and it's him. It's Ben. And my heart turns over.

Is it possible that Ben has got better looking? That television has groomed him, given him an air of confidence that he was missing before? For one tiny moment at Lauren's flat I thought that perhaps, once I'd actually seen him in the flesh, perhaps I wouldn't feel the same way, perhaps I'd just look at him, admit he's good-looking but not have it affect me, but no, no, no. I feel exactly the same way as I did six months ago, and all of a sudden I know I'm going to act like a lovestruck teenager. I'm not going to know what to say, how to be.

And I can't go over to say hello, my feet are rooted to the spot, so I just watch Ben looking round the café, ignoring the guy behind the counter who's trying to hand me my cappuccino, which I can't take because I can't bloody move!

And then finally, finally, Ben sees me, and when he does he starts to smile.

He knows me, he's recognized me! I start to walk towards him, the sunglasses still shielding my eyes, not breaking his gaze for a second, and I forget everything around me except for Ben, my love. Then suddenly he's standing right in front of me and we're both smiling. I don't say anything. I don't have to.

"I never usually do this," says Ben, as confusion crosses my face. "But I saw you last night in Schatzi on Main, and again today in the bookstore. I'm meeting a friend here in a few minutes, but I just wanted to tell you that I think you're the most amazing woman I've ever seen."

Is this a joke? What is he talking about? What's going on?

Ben blushes. "I'm really sorry," he mumbles. "I didn't mean to embarrass you," and with a shrug and a smile he turns away and sits at the table I was going to sit at, and I don't know what to do, how to tell him it's me.

"Excuse me? Excuse me? Your cappuccino?" The words float over my head, and I know that I can't go over there, not after what he's just said, I can't just say, actually it's me, Jemima Jones, and as soon as I realize this I also know that I have to leave, except my legs are still shaking, and Ben's buried his head in a newspaper and I have to leave.

And eventually, on autopilot, I walk slowly out the door and go home.

"What happened?" Lauren asks. "What are you doing back here?" And I tell her.

"Go back, you've got to go back there."

"I can't," I moan. "What would I say?"

"Are you completely nuts?" Lauren's shaking her head in disbelief. "The man you were completely in love with, you're still completely in love with, has just told you he thinks you're the most amazing woman he's ever seen and you didn't have the balls to tell him it was you? This is unreal. Get your ass back there."

I point to my watch. "He won't still be there."

"You are going to see him and, more to the bloody point, talk to him, if it kills me."

Lauren paces up and down for the next hour, and then she picks up the phone and hands it to me. "The poor guy will be back at his hotel now, wondering why you didn't turn up. Get on this phone NOW, and arrange to meet him for dinner."

"What will I say?"

"Tell him you had an emergency and you tried to get through and you couldn't. And for God's sake apologize. Profusely."

Please don't be there, I pray as I dial Shutters on the Beach, but he picks up the phone in his room after the first ring.

"Jemima?"

"Ben, I'm so sorry." I tell him the story Lauren came up with and wait for him to say something.

"Don't worry," he says finally. "I understand. These things happen. Anyway, I'm leaving town tomorrow so I probably won't get a chance to see you. It would have been nice, that's all."

"What about tonight," I say quickly, as Lauren gives me a very sharp nudge in the ribs. "I could definitely see you tonight. We could have dinner."

"You really want to?"

"I really want to."

"And you won't stand me up?"

"I swear on my life, Ben. I won't stand you up."

The rest of the afternoon seems to pass in slow motion, every second making the anticipation stronger and stronger. Lauren insists I do some serious beauty treatments "just in case," and she rushes around helping me look the most beautiful I've ever looked in my life.

And finally it's 6:45, just fifteen minutes to go before we're due to meet, and I can't stop pacing up and down, and Lauren keeps telling me off because I keep rubbing my damp palms on my dress and she's right, I might stain it, but I don't know what else to do with my hands so I just pace around, wringing them constantly.

"Well?" I say, for about the hundredth time. "How do I look?"

"You look fucking incredible," says Lauren, and, although I would never describe myself as incredible, I do know I look good in my red halter top sundress, tightly fitting at the top, then flaring out at the hips into a short, swinging skirt. It sets off my tan, and I no longer need all the makeup that Geraldine taught me how to expertly apply, just the merest hint of mascara and lip gloss. I look healthy, happy, confident and, most of all, I look like a true Californian. To be honest I'm not surprised that Ben didn't know me because looking in the mirror I don't even know myself.

But, because I've had all afternoon to prepare for this, I don't feel that nervous anymore. In a weird sort of way I feel more in control, I've already faced him, I know what I'm up against, and I know, beyond a shadow of a doubt, that I still love him.

And that knowledge has sort of given me a power, a power I never thought I had, and I know I can face him this time, I won't run away, and, although of course I'm still nervous, I'm excited now too.

This time I'm a few minutes late. I don't want to be waiting for Ben to arrive, I want to walk in when he's there, feeling strong, powerful, beautiful.

And she does walk in, and he's there, and she does feel all of the above, and she also feels brave, which is, it has to be said, a completely new feeling for her. Once again he stares at her, thinking that this must be fate, that it is ridiculous how he keeps seeing his perfect woman, how she keeps turning up wherever he is, but he looks away after a few seconds because he made a fool of himself earlier on today, and he doesn't want to do it again. But God, is she beautiful. No, he buries his head in a book. He's not going to talk to her again. He's just going to immerse himself in the book and wait for Jemima.

And as he looks at the words, for he can't possibly read when he knows this vision of loveliness is in the room, he sees a pair of taut, tanned legs standing just in front of him, and he looks up at her, and sees that this time she is giving him a warm smile, and he curses the fact that he's meeting Jemima, because right now he wants to spend the rest of his life basking in this woman's smile.

"I can't believe it's you," he says softly, frowning slightly as I smile.

"Yes, it's me," and Ben frowns, and he keeps frowning as I lean down and give him an awkward kiss on the cheek, before pulling out a chair and sitting down.

"What are you doing here?" he says, looking confused.

"What do you mean, Ben? We arranged to meet," I tease in an American accent, because I know what this is about and I'm finally starting to enjoy it.

Ben looks at me and says slowly, "How do you know my name?"

"Ben!" I burst out laughing. "It's me, you dumbass. Jemima Jones." And as I watch I see it register on his face, see the confusion replaced by sheer and utter amazement, and I'm loving this, I'm loving every single second.

Ben tries to speak, but no words come out. He just stares at me, and I can see what's happened slowly dawning on him. That I'm not fat anymore, that I've turned into the amazing woman he keeps seeing around, and through his shock and confusion I can slowly see admiration starting to emerge, and this is the best bloody feeling in the whole world.

"Jemima," he whispers, as the smile leaves my face, and then, without planning it, thinking about it, we both stand up at exactly the same time and fall into one another's arms.

Let this moment carry on forever, let the whole world disappear, leaving just me and Ben. Ben and me. I want to remember this for the rest of my life, the feel of his chest, his arms wrapped around me, his heartbeat against my cheek. I close my eyes and just cling on to him. Let me stay here forever and ever and ever.

But forever only lasts about a minute, and then, reluctantly, I pull away and sit down.

"How?" Ben starts, looking at me in amazement. "I mean, when?" He can't take his eyes off me. "It's . . ."

I laugh. "How did I get like this?"

Ben nods.

"It was after you left. I lost the weight and Geraldine made me over, as she would say."

"Oh God," Ben groans. "I made such a fool of myself today. No wonder you walked out."

"You didn't make a fool of yourself. It was lovely to hear."

"But I *knew* there was something familiar about you, I just never dreamed, never thought . . ." He tails off again, still staring at me. "You just look so beautiful. I mean, you look nothing like *you*. I'm sorry," he continues, stammering, "I didn't mean . . ."

"That's okay," I say, smiling. "I know what you meant, and thank you. You look great too. I've seen you on television. Being a star obviously suits you."

"I'm not really a star," says Ben. "Just a presenter."

"Bullshit," I tease. "Geraldine sent me that double-page spread they ran on you. You're a star, Ben. Take it from me."

"I can't believe she did that, that's so embarrassing," says Ben. "Now you know all about me."

"Your murky past," I laugh.

"I know," he sighs. "You did warn me."

"And I'm always right."

"Yup," he laughs. "You always are. God, Jemima. I've missed you," and I can hear the sincerity in his voice and I know that he means it, and I realize how much I've missed him, and not just because I love him. I've missed this, the easy banter, the friendship, and, even though I haven't seen him for months, it's almost as if barely a day's gone by, I mean, we're so relaxed we could almost be sitting in the cafeteria of the *Kilburn Herald*.

And how is it for Ben? The longer Ben sits in this restaurant with this beautiful woman, the less she becomes a gorgeous blond, and the more she becomes Jemima Jones, for Ben looks past the legs, the dress, the hair, and he sees his old friend, a friend, he suddenly realizes, he never wants to walk out on again.

I'm teasing Ben about work and we're laughing and he tells me about Diana Macpherson, grudgingly, admittedly, and even though I feel a red-hot poker of jealousy stabbing me as he tells me about his drunken mistake, I don't really mind because he's relaxed enough to confide in me, and anyway he doesn't want her, plus he tells me confidentially that he's been offered a far better job with another TV station, which solves the problem. But the funny thing is that actually I feel a little bit sorry for Diana Macpherson, this media ogre, because I know what it's like to want someone that badly, to want them even though they don't want you.

I tell him about Brad, about what it was like to finally have a boyfriend that everyone else wanted, and about how it all went horribly wrong. And yes. Okay. I did tell him about the porn pictures, I tell him very slowly and very seriously, waiting for sympathy, waiting for concern, but when I look up Ben's trying to suppress a smile.

"It's not funny, Ben," I say sternly.

"No," he says. "You're right. It's not," but he can't contain himself any more, he starts giggling, and it's so infectious and I suppose the story is so bizarre that I start giggling too, and the giggling soon becomes hysterical laughter, and the pair of us are rocking back on our chairs, clutching our stomachs in pain and crying with laughter.

"Oh God." I scrabble around for a napkin to wipe the tears of laughter away. "I never thought I'd see the funny side of that."

"Jemima, it's *classic*. It's one of the greatest stories I've ever heard," and we both start laughing again.

Neither of us eats very much. The food sits on our plates while we pick at it, raise the odd mouthful to our lips, but there's just so much to talk about, so many things to catch up on, and we hardly have a chance to breathe, we don't even let one another finish a sentence, we just let them tumble and twist, and eventually, when the waiters bring the bill, we stand up and smile at one another.

"I've had such a good time," says Ben, as we walk out.

"So have I. I can't tell you how good it is to see you." And as I turn to look at him, suddenly, the easy camaraderie of the evening disappears and we both stand awkwardly on the pavement outside the restaurant, and why do I suddenly feel nervous, what does this mean?

Ben's arm reaches out, and suddenly, and oh God I didn't plan this, but suddenly I'm in his arms and we're hugging but it's not like before, it's not just a friendly hug, and I'm very aware of Ben's breathing, of his touch, and as I stand there wrapped around him I feel him stroke my hair and I lean my head back to look at him and then everything becomes slow motion as he bends his head and kisses me, and I know it sounds naff, I know it sounds unreal, but I honestly feel that every fiber in my body is about to melt.

chapter 31

How do you know when you've found love? How do you know when you've met the person with whom you want to spend the rest of your life? How do you know it's not just two people lusting after one another, and consummating that lust in a night of unbelievable passion. How do you know it's not going to be just a one-night stand? How do you know whether your wishes will come true?

I wish I knew. All I do know, right now, when I open my eyes to the morning sunlight and Ben Williams fast asleep next to me, is that, even if I never set eyes on Ben again, this has been, and will always be, the happiest night of my life.

I know because I never dreamt that lovemaking could be so passionate, and yet so tender. I know because no one has ever cupped my face and looked deep in my eyes, and whispered how wonderful I am while moving gently inside me.

I know because I've never felt so comfortable with anyone in my life as I felt with Ben last night, because I've never felt *any* of the feelings I felt last night.

And finally I know that I will never forget what it is like to be so happy you are frightened you're going to burst.

So I just lie in bed and soak up this joy. I don't move, I'm too frightened of waking Ben up, too frightened of the magic disappearing, but as I watch him sleep he slowly opens his eyes, stretches, and then turns his head to look at me.

What should I do? I want to smile, to say something, but I can't, because I haven't got a clue how Ben is feeling, and when he blinks, smiles sleepily and holds his arm out to me, the relief is so overwhelming it practically sweeps me away and I snuggle into his chest like the proverbial cat that got the cream.

He kisses my hair, and then my shoulder. "Thank you," he says huskily, and I just smile, making small circles on his chest with my index finger.

We stay there for a little while, kissing, cuddling, completely comfortable with one another, and then Ben looks at the clock. "Shit!" he jumps out of bed. "I've got a flight to catch."

There's a knock on the door as I sit up in bed.

"Ben? It's Simon. We're leaving in ten minutes. Are you ready?"

"Nearly," shouts Ben, tripping over his shoes. "Shit!" he mutters, running around the bedroom.

"I'll help you pack," I say, climbing out of bed without a second thought, even though I'm completely naked. Ben stops and looks at me then drops his clothes and puts his arms around me, groaning, "I can't believe it's you. I can't believe last night." We start kissing again, and then Ben pulls away. "I can't. We can't. No time. Shit!"

There's no time for lazy post-coital kisses and cuddles, and within ten minutes Ben is packed and dressed, and I follow him downstairs, terrified at how we're going to say goodbye, what's going to happen next.

"He-llo," says a man I don't recognize, walking over to Ben but keeping his eyes firmly on me with a bit of a leer. "Who's this?"

"This is my friend Jemima," says Ben. "This is Simon," and I shake Simon's hand, not missing the look that he gives Ben, which Ben, being the gentleman that he is, tries to ignore.

"Simon, I'll see you by the car," he says, and Simon reluctantly walks out, probably dying to fill in the rest of the crew on the gossip.

"How long are you here?" Ben says, tucking my hair behind my ears.

"About two more months," I say, already trying to think of some way to get home, to be with Ben.

"What am I going to do for the next two months?" he says, as my heart lifts.

"I'd love to come home but I can't."

"Why not?"

I know it's crazy, but I don't want to tell him I haven't got the money, that I'm over my limit on my credit card, that in truth I no longer have a penny to my name. It sounds too sad, too like the Jemima Jones of old, so I think on my feet and come up with the perfect excuse.

"I'm doing a column for the *Kilburn Herald* and you know what the editor's like, I have to stay here, otherwise I'll lose my job."

"I'll miss you," he whispers eventually, pulling me close and kissing my forehead.

"We can write," I say in desperation. "Or phone."

"Definitely." He nods. "Can you write down your address and number?"

I pull away from him, reluctantly, and scribble down Lauren's address and number, and just as I hand it to him Simon reappears and says testily, "Ben, we've *got* to go."

We do hug, and kiss, and then Ben starts walking away. Just before he reaches the door he turns around and runs back, scooping me up in his arms and kissing me. "I'll phone," he says. "As soon as I get back home."

"What time will that be?"

"God knows. But don't worry, I'll call," and he leaves, turning back to wave as he climbs in the car, and I float back home on a cloud of sheer, unadulterated bliss.

"Well?" Lauren opens the door before I even get a chance to put my key in the lock, and I don't have to say anything, she can see from the ridiculously soppy grin on my face that last night was unbelievable.

"You did it! You did it!" She leaps up and down and throws her arms around me while I start giggling. "I want to hear everything."

"I'm so tired," I moan, collapsing on the sofa, still smiling.

"I don't want to hear that crap, I want to hear about Ben."

"I love him," I say simply, and then I say it again, just to hear the words, just to make sure it's true. "I love him."

"Start from the beginning," she commands, and I do.

I tell her about meeting him, about him not realizing it was me, and how it was like we'd never been apart. I tell her about his stories, his work, his life. I tell her about leaving the restaurant and practically leaping on one another as soon as we got outside. And I tell her about making love with him, what it was like, how I felt.

I tell her word for word, action for action, and all the time I'm talking this stupid grin doesn't leave my face, and I feel like I'm swimming in happiness.

"So you've got over Brad then?" she says, when I've finished.

"Brad who?" I laugh. "No seriously, Lauren. It was so completely different from being with Brad. I mean, the sex was amazing with Brad, but last night made me realize how that's all it was, just great sex. There was no tenderness, no love, just passion, and at the time I thought it was enough. But Ben was so different, maybe because I know him, maybe because we're friends, but I think it's more than that. I know, beyond a shadow of a doubt, that I'm still totally in love with him." I stop and sigh.

"Do you think he feels the same way?"

"I don't know," I sigh, as the insecurities threaten to strike. "I know that he was incredibly caring, and giving, and loving, but I don't know whether that means he feels the same way, but there's no point thinking about that. Anyway, he's going to call as soon as he gets home."

"What time?"

"I don't know, but I know he'll call. Oh God, Lauren. I just want to be with him. I want to go home." And I do, and two months feels like an eternity and I don't know how I'm going to cope for the next few weeks with just the memories of one night to keep me going.

"He's going to call," she says, "and you're going home in just over seven weeks. It's nothing. It will pass in a flash. Now," she says looking at her watch, "how about a celebratory brunch?"

"Perfect," I say. "I'm starving."

We go to the Broadway Deli and I dive into french toast and bacon and strawberries, and it's delicious and we go over every detail all over again, and I feel as if I'm bathed in love, as if everyone's looking at me with envy because I am a woman in love and they wish they were me.

And then afterwards we get some Ben & Jerry's frozen yogurt and some old videos from Blockbuster and we spend the rest of the afternoon and evening watching our favorite love stories, and I try to concentrate, I really do, but I'm trying not to jump every time I hear a noise because it might be the phone, except it's not, and by 10 P.M. I'm looking at my watch and starting to feel slightly sick because it's six o'clock in the morning at home and I know, I just know, that with the time difference he must have been home for ages now, and even if his luggage took forever to come through, and even if it took hours to get through customs he would still be home and he hasn't called.

And by midnight I feel the last shreds of happiness drift away from me and I think I'm going to cry.

"Anything could have happened," says Lauren, finishing off the last of her tub of Chocolate Chip Cookie Dough. "The flight might have been delayed, he might have had to work. Don't worry, he'll call." But I do worry and I am worried, and even though I know this morning I said that it wouldn't matter if I never saw him again, that the one night with him would last me the rest of my life, I know that's not true, and I know that the pain that suddenly attacks me like a knife is something I'm going to

362

have to learn to live with, because he hasn't called, and he won't call, and this is how it's going to be for the rest of my life.

A week later I'm still trying to learn to live with the pain. Sure, I'm putting on a brave face, trying to get on with my life. I don't go to the gym anymore, but I go out with Lauren, pretend to have a good time, and then every morning when I wake up the first thing I think is, something's wrong, what is it? And then I remember and the black clouds descend and the bloody things follow me around until the next morning.

You'd think I'd find some peace at night, fast asleep, but even there the pain's still present. I dream about Ben. Constantly. A mixture of memories and surreal fantasy, and, without wishing to sound overdramatic, I think I understand what it's like to be bereaved, to lose someone you love with all your heart, to know there's no possibility of ever seeing them again.

Brad was bad. That whole Brad and Jenny thing was bad. But it was nothing, nothing, compared to this. A mere drop in the ocean of grief I now feel every moment of the day, and there are days when I don't want to get up at all, I just want to lie in bed and drift into nothingness, just get it all over with.

Ben Williams cannot believe he has been so stupid. He cannot believe that the scrap of paper on which Jemima had scrawled her number and address is lost. He cannot believe that he has no way of getting in touch with her. He's left countless messages at Brad's, but he assumes they haven't been passed on because they haven't been returned. He phoned Geraldine, but the only number she had for her was at Brad's, and Sophie and Lisa weren't much use either. He even tried the editor at the *Kilburn Herald*, but he was more interested in moaning about Jemima's missing copy, and again she hadn't been in touch to tell him she'd moved.

Ben's been through his clothes, his bags, his cases with a fine-tooth comb, but he can't find the bloody thing at all.

And although he's only been back a week, he's been thinking

about Jemima Jones. A lot. In the middle of a broadcast he'll suddenly lose his train of thought as a picture will flash up in his mind of Jemima's face as she looked trustingly into his eyes when he pulled her on top of him. Or he'll suddenly remember the feel of her skin when he's in a meeting with the production team.

And there are times, late at night, every night, when he just wants to hear her voice, and he keeps hoping that she'll call him, she'll realize something's wrong, but the phone doesn't ring, and when it does it's not her. Eventually Ben—and who would have thought the divine Ben Williams had an ounce of insecurity within—starts to worry that maybe, for Jemima, it was just a one-night stand. Maybe she doesn't care about him at all. Maybe she's met someone else.

When a week goes by and he hasn't heard from her and he hasn't been able to get in touch, he tells Richard about her. He tells him against his better judgment, for Richard, as we know, is not the best person to tell your troubles to.

"She could call *you*," says Richard. "Let's face it, Ben, she knows where you work and all she has to do is pick up the phone. You should just leave it as a brilliant one-night stand and get on with your life."

"Hmm," says Ben, who sees a grain of truth in what Richard just said. After all, Jemima *could* call him, and she hasn't, so maybe he should just forget about it.

"Oh no," says Richard, looking at Ben intensely.

"What's the matter?" Ben asks in alarm.

"You're not? You can't be?"

"What?"

"You're bloody in love with her aren't you?"

"Absolutely not." Ben shakes his head.

"You are. I recognize the signs."

"I'm not," says Ben. "No way," and he looks at his watch. "I've gotta go," he says, standing up. "I'm doing an interview with the *Daily Mail*."

"What? Another interview?"

Ben sighs. "I know. After the last one I thought I'd done enough, but you've got to keep that publicity ball rolling."

"Don't tell them *anything*," says Richard dramatically.

"No," says Ben firmly. "I won't."

But Ben can't quite help himself. The journalist is so *nice*, a warm, caring middle-aged woman to whom Ben immediately wanted to open his heart, and before he knows it he tells her far more than he should.

"Please don't put that stuff in about not being able to find her," he pleads, as he says goodbye. "That's off the record."

"Don't worry," she says laying a reassuring hand on his arm. "You can trust me."

Ben refuses to think about this for the rest of the evening. How could he, when all he can think about is Jemima Jones and how to find her.

I wasn't going to phone anyone at home. I didn't want anyone to know what happened, and I knew that if I dared call anyone to tell them I'd moved, they'd want to know why, and I haven't got the strength to tell people about Brad, about Jenny and, mostly, about Ben.

But a week is a bloody long time when your heart has broken, and Lauren, great as she has been, is starting to get on my nerves. She doesn't mean to, she's lovely, it's just that sometimes I want to be on my own, to just sit and reflect on the one perfect night of my life, on the future I could have had if Ben had called me, but she won't leave me alone, and I know she's trying to cheer me up but sometimes the jokes wear a bit thin, that's all.

And then, finally, it becomes too much. I have to talk to someone who *knows* Ben. Someone who can tell me what to do. Someone who might, just might, know what he's thinking, why he hasn't called.

"Geraldine? It's me."

"Jemima Jones! Am I glad you called. Where the hell have you been?"

"Are you sitting down?"

"I most certainly am. What on earth is going on there?"

"Oh God, Geraldine. It's awful. I don't know where to start."

"At the beginning," she says quietly, so I do. I tell her about Brad, and Jenny, and Lauren, and food, and everything. And then, eventually, I tell her about Ben.

"But he called me!" she says, not even waiting for me to finish describing my pain. "I knew there was something up because I hadn't spoken to him since he left. He phoned last week to see if I had your number. Jemima, you idiot! He must have lost your number. Why the hell didn't you call me sooner?"

"He called you?" Slowly, slowly, my heart starts piecing itself back together again. "He called you?"

"Yes! Last week! I knew from his voice that something had happened. I just knew it."

"What did he say? Tell me exactly what he said."

"He didn't tell me anything, he just said he'd seen you in Los Angeles and he meant to call you to thank you but he couldn't find your number."

"What should I do? Should I call him? Oh God, Geraldine, I just want to come home."

"So why don't you?"

"I can't," I moan. "It'll cost me $954 plus tax to change my flight and I've run out of money."

"Did you tell Ben that?"

"How could I? I didn't want him to feel sorry for me, so I just said I was stuck out here writing the column."

"Oh for heaven's sake, Jemima. Why didn't you tell him the truth?"

"I don't know," I murmur. "Would it have made any difference?"

"I don't know," she echoes. "But I'm planning to find out."

"What are you going to do?"

"Just leave it to me," she says firmly.

"What? Tell me. Shall I ring him?"

"No," she says. "Absolutely not. You just sit tight and let me sort it out."

366

"Geraldine, please don't say I haven't got the money to come home. Anyway, he's probably changed his mind by now."

"Jemima, if it was as incredible as you say it was, he won't have changed his mind. Trust me. I know men." And I breathe a sigh of relief because no one knows men better than Geraldine.

"JJ? I forgot to tell you, a letter came for you this morning." Lauren dumps the shopping on the kitchen table.

"Hmm? Where is it?"

"I left it on the coffee table." Lauren comes out and lifts a magazine to reveal a large brown envelope with a London postmark. My heart stops as she hands it to me but it's not from Ben. It's Geraldine. I'd know that writing anywhere.

I tear open the envelope and pull out a newspaper clipping and a compliments slip.

Jemima Jones! As usual Auntie Geraldine has come to the rescue, and I'm sorry, I know you didn't want me to tell Ben about being stuck out there but I had to. Plus, it gave me a chance to call him a stupid bastard which I've been dying to do for years!!! (no offense . . .)

Anyway, I don't think you'll mind once you've opened this envelope, and it's not from me, it's from Ben, AND, I think you'll find the enclosed interesting reading!!! (I certainly did . . .) Lucky, lucky you!! Things still going great guns with me and Nick, will tell you all when I see you. Soon. Very soon. Ha! Loads of love and kisses, Geraldine. xxxxxxxxxx

I'm smiling because I can almost hear Geraldine speak, and then I read it again and I wonder why Geraldine's written to me, why not Ben, and, if the clipping that's attached is from Ben and not her, why did she bother writing at all, and oh my God, I don't feel too good about this and that small light at the end of the tunnel starts getting smaller, so I pick up the clipping and then I have to sit down very quickly.

"What is it?" says Lauren, sitting next to me, so I start to read it out loud, haltingly, disbelievingly.

" 'Ben Williams is cagey on the subject of love,' " I read. " 'He's "had his fingers burned," as he puts it, and doesn't want to reveal who it is. But millions of women will be devastated to hear that the gorgeous presenter of *London Nights* has fallen in love. "She's an old friend," reveals Williams, "whom I hadn't seen for a while, and then we met up recently and we became more than friends. I don't think I even knew it was love until we were apart, and now I'm just killing time until she comes home." So who is this mystery woman of his? "No one famous," he laughs. "Her name's Jemima Jones." ' "

I start shaking. I don't know whether to laugh or cry, and neither of us speaks, I think Lauren's as shocked as I am. After a while Lauren frowns and picks up the envelope, and, instead of putting it in the bin, she looks inside, smiles, and then gives it to me. I look at her, then feel the envelope, and there's something else in there, and when I pull it out I see something that looks suspiciously like a plane ticket, and why has Geraldine sent me a plane ticket? And then I notice there's writing on the cover and I remember that writing, and it says, "Come home. I miss you. Ben." And I know why Ben and Geraldine met up, and I know that this was probably Geraldine's idea because it's so typical of her and I don't care, and Ben misses me and he wants me to come home.

And slowly I look closely at the ticket and I gasp when I read it's a one-way flight from LAX to Heathrow for the day after tomorrow. The day after tomorrow! I'm going home!

"See?" says Lauren, throwing her arms around me and hugging me tightly. "I knew he'd come through for you."

"He has," I whisper, as the tears start rolling down my face. "He has."

chapter 32

And so here I am, suitcases in hand, not to mention of course the Louis Vuitton vanity case, and thank God I made it through customs—not that I have anything to hide, I just always feel so damn guilty walking through there, and, as I pile the cases on a cart and wheel it out to the waiting crowds of people, I know just how much I've missed London.

"'Scuse." A young woman pushes past me and rushes up to her waiting friends, and I never thought I'd be so pleased to hear a British accent.

Ben, I know, won't be waiting, because I phoned him before I left, in a fit of nerves and excitement, gushing my thanks at his generosity while he apologized profusely, told me he couldn't stop thinking about me, and said he just wanted to be with me. With *me!*

My Ben. Back home. I still can't quite believe that in just a few hours' time I'll be seeing him. I know I'll be jet lagged to hell by the time I actually walk in, but I also know that the adrenaline of seeing him will keep me going well into the night.

But, amazingly enough, even though it's all I've been thinking about since I got the plane ticket—seeing him again—I still managed to sleep on the plane. I suppose I was exhausted from all the emotional trauma, but nevertheless I abided by Geraldine's advice and spritzed my face, covered myself with moisturizer, and fell fast asleep until I was woken by the stewardess placing a breakfast tray in front of me.

And I realize now there aren't many things I'll miss about Los Angeles, although I will miss Lauren. She drove me to the airport, and we hugged for ages while she cried and kept asking what she would do without me. I felt like crying too, but my excitement at coming home was stronger than the sadness at leaving Lauren, so I just hugged her back tightly, told her she'd be fine, and made her promise to keep in touch.

And I do think she'll be fine, because she's a survivor. She still says she's planning to come home, but I'm not so sure. She and Bill seem to be going strong, and I've got a feeling she may well stay out there after all, but either way she's sworn she'll be back, even if it's just for a holiday, and I want her to meet Ben, and Geraldine, to see how happy I am in the place I belong.

And the funny thing is I've realized that Lauren and I aren't so different after all. That I'm a survivor too; that the experiences I've had over the last few months would surely have broken someone weaker than me. It's not that I feel terribly strong on the surface, but I know, as an absolute certainty, that deep down I have an amazing reserve of strength, which all in all is pretty comforting really.

Although standing here, looking for the taxi sign, I'm not feeling that strong. And I know it's only been six weeks, but I'm not even sure where I belong anymore. I know my home's in London, but I feel that I can't take steps backwards, go back to the life I had before. I assumed I'd go back to living with Sophie and Lisa, and in many ways I was dreading it, that really would have felt like moving backwards, but luckily that's changed too.

I phoned them last night, thinking that perhaps I'd just stay there until I found somewhere else, and—stupidly, I know—I was surprised, and slightly disappointed, when Sophie said a friend of Lisa's was staying in the room, and that they'd put my things under the stairs. They weren't expecting me back for ages, and they were really sorry but they couldn't kick this girl out.

I know it's a good thing, but I panicked for a few minutes, until I rang Geraldine, who once again came to my rescue. She's moved into her new flat, which, needless to say, is "absolutely gorgeous," and the spare room, she said, would be perfect for me.

"But what about Nick?" I asked.

"What about him?" she laughed. "You won't mind if he stays here sometimes, will you? Plus, you'll have Ben, and just think Jemima, we'll have the most amazing time. I'd love to have you as a roommate, it's going to be brilliant. I can run out to Habitat this afternoon and get some curtains, and then the room's done. It's yours."

How could I argue with her?

I clutch the piece of paper with Geraldine's new address, and get in line for a taxi, loving the fact that the cabs that are slowly lining up and pulling away are so familiar, so solid, that they are London, that they, more than anything else, tell me I'm home.

And I wait in line until finally it's my turn to climb into the cab, and as it pulls out of the airport I rest my head against the window and watch the lights on the motorway whizzing past, and the closer we get to home, the more excited I start to feel.

This is a whole new start, Jemima Jones. A whole new chapter: mine to write however I choose. And the first step is not going back to the *Kilburn Herald*. If Ben can do it, so can I. I'm going to fulfill that dream, work on a glossy magazine, and that's just the beginning. Once upon a time this would have terrified me, but now I can't wait to get started, to set off on a new journey, this time surrounded by people I love, who love me in return.

And on we go. Through Hammersmith Broadway, up to Shepherd's Bush, along the Westway. We pull off and make our way up Maida Vale, through Kilburn, to Geraldine's flat in West Hampstead.

And I look around me, and I can see that London's smelly, and dirty, and that the people look, if anything, slightly tired and harassed. The sun's nowhere to be seen, and as we drive drops of rain start slowly splattering on the windscreen, and the sky darkens with rain clouds.

No one I've seen has the remotest hint of a tan, and all along the Kilburn High Road there are people bundled up in anoraks, hurrying to get their shopping home before they get soaked.

And I love it. I'm safe here. Safe, happy, and secure. I don't care that it's the antithesis of California. I don't care that the weather's always shit. I don't care that no one, ever, says, "Have a nice day now." It's wonderful, and vibrant, and real. And most of all, it's home.

epilogue

J emima Jones is no longer skinny, no longer hardbodied, no longer obsessed with what she eats. Jemima Jones is now a voluptuous, feminine, curvy size 10 who is completely happy with how she looks. Jemima Jones now eats what she wants, when she wants, as often as she wants, as long as it's reasonably healthy.

And Jemima Jones is no longer lonely. Jemima Jones no longer dreams of the perfect romance with a man she can't have. She no longer believes that true love only exists outside herself.

Because Jemima Jones never dared to believe in love. Jemima Jones never dared to believe in herself. She never dared to believe that one of these days fate would actually take the time and trouble to pick her out from the crowd and smile upon her.

But fairy tales can come true, and just like Jemima Jones, or Mrs. Ben Williams as she's known outside of the glossy magazine where she now works, if we trust in ourselves, embrace our faults, and brazen it out with courage, strength, bravery, and truth, fate may just smile upon us too.